**Praise for the Novels
of Sharon Ashwood**

Scorched

"*Scorched: The Dark Forgotten* is a fast-paced urban fantasy that will keep you up long into the night. Hanging with the supernatural never felt so good!"
—Romance Junkies (Blue Ribbon Favorite)

"Ms. Ashwood's stories are multidimensional, and it is hard to second-guess this author. I can't wait for a third adventure in Ms. Ashwood's unique and twisted version of the world!" —The Romance Studio

"With the darkness and danger lurking on every page, it will keep readers engaged until the very end."
—Darque Reviews

"Sexual romps, fight scenes, shopping expeditions, and magic . . . *Scorched* has it all." —*The Romance Reader*

"The second Dark Forgotten urban fantasy is a terrific thriller." —The Best Reviews

"Sharp and stylish writing, plenty of action, a well-conceived and intriguing mythology, and a great sense of dark atmosphere." —BookLoons

continued . . .

Also by Sharon Ashwood

Ravenous
Scorched

UNCHAINED

The Dark Forgotten

SHARON ASHWOOD

A SIGNET ECLIPSE BOOK

SIGNET ECLIPSE
Published by New American Library, a division of
Penguin Group (USA) Inc., 375 Hudson Street,
New York, New York 10014, USA
Penguin Group (Canada), 90 Eglinton Avenue East, Suite 700, Toronto,
Ontario M4P 2Y3, Canada (a division of Pearson Penguin Canada Inc.)
Penguin Books Ltd., 80 Strand, London WC2R 0RL, England
Penguin Ireland, 25 St. Stephen's Green, Dublin 2,
Ireland (a division of Penguin Books Ltd.)
Penguin Group (Australia), 250 Camberwell Road, Camberwell, Victoria 3124,
Australia (a division of Pearson Australia Group Pty. Ltd.)
Penguin Books India Pvt. Ltd., 11 Community Centre, Panchsheel Park,
New Delhi - 110 017, India
Penguin Group (NZ), 67 Apollo Drive, Rosedale, North Shore 0632,
New Zealand (a division of Pearson New Zealand Ltd.)
Penguin Books (South Africa) (Pty.) Ltd., 24 Sturdee Avenue,
Rosebank, Johannesburg 2196, South Africa

Penguin Books Ltd., Registered Offices:
80 Strand, London WC2R 0RL, England

First published by Signet Eclipse, an imprint of New American Library,
a division of Penguin Group (USA) Inc.

First Printing, July 2010
10 9 8 7 6 5 4 3 2 1

PUBLISHER'S NOTE
This is a work of fiction. Names, characters, places, and incidents either are the
product of the author's imagination or are used fictitiously, and any resemblance
to actual persons, living or dead, business establishments, events, or locales is
entirely coincidental.
   The publisher does not have any control over and does not assume any re-
sponsibility for author or third-party Web sites or their content.

For Dad.
I wonder what you would have thought of all this.

UNCHAINED

"**A** good night to you girls, ghouls, and fangsters out there, and happy April Fools' Day. You're hearing the velvet tones of Errata Jones on 101.5 FM, coming to you from the beautiful University of Fairview campus. I'm your hostess on this nighttime ride on CSUP, where we put the *super* in supernatural.

"On tonight's show, our guest will be my own good pal and computer-savvy werewolf, Professor Perry Baker. Perry's going to tell us about the new UnWeb for the Undead, how you can log in, and what it can do for you. So listen up and get your bytes on.

"But first, for those of us who've never met a conspiracy theory we didn't like, we're going to spend some time talking about a portal into another world—a dark and dangerous world—that has appeared in our very own downtown core. That portal leads to a prison called the Castle. This is no April Fools' joke, but the biggest news for the nonhuman community since vampires and shifters came out of the crypt and hit the talk-show circuit in Y2K.

"There's a lot about this Castle we don't know. Those of us in the news biz thought the secrecy would end last fall, when Fairview locals took over management of the prison and immediately released hundreds of inmates they felt had been unjustly incarcerated. However, the new administration reluctantly admitted that this was only a small percentage of the total prison population. Apparently there are demons in there who'd eat us up faster than a high school ball team would a meat lover's pizza.

"What exactly is the prison administration doing to make sure these demons don't get an unscheduled day pass?"

Chapter 1

E vil lurked in public bathrooms.
It wasn't just the bad lights and weird green soap. Predators loved hidey-holes where folks could disappear from view and no one thought anything about it. Any slayer worth her salt—and Ashe Carver was a pro—knew to look for monsters in those boring, ordinary, deadly places.

Ashe hugged the outside wall of the brick building, her boots sinking into the carefully tended tulip beds. It was dark, damp, and cold. She could smell the green tang of the crushed plants mixing with an antiseptic stink leaking from the vents. The washroom had been recently cleaned, probably just after the Fairview Botanical Gardens had closed for the night.

Thankfully, lurking evil had waited until late to pay a visit. On any day of the week, thousands of tourists came through the Gardens' rose-decked gates, swilled overpriced soft drinks, and headed straight to the restrooms. Tonight, timing alone saved them from an encounter with worse problems than an empty towel dispenser.

Around nine fifteen that night, something had eaten the concessions clerk. He'd been identifiable by the name embroidered on the pocket of his candy-striped shirt. Security guards had dialed 911. Police had called a supernatural expert—aka Ashe's vampire brother-in-law— who had called Ashe. As he put it, carnage was her thing.

First stop, she had looked at the body. In a word, *ick*. She'd never seen bite marks quite like that, but bet on a werebeast of some kind.

She cursed the flowering bushes that obscured the ladies' room entrance. The blooms were pale in the dim light, and blurred into the shadows like watercolor stars. Pretty, but a security no-no. She crept toward the entrance one step at a time, eyes and ears tuned to the slightest disturbance. The problem was that the garden clamored with bugs, birds, bats, rodents, and a dozen other noisemakers, even at night. Most predators could hide beneath that rustling chaos.

The human noises were worst. Even from a distance, voices and motor sounds carried in the dark. She'd called in her location and switched off the radio the guy at the gate had given her. If there was something lurking around the corner, a sudden spew of static could give her away. Besides, she'd been born a witch. A bad spell had broken most of her powers when she was a teenager, but she still had a sixth sense that had saved her backside time and again. Electronics messed with that.

Ashe stilled, straining to pick up the slightest whiff of Nasty Critter. A light breeze chilled the sweat along her hairline. Her heart hammered hard, but her thoughts were clinically calm. If you were going to kick the ass of anything bigger than a garden sprite, discipline was key.

Another two steps, and she was behind the door-guarding rhododendron. The petals kissed her skin, the cool, soft touch making her shiver. She shifted her grip on her Colt automatic—a custom make loaded with the best silver-coated ammo she could afford—and smacked open the bathroom door with a sideways kick.

Her foot *blammed* against the wall, the noise meant to shock her quarry into revealing itself. Her gaze went first to the ceiling—you just never knew—then scanned across the long rows of sinks and stalls. It looked pin-neat, gleaming, and empty. Ashe shuffled inside, crouching, gun ready, letting the door swing shut behind her.

The echo of the door slam faded to the buzz of a faulty light ballast and the *drip-drip* of a tap. The suggestion of water made Ashe lick her lips. Her mouth was dry because of her nerves, but that was okay. Fear made her careful.

A quick look told her no feet showed beneath the stall doors. Of course, any high schooler knew that didn't mean a thing. Next, she would have to go banging open each door in the double row of stalls, which meant the monster in the last stall could jump her while her back was turned.

That had happened once. That was so not going to happen again.

Ashe took one long step onto the countertop, and from there cautiously pulled herself up the metal side of the first toilet stall. Yup, it was empty. With a heave, she hooked one leg over the side and used the wall for balance. In a very few seconds, she had gained a good aerial view of all the stalls. They were empty. Too bad; from up there it would have been like shooting fish in a barrel.

Werewolves in a can? She winced at her silent joke.

So the bathroom was a bust. Time to move on. Carefully, Ashe twisted to look behind her, gauging the distance to the countertop. She caught a glimpse of herself in the full-length mirror against the wall. Heavy boots, black-on-black clothes, blond hair straggling out of her ponytail. Yep, she was workin' the black ops chic. While dangling from the side of a toilet stall.

Good to know she'd put those junior high modeling classes to good use.

Ashe dropped back to the counter just as the outside

door swung open and someone walked in. In a flash, she aimed her gun in a two-handed grip.

Then she froze. *Oh. My. Goddess.* But she let her surprise last only a microsecond. Her eyes on the newcomer, she hopped to the floor. "What are you doing here?"

Captain Reynard gave a slight bow. "I am looking for you." His so-English accent sounded like something off *Masterpiece Theater*, but that baritone voice was pure seduction.

"Oh." For a moment, her mind hydroplaned. *Looking for me?*

The last and only time she'd met Reynard, he'd taken a battle-ax to the gut. He should have died. At best, he should still be moving like a cripple.

Now Reynard looked more than fine. No, that didn't cover it. He was Sleeping Beauty's dreams made flesh. The gold braid of his scarlet uniform glinted in the light. He wore his dark, thick hair pulled back into a neat queue, showing the angles of his lean face. His steel gray eyes were guarded, promising a thousand secrets, and enough bad boy lurked in the set of his mouth to make any red-blooded woman lick her chops in anticipation. If she was really, really naive.

Ashe turned her mental sprinkler system onto cold-shower mode. The guy looked her age, but for all she knew, he might have been three hundred. Reynard wasn't human anymore, but some kind of immortal. Who knew what that scrumptious packaging hid?

The muzzle of her gun was still aimed squarely between his eyes. He just stood there, ramrod straight, and made no move to draw his sword or raise the long firearm he carried. The piece looked like it belonged with the uniform—several hundred years out-of-date.

"I trust you are well?" he asked blandly.

She dragged her gaze away from the weapon and back to his face. "I didn't think you could leave the Castle, Captain Reynard. From everything I know, you shouldn't be here."

Reynard gave a smile more lethal than any gun. "Do you think this is a demon wearing my appearance?"

"Can the charm. I don't know. I don't know what happens when you leave your prison—and something deadly is stalking these grounds. Sue me for being cautious."

He glanced at her Colt, and a slight flicker of expression showed both amusement and annoyance. That annoyed her right back. He didn't think, or didn't care, that she would shoot. He didn't go for his own weapon—gun, knife, or anything else. No one was that cool unless they were crazy or a liar.

He met her eyes. Liar. Crazy. Iceberg. She couldn't read him. He was granite. *Damn.* Reynard studied her, his body nearly as still, as *not there*, as that of a vampire.

"I can leave my post for an hour or two. Nothing happens. I'm a guardsman, not one of the Castle's prisoners." With his free hand, he tapped the hilt of his sword, the gesture reminding Ashe of a detective flashing his badge.

"Why are you looking for me? How did you find me?"

"Word reached the Castle that you were on this case. I found you because, well, that is what guardsmen do. We find our quarry." He gave a ghost of a smile that didn't soften his face. "I take it you're not pleased to see me. I'm devastated."

Ashe ignored the last bit. "So you found me. Why are you looking?"

"I am here to help with your search. I suppose I should value the novelty of a trip to the world outside the Castle realm." Reynard somehow managed to glance around without completely looking away from her trigger finger.

"Uh-huh."

Now Reynard showed a sliver of uncertainty, a slight downturn of his mouth. "This looks very different from anything I recall."

"It's the women's bathroom."

He looked puzzled. "Bathing room? I don't see any tubs. No lady's boudoir ever looked like this."

Oh, Goddess. Ashe gave up and lowered the gun. "Why did you come to help?"

Reynard gave a small shrug, barely acknowledging the end of their standoff. Ashe tried to bury her temper. She was showing the guy some trust. This was the new, improved Ashe Carver, the one who didn't stake first and ask questions later. He should be grateful.

He leaned his old firearm against the shining tile wall. "The guardsmen know something about the creature you hunt."

Reynard folded his hands behind his back, the gesture very old-fashioned, but somehow commanding. Masterful suited him. It occurred to Ashe the title of captain might be a leftover from his human life.

"Go on," she said, forcing herself to concentrate past her ecstatic hormones.

"The creature escaped from the wilds deep in the Castle. I don't know why or how. It would not normally approach an inhabited area."

"So why did it?"

"I suspect someone turned it loose, but that is tomorrow's investigation. Tonight, we catch the creature, and that won't be easy. It's fast. It took only a moment for it to burst past our men and through the portal into your world." He stood, if at all possible, even straighter. "It escaped on our watch. Therefore, we must help with its recapture."

Ashe pushed her hair back. He followed the gesture with his eyes. Something dark and very male crossed his face, then was gone. The closed book of his expression had opened for just a second, but what she'd seen had made her whole body tighten. No, the guardsmen didn't get out much. The Castle kept them immortal, but it also kept their animal appetites under iron control.

But he wasn't in the Castle now. He'd claimed nothing would happen when he stepped outside its walls. *Bullshit.* That bad boy she'd glimpsed wanted out.

Caution flooded back, stiffening her shoulders. Caution and curiosity.

"What kind of creature is it?" she asked, and wondered whether she meant the man or the beast.

"A phouka."

Ashe tried to remember exactly what that was. She'd never encountered one, but thought it was a kind of animal. That would fit with the savage attack. "Can it talk or fire a gun?"

"No. It has no offensive magic that I know of, either."

"The best news I've heard all night." There were more questions to ask, but time was short. "So what's the plan?"

"To chase it back to the Castle. Mac doesn't want it killed. He says it's too rare."

Mac was the Castle's head honcho, Reynard's boss, and not a bad guy for a fire demon, but still ... "That's it? You're kidding. Surely you guys know what these creatures can do to a human body?"

Reynard gave a slight shrug. "He is my superior. I respect his orders. Mac does nothing lightly, and someone will pay for this breach of security. That is certain."

The memory of the chewed-on concessions clerk oozed through Ashe's imagination. "Okay. Fine. How do we get it to go home? Whistle? Rattle its kibble bag?"

"I'll open a portal to the Castle."

"Don't you need a key for that?"

"The old guards do not need keys. We can open a portal at will."

Ashe knew almost nothing about guardsman magic. She would have to accept that one on faith. "Okay. So, then what do I do?"

"You chase it through. Mac will have men waiting on the other side."

She gave an inward sigh. She didn't like working with others, much less turning control of the hunt over to someone else, but Reynard had a plan and she didn't. No points for her. "All right. C'mon."

Ashe pushed past him, through the door and out into the night. He followed silently, carrying his long firearm in one hand.

She turned and looked at it curiously. "That's a musket, right?"

He glanced down, like he just remembered he was carrying it. It was a part of him. "Yes."

"How many shots does that thing get?"

"Just one."

Okay, he might have a plan, but his weapons sucked. Points even. "Guess you don't get to miss."

He made a soft sound, not quite a laugh, that raised the hairs on her arms. There was something predatory in it. "I would rather count on hitting the target than need a second shot."

"Can't argue with that." But she did, and her tone said so. The thing belonged in a museum.

Reynard gave her a sharp look. He was tall but so was Ashe, and the full force of his gaze caught her straight on. His gray eyes looked darker in the uncertain light. "Do you find fault with me?"

"Not with you. That weapon is old and, forgive me, primitive."

"You have no reason to worry." His voice wasn't quite so friendly now.

She let the subject drop. She'd said what she had to say.

They'd reached the sidewalk that snaked along the perimeter of the buildings. Gift shop. Coffee shop. Ice-cream stand. Art gallery. Restaurant. All the windows were dark, except for the odd security light. It made Ashe think of a movie set after the cast went home. By contrast, the workers left the gardens lit for the search. Colored lights peeked from the flower beds and dotted the paths, making a fairyland of the night garden. Floodlights of red, green, and blue washed the branches of the trees. It was beautiful, but tricked the eyes. There could be anything hiding in that fantasia of color.

The night air was cool enough for her to feel the heat

from his body as they walked side by side. He smelled faintly of gun oil, as if he'd been cleaning his weapon before he came. She liked the scent. She'd been drawn to him from the moment they met last autumn—he'd been brutally wounded; she'd been one of the fighters defending the Castle. She'd guarded him until help arrived. The stuff of action-movie romance.

But I got over it. Besides being a not-quite-human guy from another century, Reynard was doomed to eternal servitude in an alternate dimension. Talk about geographically incompatible. No, drop-dead gorgeous didn't make up for everything.

Besides, she'd had to change. The old Ashe Carver—aggressive, mouthy, with a free-range libido—had been forced to grow up now that her daughter was living with her. She was less eager to start a fight just to see what would happen. It mattered if she took a bullet, because she had to work a regular job. Most of all, having a kid had made her picky about whom she spent time with and utterly paranoid about whom she brought home.

So she wasn't going to lose her cool over a little eau de gun oil. Ashe tried to shift her weight away, put a few inches between her body and Reynard's, but he touched her shoulder and gestured silently. Across the lawn, something flickered through the darkness, barely a ripple of shadow. Their quarry had speed on its side.

She nodded. In silent agreement, they took off after it. Reynard bolted ahead of her, incredibly fast. The not-quite-human thing obviously had perks.

She cut a steeper angle across the lawn, trying to shave off distance, leaping over the beds of tulips and English daisies. Reynard held out a hand, slowing, crouching. Ashe skidded to a halt, dropping to one knee on the ground beside him. The cool air felt good in her panting lungs, chill and tangy from the nearby ocean.

"It's up there," he said. "It's trapped in the dead end."

Ashe squinted. Directly ahead there was an arbor the size of her bedroom at home. About forty hanging baskets ringed the area. Behind them was a wall of rock. The phouka was moving beneath the baskets, making them swing like silent bells.

She'd expected something with the liquid grace of a predator. She couldn't make out much except that it seemed to be far less coordinated when it wasn't running. The shadow bunched and shuffled as it went.

"Can we corner it?" she whispered, so softly that her lips almost touched his ear.

The shadow that was the thing stretched tall, making the baskets dance on their chains. Reynard put a finger to his lips. Whatever that creature was, it had superhearing. *Crap, we're busted.*

They waited, stock-still, as the breeze fluttered the grass. Fortunately, they were upwind. The creature relaxed, seeming to snuffle at the plants around it. Ashe wished she could use her flashlight without giving them away, or that the creature would move into the beam of a floodlight. Not being able to see what she was hunting was getting on her nerves.

Reynard pointed to himself, pointed to the stone wall, and made a circling motion with his finger. He was going to move ahead and get ready to open a portal. Ashe gave a thumbs-up. He stood very slowly, silent as a ghost, the gold braid on his coat mere stripes in the darkness. She tensed her muscles, ready to sprint into action the moment she needed to surprise the beast into the Castle.

Reynard froze. "Where did it go?"

Good question. The baskets were still, the platform empty. Ashe's hands felt suddenly cold, clammy, as if her blood were trying to flee her body. She squashed her fear down, swallowing hard. "Shit."

She let out a long, frustrated breath and rose to her feet. In the moment it took to exchange hand signals with the captain, the creature had slipped away. Good thing there were only two directions the beast could have gone.

"Up there." She pointed to her right. "The only other

choice is the front gate. It won't go that way if it doesn't like lights and people."

Reynard followed her pointing hand. "Where does that path lead?"

"There's a sunken garden—it was a quarry once. Steep stairs. Blind corners. Tons o' fun."

Even in the dark, she caught the depth of his frown.

"Not ideal, I know."

He shrugged, his face returning to its usual shuttered expression. "My father wagered I'd meet my death in a foolish hunting accident."

"Oh, yeah?"

"I dread the thought that for once he was right about me."

Ashe wasn't sure, but thought he might have made a joke. He was damned hard to read. "Follow me."

Ashe started up the path at a quick, crouched run. She moved almost silently, weapon drawn and ready, two-handed grip, muzzle pointed skyward. Wouldn't do to slip and murder the bushes in cold sap.

Reynard followed without a fuss about who took point. It was a refreshing change after some of the other slayers she'd met. Give a boy a stake and he thought he was Rambo, Doctor Doom, and Lawrence of Arabia rolled into one spray-tanned package.

"What is that stench?" Reynard said under his breath, the words faint ghosts against the whispering leaves.

Ashe stopped cold. Bad smells might mean dead bodies. Poison. The musk of unspeakable monsters. She caught a whiff of the offensive scent and relaxed. "It's the burger stand. They need to clean the grease trap."

"That's food?" The whispered word dripped with doubt.

"Sort of."

"It seems I have not tasted it for too long. It did not seem familiar."

Sarcasm dipped in sugary innocence. Not hard to read that time. "I thought Mac changed all that. I thought you guys could eat and drink these days."

"That applies only to the new guards."

"Not you?"

Ashe forgot her caution for a split second and glanced behind her. Reynard stood beneath a Garry oak just coming into leaf. A red spotlight illuminated the twisting branches like gnarled, bloody fingers. The strange light made the path seem even darker. She could barely make the captain out, just a faint red sheen reflecting from the buttons of his uniform. It looked like a row of glowing eyes.

"Our terms of service have not changed."

The words were more of a rebuff than an explanation. The old guards didn't need pansy-assed creature comforts like food. His tone made her suddenly cold, like an unexpected breath against her neck. Unsettled, she turned and started moving forward again.

"Yeah, well, my daughter loves those burgers," she said, a little gruffly.

For a split second, she imagined Eden's ten-year-old face, the child's animal delight in ravaging the oh-so-unhealthy treat. She switched off the image, ducking the emotions it brought. Doubt. Anger. Fear of loss. Custody issues were a bitch.

If Ashe didn't concentrate, she'd put herself and Reynard in danger.

To their left was a high wall of rock. To their right was a swath of flowers that rolled away into an expanse of lawn. The wind in the spring grass was a ruffling swish. The beast, if it was nearby, was utterly silent. Ashe searched everywhere, her eyes aching with the strain of looking so hard. A minute or two passed.

"You have a child?" Now Reynard's voice was careful, as if he'd been mulling over that idea and couldn't quite believe it. She could almost hear his good manners choking him.

"Yeah. So I don't fit the maternal profile. Live with it."

She heard him draw breath, but he didn't reply. Smart guy.

The path wound around a sharp bend, turning away

from the lawn. Now both sides were hemmed in by steep rising slopes, trees and bushes obstructing their lines of sight. This was the stretch that most worried her. An attacker would have the advantage of surprise and higher ground.

Reynard caught up until he was more beside than behind her. They stopped talking, all their attention fixed on the night around them. They'd instinctively divided the compass. Reynard watched to the right and behind them, Ashe to the left and in front. Ashe could anticipate his moves and mirrored him, weapons sweeping in deadly symmetry. In other circumstances, they would have danced well together.

The thought almost made her smile—a deadly, cold smile suitable for a hunt, but a good one nonetheless. It barely made it to her lips before they were leaving the blind passage and relief pushed out every other emotion. And then the moon-washed vista below gave her something new to worry about.

"There it is," breathed Reynard, the words hot against her ear.

Oh! She cringed at what she saw, every muscle screaming to turn away.

The beast crouched on the top landing of the concrete stairway that led down into the sunken garden. What the moon didn't show, the safety lights along the steps did. Crouched on all fours, it looked bulky and round and at least as tall as Ashe's ribs. It had a pretty, soft brown and white coat.

"Oh, now, that's just wrong," she murmured, her words barely audible.

The twitch-twitch of its nose made Ashe queasy. Or maybe it was the clots of blood around the whiskery muzzle, or the glittering black eyes.

"It's a hell bunny," she croaked. "A bunny ate the concessions clerk."

"Indeed," Reynard replied.

Monsters were supposed to look like monsters, or tried to fake being human. This was just confusing.

"I wish you'd warned me. Those floppy ears are awfully cute." Ashe tilted her head, as if the angle could somehow make the view better. She really hoped it didn't have a cotton-puff tail. That would just make it harder to blow its head off, if push came to hop.

"Don't underestimate it. We tried offering it a carrot," Reynard whispered, his tone dry as grave dust. "It prefers something less crispy."

With that phrase, he warped all her happy Easter memories. She used to love those marshmallow-filled bunnies wrapped in pink foil. She never would again. "Next time, I am so going to bite the head off first."

Reynard gave her a puzzled look. "I wouldn't do that. It has a deadly kick."

Ashe closed her eyes, opened them again, forced her thoughts into neat rows. "Okay. We are bunny doom. How do you want to play this?"

The rabbit suddenly started and bounded down the stairs. The stealth portion of the evening was decidedly over.

Reynard bounded after it, vaulting over the guardrail and dropping to the stairs. A dangerous move, but it put him yards ahead of Ashe.

"Cut it off at the water up ahead!" he bellowed.

Ashe scrambled, leaped off the last few stairs, and sprinted over the lawn, angling to the right of the path. The garden was shaped like a doughnut, a spire of rock forming a lookout in the center. On the far side of the doughnut glittered a water garden. Ashe could hear a waterfall muttering like a distant conversation.

Her boots thumped on the grass, skidding as she leaped over a flower bed. Reynard had gone to the left, circling the other way. No blind corners here, but there were too many bushes for her liking. She made it past the lookout and headed for the pond, the colored lights in the flower beds splashing her legs green, then blue.

She sensed the hell bunny almost as she reached it. A thrill of energy down her skin told her she was far too close. *A creature of the dark fey.* A day late and a dollar short, everything she'd read about phoukas was coming back to her.

It reared up from the hydrangeas like a Beatrix Potter nightmare, front paws tucked against its fuzzy chest, nose working. A glob of flesh clung to one whisker, weighting it down.

Ashe stumbled back three steps, weapon already aimed at Vlad Cottontail. "Where's that portal?"

"Nearly ready," Reynard shouted back.

She felt a second thrust of energy from his direction, ants skittering over her flesh, biting, stabbing. The power rushed to her head like a slug of whiskey. Ashe gripped the Colt, using her own shredded magic to shove the high out of her brain.

An orange disk of light began to flare, hanging in space just above the lily pond. The portal spiraled from a bright pinpoint to the size of a hubcap in seconds. She prayed Reynard could get it open fast.

A charred smell filled the air, as if the wall between Earth and the Castle's dimension were burning away. Ashe could see the portal growing behind the rabbit, outlining its floppy ears like a bright harvest moon. The beast was shifting its backside the way a cat does before a pounce.

"Hurry it up!" she yelled.

"Drive the beast this way!" Reynard answered.

"Haul ass, Cottontail," she snarled, sighting down the gun.

The rabbit bared choppers and snarled right back.

Crap.

The demon rabbit seemed to sense the portal, because it hunkered in on itself, glancing from the gun to the ballooning orange glow. It looked angry and miserable. Ashe felt a moment of pity, and then thought of all the tender, juicy kiddies coming all too soon for the Easter egg hunt. Yum, yum.

"Okay, bud, do it the hard way." Ashe shot the dirt at its feet.

It launched straight for her throat. Scary fast.

Shit! Ashe dropped to the ground, rolling out of its way and back to her knees in time to fire three shots at its head. They went wide. The rabbit flew over her, unable to stop its momentum. She heard Reynard shout, then a shot that wasn't hers. She rolled for the flower bed. Two more shots bit the earth behind her.

Ashe panted, hot confusion sparking over her nerves like live voltage. Those shots weren't from Reynard's musket. His gun would fire only once, and it wouldn't sound anything like a high-powered automatic rifle. Neither would anything the local security carried. *What the hell?*

She tucked her feet under her, coming out of her crouch an inch at a time. The bushes, so dense when she was hunting, now seemed woefully sparse. Her knees were steady, but she could feel a fine trembling in her muscles from the cocktail of adrenaline and hard running. The night was full of edges, sharp, clear, honed by danger.

A bullet sang by her ear, another spray of splintered bark. She did a face-plant in the dirt—pure reflex.

More shots came. The rabbit thundered by, claws barely missing the flesh of her arm. Ashe tracked it with her eyes, her cheek pressed into the soft, damp soil. The beast headed straight for the portal, leaping through the orange whorl. As it arched through the vortex, she saw the powder-puff tail on its vanishing backside.

She thought she heard someone shout on the other side of the orange glow—maybe Mac and his men playing zookeepers on the other side. Like a spiraling lens, the portal closed, the orange glow shrinking to nothing.

Then Reynard was in the dirt beside Ashe. The charcoal scent of the portal's magic clung to him like cologne. He put a hand on her shoulder, a hot, firm touch. "Are you hurt?"

"Get down!" she barked, dragging him by the collar of his fancy coat.

The next shot missed his head by a whisker.

Chapter 2

She could smell his sweat, the dirt, and the tang of crushed plants. She'd landed in a herbaceous border, destroying the gardeners' careful work. A mound of thyme was bleeding spice into the night air.

She could hear the clock tower of the main building chiming eleven. Time to be home watching the late news, not chasing monsters around a tourist trap. Wait— they'd bagged the monster. So why was someone still shooting at them?

Reynard gripped her arm. "Are you hurt?" he repeated.

"No." She turned to look at him, careful not to raise her head too far. "How about you?"

"No."

They lay still for a moment, breathing, listening to the dark spring night.

"Anyone trying to kill you these days?" she asked.

"Not outside the Castle."

His eyes glittered. It might have been humor. She couldn't quite tell. He was too closed, too different, like a map with no street names or landmarks. Just a lot of really nice geography.

Ashe swallowed hard, willing her jackhammer pulse to slow down. "Then the shooter must be after me."

"A common occurrence?"

"Not since I moved to Fairview." *Shit. Shit.* This was all supposed to be in the past. She had relocated, given up life on the road, scaled down the hunting to almost nothing—just the odd case. She'd let the word go out that she was retired. Sure, there'd always be some unhappy campers—friends and relatives of the supernatural monsters she'd exterminated—but even they'd grown quiet.

Quiet enough that Ashe had taken the risk of sending for her daughter.

Shit.

Ashe crawled backward, a slithering motion that brought her to the shadow of a thick bush. She rose into a crouch, molding her body to the shape of the greenery, hiding in the dense leaves. She guessed at the angle the bullets had traveled. That put the shooter high up the tall column of rock that formed the lookout in the center of the sunken garden. She knew there was a nearly vertical staircase that led up to the platform at the top, but it wasn't lit at night. All she could see was the dark spire of stone blotting out the stars.

Reynard moved to her left side, noiseless as a phantom. Wisps of dark hair framed his face. His neck cloth had come untied. Ashe couldn't help noticing messy looked good on him.

He rested on one knee, raising the long musket. "Stay down," he said quietly. "I'll take care of this."

A sour burn of impatience caught in Ashe's throat. "There's no way to make the shot at this distance."

"No?" There was that sarcasm again.

"It's dark."

"I live in a dungeon. I've adapted to the dark." He sighted down the long barrel as confidently as if it had one of the super-duper, high-whatever nightscopes Ashe had seen in the latest mercenaries' mag.

They were wasting time. Firing would give away

their position. They'd be better off sneaking up on the sniper. "That thing has a range of two feet. A crooked two feet."

He sighed lightly, and cranked back the hammer. It was at that moment she saw it had a real, honest-to-Goddess flint secured in the jaws of the mechanism. This thing relied on sparks and naked gunpowder. They'd be lucky if it didn't blow up.

"They won't be expecting us to return fire," he said evenly.

"Because it's not possible! I have a real gun, and I can't make that shot."

Thoroughly ignoring her, Reynard pulled the trigger, jerking as the musket recoiled. It banged like a giant cap gun and smelled like a chemistry set gone wrong. Ashe opened her mouth to protest and got a mouthful of foul-tasting smoke.

And there was a distant, sharp cry of pain. Reynard had hit his mark.

"That's not possible!" She realized she sounded annoyed.

He made a noise that was almost a laugh. "Just a touch of a spell. I thought witches were open to magic."

"I'm not a witch anymore."

He gave her a look, grabbed the musket, and slipped into the darkness. Swearing, Ashe ran to catch up. The entrance to the staircase was on the other side of the tall spire of rock, forcing them to circle its base. The colored lights that illuminated the flower beds dwindled, then stopped as soon as they left the footpath. Ashe tripped, nearly going down on one knee before she bumped into Reynard.

He steadied her, and she could feel the remnants of magic clinging to Reynard's long, strong fingers. But there was more than that; she felt power spilling over her like sand in a windstorm, stinging in a thousand tiny bites. Whoever—whatever—had been shooting at them was hurt, and not human.

She thought again about her daughter, and knew fear.

Reynard took a step forward. Ashe grabbed his arm. "You had only one shot in your musket. I should go first."

He pulled what looked like a very modern Smith & Wesson—it was hard to tell in the dark—from a holster hidden at the small of his back. "I could reload. I also carry a backup. As Mac is so fond of saying, shit happens."

The obscenity sounded wrong coming from him. Of course, every assumption she'd made about him so far that night had been off base. Not a good thing when they were supposed to be covering each other's backs.

Reynard started up the stairs, showing just how good his night vision was. Ashe brought up the rear. There was an iron railing to her right, but that was her gun hand, so she left it alone. Her skin crawled, not just with power but with vertigo. Normally she didn't mind heights, but all that changed when she couldn't see where she was putting her feet. She felt for the steps and counted each one. Good to know how many steps she'd climbed in case she had to reverse course in a hurry. Thinking you were at the bottom of the pitch-dark stairs when you weren't could be a problem.

More plants and bushes grew on the rock spire. Leaves brushed her face like slick, green fingers. They reached the landing, where the stairs took a sharp turn. Overhead was a wash of stars, thick and bright because the gardens were outside the city. Above the canopy of trees, the waxing moon gave a thin wash of light. Ashe saw Reynard hold up his left hand, then point. His right hand was curled around his weapon. Ashe grasped her own gun in both hands, reassured by its cold, heavy weight.

They went up the last dozen stairs. At the top was a kidney-shaped platform surrounded by an iron railing. It was like another small garden. The flower bed, maple tree, and bench would have been lovely in daylight. At night, the scene was eerie.

Reynard turned right and swept his gun downward

to point at the fallen shooter. Ashe aimed at the figure sprawled facedown on the ground. He was twisted as if an effort to duck had spun him around.

Vampire. Now that she was close, Ashe could almost taste his essence. His energy was pouring needles of power over her like the skitter of insect feet on her skin. She glided to the left of the figure, Reynard to the right, until they stood on opposite sides of their quarry.

What happened next depended entirely on the vamp. Why had he shot at her? She wanted an explanation. She'd be happy to keep him alive—vibrantly undead?— at least long enough to question him. Longer if he played nice. Then again, he'd tried to kill her already. If he attacked, there'd be no messing around.

The vamp was male, medium height, dressed in jeans. A scatter of weapons and a tripod were strewn around him. She smelled blood, but saw only a shining stain on the back of his jacket. It was too dark to see color. He was motionless, but still she kicked his rifle out of reach. It was a sniper's piece—nightscope and all the fancy fixings.

"Weapon says he meant business," she said softly.

"It seems your enemies put forward their best efforts," Reynard replied.

"I'm so flattered." Ashe took another quick inventory of the vamp. Short leather boots. The glint of a fancy watch. Dark hair, collar length. "Y'know, at first I wondered why someone would shoot from a place with only one escape route."

As she spoke, she shifted the Colt to her left hand and reached into the pocket that ran up the outside of her right thigh. Familiarity washed through her. Slaying wasn't her happy place, but it was one she knew inside and out. And it was the place where a bad guy ceased to be a "he" and became an "it." It was easier to take them out if they weren't people.

Ashe pulled out a long, straight, sharp stake. "Then it came to me. Vamps can fly. And then I thought of another thing. I was called out here on an emergency. How did an assassin know where I'd be? Somebody's been doing some planning, and I'm going to want names."

The vampire struck. The speed was breathtaking, lifting it from a facedown sprawl to a frontal attack in less than a second—but she'd been expecting that. Ashe felt the thing's body pound into the stake, and she used its own momentum to drive the weapon home. All she had to do was brace her feet against all that brute force and lean into it.

The vamp flailed its arms, trying to change direction and pull away, trying to slash and bite and escape all at once. She'd judged the vamp's height fairly well, but the stake had entered just below its heart. Ashe felt her feet skid on the stone beneath her, sliding far too close to the iron railing and the sheer drop beyond.

Reynard yelled, grabbing the vamp from behind. In a flash of moonlight, she could see the vampire's face—features twisted in pain and rage. Reynard was managing to pin its arms, something no human should have been able to do. That seemed to scare the monster even more than the stake.

Ashe twisted her weapon, driving upward. The vampire gasped. She stopped a hairsbreadth from skewering it, praying Reynard's strength would hold. She was taking a risk, pausing like this, but a chance at information was worth it.

She could feel his—its—breath on her skin, catch the faint, sweet smell of its venom. A vampire's poison was so addictive, its erotic high made its victims slaves after just one bite.

"Why were you shooting at me?" she demanded.

It bared fangs, giving a rattling hiss.

"Scary, but I've seen better," she said.

Reynard did something that made the vampire wince. "Answer."

"Abomination!" it snarled, and gave one last lunge at her.

"Last" being the operative term. Ashe slammed the stake upward just before its fangs could reach her flesh. She heard the snap of its teeth as they closed on air.

The vampire was suddenly deadweight. Reynard let the body drop, wood still protruding from its chest.

Ashe looked down at the vampire. She knew she would feel plenty later—anger, triumph, regret, pity, self-justification—but at the moment she was blank. She'd done what she had to do. Once the adrenaline wore off, the rest could engulf her.

The vampire had called her an abomination. She opened her mouth to comment on how strange that was, coming from a bloodsucking monster, but closed it again. It was weird enough that she didn't want to even think about it. Besides, there were other, more pressing questions—like why had the vamp chosen to die rather than talk?

It could be vengeance. It could be something else. Whatever it was, it was personal. That thought made her queasy.

"Are you all right?" Reynard asked.

"Yeah," Ashe said, keeping her voice light. "It went down easily enough."

Reynard sat down on the bench, head bowed. Ashe looked away. He looked glum, but skewering the enemy wasn't a cheery kind of thing. And then again, you didn't get into this kind of work to talk about your feelings.

Ashe turned to lean on the railing. Below was the garden, bathed in starlight. A much better view than the vampire. The body had already started to shrivel. In about twenty minutes, it would be a pile of dust. It was like time caught up with the vamps, grinding them to nothing. Once it was gone, they would search the vamp's possessions for clues.

Above, the stars glittered like sequins on a torch singer's evening gown. Below, the gardens glowed like a fairy kingdom. It seemed distant and surreal, a pretty mirage she could look at but not touch. She was made from a different element—something far less appealing.

At some point along the way, when her parents died,

or when her husband died, or maybe when she'd bagged her first monster, Ashe had let herself slide into the darkness. Now that her daughter was home, she had to snap out of it. Kids needed a bright, shiny world. Eden needed something besides a monster-slaying action figure for a mom. Too bad Ashe didn't know how to be anything else.

She would try. Goddess knew she would try. She would strive to see the beauty in the world and look away from the shadows. It was her duty as a parent.

She heard Reynard shift on the bench behind her.

"You should come see the view," she said.

"No, thank you." His voice was quiet. The dark made it oddly intimate.

"Why not?"

He was silent for a few heartbeats. "I have to go back to the Castle."

"So?" She turned, leaning against the rail to face him.

He raised his head, but didn't meet her eyes. "Whatever I see out here will make me restless, and I don't have a choice about going back. It's best I see as little as possible."

There was so much regret in the words, it bruised her. Regret—that, she knew. She could almost taste it like coppery blood on her tongue, sharp and familiar.

Now, finally, there was something about him that she understood.

And, Goddess help her, she suddenly wanted to fix it.

Chapter 3

"This is Errata Jones at CSUP, the station that defines the supernatural in the beautiful city of Fairview. It's eleven-oh-seven, just after the late news, and we're back to talk some more about what the presence of the Castle in our town means for us.

"The new head honcho at the Castle—that would be our very own ex police detective Conall 'Mac' Macmillan—has been hiring locals for guards, and a number of our Fairview boys have signed on.

"Well, girls and ghouls, that sounds like a great way to earn money and meet interesting people, doesn't it? But I'd still ask a few questions before picking up my staff ID card. My sources have learned that, up until this recent hiring spree, the last man to join the guardsmen was Captain Reynard, back in 1758. Why did recruiting stop for two and a half centuries? And why do we so rarely see the guards outside the Castle walls? After that long, you'd think those guys would want a breath of fresh air.

"So, what exactly are our poor mortal lads getting themselves into? Once they're in, there's a confidentiality clause that forbids the guardsmen from talking to us. What doesn't the Castle administration want us to know?"

Inside the Castle, Reynard found himself alone. He paused, letting the portal drift shut behind him. It closed with a faint popping noise that reminded him of smacking lips. The Castle had swallowed him up again.

He straightened his clothes, dusting mud from his sleeve. The light was low enough that his eyes barely needed to adjust from the dark outside. The area where he stood was a round, empty chamber, chosen because it was large enough to corral and capture the rabbitlike creature. Like most of the Castle, it was built of rough gray stone and lit by ever-burning torches that cast barely more than a flickering orange glow. He had expected to find some of his fellow guardsmen, but apparently they had bagged their quarry and left.

Well, he'd done his part already. Captain of the guardsmen who patrolled this section of the Castle, he had gone into the world and recaptured an escaped prisoner. He had done it a thousand times, and would do it a thousand more. His duty ended only if he was killed or the otherworldly magic of the Castle prison wound down. These retrievals were his only break in routine.

One would think he'd welcome them. Instead, he hated leaving the Castle. He hated coming back in. It was a cruel thing to taste freedom and then to walk away from it after only a few hours.

The outside world held everything he had lost, and everything he might be tempted to take. The Castle robbed him of much—hunger, thirst, lust, joy—as part of the ancient magic that prevented overpopulation by the inmates or the gobbling up of weaker species. Perversely, anger and bitterness remained. The Castle had little love, but much war.

In contrast, the outside world sharpened his appetite after decades of nothingness. Sensation—the scent of grass, the wind against his cheek—vibrated in his bones like colors long forgotten, clinging a moment before they crumbled into the dust of memory.

Desire, so heady minutes ago, still clung to his imagination. He envisioned Ashe Carver's body under his, warm and female, the spice of thyme washing around them. She was strong, but no match for a guardsman. He could think of a thousand ways he'd like to show her that strength. He savored the hunger, imprinting it on his mind before it, too, fell to cobwebs.

Reynard had a reputation for iron discipline. Few considered why it might be necessary, or what would happen if that discipline slipped. On the other hand, he remembered who and what he'd been before he got there: angry, womanizing, a gambler, a duelist, and every other hazard a debutante's mama might think to warn her baby chick against. That man was long gone, but every so often he felt that devil stir.

He wiped the light sweat that clung to his face and started walking down the corridor, barely bothering to look around him. There were no windows, no views of another landscape. There was only an inside to the Castle, an endless maze of shadowed corridors and vaulted rooms. The stone dungeon had lost its novelty value approximately two and a half centuries ago, but what could one expect from an eternal curse? From what he could tell, curses all began with great fanfare, but were one-note songs. Eventually they faded to the background, like a ticking clock: *doomed, damned, doomed, damned.*

A crashing bore, really.

From a chamber or two away he heard Mac singing— if it could be described as such—at the top of his lungs, "Kill the wa-a-a-a-abbit!"

Despite himself, Reynard smiled. Mac had been a human officer of the law, become a fire demon, and now described himself as head of Castle operations. There was much to admire—courage, loyalty, and a shrewd mind. There was also much about him that puzzled Reynard.

"Kill the waaabbit!"

Puzzled him a lot.

Reynard turned the corner. Mac was in a small room to the left, writing on the duty roster he had pinned to the wall. Mac was large—a head taller than Reynard and bulky with muscle. He was wearing the same modern clothes many of the outsiders wore—jeans and a T-shirt that left his tattooed forearms bare. But Mac was no outsider. He was as close to a friend as Reynard had known for at least a hundred years.

"Did you kill the wabbit—er—rabbit?" Reynard asked. "I thought you merely wanted to recapture it."

Mac gave him scandalized eyes—an odd look, since they held a glint of demonic fire. "Of course I didn't kill it. We took it back to its habitat. Some idiot had left the gates open."

"Then why are you singing about putting the creature to death?"

"I'm quoting Elmer Fudd."

"One of your modern poets?"

A look crossed Mac's face. "Not really."

"Do I surmise that this is one of those cultural gaps no amount of explanation will close?"

"You got it."

Reynard could hear the hubbub of the guards' quarters a short distance away. Since Mac had arrived, the anti-appetite magic had been reduced in the quarters of the common men. Something close to a normal, noisy, messy life had returned—at least for the new recruits. For the old guard, as he'd said to Ashe, things never changed. They were subject to the Castle's laws, but there was other, additional magic that ruled them—spells that denied them any benefits from Mac's kindlier regime.

Reynard could smell the oily stink of roasting meat and hear the muted babble of one of those *television* devices. He edged a few inches away from the sound. They had a way of hypnotizing a man. He'd find himself wasting hours unless he was cautious, lost in images of things he could never have or do.

"How was the trip?" Mac asked.

"It was successful."

"That much I got from the sofa-sized rabbit hurtling through the portal."

Mac made a notation on a clipboard that hung on the wall, using a mechanical pencil leashed to the board with string. *As if that would stop a thief.* The Castle residents were notorious for stealing pens, flashlights, and anything else that was new. Such small wonders were as candy to children. Try as he might to ignore modern fripperies, even Reynard knew about cell phones and netbooks. And—he was ashamed to admit—he had been known to carry off the occasional roll of duct tape. That stuff could be used for *everything*.

Mac glanced up from writing. "What I'm asking is whether you enjoyed your trip."

"It is better if I do not enjoy myself. It makes returning all the harder."

"Ever hear of the concept of vacation?"

"It's different for us." Reynard had seen soldiers go mad once they reached the open air, throwing civilization aside like barbarians sacking a town. "Killion left on a mission and murdered five farmers before we took his head. At the end, he was babbling about too much open space."

"I think he was at the extreme end of the sanity bell curve."

"Killion was not an isolated case."

"You think your head would explode if you took a few weeks for yourself? Everyone deserves time off. I mean, it's up to you, but you're not one of the men I worry about."

"Thank you, but no."

Reynard thrust the idea aside before it could infect him. He liked to say he had two and a half centuries of overdue leave, but Mac didn't understand. As capable as he was, there were things he didn't know about the Castle.

The old guards had their secrets. There was a reason they never left.

One of the new guards walked by, pierced and tattooed, with a chain-mail shirt, leather kilt, stainless-steel coffee mug, and Doc Martens. He waved a hand at Reynard. "Hey, there, Cap'n."

"Stewart." Reynard nodded, overlooking the easy familiarity of the boy. Like the other new recruits, Stewart was a mere puppy, full of jokes and fun. Mac hired men as good with people as they were with weapons.

Stewart stopped, grinning sheepishly. "I'm going to need to book some time off in August."

Mac looked up. "Yeah, what for?"

The boy's eyebrows lifted, pierced rings and all. "Honeymoon. Becky said yes."

"Well, all right!" Mac said, thumping Stewart on the back. "Did you make her sign an insurance waiver? Y'know, hold harmless against risk and all that?"

"Why, do you think marriage to me is as bad as an extreme sport?"

"You tell me." Mac waggled his eyebrows.

"Ha, ha. Maybe I should sign one. She said she'd break my neck if she doesn't get two weeks in the Rockies."

"Congratulations! All the best wishes to you and the fair lady." Reynard shook his hand. "So, you'll expect your wedding day off work as well?"

"If you don't mind."

"We'll consider it," Reynard said, deadpan. "It might cause some problems with the schedule."

Stewart grinned, showing the even, white teeth that all the new men and women seemed to have. "I know you'll do your best, Cap'n. And I want you at the wedding, if you can come."

"Thank you." Reynard was unexpectedly touched by the invitation. He didn't bother to say it was impossible to accept. That could wait.

Stewart ambled away, lifting the mug to his lips as he walked. Reynard studied the young man as he disappeared down the hall. New recruits were desperately needed, but it was all one could do not to resent them for the life they had. Stewart had a woman he went home to every night. He was also mortal and utterly fragile without the devil's bargain that made the old guards ageless, indestructible, and trapped.

Trapped. The best he could ever hope for was a dull contentment and devotion to his duty. *Stop dwelling on it. Get over it.*

He was picking up these modernisms at a shameful pace. Soon he would even talk like one of these boys.

That might be fun.

He imagined himself hurrying home to a woman after a hard day's work. What would Ashe Carver be like stripped of all her weaponry? There was something of the pirate queen in her fierceness. Would she be soft and womanly between the sheets? Or just as much an Amazon as she had been tonight? He let that question melt on his tongue, savoring all the possible answers and loving the fact she was so different from any woman he'd ever met.

Evidently, even a brief exposure to the outside world had affected him. Or maybe some of that was just the woman herself. Either way, his imagination was going places he'd all but forgotten.

Mac finally finished writing. "There. I've taken you off the next watch."

Reynard wrenched his mind back to his cold, stone reality. "Why?"

"Someone let that rabbit beastie out of its habitat. I want to go look at the gate again. Come with me."

"Are you looking for something specific?" Reynard unhooked the clasp of the leather cartridge box slung across his left shoulder, taking out ball and cartridge and reloading the musket in a drill he'd performed thousands of times. Cartridge. Prime. Load. Ram. If they were walking into the depths of the Castle, he was going to be ready.

"Specific?" Mac mused. "Maybe. Or maybe just a general vibe. I want to know who opened that gate, and why. You know the residents of this place far better than I do. You might see a clue that I would miss."

Reynard slid the ramrod back into its holder beside the barrel of the musket. "Perhaps it was sabotage. By a strange coincidence, there was a vampire hunting Ashe Carver at the exact second we were there chasing the creature. That led us on a merry little dance."

Mac was checking his own piece, a SIG Sauer automatic. His eyebrows shot up. "What? Full report, soldier."

"She was not harmed."

"Of course not. You were there."

Reynard allowed himself a small smile. "She would have skewered her vampire with or without me. I was merely a convenient accessory."

Mac gave a dry laugh and set off down the hallway, gesturing for Reynard to follow. "That's Ashe, all right."

"I'm serious. I might have stayed home with my feet up. Most cutting to a man's sense of self-worth. It's not as if I haven't killed my fair share of men and monsters." In fact, considering his duels, battles, and years in the Castle, he'd simply lost count.

"Just think of the pleasant conversation you'd have missed."

"Are you referring to the part where she threatened to blow my head off, or when she insulted my Brown Bess? There was no time for pleasantries. She didn't even refer to the battle for the Castle, or that we had met before." *Or that she had nursed me in my hour of need, saved my life, kept me from bleeding to death. Such pathos, utterly wasted on the woman.*

Mac shot him an amused look. "Disappointed?"

Yes, bitterly, but he hid it. "Perplexed. It's true we were busy, but anyone else would have at least asked after my health."

"Dude, she's a killer."

"Some of the most pleasant people I know are flesh-eating werejackals. There is no excuse for bad manners. Did you know she has a daughter?"

"Sure. Her name's Eden. Cute kid. Calls me Uncle Mac."

"Ashe is a widow, is she not?"

"Yup."

"Hm." Reynard stopped there, refusing to indulge his curiosity about the woman any further. It wasn't as if he could put any of the information to good use. Opportunities for seduction were long lost to him.

Mac sighed. "Let's just focus on the hell bunny. Tell me what happened. From the beginning. What was Ashe doing there, anyway?"

Reynard fell into step beside him. The conversation, however much it was about the task at hand, lightened his mood. They passed a pair of guardsmen returning from patrol, the torchlight throwing strange shadows across their weary faces. They paused and exchanged a few words. Brief, efficient, factual, but friendly—the way Reynard liked it. Morale was important but hard to maintain.

They moved on. Reynard told Mac what had happened in the gardens that night, step by step. They passed another group of guardsmen, but this time Mac just waved a greeting. Reynard had reached the part where they'd killed the vamp.

"What the hell?" Mac grumbled. "This was no coincidence. Who would be working inside *and* outside the Castle? Who would know that Ashe would get the call to go investigate?"

Reynard hated the fact that she'd been tricked. He would, come what may, teach that unknown villain courtesy to a lady. "Someone who knows she is in Fairview, obviously."

"More than that. Someone who knows her family. The police wouldn't call her directly. They'd call her brother-in-law first."

"Then why did he not come instead?"

"There's a new baby in the house."

"Of course." A witch and a vampire had produced a baby girl—a miracle by anyone's standards. Even the Castle guards had heard that snippet of gossip. Odd how even the most seasoned warrior could be moved by word of a birth. Soldiers were surprisingly sentimental.

Mac and Reynard had walked beyond the guards' quarters and were crossing through a long cavern that sloped gently downward. The atmosphere changed, growing almost cavelike. The ceiling was the height of several men, but at least half of that space was black with shadow. Whispering echoes sighed like the breath of some nightmarish sleeper.

Dry, dead, gravelike . . . but not quite.

Once, the Castle had been a living universe, green and pleasant, until one of its creators had stolen the life force from it. After a long, slow decline, the Castle had become nothing but hewn stone, a true dungeon. It had been that way as long as Reynard could remember. Then, last autumn, there was a battle. Reynard had nearly died and Mac had sacrificed the last of his humanity, but the life force that had once made the Castle a living world had been restored. The effect was gradual. The rebirth that stirred deep in the Castle had not reached this far. Still, Reynard could feel it like the intimation of mist against his skin.

A hint of something. A spark. For the first time Reynard could recall, the breeze that swept the dust from the bare floor carried the sharp scent of mud and moss. Here and there, freshwater springs bubbled out of the earth and trickled over the stones, murmuring of a future.

It made Reynard restless, like a stallion catching the first whiff of spring meadows.

It made the darkness seem heavier.

They'd reached the gate of the enclosure. It was a huge, arching thing of wrought iron. Each post was thick as Reynard's forearm and crusted with a layer of dead moss. Beyond was the corpse of a forest, a skeletal wasteland of bare branches festooned with luminous fungi. The place smelled fetid, like a rotting woodpile where something furry had died.

Mac shifted uneasily, red demon fire glinting in his

eyes. Reynard understood. Strange creatures lived in the depths of the wasteland—most with names long lost to mankind. This was where the demons too dangerous to mingle with the other monsters were kept. God's teeth, even the trolls feared to venture past the rusty padlock that held the two halves of the gate together. So who had wrenched the lock open, leaving it a mangled bit of scrap on the ground?

The tension between Reynard's shoulder blades bit deep enough to crack his spine. They peered between the bars of the gate. Its massive height made Reynard feel no bigger than a schoolboy. Someone had secured the gates with a thick chain and a shiny new lock. The lock looked blindly optimistic.

"Charming place," Mac said dryly. "Great site for a romantic getaway."

"Only if you wanted it to be your last. If a monster didn't finish you, I'm certain Constance would."

Mac chuckled at the mention of his woman. "Yeah, too Gothic even for a vampire."

"Especially one so fond of shopping." Reynard stepped back from the gate and looked around uneasily. "Not a boutique in sight."

There wasn't much to see, period. A few more dead trees. Some boulders. Dust. It was no wonder the rabbit beast had bolted for freedom. Reynard gave a helpless gesture. "I see no clues. There's nothing to suggest who broke the lock."

Reynard could feel the heat radiating off Mac, a sure sign of a fire demon on the edge of losing his temper.

Mac swore. "I want an arrest for this."

"I want someone's head on a pike. I haven't had a piked head for ages."

"I've heard about English cooking." Mac sat down on one of the boulders. "Crap."

"Indeed."

The demon heaved a frustrated sigh. "It's a crime scene. I could print the broken lock, but no one from here's going to be in a fingerprint database."

They were silent for a moment, and then Mac spoke again. "You know, I've tried to loosen security up a bit. Make the administration approachable. I've always figured that if you treat people like you expect them to behave, well, they usually do. But here in the Castle, I'm not so sure that's working."

"Change is a slow process," Reynard offered. "You are taking a place ruled by brute force for thousands of years and trying to bring it enlightenment. That may take decades to accomplish, and you've been here six months."

"If folks think they can get away with this bullshit," Mac said, kicking the broken lock, "I'm rethinking my approach."

Something tugged at Reynard's senses, making him look over his shoulder. A figure was ambling toward them, as unhurried as a sightseer out for an afternoon stroll. In a place where every rock was a hiding place for fanged death, that casual air reeked of trouble. Reynard raised his musket.

Mac got to his feet. "Who is it?"

Reynard sighted down the barrel, using the moment to study the set of the figure's head and shoulders. What he saw made every fiber of his body go still and quiet as a hunted bird.

Though it was a prison, there were few cells in the Castle. With some exceptions, thousands of inmates roamed free to form alliances and enemies, kingdoms and armies. Power and territory were in constant dispute. Thugs became warlords; warlords became petty kings.

Guardsmen kept the peace, but a handful of dangerous troublemakers always flouted the rules. The figure strolling toward them was at the top of that list, underlined twice.

The figure drew closer, his steps unhurried. He was tall, but not overly so, strongly muscled without an excess of bulk. He looked to be in his late thirties, but had probably seen King Arthur pull Excalibur from its stone.

Reynard doubted their visitor would have been on Arthur's side.

"Prince Miru-kai," Mac said neutrally.

The prince stopped a dozen paces away and bowed.

"Your Highness," said Reynard, polite despite the musket aimed at the center of Miru-kai's skull.

The prince straightened. He was dark, hawk nosed, and black eyed with long, fierce mustaches. A circlet of gold sat on his brow. Black hair fell in a braid down his back, bound in casings of beaten gold and silver. His robes were red silk stitched with a design of running stags. A curved sword hung at his hip, the scarlet tassels on the sheath shivering as he moved. If he had been human, one might have mistaken him for a Turk or a Magyar or any of the wandering tribes that warred in the lands where Christendom met the East in ancient days.

But he wasn't human. He was dark fey—dangerous and unpredictable.

Reynard kept the musket steady.

"Demon lord," the prince said, "I greet you. And you also, Captain."

His voice was smooth, polite, educated. One might never have known he was the most dangerous warlord in the Castle. He was not just ruthless, but a master of warcraft and sorcery.

"You are unattended," Reynard observed. "I believe this is the first time I have seen you alone." *Perhaps I could even kill you.*

"My attendants can sometimes be excitable. That is of no help to me today. I ask for parley."

Parley had to be honored. Frustration ached in Reynard's bones as he lowered his musket. "Don't make me regret observing fair play."

"But, Captain, you are the byword for gentlemanly conduct. Fair play is what lightens your grim nature."

Reynard narrowed his eyes. "To borrow the modern phrase, sometimes fair play sucks."

Miru-kai laughed, a slash of white teeth in his dark face. "I never tire of you, old fox."

"What do you want?" Mac demanded before Reynard could change his mind and put a musket ball in the prince's sarcasm.

Miru-kai inclined his head. "I heard the gates had been breached and that one of the creatures escaped."

"We caught it and put it back," Mac replied, folding his arms. "So?"

"That is good. The phouka are dangerous."

"Ya think?"

"They are beasts from the fey kingdoms. They don't belong in this world. It is not their fault humans taste sweet to them. They should have been returned long ago to their proper homes."

"And why weren't they?" Mac demanded.

Miru-kai gave a smile that revealed nothing. "If you find a map leading to that door, let me know. We of the fey have strained our eyes for a glimpse of the Summerland since the dawn of human rule."

"You are dark fey," Reynard replied.

"That does not make me any less homesick." Miru-kai shrugged. "But that is not what we are here to discuss. I have smelled life in the wind. I have seen moss beside the water and know someday soon there will be grass under the soles of my feet. The Castle wakes. The warp and weave of the universe changes."

Mac raised his eyebrows, as if waiting for a punch line.

The prince shifted impatiently. "You sacrificed much to bring the Castle back to life. For what you have done, I step forward to share what I know."

Mac was unimpressed. "You're a warlord. Peace is gonna put you out of work."

"After the first few centuries, war is a dull occupation."

Does he take us for fools? "You are an old dog, Miru-kai," said Reynard. "You cling to old tricks."

"You are a cynic, fox."

"Whoa." Mac waved his hands to silence them. "Sorry

to break up your mutual admiration, guys, but what does any of this have to do with the phouka?"

"Who was trifling with the locks?" asked Reynard.

Miru-kai held up a hand, as if to halt their hostility in midair. "Someone who freed a deadly beast in order to set a trap. Or perhaps create a diversion?"

Mac unfolded his arms, drawing himself up. "Yeah? A diversion for what?"

"Thievery!" Miru-kai exclaimed in an exasperated tone. "What else? Have you no idea of what riches are stored in this place? Collectors outside the Castle slaver like wolves. They cannot wait to plunder your treasure rooms."

"How do you know that?" Mac protested. "You're stuck in here!"

Miru-kai rolled his eyes with theatrical impatience. "How do you think I was trapped here, you buffoon? I broke in and never got back out! The fey cannot leave, not with any magic or trickery."

Mac shook his head. "Then what was stolen? Nothing's missing. There's nothing in the forest worth taking."

Miru-kai waved his hand in a flowery gesture. "You are brave to a fault, honorable, witty, but utter dolts. There is no sign above the door of the greatest treasure hoard."

"What are you talking about?" Reynard snapped.

A silence fell. Deep in the dead forest, water dripped slowly. Miru-kai studied Reynard, dark gaze scanning back and forth, searching his face. *What for?* Reynard wondered. *What does he see there that he hasn't seen before?*

At last the prince spoke. The words came quickly, as if that was the only way they would come out at all.

"Captain Reynard, while you were out chasing a carnivorous rabbit, someone slipped into the Castle vault and stole your soul. If you don't find it, you're going to die."

Chapter 4

Reynard's mind was numb and reeling at once. *Someone took my soul? Who? Why?*

He didn't wonder how. He knew that: They called it the guardsman's sacrifice—and those memories were enough to bury a man's courage like a corpse under January snow. Not that Reynard let one shred of horror show on his face. That was private, both from friend and foe.

He pushed aside those useless, tattered images from his first days in the Castle. That was so long ago, it was a wonder they hadn't rotted from his brain. They had no right to still be vivid as a fresh wound.

Miru-kai wheeled on one boot heel. "Follow me."

This time his voice wasn't insinuating, smooth, or oh-so-reasonable. He followed the command with an imperious glance over his shoulder. Mac looked at Reynard and shrugged, the look on his face clear. It might be a trap, but only fools would try to ambush a fire demon and the captain of the Castle guards.

Still, Reynard kept his weapon ready. Fools were everywhere.

They followed Miru-kai back the way they had come.

The fey turned right down a narrow side passage. Like everywhere else in the prison, it was lit by undying torches. They flickered weakly, their light never quite bright enough to see by but still too persistent to allow the comfort of real darkness. Here, they were smaller, closer together, like the beat of a drum growing faster, a double-quick march to lead Reynard to the site of his doom.

He knew what lay at the end of the narrow passage, even though he'd been there only once, centuries before. No guardsman went there of his own accord.

It was a room with no name, just the guardsmen's symbol, a six-pointed sun, painted in gold leaf above the arch of the door. The door itself was covered with another black iron gate strong enough to keep out an army of thieves—which was no doubt why it thoroughly interested Miru-kai.

"I had no idea this was here," said Mac. "What is it?"

"One of the guardsmen's many secrets," Miru-kai responded, sweeping a hand before him like a showman revealing a three-headed calf. "Behold a treasure trove, my demon friend."

"Treasure trove? I'm in charge of the place. You'd think I would have known about it," Mac grumbled.

"It's not Castle business," Reynard said, his voice quiet. He gripped the stock of his musket tight, trying to hide the fact that his hands were shaking. "This belongs to the guards."

He shouldered past Mac and Miru-kai to reach the iron grille. It wasn't fancy, just a crisscross of black metal bars set into the gray Castle stone. The top of the grille was tipped with spearheads. The lock was as big as his fist and firmly in place. He let loose a relieved breath. "There's been no theft here."

"Look more closely." Miru-kai's dark eyes challenged him. "There is no dust on the lock. The grit beneath the gate has been recently disturbed, I think. And look," he added, bending to pick up a sliver of something bright. "A fragment of painted pottery, yes? The edges look clean and fresh, as if this was broken mere hours ago. These are not begrimed with the grit and dirt of years."

Reynard stared at the shard. Like the symbol above the door, it had been decorated with gold leaf. Like the symbol, it held great significance to the guards. A sick anger filled him all over again. He grabbed the fey's wrist so hard, he felt a shifting of bones beneath his grip. "Perhaps because you broke it yourself? Do you know what a broken urn means?"

"No, what?" Mac asked, but Reynard's attention didn't waver from the fey.

The muscles under Miru-kai's eyes tensed from pain. The dark fey curled his upper lip, baring teeth sharp as a vampire's. "I did not do it. This door is warded with magic, as well you know. I cannot cross its threshold. I can't even pick the lock. Not with the wards in place."

"Then who got in?"

"Cockroaches go everywhere."

"A cockroach broke that urn?"

Miru-kai jerked his arm free. "With proper instructions, a minor demon could have wormed his way inside. That has always been the weakness of great sorcerers. They set wards to keep out powerful enemies, not the village scoundrels."

"And no *scoundrel* has attempted this lock before?" Mac asked pointedly.

"Not one with the right mentor." Miru-kai gave his cuff a sharp, irritated tug. He locked eyes with Reynard for a long moment, glaring his displeasure. After a few heartbeats, the fey looked away. "Every thief here has tried it at least once."

"So this villain is more clever than the lot of you." Reynard gave the lock a vicious pull, but it held fast. Now frustration as well as alarm vibrated through his blood, making his ears pound. He kept his face away from the others until he could smooth it into its customary cool lines. "You're saying this thief set a distraction by turning the phouka loose and then thoughtfully locked up this room behind himself?"

"Well planned, don't you agree? Without me, you might have missed the whole event."

"I don't believe you," said Reynard. "None of this makes sense. No one would ever think to look here for a robbery. Why would a thief need a diversion?"

Mac folded his arms. "Why did you tell us about this robbery, again? Just because we're such good guys?"

Miru-kai smiled. "Perhaps there's a touch of professional jealousy involved. I've always wondered what treasures gather dust behind this door."

"I'd guess you already have the catalog," Mac said affably. "If this door is warded, how do we get in to see what's been taken?"

"You are head of Castle operations, are you not?" Miru-kai asked Mac. "I believe you have a master key that will work even on this door. Ordinary keys to the Castle will not."

"How do you know?" Reynard asked. There were only nine keys, and he knew where most of them were—but not all.

"They've been tried," Miru-kai responded. "It will take a master key, or—"

Reynard turned quickly to Mac, cutting off the prince. "Do you have it with you?" He hated the eager desperation in his voice.

Mac's gaze slid to Miru-kai. "Take him aside."

Reynard raised the barrel of his musket with a mix of impatience and dark satisfaction. "Walk back down the corridor until I tell you to stop."

Miru-kai raised his hands with an aggrieved huff. "Such thanks I get for my assistance. I would not have taken you for such a boor."

"Farther."

The prince turned and walked with exaggerated strides, making sure Reynard saw each one. The fairy prince had missed his calling as a comic—but Reynard wasn't in the mood. He'd sooner plant his boot in the prince's backside.

"Farther."

A flare of white light washed the corridor for a heartbeat. The magic of Mac's key had unlocked the wards. Reynard blinked tears away, blinded by the sudden brightness.

Miru-kai turned. "Did it work?"

Mac pulled on the gate. It swung open on silent hinges. The heavy wooden door behind it surrendered to a shove from the demon's bulky shoulder. Both Reynard and Miru-kai hurried forward.

There were torches inside the chamber, casting the same eternal, flickering glow as those in the Castle's corridors. Reynard took a step into the chamber, his boots scraping on the marble mosaic that covered the floor in a pattern of dark and light squares. The space was octagonal, the stone ribs from each corner making a high, domed vault above them. From floor to ceiling on each side were rows and rows of narrow stone shelves filled with pottery urns.

"What the heck is all this?" Mac asked softly. The mysterious atmosphere of the shadowy room demanded low voices. "And why didn't I know about it?"

"Each urn holds someone's essence," Miru-kai said quietly, entering the room behind them. "A life. A soul. Call it what you like. The old guards keep it a secret because what you see in this room makes them vulnerable."

"Be quiet!" snapped Reynard, suddenly furious. He felt violated, invaded. "This isn't your information to share."

The prince ignored him and looked at Mac instead. "When the guardsmen—the old guardsmen, not your new men—arrived at the Castle, they surrendered their souls for safekeeping. It made them immortal, but it chained them to their duties. That is why they cannot leave for more than an hour or two before their powers begin to weaken. Once separated from their soul vessel, the guardsmen slowly begin to die."

"Why?" Mac demanded.

"A very clever system." Miru-kai went on. "Man and

urn must both be in the Castle. The magic that holds them together fades in the outside world, and in a matter of weeks the guard is dead. Man in one dimension and urn in another hastens death from weeks to days. I suggest you get busy, Captain Reynard, and find your pot."

Mac flushed with anger. "Whose stupid idea was this?"

"Those who created the guards wanted to keep them obedient. Those men who leave their post perish."

Mac turned, staring at Reynard in bewilderment. "Seriously?"

Reynard gave a single, stiff nod. "I came to this room like all the rest. I did what was necessary. It was required of us."

Thunder gathered in Mac's face. "Who was doing the requiring?"

Reynard turned away, walking toward the shelves and setting the musket down on one long shelf. He was sweating with panic, the soft fabric of his shirt clinging as he moved. "It's all in the past now." His tone brooked no discussion.

He didn't want to think about it.

"I want to know—"

"Look," the fey interrupted, pointing to his right. "Some of the urns are broken."

Reynard whipped around, filled with fresh panic.

"So what *does* that mean?" Mac stooped, picking up a broken lid, bits of wax seal still clinging to its lip.

Reynard answered. "Those men are dead. They were killed when the urns smashed."

Mac spared an incredulous glance at the broken pottery. "Then who died? And when? Whose urn was outside?"

"No guard has died in several months. Those vessels were empty when they broke."

Mac shook his head. "If each urn represents a guard, then a lot must be empty. There are thousands of jars here. There aren't more than a few hundred of the old guards left."

Reynard narrowed his eyes, struggling for the shreds of his self-control. "Some of the urns have . . . lost their contents. We do not age. That does not make us inde-structible. Most of us have fallen in our battles with the warlords. Like *him*." Reynard glared at the prince.

"Your vessel is obviously unbroken," said Miru-kai, looking around the room with a mischievous glint in his eye. "But where is it?"

Beside each shelf was written a span of years from a calendar far older than the one Reynard had learned as a boy. His shelf was the last to be filled, his urn the last to be placed there. He covered the distance to that row in two strides. He snatched up one vessel after another, reading the names inked onto each potbellied side. *Where is mine? It should be right here!*

Or here.

Or here.

His heart was racing, making his head swim. He stopped handling the fragile pottery, afraid he would drop one of the vessels. He turned to Miru-kai, his face feeling slack with fear. "How do you know mine was taken?"

"Do you see it there?"

Reynard's breath failed him for a moment. "No."

"Don't you feel its absence, like a hole in your belly?"

Reynard didn't answer, because he couldn't. He felt so sick with apprehension, he couldn't tell whether any-thing else was wrong. "How do you know?"

"Call me clairvoyant." The fey gave a predatory smile, his affable facade falling away. "Or a ferocious gossip."

Reynard dove for him, snatching at the front of Miru-kai's rich robes. The force of his anger lifted the fey from the marble floor, dangling him in the air. The violence felt so good, a moment of release. Rage was one base instinct his curse hadn't stolen from him. "What do you know?"

"Reynard!" Mac shouted.

Miru-kai lowered his eyes, looking down at Reynard

with cool mockery. His glittering stare was inhuman, hostile. "What a prize the soul of the guards' captain would make. A jewel for any collector. A collector who has carried it right outside these walls."

"Who took my soul?"

"Better to ask why, and what else might have escaped the forest. That gate was opened before today."

"Why?" Reynard roared.

Miru-kai was starting to wheeze under the iron clench of Reynard's grip. "Ah, you have me there, old fox. I don't know why the phouka was set free, but I'm glad it was. It gave me the perfect excuse to connive my way into this room."

Mac was beside Reynard now, one hand on his arm. "Put down the enemy warlord and step away. He can't talk much longer with you strangling him."

The prince gave a jeering smile.

"Wretch!" Furious, Reynard threw Miru-kai to the ground, using all his strength to smash the fey like one of the shattered urns.

Miru-kai vanished before he hit the ground. Reynard heard him land, saw a shimmer, but his prey was gone. Reynard stumbled forward, swinging at the empty air with his fists. "Where are you, son of a whore?"

Blood pounded in his head. He stomped, driving his boot heel over and over into the floor, hoping to catch a limb or—better yet—Miru-kai's sneering face.

"Forget it; he's gone invisible." Mac gave an experimental kick at where the prince should have been. Fire blazed in Mac's eyes a moment, the heat of anger bringing his demon to the surface. "I had no idea he could do that. No wonder he made such a good thief."

"Blasted fairy!" Reynard whirled, smashing his boot heel into one of the empty shelves. The stone split with a sharp crack, chunks crashing to join the broken urns below.

Mac grabbed his shoulder. "Cool it!" He swung Reynard around, looking him up and down. "We're going to fix this. Somehow."

"He knows!" Reynard snarled. "Someone stole my life and that thrice-damned fairy knows who it was."

"Yeah," said Mac. "But I doubt he came along just to gloat. Why was he so anxious for us to let him in here?"

Thursday, April 2, 12:30 a.m.
The Castle

Reynard stormed through the gloomy corridor, heading back to the guardsmen's headquarters. He needed to know who was patrolling this section of the Castle over the last week. Somebody saw something; they just didn't know it yet.

"How clearly are you thinking right now?"

Reynard turned on his heel, wheeling around to face Mac. Anger ripped through him, leaving his thoughts in dangling shreds. Striking out would be a relief, whether or not Mac was the right target. He had to look up into the demon's face, but that didn't faze him. He'd taken on bigger creatures and won.

"I commanded this guard for a very long time before you joined us." The words were polite, but Reynard's tone was ice. "I know the workings of this place better than anyone. I'll find this thief."

Mac's expression was carefully neutral, torchlight playing on the planes of his face. "Cut yourself some slack. You're going to need help on this one. Even from a newbie like me."

Hauling in the reins of his self-control, Reynard turned and started walking again, his footsteps echoing in the darkness. "No one can help me."

"Is that so?"

Reynard stopped dead. Fury was a cold thing, freezing the flesh from his bones. "The guardsmen have carried on, decade after decade, heading out to fight monsters we cannot possibly defeat," he said quietly. "It does not matter what bites, wounds, or claws us. We heal and keep going back for more until we're torn to pieces so thoroughly that even we cannot mend. That is the service we owe."

Mac said nothing, just listened.

"It is not right." Reynard paused, breathing hard. "*Not* right that we should die because our soul vessel smashes like an old teacup. It's bad enough that some foul thing has stolen my life, and that I am passed around from seller to buyer like cheap goods at a county fair. If someone drops or damages the urn, then it's good-bye, Captain, and fetch the broom and dustpan. I am the head of the guardsmen, a warrior with centuries of skill, and I am vulnerable as an egg."

Mac shook his head. "Yep, that sucks."

"It's bloody ironic." Reynard's rage ebbed a little, enough to feel the fear beneath. Amazing that he still fought to live, when hope was such a cruel joke in the Castle. "It's bloody embarrassing. A man should be a bit less breakable."

"How come you've never mentioned any of this before?"

"The prince had it right. The magic that rules the guardsmen binds us to this dungeon more securely than if we were one of the prisoners. We vowed to keep silent about the soul vessels for our own protection, and the secret unites the old guards like nothing else could. Nevertheless, that vow must have been broken, if every thief in this place has an eye on our vault."

Mac clapped a hand to Reynard's shoulder. "We've gotta get a handle on this. What was that Miru-kai was saying? There's a collector involved?"

"Unless he was lying."

"But if he isn't, that means your life essence—soul, whatever—has left the building."

Reynard took a deep breath, realizing Mac had somehow calmed him down. Directed his anger to a practical problem. He wasn't the kind of superior Reynard was used to, but he was damned effective.

Reynard gave a tired smile. "I would bet all two and

a half centuries of my overdue pay that there is a con-spiracy in the Castle, and Miru-kai is in the thick of it."

The two men shared a look. Demon fire smoldered in Mac's eyes, a sign of temper.

"Yeah," said Mac. "Okay. First, who or what else is in the forest that might have escaped? I'm thinking oppos-able thumbs here. Someone who could be a thief, per-haps coached by our fairy friend."

"A demon would be the most likely candidate, but the forest is vast. There are thousands of hellspawn, and no means of checking to see if one is missing."

Mac grunted unhappily, and Reynard could see him adding "demon inventory" to his mental list of projects.

"Perhaps a demon got out first, and then the phouka today," Reynard added.

"That's right. Someone had to let the phouka loose. A flunky demon had to open the lock to the guardsmen's storage room. A sorcerer had to know how. And then someone else had to have a connection on the outside. While it's remotely possible that was all one or two peo-ple, I highly doubt it."

Reynard considered that. "And in the outside world, there is a collector and the vampire assassin hunting Ashe Carver. Two very different interests. There is more than one player beyond these walls as well."

"See, I said you needed help tracking down all the answers." Mac swore under his breath. "I'll bet this is the tip of a nasty old iceberg."

They began walking again. Reynard felt his sense of purpose trickling back. "When I'm done with the guards, I will begin questioning the known thieves."

"Dude, I'll cover the stuff inside the Castle. You've got to get outside and find your soul. We don't know exactly when the urn was taken. I know it can't be too long because you're still okay, but . . ."

Reynard jerked, the words cleaving him like a broad-sword. "Outside?"

"If it's separation from your urn that's the problem, you need to be wherever it is. If it's left the Castle, you have to follow it."

"Wonderful. Just bloody wonderful. How am I supposed to track the wretched pot through a world I don't know anymore?"

"Ask for help. We've got friends. Ask Caravelli. Holly."

Freedom. A sudden chill seized him, making gooseflesh. Anticipation or fright, or both. If he left the Castle for too long, would he be strong enough to come back to eternal duty in a dark dungeon? Or would that much freedom drive him mad, like poor Killion? "This isn't how I envisioned getting a few days' leave."

"Ain't life a funny old thing."

Reynard swore. "I'll get the job done. I always do."

As the spike of panic faded, he realized suddenly where they were. This was the place where Ashe had stood guard with her rifle, waiting for help while Reynard bled his life out on the stone floor. It looked like any other place where two corridors crossed. Nothing remarkable, except in his mind. What he remembered most was the pain of Bran's ax wound to his gut, but through that he recalled Ashe's cool touch. She'd given him water to drink. She'd held his head. It had been so long since anyone had shown him compassion, and when he needed it most, she was there.

Any more detail than that was the needless embroidery of his imagination. What counted was that, for once, someone had looked after him. Not the kind of woman he'd loved before, all soft sweetness, but the right woman for that moment: brave, strong, and fierce.

"Do you think Ashe Carver would be willing to help me?" Reynard asked with casual curiosity.

Mac opened his mouth to answer, but a bellow thundered in the stone vault of the corridor. As one, they sprang forward, racing toward the sound.

"That was human," Reynard shouted. "One of the men!"

They were heading to a place where one corridor

crossed another. A few paces ahead, Mac slowed, skidding as they reached the intersection. It was impossible to see around the corner, and the dark, blanketing shadows only increased the danger of being caught in a trap. Mac drew his nine-millimeter SIG Sauer automatic. Reynard slid to a stop and dropped to one knee, sighting with his musket and using the corner of the wall for cover.

For a moment, there was utter silence. Reynard could taste the dry dust of the stone, smell the faint scent of thyme still clinging to his clothes from his adventure with Ashe. His pulse was hard and steady.

Then he heard the scuffle of feet, an uneven rhythm that ended in another yelp of pain down the righthand—eastern—arm of the corridor. Reynard eased around the corner, trying to see without exposing his position. He exchanged a nod with Mac and rounded the corner, flowing silently into the shadows.

A tangle of shapes wrestled beyond the smear of torchlight a few feet ahead. The flickering illumination only made the corridor beyond twice as dark. It wasn't light, but a mockery of it.

Behind him, Mac yelled and fired the SIG Sauer, the report a physical slap. Reynard slammed his back to the wall and turned enough to see two figures rushing Mac from the western arm of the crossroads. Another assailant burst from the north side, cornering Mac.

Trap!

In one motion, Reynard sighted and fired. The Brown Bess banged, coughed smoke, slammed into his shoulder. The third attacker dropped.

As it fell, Reynard could see the maw of needle teeth where the mouth and nose should have been. *A changeling.* One of the hideous, twisted mutations of the vampire species. They had all the vampires' appetite with no humanity left to temper it. Few things would kill a changeling, but blowing the skull to bone shards generally worked.

Mac kicked one of his attackers in the head. It was a

green thing, a kind of frog-man with claws and teeth. A creature that grotesque had to be some kind of dark fey. *Miru-kai is behind this*.

Mac's other assailant was a tusked goblin flailing a two-handed sword. Reynard dropped the musket, pulled out his sidearm and his sword. He'd trained himself to use either hand to fight with sword or pistol, but still preferred the blade on his right.

As he rushed to help Mac, the demon tossed a stream of flame into the goblin's face. The creature fell back, raising its hands to protect its eyes. Mac kicked the sword out of its grasp.

The frog-thing scrabbled for it, but Reynard lunged, sliding his blade between the creature's ribs and out its back. It screamed piteously, mouth opening wide to reveal fangs like a cobra's, so long they must have folded up inside its mouth. Reynard pulled back on the blade, feeling bone and the pull of flesh against steel.

The screaming didn't stop. The creature was a mercenary, a soldier, but it still felt pain and death. He shot it in the head, over and over, until the screaming stopped.

"Hey!" Mac dodged as the huge goblin swung with its tusks. The face was grotesque, man crossed with pig and decorated with a dozen piercings. Squares of metal were sewn to its tunic, overlapping like scales. Mac hoisted the sword, letting flame leap along the blade.

Reynard backed up, giving him room to swing.

"I've got this," yelled Mac, who looked like he was starting to enjoy himself.

Now that the odds were even for his friend, Reynard turned and bolted the other way, back toward the source of the first cries. He had delayed only a moment to help Mac, but every lost second tore at him with frantic claws.

Abandoning stealth, he pelted through the torchlight. The cluster of figures who had struggled in the darkness beyond was gone. Something lay on the ground. Reynard paused just long enough to glance at the object.

A circular silver pin decorated with a sprig of heather. *Stewart!* He had dropped it as a clue.

Or else it was a whole new trap, meant to lure Reynard deeper into the Castle.

Bloody hell. There had to be more than one attacker, because Stewart was a good fighter. Reynard slowed his pace just enough to scan the ground as he went, searching for some indication of what he was up against. The bare stone told him nothing.

The next junction in the corridors was shaped like a T. Left or right? Reynard listened intently, letting his vision go soft, letting sounds come to him rather than seeking them out. Perhaps it was magic, perhaps not, but it was something he'd been able to do since he was a boy. He heard things that should have been impossible to detect.

Like the jingle of a goblin's scaled armor along the left-hand passage. Reynard shifted his bloody sword to his left hand and put the Smith & Wesson in his right. If he was fighting a goblin, bullets were a better choice.

He sprinted down the corridor, willing himself to catch up. Stewart's bride was waiting for him to come home, and Captain Reynard did not leave his men behind.

The passageway curved, the monotony of stone blocks and darkness creating a blind corner. He slowed to long, walking strides, gun ready.

They were waiting for him, a changeling and a goblin. Stewart lay like a huddle of laundry at their feet. His neck was savaged.

Suddenly Reynard's mind was crystal clear, his anger snuffed out. Battle brought out his icy control, and he needed every strength he had right then.

Stewart needed it.

Reynard fired the gun. The changeling flew backward, but Reynard already knew he had missed the head. *Damnation!*

The goblin fell back a step at the sound of the shot, but drew a bronze knife the length of a man's forearm.

The blade was serrated in long, wicked notches, meant to catch and tear as it sliced. Worse, the goblin handled it with confidence. Anticipation came into its piggy eyes. Its lower lip—stomach-churningly human—sagged a little as the upper mouth lifted, showing off the sweep of its gold-studded tusks.

Was that a goblin smile? Leer? Evil grin? *The devil only knows*.

It all took less than a second; then the goblin was on him. The thing was at least seven feet tall and smelled like rotten ham.

It crashed forward like a falling boulder armed with a knife. Reynard ducked, but not far enough. A tusk slammed the side of his head, making his ears ring and sending him stumbling to the side. They careened into the wall, their combined weight driving the air from his lungs in a whoosh.

Reynard sagged enough in the creature's grip to bend his knees, then used the full force of his body to drive the heel of his hand into the goblin's snout. Its head snapped back. He'd caught it by surprise.

Reynard shoved his gun into the soft flesh beneath the goblin's jaw and fired three times. As the top of the goblin's head sprayed the wall, a single, convulsive jerk smashed its bulk against Reynard. It felt like a seven-foot bag of stone. Reynard twisted, using the goblin's own weight to send it crashing to the floor.

Flecks of blood and bone were everywhere, over the walls and floor, over Stewart's still form, glistening in the torchlight.

The changeling was gone.

The Smith & Wesson was empty, and he didn't take the time to reload. Swords were better with vampires.

Reynard spun away from his position, searching the shadow for the glow of pale yellow eyes. *Nothing. Nothing*. He dropped the gun and took a firmer grip on the sword.

Instinctively, Reynard looked up just in time to see the changeling drop from the ceiling like a massive, pale spider. Reynard sprang aside, but not quite fast enough. Claws hooked in his sleeve, pulling him forward. He landed hard, the shock of stone on his knees stealing his breath.

Reynard threw himself into a roll, knowing motion was his best defense against the changeling's massive strength. A swipe of long claws missed his face by a whisper.

Then he was back on his feet. The changeling circled, its gait oddly crablike. Hunched, bald, barrel-chested, it looked frail and slow. It was anything but. Now it had picked up the goblin's knife.

Blood stained its maw. Stewart's blood.

"Who sent you?" Reynard demanded, more to buy time than anything else.

The thing hissed and pounced; Reynard ducked, bringing up the sword to block and turning into the motion. Not the most elegant move, but it put cold steel between his flesh and those needlelike fangs.

As he planned, the changeling landed against the sword's honed edge. For the second time that night, Reynard felt flesh give under the blade. Claws tore at Reynard, raking through his hair, down his sleeve. The changeling staggered back, wrenching free of the sword's bite. No scream of pain this time, just a wheezing gurgle.

Reynard straightened, raised the sword again. The changeling tripped on Stewart's body, then fell backward.

Reynard took its head with a two-handed blow, feeling the crunch of the spine vibrate through the blade.

Lungs heaving, he stood a moment, half-drunk from the sheer savagery of the fight. Then he dropped the sword and pushed the changeling's body aside.

Mac was suddenly there, kneeling beside him. "Is that Stewart?"

Reynard felt for a pulse, his own heart racing in his ears. Hot blood made his fingers slippery, frustrating his search. "I can't tell if he's alive."

Then he found it, weak but steady. Reynard felt a tremor down his limbs as the tension he'd been holding released a notch.

"You saved him," Mac said.

"Barely," Reynard replied.

Mac shot him a look. "Taking on a goblin and a changeling at the same time? That was damned near suicidal, even for you."

Reynard shrugged, allowing himself a moment of cold satisfaction. "I knew you'd catch up eventually. Now let's get this boy to a doctor."

The chambers of Miru-kai, prince of the dark fey, were farther into the Castle than the guardsmen's quarters. The prince ran, invisible and fairy-fleet, through the darkness and torchlight. He had his prize from the guardsmen's vault. All that remained was to avoid the fire demon and the old fox. Along the way, he met up with his guard and ordered them to delay any pursuit.

They obeyed at once, not just because Miru-kai was their prince, but because he led them well. He never gave them instructions without a reason. The respect between them was mutual.

That taken care of, he ran all the harder, because he was running to a problem, not away from one. Fear of something far worse than capture nipped at his heels.

Miru-kai slowed to a princely pace only when he was through the tented encampment that guarded his territory. Behind the rows of silk structures, faded and tattered by time and war, was the cluster of stone chambers he called home. There lived the court of the dark fey.

Outside his great hall, tusked goblins stood sentry. He waved them aside. The room was furnished with cushions and stools, a nomad's quarters. Easily packed, quickly moved. Such was the life of a Castle warlord, where borders wavered on the edge of a sword.

Surprised, the courtiers in the hall jumped up from their cushions, making a hurried bow as Miru-kai passed. He gave a distracted greeting, barely slowing his stride.

His destination was farther on, in a bedchamber next to his own. A servant woman sat outside the door. When she saw the prince, she rose, curtsying low.

"How does he fare?" asked Miru-kai.

"There is no change, my lord prince."

Miru-kai nodded and passed her, entering the cool, dark room. He picked up a candlestick and blew lightly on the candle. Flame blossomed from the wick. He stood a moment, using his hand to shield the light from the figure sleeping in the bed. It was an old, old man.

A mix of sorrow and fear twined around Miru-kai's heart. Each breath the sleeper took seemed too loud, too wet. Age was drowning him with each tick of the clock.

Yes, the Castle had changed in the last year. Much of it was for the better. Spring was in the wind, like a brilliant green madness. Sap ran in forests long dead. But for those who were not truly immortal, the irresistible current of time had taken over. With nightmare fascination, Miru-kai watched mortal friends wither and die, day after day after day. The return of life to the Castle had a blood price.

Part of him was willing to pay it. He understood change. It was necessary to be truly alive, even for the dark fey. But this—this was one change he could not accept.

"Simeon," he whispered, at once wanting to wake the old man and yet wanting him to sleep on. There was no pain in sleep. This man, this mortal warrior who had laughed and drunk ale and been the hearty, backslapping father Miru-kai had craved, this *hero* did not deserve a mortal's insignificant, sour-smelling death.

The man's eyelids, wrinkled as winter leaves, flickered open. "Kai?"

The prince set the candle on a bedside table and knelt to look at the old man. "Simeon, how are you?"

"I am content."

"There is no need to jest now, old friend."

"I don't. The sentinels brought news of rain."

Miru-kai frowned. "Rain?"

Simeon's hand emerged from the covers, tremulously seeking that of his prince. "There was rain to the east. The Castle is truly coming back to life. The sentinels caught the rain in their helmets and drank it. They said it was the sweetest taste that had ever crossed their tongues."

"Of course, I hesitate to think where those tongues have been."

Simeon squeezed his hand, a feeble gesture, and let go. "Kai, be serious for once. This is a good thing. Something to celebrate."

"Of course, and we'll celebrate in fine style. Just as soon as you're well again."

Simeon closed his eyes. He didn't need to speak the words Miru-kai had heard so often: *I'm going, my boy. Fare thee well.*

Miru-kai was the mightiest of the warlords in the Castle, but what did that mean? The dark fey had few friends—such was their solitary nature—and the few he had were mortal boon companions, pirates and thieves like himself. Like Simeon, who had taught him the ways of the sword, of parley and battle.

Miru-kai had seen the *television*. The world he and Simeon had known was gone, replaced by an utterly alien landscape. Too much was happening that he didn't understand. He needed Simeon with him. His old friend could make sense of so many puzzling things—those problems that sorcery or trickery couldn't solve. Matters only a mortal heart could unravel.

So the prince would change what he could not accept.

The fey believed in a weave of cause and effect, of natural laws and divine commands they called "the pattern." It dictated what could be governed by choice and what was destiny.

They also believed that weave could be altered, either through good deeds or bad. When Mac sacrificed his humanity to save the Castle, he had changed the pattern. Where, once upon a time, the cycle of life and death had been snipped away from the Castle's design, now it was sewn back in.

The same sacrifice had ended Simeon's thread, but Miru-kai was willing to play weaver. He was a master of magic, both light and dark.

Miru-kai drew an urn out of the folds of his robe and prepared his mind for sorcery.

By the time Ashe left the Gardens, picked up her daughter from her sister's place, and got home, it was midnight. Eden had fallen asleep in the car. Ashe had put her to bed feeling guilty for keeping her up so late. Just another reason to stay away from hunting jobs—especially ones that blew the lid off the weirdness scale.

When she got to bed herself, she fully expected to lie awake worrying about rabbits and assassins, but every muscle welcomed the springy oblivion of her mattress. Exhaustion won out in minutes.

Ashe dreamed she was sleeping in her own bed, the room, the dark bedcover, her entire apartment exactly as it really was. That made the sensation of someone else slipping between the sheets all the more strange. At first, an illogical part of her thought it was Roberto, coming in late as he sometimes did.

But her husband was long dead. The realization wrenched her gut with anger and grief as raw as if that loss were new. After close to five years, that wound re-opened now and again, bleeding afresh.

It seemed to take forever for her dream-fogged mind to turn away from that thought to wonder who, then, was beside her.

She felt a cool hand slide down her arm, leaving a wash of pinprick electricity in its wake.

Vampire. Oh, Goddess.

She needed to turn her head, to see the face that belonged to the hand, but terror had fused her neck into one stiff column. That cold hand was freezing her in place as it slid over her hip to caress her belly. She willed herself to leap up, smash her elbow into the jaw of her attacker. Run.

Fear for her daughter began to pound through her with every heartbeat. If this was happening to her, what was happening to Eden?

"I didn't know we were both watching you. You should be more careful." The whisper was so soft, she barely heard it.

Ashe felt the slide of lips against the back of her shoulder, nuzzling higher and higher to reach the soft down of hair at the nape of her neck. Then the hot, intimate pinprick of fangs. Ashe exploded out of bed, sheets flying, grabbed the handgun on her nightstand, and whirled.

With sweat cooling on her skin, she realized she was threatening an empty pillow.

Goddess, she hated anxiety dreams.

Chapter 5

The plaque beside the glass-paneled door told Ashe that she'd arrived at her destination: BANNERMAN, WISHART, AND YEE, BARRISTERS AND SOLICITORS.

The eleventh floor of the sleek Benoit Tower was definitely outside her comfort zone. Tired as she was from so little sleep—there had been no falling asleep after her nightmare—anxiety had her wide-awake. Ashe hesitated. Her hand looked bare without a stake. For an instant, she wanted to bolt, but running never got rid of monsters. It just made them chase you.

Which would be bad, since she was wearing high heels. She'd forgotten how much she loathed them.

Gripping the door handle, she bit her lips and tasted the unfamiliar sweetness of lip gloss. Putting on her game face, she stepped into the hushed office suite, closing the door behind her. The lighting reminded her of an expensive salon—subdued, calming, almost metallic in its urban polish.

Ashe was glad she'd worn the winter-white skirt suit.

At least she looked like she had a right to be there. She'd even remembered her pearl stud earrings, a wedding present from her husband. She straightened her shoulders and advanced through the reception area, doing her best not to fall off the heels.

An older woman sat behind a mahogany counter, guard-dog alert.

"Good afternoon. I have a two-o'clock with Mr. Bannerman," Ashe said. "My name is Ashe Carver."

The receptionist tapped her mouse and glanced at her computer screen, a confused expression pleating her brow. "I show your appointment as being canceled."

New anxiety rippled through Ashe's stomach. "There must be some mistake." She'd paid a fortune to retain this shark, an expert in both supernatural matters and family disputes. He'd damned well better see her.

"That must be the case. No one else has booked the time. I'm sure Mr. Bannerman is available."

Ashe nodded. With a brisk air, the receptionist picked up the phone and relayed the your-client-is-here message. Ashe looked around, noting that the landscape art on the walls was original, not prints. This was the twilight world of settlements and affidavits. No flamethrowers, submachine guns, or missiles allowed.

I'm so screwed.

"You can go right in." The receptionist gestured to an interior door, graceful as a game-show demonstrator. *And behind door number one . . .*

A death grip on her useless clutch purse, Ashe entered the lawyer's office, pumps silent on the plush carpet. She tried to take a deep breath, but her ribs just wouldn't relax.

Lawrence Bannerman was waiting beside his desk. He gave her the once-over, his eyes sticking here and there. Ashe was tall, blond, and slender, but more Amazon than bikini babe. When his gaze reached her face, she saw the flicker of judgment. She wasn't a dewy twenty-two anymore, either.

Well, screw you. I can kick Godzilla's ass.

"Ms. Carver," he said in a friendly-friendly voice.

"Mr. Bannerman," Ashe replied, remembering to shake his hand like a woman instead of a wrestling champ.

"Please make yourself comfortable."

She sat in the client chair in front of the lawyer's desk, the leather upholstery sighing as she sank into it. She glanced around, assessing what the man's territory said about him. Bright summer sunlight streamed in through the wide windows of the corner office, showing off the clean lines of the Japanese-inspired furnishings. Expensive. Tasteful. Sterile. Even the bonsai on the coffee table looked buffed. *Stepford bonsai. Goddess save me.*

Bannerman shuffled some folders together, propping them in an upright holder to his left, which was angled just enough for Ashe to see the color-coded labels. The file in front read *Book Burrow* on the tab.

The lawyer turned his full attention to her. "You have a most interesting case."

"That's one way of putting it." She started to cross her long, tanned legs, then remembered she was wearing a short skirt and stopped herself. Now was the time for discretion, self-restraint, and all the other civilized qualities she so utterly lacked.

Part of her still wanted to flash him out of sheer perversity.

Bannerman pulled another file out of the upright holder and opened it. In his mid-forties, with chestnut hair just graying at the temples, he looked every bit as polished as the silver frame around the family photo on his desk.

"All right," he said. "We spoke on the phone, but I'd like to review the basic facts, just to get started. Eden is your only child, correct?"

"That's right. She's ten now."

"And you were legally married to her father, Roberto de Larrocha?"

"Yes. I went back to my own name after he died four and a half years ago."

"And you put your daughter into boarding school. . . ."

Ashe was tired of explaining all this. "When she was eight. At the time, it was necessary. After Roberto died, I'd started doing missing persons work rather than relying on my in-laws for support. Eventually, that led to hunting supernatural killers, and the local vamp clans began to threaten us."

"So you put Eden in school?"

"Saint Florentina's Academy is designed for security against supernatural threats. It also provides a first-class English-language education."

Bannerman gave a slight smile. "You sound like an advertisement."

Ashe shrugged. "Saint Flo's gave her safety and a future. It cost every penny I had, but it was the best thing I could do at the time." It had cost everything she'd earned along the way, too. The crème de la crème of schools didn't come cheap, and now, after Bannerman's fee, she would be almost broke.

"Why didn't you just stop hunting vampires?"

"They were killing people at the rate of three and four a night."

"You felt it was your duty?"

"Yeah. And that kind of work is addictive. There's always one more monster to take out before you're done. Then you look up and you realize the hunting has eaten away your life."

Bannerman gave her a long look. Ashe felt her scalp prickle, sensing the courtroom predator beneath the lawyer's smooth surface. She could feel the adrenaline in her blood responding to that gaze.

He turned his pen over and over, rubbing its brushed-gold metal between his fingers. "Apparently you're good at death. The Internet is full of stories about the powerful magic of the Carver sisters and your exploits as a monster slayer."

As she'd told Reynard, Ashe didn't have magical powers to speak of, but she found the badass-witch reputation gave her a psychological advantage, so she'd let the tales spread. "The witchcraft is more my sister's thing."

"Don't be modest. The Carver bloodline is famous. You've taken jobs all over the world. You're sure it was just monsters you were killing?"

"Completely. I stayed within the law."

Bannerman regarded her as if reconsidering his assessment of her beauty. Ashe knew what he was thinking, had heard the line a nauseating number of times before—there was something sexy about a lethal woman. *Men are so weird.*

Ashe cut to the chase. "I've pulled myself together. I'm done saving the world. Now I just want to raise my daughter in the loving home she deserves, surrounded by her family. If I have to rethink my life to give her that, I will do it."

Without taking his eyes from her, Bannerman riffled the pages of a thick document, "Your in-laws have recounted at great length all the reasons they believe you're an unfit mother. Since you have removed Eden from school, and from Spain, they feel compelled to seek custody."

Ashe felt her face freeze. He wasn't saying anything new, but the words still tore like the jaws of a hellbeast. "What's the law around international custody cases?"

"Not relevant. Your husband's father is from here, so any trial would likely be in our own courts. On the good side, that's less complicated than it could be."

"Papa de Larrocha always disliked me. So does Mama, maybe even more."

"Why?"

"I was born a witch. They consider that a taint. They think if they can keep Eden away from her witch heritage, she'll grow up completely human."

Ashe wanted Eden to grow up proud of everything she was. A child of warriors.

"Is that possible?"

"No. She's at the age when her magic will start to

manifest." That had been the final push for Ashe to bring her back to Fairview, where Eden could be around other witches. That first flush of power was a delicate time for a child.

Bannerman tapped his pen on the pile of legal papers. "Given your family's heritage, arguing to retain custody isn't going to be an easy sell to a judge."

Ashe met his eyes. "What do you mean?"

"Every similar judgment to date has weighed against the supernatural."

Ashe swore, dropping the civilized act. "That's a rights violation."

Bannerman narrowed his shark eyes. "Perhaps, but human rights are the only ones enshrined in law. Technically, you're not human. But I'm a very, very good lawyer."

Ashe let out a shaky breath. "Good to hear it."

"You've got to demonstrate that you can live a life that even a prohuman judge will find faultless. There are a few things you should do."

"Name them."

He weighed his words. Nervously, Ashe scanned the wall behind him, trying to stay steady. She'd never understood the whole thing about wringing one's hands until now. Ironic her family had so much power, and yet magic was useless against law.

There was a movement in the shadow between the wall and the window, probably a stray cloud brushing the sunlight. Her eyes tracked it, her predatory senses on automatic. Her conscious mind was busy panicking at the lawyer's words.

"First, you'll require a proper residence with everything Eden needs. Her own room. A decent school. Good clothes."

"Got all that." Ashe was really noticing the shadow now. It was sliding down the wall, like a drip of paint. *What the hell is that?*

Bannerman was oblivious. "How's your daughter adjusting?"

"She misses her friends at her old school, but her grades are good." Ashe blinked, wondering if her eyes were playing tricks. Stress did funny things.

"You'll have to get an ordinary job. Show you can put food on the table the old-fashioned way."

"Already taken care of." Schlepping books at the local library, but whatever.

"Good. Do you have a support system in Fairview?"

From where Ashe was sitting, it looked like the drip was behind Bannerman's right shoulder. It was getting larger as it moved, gathering mass. *Something's wrong.* She shifted in her seat, balancing her weight in case she had to move fast.

"Do you understand the importance of this, Ms. Carver?" The impatience in Bannerman's tone was clear.

Ashe's attention snapped back to the discussion. "My grandmother lives here. So does my sister, Holly. She has a partner and a new baby."

"Alessandro Caravelli's child." Bannerman sounded resigned. "Having him as a relation isn't exactly a plus."

The sun came out from behind a cloud, brightening the room. Now she could see that whatever was sliding down the wall was a sparkly blue-green. It looked like the sort of goop Eden used for arts and crafts.

Except this was the side effect of something deadly.

Ashe flicked her gaze back to the lawyer, then back to the wall. "Caravelli is a good man."

"Caravelli's a vampire," Bannerman pointed out. "As far as your case is concerned, he's a liability."

"We can't pick our in-laws. Just ask the de Larrochas." She got to her feet, kicking off her pumps. She hated the damned heels. "Do you have ghosts in this neighborhood? Or demons?"

Bannerman swiveled his chair, trying to see what Ashe was looking at. "What are you talking about?"

"There." She pointed. The drip had just reached the floor, oozing over the carpet like melting ice cream. Another drip was forming near the ceiling. "Ectoplasm."

This drip traveled faster, whizzing down the wall like

a toddler on a slide. It plopped on top of the previous puddle, rippling a few inches farther onto the dove gray carpet. Sunlight dazzled on the edge of the sticky pool, making rainbows on the wall and ceiling.

Once the sun struck the goo, the air smelled of very, very rotten pork.

The lawyer sprang up, marching toward the ooze. "What the hell?"

"Don't touch it with bare skin," she warned. "It can make you sick."

He wheeled, a revolted look on his face. "Impossible. Something must have followed you here. We don't have slime at Bannerman, Wishart, and Yee."

Ashe bit her tongue. There were just too many lawyer jokes in the world. She stripped off her winter-white suit jacket, folding it neatly over the chair. Ignoring Bannerman's stare, Ashe grabbed the pen off his desk and crossed to the corner, shouldering him aside. She poked the pen in the goop, twirling it around like honey until she had a glob she could take a closer look at. She held it to the light, careful not to let any drip on her freshly dry-cleaned skirt.

There were solid specks in the blue-green gel. Ghostly ectoplasm had no inclusions. This was definitely demon. *Rotten pork with floaty bits. Yum.*

"What are you looking for?" Bannerman snapped. "What kind of creature caused that?"

"Ectoplasm is a by-product of magic, just like exhaust comes from cars. It's not alive, but it tells us there's a demon working mojo nearby." She dropped the gold-plated pen into the puddle of ooze. It bobbed a moment, then upended and sank like a ballpoint *Titanic*.

Ashe folded her arms. "You should evacuate the office."

"Can't you do anything?"

Ashe met his angry gaze, but refused to flinch. "I can give you the number of a good carpet cleaner. I had my apartment done when I moved in."

"Make this go away."

"I didn't cause this, Mr. Bannerman."

The lawyer's gaze shifted away. Ashe's instincts pounced.

"But you know who did," she said quietly. "You've been dealing with a devil, haven't you? Got yourself an unhappy client."

He turned, walked away a few steps, then turned back. His face was expressionless, except for his eyes. A great white had nothing on that glare.

"Hunt this down."

"I don't do demons."

Bannerman's face twitched, as if in sudden pain. "How badly do you want to win custody of your daughter, Ms. Carver? Take care of this and I'll waive my fee."

Ashe had a demon to hunt. Well, she'd hunt it if it turned out to be a little one. With big demons, it was best to just run like hell.

Bannerman had promised to give her file top priority, the gold standard, red carpet, and a five-diamond rating if she'd make the demon go away. That was enough to make her agree. He'd also given up just enough details to tell her he was holding something back. Probably some client confidentiality thing. Alarm bells had gone off, but she was crossing her fingers that she could pull off the job anyway. It would be worth the hassle if it meant Eden was hers.

That meant she had vindictive in-laws, a demon to bag, and a lying if brilliant lawyer to cope with—not to mention someone had sent a vampire to assassinate her. Good thing it was her day off.

And that didn't even cover her family responsibilities. The whole sandwich-generation thing was tough. Grandma, bless her, was starting to need more help with things like getting groceries or a ride out to the hairdresser. Holly needed help—she had a new baby, the ghostbusting business, and she was still taking classes toward her business degree. Alessandro was great with midnight feedings, being a vampire and all, but completely useless during the day. Ashe had stepped in more than once just to give Holly a break.

And then there was Eden.

With vampires on the hunt and now a demon in the picture, there was no way Eden was walking home from school. *Am I going to have to send her away again?*

She pushed that thought away before it could burn her like the acidic thing it was. Nothing was that dire yet. And it wouldn't be. Not if she was smart, and fast, and strong enough. Not as long as she could fight.

Ashe eased her red Saturn VUE into the line of mom cars outside Richard Bellamy Elementary. It had started to rain, and the schoolyard was full of mud puddles and happy babble. Kids plus dirt plus water. If the homework fell into the sticky mess, so much the better. Some things hadn't changed much since Ashe was ten.

She turned the heater on to clear the fog from the windshield. She preferred riding her motorcycle, but she'd gotten the VUE as well when she moved to Fairview. It looked like a mom car, it had more air bags than a roll of packing bubbles, but you could still fit a shitload of weaponry in the back. There were even cute little grocery holders to keep the smaller stuff tidy. Still, it was so not her. It cornered like a box of crackers on wheels. *Suck it up. Be the adult.*

The line of cars scooted forward, and Ashe pulled in to the curb. The VUE ambled to a stop like a fat, sleepy carthorse. She ducked to survey the crowd of waiting children. Kid-sized umbrellas in pastels and plaids hid too many faces, so Ashe went by size and clothing. Eden was small for her age, tomboyish but delicate. Ashe had been exactly like that until she hit thirteen, and then she'd shot up six inches in one summer. There was no doubt Eden was hers, down to the stubborn, pointed chin.

There was Eden, dressed in a jean jacket and black camouflage pants. She was standing with an MP3 player in one hand, a backpack in the other. Alone. Drenched.

Sulking. Yup, that was her kid. Ashe couldn't hold back a grin at all that drama in one small package. Her very own baby Goth.

She had a momentary flash of memory: Roberto sleeping with Eden on his chest when she was still a baby. When he was still alive. Ashe swallowed hard, wondering what he would think of Eden now, what they might have done together, father and daughter. Eden was smart and growing up so fast, one moment a teen and the next back to child mode. "Handful" was an understatement.

She lowered the passenger window so she could call out, letting a gust of cold, wet air into the car. "In you get, sport."

Eden crawled into the backseat of the car, dumping the damp backpack on the seat beside her. No eye contact. Ashe could hear the tinny voice of a rapper trickling from Eden's headphones, like there was a mosquito-sized gangsta hiding in the music player. When had Mr. Bad Bug Man found his way onto Eden's playlist? She'd checked that thing two nights ago. Mr. Bug had better have a clean mouth, or he was so deleted.

Ashe raised the window again, shutting out the rain, and watched her daughter in the rearview mirror. Eden was fair-skinned with pale freckles, like Ashe, but her hair was brown and her eyes the hue of hot chocolate. That coloring came from Roberto.

"Headphones off in the car."

Eden gave her a filthy look, but switched off her player and buckled up.

"Genghis Khan."

"You bet," Ashe said cheerily, putting the car in gear. "That's me, Genghis Mom. Now I'll take you home for your daily meal of bread and water; then I'll lock you in the basement and let the rats gnaw your bones. It'll be fun."

Eden sighed and lolled against the car seat like the

victim of a particularly bad vampire attack. The thought made Ashe go cold inside, but she kept her smile in place.

Eden lifted her head a little. "You're dressed up."

"Had to go see a lawyer. Boring grown-up stuff. How was school?"

"Dumb." Standard response.

"What kind of dumb? Other-kid dumb? Teacher dumb?"

"This place is just totally stupid. I did all these classes already at Saint Florentina's. I'm bored, bored, bored-boredbored. I want to go back. I've only been gone a few months. I'll catch up."

Ashe understood. The school hosted students from all corners of the globe and had an excellent academic program. It taught its charges to stand out, not fit in. Adjustment to a regular school wouldn't be easy. "If you went back, wouldn't you miss Grandma and Aunt Holly?"

Eden shrugged, fiddling with her music player. "I guess."

"But you miss your old friends, too," Ashe said gently. "I get that." She signaled and pulled into traffic slowly, cautious in case some young'un dashed out from behind a car. One of the mothers waved. Ashe waved back with a bright smile. *See, this mom thing isn't so hard.*

"Yeah, I miss them. A lot."

Poor kid. New school, new people. New country, even. A mom she'd half forgotten. It made Ashe feel like every conversation was open-heart surgery, and she was wearing boxing gloves. Eden had run away when she first arrived, making it as far as the bus station. Something Ashe hadn't mentioned to Bannerman, because she prayed it would never happen again. "Have you met anyone here you like?"

"They know I'm not from around here." Eden said it with the acid bite of someone far older.

Oh, crap. What has been going on that I don't know about? "I guess that makes you exotic."

"Yeah, right." Eden sat up, ending the rag-doll act.

"I'll wear black lace and dance the flamenco." She giggled at her own joke, raising her arms like someone holding castanets. *"Viva España."*

Slowly, the tension in Ashe's gut uncramped, as if that laugh were a powerful drug. "You should be showing off all that high-class international education."

"Yeah, well, Marcy Blackwell and her friends laugh at me because I know all the answers in class but I don't know the names of all the stupid baseball players."

Then kick their heads in. No, wait, wrong answer. Bad mother. No cookie.

"You'll learn about North American sports, and you don't want to play stupid to please somebody else. Trust me on that one. It never pays to pull yourself down so that someone else feels better."

"I want to go back to Saint Flo's." Eden turned her face to look out the window. "At least they don't call football soccer."

"Barbarians." Ashe drove, forcing herself to pay attention to the mechanics of driving. Past the corner store with buckets of flowers on the sidewalk. Past the coffee shop and the place with Jamaican food. The neighborhood where they rented a suite was filled with narrow streets and too many suicidal cyclists to let her mind wander.

"Why can't I go back?" Eden asked.

"You're that eager to go?" Ashe said quietly. *Why are demons easier than kids?*

"I just make you feel weird. You don't like being my mother. That's why you sent me away, right?"

Ashe gripped the wheel hard, a hot, guilty flush making the back of her neck prickle with sweat. "Of course not."

"Then why?"

"It was for work."

"Slayer work?"

"Yeah."

"Huh, well, hard to know. You used to say you were a giftware sales rep."

Ashe bit her lip before she could swear. "You were too young for a lot of the details, Eden. I didn't want to scare you. Slaying isn't a pretty job."

"And it's hard to do with a kid tagging along."

"It's dangerous, Eden. The vamps didn't like me coming after them."

"Well, duh. Big pointy stick and all."

"I was worried you'd be hurt if they came after me."

"Well, why won't I get hurt now?"

Ashe swallowed hard. "I quit doing that job. I'm hoping they'll leave us alone."

She turned onto their street. Huge chestnut trees made a nearly perfect canopy over a road designed for a single lane with a horse and carriage. The century-old houses here had been beautiful once, but these days the owners were opting for funky.

"Why can't I go back to Saint Flo's?"

Ashe was irritated. Funny how a kid could make you feel so small. "I thought maybe we could be a family for a while. Y'know, give it the old college try."

She turned the steering wheel to navigate the sharp angle into their driveway. At the same time, she could almost hear the wheels turning in Eden's head. Ashe parked, braked, and turned off the motor. There was a sudden bubble of silence.

She unbuckled and turned in her seat to look at Eden. "We're going to get to know each other, okay?"

Eden looked suspicious. She had those scary-smart eyes kids get when they've had to grow up too fast. "I'm getting to know you, Mom. Whatever you're telling yourself, you put me in boarding school when it suited you and took me out when it suited you. What suits me never crossed your mind."

Ashe felt her jaw drop. The words were both true and not true in a thousand painful ways. *How did this get so messed up?* "There's too much you don't understand."

Eden opened the door and grabbed her backpack, pausing only to lock gazes.

"I hate you."

"Eden!"

This had to be one of those extra-early teenage moments that had started to crop up. Her daughter slouched out of the car, resentment following her like a black fog. Ashe squeezed her eyes shut, looking for the calm that helped her smack down werewolves, and not finding it.

Goddess, I don't know how to be a mother.

Chapter 6

A she got out of the car too quickly, forgetting the short skirt and high heels. It took her a moment to find her balance and by that time Eden was up the front steps. Ashe followed at the slower pace demanded by the shoes.

Eden slammed the door. The loud, spiteful *wham* pushed Ashe from guilt toward anger. A hot flush scalded her cheeks. *Slow down, deep breath. Don't make it worse.*

She went up the porch stairs and into the front hall. The first floor was divided into two suites. On the left was the English Mrs. Langford, who pronounced the existence of the supernatural "stuff and nonsense" no matter what the television and newspapers said. The tiny apartment on the right belonged to a real estate guy who was never home. Ashe and Eden had the whole upstairs.

Ashe climbed the stairs to the second floor, wishing she were back with Reynard and chasing the vampire. That was simple. Reynard was easy to work with. She knew what she was supposed to do.

Anger was swinging back to guilt and grief, getting

tangled up with an urge to justify herself to someone too young to understand. Hell, Ashe didn't understand half of why she did what she did when Roberto died. Her first instinct had been to die right along with him, but there was Eden. Kids put a whole new face on the need to survive.

So many emotions crammed her throat that Ashe couldn't speak. Eden was sitting on the floor of the landing, her back to the suite door and a look thick with distrust in her eyes.

Ashe clenched a tight fist around her temper. It would be too easy to explode and turn a spat into a war. A war that could end up with Eden running away again. Wordlessly, she reached over her daughter and unlocked the door.

Eden stood up, grabbing her backpack, and ran to her bedroom.

Being alone for a moment was a relief. Ashe kicked off her shoes and shed the suit jacket. There was a brief span of quiet, nothing but dust motes spinning in a shaft of light.

The living room was warm because it faced west. There wasn't a lot of furniture, but the apartment had a comfortable feel, with fir floors, built-in bookshelves, and lots of light. Ashe had done pretty well, finding this place. There was even a big park down the street with other kids to play with.

I try. I really do.

Which meant she had to put an end to the day's skirmish. She tapped on Eden's door. "Hey, you."

"Go away."

For a moment, Ashe was reminded of her little sister, Holly. Was there a bratty gene? Had Ashe had it at that age? Ashe turned the handle and invaded. Eden's room was decorated with a mix of stuffed animals and posters of pouting pop bands barely old enough to shave. A scattering of books. No more than a day's worth of clothes on the floor. Nothing to alarm the mother unit.

For now. She wondered how long it would be before

the boy bands came down and someone less appealing appeared in poster form. It was hard to know what was a miniphase and what would stick.

Eden was facedown on the bed, picking at the strap of her backpack. Ashe perched on the edge of the bed bedside her daughter, smelling the mix of schoolroom and peppermint gum that clung to all Eden's clothes. The storm of her emotions died as suddenly as it had blown in. She put a hand on the back of Eden's head, caressing the soft brown curls. *Goddess, I love her.*

Ashe drew a long breath. "I sent you away because I couldn't protect you, and I'm sorry for that. But if I didn't go on with the work I was doing, a lot of people would have died. I couldn't let that happen. That's all I can really tell you, because that's all I understand myself."

Eden hunched her shoulders, inching away from her mother's touch. "Won't people die now that you've stopped being a slayer?"

Ashe removed her hand. "Maybe, but some things are different now. Vampires and the rest of the monsters have been out in the open a few years. They've got ways to police themselves that they didn't have before. The good vampires don't want bad vampires causing problems any more than we do."

"Why not?" Eden stopped picking at the backpack, actually listening now.

"They're trying to fit in. It's not easy living in secret, especially when there are so many of them. If the vampires behave themselves, they get to have jobs and credit cards and all the advantages humans have. It's to their own benefit to be good citizens."

Eden finally turned to look at her. "Is Uncle Sandro a good vampire?"

"Yeah." Ashe sighed, thinking of the many times she had butted heads with Alessandro Caravelli. "He's a good guy. I didn't like him much at first, but he proved himself to me."

Eden nodded slowly. Ashe could see her thinking, putting pieces together. The girl rolled onto one elbow and propped her head in her hand. "So Uncle Sandro is with Aunt Holly, and she's a superpowerful witch and she put a no-biting spell on him and stuff and they even had a baby, which vampires aren't supposed to be able to do, right?"

"Uh, right."

"And I'm going to be a half witch someday."

"You're already a half witch. You'll get your powers soon. You're the right age."

There was a flicker of buoyant excitement, but Eden didn't say anything. Ashe knew there would be a million questions, but not now. Not until Eden had a chance to mull things over and plan her attack. She had a great future as a prosecutor.

Right now, she was giving Ashe the third degree about something else. "So how come you don't do magic? I know you can feel ghosts and stuff, but how come you don't cast spells like Aunt Holly?"

Crap. Ashe made herself smile, as if she were okay with the topic. "I told you that. When I was sixteen, I did a really stupid spell and blew up my own powers. I nearly nuked Holly's, too. She had trouble with her magic for a long, long time."

"What kind of spell?"

Ashe swallowed hard. The weight of the memory dragged like shackles. "It was for personal gain. They say you should never do magic for yourself, and that's not entirely true, but you can't mess with other people. The first rule of magic is to do no harm. I did harm, for a bad reason, and it came back on me big-time." *But not as much as it should have.*

"Did you get in trouble?"

"Sure I did. I let everyone down. They thought I was a better person than I turned out to be and, to tell you the truth, that was the worst part. I had to live with what I'd done."

"Mom, what did you do?"

Ashe felt the question like a noose, but now was not the time to lie. Not when they were finally talking. "I wanted to go out to a concert instead of babysitting Holly, but I knew I'd get in trouble if my parents got home and found me missing. I gave them car trouble so they'd come home late."

"That's it? That's all? You lost your powers because of that?"

How much could you tell a ten-year-old? How much did she have the guts to say?

"The spell backfired." Ashe looked Eden in the eye, willing herself not to flinch. "I thought that because I was pretty and popular and got good grades I couldn't make mistakes. Remember that when you start casting your own spells. Magic doesn't care about the surface stuff. It knows what's in your heart. The spell knew I was being stupid and it took away my active powers."

Eden's face softened a bit. "That sucks."

"Yeah, it sucked pretty bad. Really awful, and for a lot of reasons. I didn't even start to get over it until I met your dad." Ashe touched Eden's cheek lightly. For once her daughter didn't pull away. "He didn't see a broken witch. He saw a whole person. I remembered how to be happy when I was with him."

We called you Eden because we thought we were in paradise. Sappy, but true.

Eden squirmed into a sitting position, close enough now that Ashe felt her warmth. They weren't touching, but the girl's body wasn't rigid anymore.

"I miss Dad."

Ashe swallowed hard, and it felt like something jagged caught in her throat. If she didn't get out of this conversation, she was going to start crying. With her world already upside down, a weeping mother was the last thing Eden needed.

Besides, real slayers didn't cry. *Yeah, right.*

She slid off the bed. "I miss him, too, babe. Every day. Now I'm going to get out of this monkey suit and cook us dinner, okay?"

Ashe headed for the door. She heard Eden shift, the bedsprings squeak.

"Mom, did the spell work? Even if it blew up?"

Ashe froze and didn't turn around. "Sure. It worked just fine."

Better than fine. Her parents' car had crashed, killing them both.

But how was she going to tell that to her kid?

Friday, April 3, 1:00 a.m.
Ashe Carver's apartment

That night, Ashe went to bed counting on exhaustion to give her a solid eight hours' sleep. No anxiety dreams. For extra insurance, she had a shot of whiskey to make sure she conked right out, but only one so she wouldn't wake up later with postalcoholic insomnia.

It was a good plan, but it didn't work.

This time she was aware of standing in a white room. It looked blank and a bit misty, like the backdrop of a picture no one had bothered to paint in. *This is lame. I can dream better than this.*

There wasn't time to worry about the decor. Prickling danced over her skin again, kicking her survival sense into high gear. Her invisible vampire was back. She realized she was wearing her fighting gear, and whipped out her stake.

"There's nothing you can do that will hurt me," said a deep, soft male voice.

Startled, Ashe looked around. *Son of a bitch.* The bastard could see her, but she couldn't see him. It wasn't like there was anything to hide behind, and yet she could swear he was within arm's reach. Ashe shifted the grip on her stake, turning in a slow circle to catch the slightest hint of where he might be.

"Come out, come out, wherever you are," she growled. "You're spoiling all the fun."

"Are you always this tense?"

A crawly sensation went up her spine. She could smell that sweetish venom scent—a bit like sour Gummi bears, sweet and sharp at the same time. If she could smell him, that meant he *had* to be close. She lifted the stake a little higher. "Who are you?"

"Life and death."

"No self-esteem problems on your account."

She felt, rather than saw, his smile. It twisted through her body, as if he were somehow inside her.

He chuckled. "You have a quick wit. I like that."

"Get out of my dream."

She thrust outward, deciding to use her powers. Hey, if she was dreaming, she could have whatever she wanted. But they didn't work, not even here. She'd killed her parents. Her magic had died with them. Those two facts were irrevocably linked.

Guilt filled her mouth with a taste like ashes, followed by a chaser of sour fear. Her skin crawled, as if her unseen attacker were watching her from all sides.

Go away, go away, go away.

Ashe didn't see or hear any change, but the atmosphere shifted, as if the air had suddenly lost density. Had her prayer worked, or had her watcher simply chosen to back off?

A cry of surprise and pain sounded behind her. She wheeled around to find a corridor that hadn't been there before. It looked like something out of the Castle, all stone and torchlight. With the certainty of dreams, she knew Reynard was down that dark passage, injured and bleeding, just like he had been last fall.

She raced into the cool shadows, terrified she wouldn't get there before he died of his wounds. She would bind up his injuries, just like she'd done before. Give him water. Guard him. She was a hunter, so she treasured those chances she had to heal. Maybe it erased a bit of the stain on her soul left from her parents' deaths.

There he was, curled on his side, the bright blood lost on his red coat. She raced to the still form, gently turning him over.

Oh, Goddess! Horror shrilled through her. It wasn't Reynard. It was her husband.

Oh, Goddess! His face had the same waxy pallor as

when he'd died, organs crushed. Furious, hurt, lost, she'd sat by his hospital bed and held his hand as his magnificent body failed. Her husband had conquered every mountain, snowstorm, and cave worth the challenge. They'd done most of it together.

But his work was as dangerous as his play. He'd chosen to stay in Spain because it offered the most exciting, most glamorous occupation he could find. One with enough peril even for him—he had been a matador.

He hadn't survived his last fight. The bull had trampled him to death.

Anger and grief ripped through her, a repeat of everything she'd felt when his heart had stopped, leaving hers to beat alone.

She had loved him so much.

Ashe woke up in tears. He was gone. He would always be gone.

She hadn't been able to save him.

Friday, April 3, 8:30 a.m.
North Central Shopping Mall

The next morning, a very tired Ashe trudged from the parking lot to the mall, stopped at the Beans! Beans!Beans! Coffee Bar, and carried on through the food court to the library. The North Central Branch was attached to a shopping mall, its entrance between the washrooms and the fast-food kiosks. The popularity of any front-rack bestseller could be determined by the number of ketchup stains and ice-cream smudges.

Sadly, slaying library patrons wasn't allowed. Bad customer service and all.

Ashe had landed a job as circulation clerk mostly because she'd volunteered at North Central in high school. She had no other real qualifications. Fortunately, the head librarian remembered her and liked the fact that she was fluent in three languages. Plus, Ashe was great at keeping even the snarliest mall rats at bay. The pay was average, dismal compared to her contract fee as a kick-ass monster killer.

On the upside, "library worker" would go over well in family court. It sounded responsible, learned, and harmless. Obviously, no judge had ever been to the staff parties.

Ashe yawned, her body objecting to the fact that she'd fallen asleep again at three and been up at six to get Eden off to school. She'd dreamed about Roberto's death before, but not as often now as she used to. Lately, the nightmares seemed to come up in times of stress. Or whenever another attractive man crossed her path—like Reynard. Guilt, maybe?

If so, the guilt was needless. Roberto would want her to move on. He'd lived in the moment far more than Ashe had—he'd never understood things like photographs and albums before Eden was born. He'd always said the heart was enough of a scrapbook for him, with an infinite number of pages.

Yeah, it was hard to let go of someone who could just look at you, and you knew your image was recorded in their heart forever. That was a tough act to follow.

And yet, Ashe was lonely. It had crept up on her since she moved back to Fairview. Maybe time had finally buried her grief deeply enough for her to feel again. Or maybe it was hanging around Holly and her immortal hunk o' vampire love. They were nauseatingly pleased with each other. Watching them had revived longings Ashe had thought were over—everything from a steady supply of hot sex to the wish that someone else would pick up milk on the way home.

As for the vampire dreams, she was just damned sick of those. Obviously the fight with the assassin had scared her worse than she thought.

She stopped, swallowing a slug of scalding coffee. The hot liquid burned down her throat and she blinked hard. The mall was gloomy, shutting out most of the spring daylight. At the other end of the food court, the janitor was pushing around a noisy floor polisher. The place smelled of junk food and industrial cleaner.

With a shudder, she resumed her course. She went a few steps before she saw the Battle of the Pranksters (library versus mall bookstore) was alive and well. Sort of.

Ashe shook her head sadly. *Lame, guys, really lame.*

There was a forest of life-sized cardboard people—courtesy of various book publicity campaigns—in front of the library. Legolas, some guy in shades, a studly romance hero with no shirt, and a cartoon pirate. The pirate had an Easter basket looped over his cardboard arm. A sea of little chocolate eggs covered the floor. They must have bribed the janitor.

Someone had already stepped on a couple of the eggs. Sticky filling smeared the floor like bird droppings. *Okay, gotta give 'em points for the yuck factor.*

The bookstore nerds still hadn't topped the green coffee incident on Saint Patrick's Day, and Ashe's team wasn't divulging their nefarious chemical secrets. War was war, and the librarians had a reference section on their side.

Ashe shouldered her way between manly cardboard men, tiptoeing around the eggs and fishing in her coat pocket for her keys. Looked like she was the first one there.

"Good morning."

Jeez! Ashe jumped, managing to splatter coffee despite the travel mug's lid. She spun around, crouching, keys held like a weapon.

It was Reynard, standing so still that in her morning fog she'd mistaken him for one of the cardboard cutouts. *Crap!* Her heart pounded madly, partly from the fright, partly because it was him. Whatever her brain was saying, her neglected libido was very aware of his good looks.

"I'm a bad person to startle," she said grumpily. At least she was wide-awake now.

"So it seems." He gave her a slight bow, all grace and manners, but there was that hard edge underneath.

Oddly, he was wearing shades. That and the fact that

he'd been standing behind the pirate were why she hadn't recognized him. "What are you doing here?"

"I require your assistance." He turned to look at Legolas, then the bare-chested stud. "What are these things?"

"Decoys. All the librarians are hoping the real thing shows up."

Reynard looked confused, but that slowly gave way to amusement. "Is that why you scatter food on the ground? I had no idea shirtless men were in season."

Ashe ignored that and undid the lock. Like all the storefronts in the mall, the library door folded away like an accordion, disappearing into a pocket in the wall. The clatter of it echoed over the cavernous food court. Reynard watched with interest, apparently fascinated by the track mechanism. *Boys and mechanical stuff. Guess it goes way back.*

"Come on in," she said, setting her coffee on the front desk and flicking on the overhead lights.

When she turned back to her visitor, she froze, the palms of her hands suddenly tingling like she'd touched a live wire. She grabbed her mug, taking another swig just so she didn't stand there like an idiot. It was the first time she'd seen him in decent light, and even hidden behind the sunglasses he was drop-dead gorgeous. *Don't even go there.*

She wasn't in the market for men. After the dream last night, it was obvious her emotions weren't ready. But she couldn't help it. There was no threat to distract her, like there had been at the gardens. She could give all that studly goodness her full attention. And that accent . . .

And she was lonely. She'd said that to herself just minutes ago.

Ashe wanted to throw Reynard down on the circulation desk and, well, circulate. Check him out. Crack spines and bend pages. Granted, she'd been alone for a long time, but a guy had to be hot to get her attention before she'd finished her first cup of coffee.

He pulled off the shades and immediately started

blinking against the light. Back on went the sunglasses. "I apologize for wearing these ridiculous things, but Mac insisted I borrow them. Fortunate that he did. I'm not used to the light any longer."

She'd never seen a guardsman in daylight. Now she knew why. They were blind as cave bats. "Don't worry about it. Let's go back here." She grabbed his sleeve and dragged him into the dim staff room.

The bulk of muscle under the wool of his jacket was unmistakable. Feeling even more deprived and frustrated, she pushed him into one of the plastic chairs and then took a step back, folding her arms to keep her hands to herself. *What is the matter with me?*

She gave Reynard the once-over as he took the glasses off again and rubbed his eyes. He was still wearing his uniform, but at least he'd left the musket and sword behind. Mac must have frisked him at the Castle door for things that would upset the natives.

The demon should have made him change clothes, too. The uniform had been on its last legs generations ago. Reynard was deathly pale, like he hadn't seen sunlight for, gosh, centuries. The circles under his eyes said he hadn't done much sleeping, either.

Take that, hormones. Ragged and pasty. Bad mating material.

Yeah, right.

She'd thought his eyes were icy gray. During that moment when they had been in full light, she'd seen they actually had darker streaks, giving them a changeable, stormy cast. And his hair was more brown than black. The Castle's shadows had robbed him of color.

A memory flickered through her mind, a picture from the battle last fall, when she'd held Reynard's head in her lap. No one was sure he'd live. She'd nursed him out of sheer perversity, willing him to beat the odds. She'd never seen a man cling to his courage like that.

Ashe gripped her elbows like she might fly apart. "So what's up?"

He stopped rubbing his eyes and squinted at her. The

watering eyes ruined his panache. "I am sorry for disturbing you."

She grabbed another chair and sat down. "It must be important, or you wouldn't have come."

He was silent, head lowered, hands resting on his knees.

"More bunny problems?" she prompted.

She caught a glimpse of his wry smile, the merest twitch of lips. "A thief has escaped from my world into yours. And, though I'm not sure if or how it is related, the phouka was deliberately released."

Her eyes lingered on his mouth. In a face made up of blade-sharp angles, it hinted at melting sensuality. *Stop it! This is a serious conversation!* She coughed. "Huh. I assumed the phouka was connected to our lone vampire gunman."

"My *informant*"—Reynard said the word acidly— "is a prince of the dark fey. I would not be surprised if the vampire assassin was involved with the phouka or the thief as well. Dealing with Miru-kai is like seeking a door within a hall of mirrors. There is always the reflection of truth, but you find substance by pure chance."

"So we're dealing with a bunny-releasing, hit-man-hiring thief?"

"Perhaps. I am only guessing that there is a connection. Miru-kai hinted that there is a collector from your world involved. If there is such a collector, he hired the thief. The time line, such as I can determine, is that a thief—most likely a demon—escaped and committed his burglary several days before the incident with the phouka and the assassin."

This was getting complicated. "What was stolen?"

Reynard's face was carefully neutral, but panic was leaking around the edges of that perfect blankness. "It is difficult to explain, but I'll try."

Ashe listened, her slayer senses going on high alert as Reynard spoke. *What the hell is he saying?* But she could hear the strain in his voice. That more than anything told her his crazy story was real.

She sat speechless after he finished, not able to find anything helpful to say. *What dumb-ass idea ever made them put their souls in jars?*

So she came out with the first thing that wasn't an outright insult. "If your soul—or whatever—is out here somewhere in my world, that means you're not tied to the Castle anymore, right?"

"Not exactly. Ordinary prisoners can leave the Castle and carry on with their lives, free of its magic. Guardsmen cannot. First, the magic that allows our bodies to survive separated from our life essence begins to dissipate once we've left that dimension. Second, we cannot stray too far from the vessel that contains our life essence. If we do, we start to fade." He said it coldly, softening nothing.

"Fade?"

"Die. The bottom line, as they say, is that I have to find my urn and return to the Castle as soon as possible."

Die. The word clutched, cold and hard, in her gut. She forced her dismay down, covering it with gruffness. "How long have you got?"

Reynard gave a slight shrug, his face a complete mask. "I don't know. I can feel the urn's absence. It's like something you're trying to recall, but can't. A nagging sensation. But that's all." He made a weary gesture. "I assume it will grow worse with time. Being outside the Castle helps. At least I'm in the same realm as my soul."

"I'm sorry," she said. *Goddess, Ashe, that was lame.* "What can I do?"

"I was hoping you would offer your aid," he said tentatively, finally letting his storm gray eyes meet hers.

It was suddenly hard to breathe.

"You helped before," he said quietly. "When I was hurt."

A girl could drown in those eyes.

"Yeah." She ducked her head, not wanting to think about him dying a lingering death because some maniac had taken his urn. A man's urn should stay in his Castle.

Or whatever. A sick sensation, part anger, part helplessness, made her momentarily dizzy.

"Since I found out about the theft, I checked the vault where the guardsmen's souls are kept. I examined every vessel. Mine is not there. Mac is questioning the Castle residents thoroughly."

Ashe swallowed hard. "So now you have to comb through the whole of my world looking for your thief?"

He spread his hands. "I don't know this world anymore. I'm not helpless, but I don't know where to start. I am hoping you can guide me."

"Why not Mac?"

"Besides being an overlarge fire demon with a full-body tattoo and therefore highly conspicuous, he has a prison dimension to run. His contacts in the human police department are checking their contacts, but this is really a supernatural crime. I would benefit more from the advice of someone familiar with the nonhuman world."

"Plus," added Ashe, "this sounds like there was someone on the inside. Mac needs to find out who in the Castle set this up."

"And what they hoped to gain." His eyes went hard with anger, giving them a gunmetal cast.

Just then Gina Chen, the other clerk on shift, stuck her head in the door. "Hey, Ashe, you here? What's with the cardboard people?"

The young woman, all sleek black hair and almond eyes, caught sight of Reynard. "Oh, hi." She smiled slowly, like a toddler spying a ginormous ice-cream cone. "I don't think I've met you before."

Ashe nearly growled. All of a sudden Gina was far too young and exotically pretty. Reynard was out of his element and vulnerable to the wiles of clever circulation clerks.

"I'll be right out," she said. At least the spike of hostility had put her back in charge of her emotions.

"Neat outfit," Gina persisted.

"He's in a play," Ashe snapped. "Early rehearsals."

"An actor. Cool."

Reynard was watching the two women cautiously, looking from one to the other as if he were following a tennis match—or perhaps he was a cat choosing between two birds. His expression wasn't entirely innocent.

"I'll be out to help with the returns in a minute," Ashe grumped.

Finally taking the hint, Gina huffed and went back to the desk.

Ashe turned to Reynard. "I have to work. I have to think about what you've said."

Images flitted through her head. Eden. The vampire in the gardens turning to dust. The piles of books waiting to be checked in. Eden. Bannerman's waterfall of slime. Kneeling beside Reynard in the Castle, watching him bleed. Eden. There was too much crowding in on her.

Reynard frowned, seeming to sense her tension. He took her hand lightly, just holding it. Drawing her in with the touch of his warm fingers. "Please take the time you need."

"I've got a lot going on right now." She should send Reynard packing. She didn't need his problems on top of her own—too many demands made it easy to drop the ball. She couldn't afford that. Not with assassins and lawyers on her case.

Just standing in Reynard's presence, she felt as if she'd run a marathon. There was a sudden frisson of fear, desire, and schoolgirl nerves.

He let her go, the tips of his fingers sliding along her palm. "I'll take whatever advice you can offer."

Her mouth went dry. Well, at least she wasn't salivating. *Just pick a problem, Ashe; pick something and fix it.* "You need new clothes. You stand out too much dressed like that."

He looked affronted. "As I told Mac, this is my uniform."

So Mac had already lost this argument. Too bad.

"You're going to attract attention. You came to me for advice; I'm giving it to you."

He frowned, looking very Mr. Darcy.

"Don't be stubborn." Ashe used her mom voice.

She watched him back down. That was a lot of pride to swallow, but he did it. Good for him.

Grabbing control made her feel better. "Look. There's a store in the mall called Workrite. Ask for Leslie and say I sent you for some casual clothes. Enough for a couple of days. Tell her I'll come by later and take care of the bill."

He shied from that. "I can't . . ."

"You can, and Leslie will be discreet." She was also very gay, which kept things simple in Ashe's mind. Plus, she'd give Ashe a discount. "It's the least I can do."

It was a tiny thing to do. Not enough by any standard, but at least it was concrete and immediate. Best of all, sending him on an errand bought her time to think.

Reynard met her gaze, appeared to consider a moment, and nodded his agreement. "I shall repay you. My word of honor."

All very proper, gentlemanly. But with a shock that hit low in her body, she saw her own mix of eagerness and reluctance in those storm-cloud eyes. A faint upturn to the killer lips. There was that bad boy again, wondering if he was welcome.

Ashe stood, needing distance. "Let me know how it goes. Stop back here later."

He rose, standing so close in the tiny staff room, she could feel the male warmth of him. "I am at your disposal," he said mildly.

In my dreams.

Chapter 7

Late afternoon only brought new complexities.

Ashe had spent most of the previous day—when not dealing with lawyers or children—making phone calls and lurking in her favorite hangouts swapping gossip. If there were hit vampires and slime demons afoot, surely somebody must have noticed.

Of course, the only problem with calling people and asking for favors was that they might call back. Especially when they were your sister, a new mom, part-time university student, and primary agent of the family ghostbusting business.

"Ashe, I'm begging you," Holly said, sounding like death warmed over and spread on toast. "My magic is still all messed up from baby hormones. I've got a paper due. I haven't slept for days. Alessandro's great about doing his daddy bit, but he's got to work, too, and he's not much use in the daytime."

Ashe peeked around the staff room doorway, checking the lineup at the front counter. It was getting close to closing time, and the late rush was in full swing. Gina was handling it okay, but it wasn't a good time to be on the phone. Cloying sweetness radiated from the crumpled muffin bag on the lunch table, making her feel a little ill.

She'd expected Reynard back from Workrite long before now. Where was he?

Ashe suddenly realized her mind had wandered and Holly was waiting for a reply.

Just say no to more crises. "I'm sorry, Hol, I really am. I have to see my in-laws' lawyer tomorrow afternoon, and it was really tough to get a Saturday appointment. Besides, I'm trying to prove I'm a fit mother, and I can't do that covered in ectoplasm."

"It's only a *little* ghost. In and out. I promise. An hour tops. I'll load you up with everything you need. All you have to do is check it out and set up charms if they're needed."

Holly and their grandmother had come up with some prefab charms that even Ashe's limited magic could activate. Kind of like witch grenades. "Holly, I've got so much going on. . . ."

An honest answer, but it still swamped her with guilt.

"Ashe . . ."

She could hear the strain in Holly's voice. She remembered that new-mom state of mind, when Nirvana was a full night's sleep and a drool-free outfit. *Oh, crap.*

"Is it in town?" Ashe asked, knowing she was helplessly sliding into Holly's clutches. Damn that guilt, anyway.

Paper rustled on the other end of the line. "On Fort and Main, a store called the Book Burrow. New owner. Says he has an attic haunting."

Ashe glanced at her watch, at the pile of work she had left to do before she went home. *Just say no. Just say no.* "Okay, I'll take a look."

Holly let loose a gusty sigh. "Blessings on you. Gotta go: Robin's starting to fuss."

"'Kay, bye." Ashe clicked her cell phone shut, feeling glum.

How did this get to be my life? She was a slayer—

hot, blond, lean and mean. She should be traveling the world, leaving a trail of vamp-kebabs in her wake.

Ashe took a deep breath. *Suck it up.* Holly needed one favor. If Ashe didn't want to be a lone wolf anymore, she could learn to juggle appointments. That was the life of a single mom, a sister, the family member. She loved her family, especially Holly. Connection meant complication, but it was worth it. *I just wish I could clone myself.*

Her conversation with Reynard came back in a rush. He was today's other waif in need. *Where is he?* He was far too good-looking to leave unattended in a public place. The mall was packed with unscrupulous women.

What was she going to do about him? Maybe she could find someone else to help him out? But all the competent folks she knew were either monsters—who hated the guards—or slayers, who couldn't be trusted in a monster-friendly place like Fairview. Delegating could result in a bloodbath. *Gah!*

She pulled her datebook out of her purse and jotted down the time of the ghostbusting appointment. Ghost at two thirty, lawyer at four. That shouldn't be so bad.

She stuck the book in her purse. Time to get back to work. Stacks of books rose from the work counter like stalagmites, waiting to go into plastic bins marked, *Hold.* They would get picked up for shipment to other branches in about fifteen minutes. Ashe grabbed a fat novel, determined to finish the job on time. If the City of Fairview was paying her to sling books, sling books she would.

Crime and Punishment dropped with a thud, the empty bin echoing like a tomb. The Russian master was followed by a children's reader, a Polynesian cookbook, and a decades-old but still popular *The Apocalypse and You.*

Apocalypse bounced on the rim of the bin, landing on the floor with a sad flop.

Ashe walked over to pick the book up. She could hear patrons shuffling at the front counter and the crinkle of laminated bindings as covers opened and closed. Bar-code readers beeped; due-date slips chugged out of the printer. Ashe glanced through the doorway. Gina's long dark hair swung as she swiped books over the de-magnetizer to disarm the security chips hidden in their bindings.

Ashe inspected *Apocalypse.* She'd bent the cover. *Damn.*

"Don't be ridiculous. You're dead," Gina snapped at someone.

With an alarmed jerk, Ashe raised her head. *And I thought I was queen of snarky customer service.*

A male vampire hovered before the desk like an evil intention. *He's up early*, Ashe thought. He was pulling off sunglasses and tucking them in the pocket of his hooded coat—the hood no doubt how he had made it through the fading afternoon light. It was cloudy outside, but the sun wouldn't properly set for at least another hour. He pushed back the hood and looked around, as if he ex-pected to see someone.

The guy was fresh from Vampire Central Casting: overlong hair brushed back from his forehead, leather coat, high cheekbones, and broody lips. Cute, but Ashe tensed. Just because there were vamps who tried to get along with the rest of the world, she wasn't rolling out the red carpet for every bloodsucker who flapped by. Still, he was a patron.

"What's the problem?" Ashe dropped the book in its bin and hurried to the front counter.

Gina was gearing into full snit mode. Ashe could tell by the way she was vengefully gnashing at her gum. "He wants a card."

Not a surprise. Most vamps, stuck inside during day-light hours, were big readers. Ashe turned to the guy. "Got some ID?"

Gina turned to help Mrs. Fanhope, an elderly patron with a taste for gory murder mysteries. Wordlessly, the vampire took out his wallet, thumbing out a driver's license and handing it over. Apparently his name was

Frederick Lloyd. Ashe glanced up, noting the defensive jut of his jaw. He probably had a hassle getting help from most human institutions.

"I'm within my rights. I don't need to be legally alive to check out books."

"You're right," she said, careful to keep dislike out of her tone. "But something with a local address would be good. This is an out-of-town license."

"I just moved here."

Ashe took a subtle step back. Unless they were part of a visiting royal court, vamps didn't move around. This one had come from the King of the East's domain, a large territory that stretched from Detroit to the Atlantic and as far south as Virginia. What was going on? Did Alessandro—Mr. Vampire Law and Order—know that there was a stranger in town?

The heating system came on, blowing a gust of air against her skin. She gave an involuntary jump. *Get a grip.*

Frederick Lloyd was watching her with feline patience. His eyes in life had probably been brown, but had lightened to amber. Dark lashes swept over them like wings. He was staring so hard, he had forgotten to breathe. He bit his lower lip, the point of one fang protruding.

Great, a flirt. She thought about the vampire sniper. Suspicion scuttled across her thoughts like a dark, foul beetle. Were those dreams she was having just anxiety, or something more? Ashe looked around. It was close to closing time. The general public was clearing out. The last few patrons were lined up in front of Gina, oblivious to the predator mere feet away.

He leaned closer, putting his elbows on the counter. His chin lifted slightly as his nostrils flared. Only because she knew the species, Ashe could tell he was trying to catch her scent. *Hunting.* She reached for the shelf beneath the counter. Her fingers brushed over a tape dispenser, a stapler, then closed on the wooden ruler she'd put there the first day she started, just in case. It had a nice metal edge—not as good as a real weapon, but circulation clerks weren't allowed to carry an Uzi on the job.

Try to get him the hell out of here. "We can give you a temporary card until you're settled."

"I'd rather have something permanent," he replied, spooning on the innuendo like fudge sauce.

"That's our policy. If you take our books, we have to be able to track you down."

"Do you plan on paying a personal visit to collect your overdue fines?" He gave a sly grin.

Oh, lord, this guy believes his own press. "Believe me, if I decide you're overdue, I'm checking you out once and for all." She handed him back his license. "Your choice. Take a temporary card or come back with current ID."

"You don't look like the type who plays by the rules."

"I do when it suits me."

"You don't bend them just to be nice?"

"I'm not a nice person."

"Unfortunate."

"Sue me."

Slowly, he put his wallet back into his coat pocket. Too slowly. He was stalling. "You smell like a witch."

"All the better to hex you, bloodsucker," she muttered under her breath.

"You must be Ashe Carver."

"How do you know that?"

He gave a smoking look from beneath the long eyelashes. "I'm looking for you."

Alarm hit like an electric shock, but she leaned across the desk, speaking just above a whisper. "What's the matter? Did I stake your BFF?"

Lloyd gave a Cupid's smirk. An evil, twisted Cupid. He dropped his voice, too, leaning in so their faces were mere inches apart. "Rumor has it a Carver witch just bore a vampire's child. Defied nature itself. Some call it an abomination; others call it . . . interesting."

Ashe froze, feeling his cool breath on her face. *Abomination?* That was what the vampire in the gardens had called her. She snatched a quick glance at Gina. She was staring openmouthed at the vampire, the book scanner in one hand. Mrs. Fanhope and a scruffy, university-aged girl were standing to one side, their expressions somewhere between scandalized and riveted. *Great. They think we're hitting it off. The Carver name makes the tabloids once again.*

"That wasn't me," Ashe murmured. "I'm not into dead guys."

Lloyd's eyebrow twitched. "I wasn't asking what you liked."

"Then what are you asking?"

"My king wants a child of his own. Your family has the right kind of power to give him an heir. Our sources tell us you are unattached. Not that the king cares, but who likes a Jonathan Harker type getting all stakey on your ass?"

Oh, ick. Ashe jumped back from the counter, letting Lloyd see the wooden ruler clutched in her hand. "Did you also hear I'm hell on bad dates?" she said in a clear, loud voice. Public embarrassment was sometimes as good a weapon as anything else.

"Wow," said Gina, looking like all she lacked was popcorn and a soft drink. All three, even Mrs. F., were wide-eyed with fascination.

He gave another slick smile, eyeing the ruler with disdain. Obviously, publicity didn't faze him. "You have a reputation as a dangerous woman. That's why my lord sent an emissary in advance."

"Smart man."

"I'm here to open negotiations. Will you listen to his proposal?"

"Get out of here, Lloyd. You're not here for the books, and it's closing time."

"I think we should all stay and chat, don't you?" he suggested smoothly, then flashed a full, sharp-toothed smile at the others. The university student squeaked, hugging her backpack like a teddy bear. Fear seeped into Gina's pretty face.

Ashe glanced at the glass door to the mall. Plenty of pedestrian traffic out there.

Plenty of potential victims.

Nothing but a ruler between a vampire and her gene pool. *Give me a break*.

Ashe stalked around the end of the counter but left a good chunk of carpet between her and Lloyd. "Look," she said in a constrained voice. *Goddess, this is awkward*. "Even if I wanted to, I can't help your lord."

Lloyd draped himself against the counter like an expensive fur coat. "Why ever not?"

"I don't have the power to make a baby with a vampire. That's extremely rare, and I barely have any magic at all. So go tell his fangship to stick it someplace else. I'm no help to him."

The bystanders watched with open mouths. Ashe had a high embarrassment threshold, but she could feel the blood mounting to her cheeks.

Lloyd curled a lip. On his pretty face, the sneer made him look like an underwear model mugging for the camera. "And you think I'm going to go home to my king empty-handed?"

"The drugstore sells souvenirs. Get him a key chain."

He gave a low, self-satisfied chuckle. "Try again."

After leaving Ashe, Reynard portaled back to the Castle to update Mac, but became swept up in the interviews Mac was conducting. So far, none of the residents he had questioned about the forest gate or the burglary had produced useful information, except for one fact: A goblin's cousin-in-law had been hired the night before to free the phouka. The other goblins, annoyed to find a traitor in their midst—though Mac had no luck establishing who the goblin was allegedly betraying—had torn off his head. So much for questioning *that* material witness. No one had a clue who had done the hiring.

Mac had put his fist through the interview room table,

then accidentally set what remained of the furniture on fire.

As interesting as it all was, Reynard was wasting time watching Mac work. Yet, he allowed himself to linger. Part of him wanted to test how soon he would feel the effects of being in the Castle while his urn was in the outside world. His answer: three hours. From what he could tell, that meant he was still in relatively good shape.

By midafternoon, he made his escape back to the mall to fulfill the first part of his mission: an effective disguise. He understood the necessity, but hated abandoning his uniform. After so long, it was an integral part of him.

Reynard had no trouble finding the store or Ashe's friend Leslie. She was more than efficient in supplying a range of clothing. He recognized a lot of it from what the younger guards wore: lace-up boots and blue jeans. Not a gentleman's wardrobe, but sturdy, convenient, and comfortable. It would serve its purpose.

He would never have accepted the gift of clothing from anyone else. As it was, he would pay back its worth. But accepting the clothing from Ashe pleased him more than he liked to admit. It was intimate next to his skin.

Not the sort of thought he was supposed to be having. Duty, dignity, and death. That was the guardsman's creed. If he was going to die hundreds of years and miles from home, he wanted an honorable end, sword in hand.

He must remember those three Ds the next time he looked at Ashe Carver's lithe, sun-browned figure. He all but snorted out loud. Even if he wasn't shriveling up and dying quite yet, a few hours out of the Castle were eroding his self-control. That didn't mean he could escape his duty. His life, such as it was, belonged to his curse.

But, as he stood in Workrite with the fluttering salesgirls, the Castle seemed far away. They were reminding him what it felt like to be seen as a bedworthy man, and that made him dream of the blond-haired huntress.

The stretchy shirts the girls brought him seemed too tight—but every one of them insisted that was the proper fit. He wasn't an idiot. It showed off his chest and shoulders. Who was he to argue? After so long, he was enjoying the attention. It seemed almost a shame to cover that tight shirt with the short leather jacket Leslie brought.

One more thing. He unbraided his hair from the tight queue that had been fashionable in his day. He let it fall loose in shoulder-length waves. *No, that would get in the way in a fight.* He tied it into a simple ponytail, like some of the modern men he'd seen. *There. I am thoroughly camouflaged.* Last, he put the sunglasses back on.

After leaving Workrite, he walked around the mall. It was an odd building, so dark that it might have been built under the earth. It seemed to wander forever and had no windows, much like the Castle.

The first time he had portaled in, he had arrived only moments before Ashe. Now he took the time to survey the location of the exits, hallways, and blind corners to consider if he—or they—were attacked. Habits died hard.

Reynard felt naked without his weapons, but Mac had insisted he leave them behind unless he was with someone who knew the local customs. Unnecessary. He had once had a taste for dueling—over cards, over women, over anything at all—but that was long ago. He'd had his fill of killing now. He was more interested in what the world of the living had to offer.

Fascinated by everything he saw, Reynard crossed through a noisy area filled with white tables and chairs. There were gossiping mothers and squalling children. A number of the mothers turned to stare as he walked past, running their eyes up and down him as if he were a horse they wanted to purchase. Out of sheer deviltry, he gave them the same look back, tipping up the glasses to get a better look. They didn't seem to mind in the least.

The repressive magic was wearing off, and his senses were reeling. The atmosphere of this world was as addictive as the opium poppy. He wanted more and more: to run for the pure satisfaction of weary muscles, to stand under the rushing leaves of an aspen tree. Everywhere he could hear a strange music that seemed to come from the ceilings. Even though part of him knew it was the simplest of tunes, the lilt of it brought sweet melancholy like an unquenchable ache. He wanted to *live*.

You don't deserve it. You went through women the way other men ate a bowl of fruit. Once the soft flesh was consumed, it was time to move on to the next. And that was but one of your failings. The Castle taught you duty, self-denial, and honor. Would you turn your back on that now? Would you go back on your bargain?

He could. He had the option of simply walking away. His life would be short, maybe only days, but it would be his—until separation from the urn killed him. Was that what he desired? Was he still the same man who would break an oath to feed his addiction to pleasure?

No, that wild young officer had burned down to dead ash during his first few months in the Castle. After that, horror had become commonplace. He had done terrible things in the name of duty. He'd had to bargain with villains like Miru-kai, trading for the welfare of the weaker inmates the warlords took as slaves. He'd had to wage war against gangs of inmates, and sometimes against his own men. But it was the small things that cut deepest. Constance, Mac's woman, had adopted a son, and for a time Reynard had been forced to take the youth prisoner. It had been necessary to maintain order in the Castle, but that didn't make the wrench of separation any easier for mother or son.

Though the Captain of the guardsmen could not show one scrap of what he felt, that episode had nearly broken what was left of Reynard's heart, and he'd regretted it ever after.

So many, many times, it would have been easy to give in to despair. Discipline was the best shield he had against complete moral collapse. Honor. Duty. Dignity. Death. His father would have been pleased at the change a few centuries of servitude had wrought in his troublesome son.

Reynard walked past a shop filled with televisions and electronics—a land of incomprehensible wonders. Then a tobacco shop that informed him that snuff had fallen out of fashion in the last centuries. Then a bookseller's— finally, someplace he understood the merchandise—and then he lingered a long time in front of a toy store.

They had tiny, brightly colored knights on chargers, all ringed around a paper castle. A little green dragon grinned down from the parapets.

They've obviously never seen a real dragon.

"Are you looking for your own boy?" asked the shop girl.

"No," said Reynard, realizing he was just another man to her. Someone with an ordinary story, children of his own, nothing grim, nothing bizarre.

He surprised himself by smiling. "I'm really looking for myself."

She laughed, and it was wonderful. She had a simple, merry, human laugh. A sudden joy overtook him, the sheer seduction of being nonsensical. He laughed with her until he felt his cheeks flushing, suddenly self-conscious.

Rattled, he thanked the shop girl and left the store. He had no money, or he might have bought something to prolong the charade. It was too easy to let himself pretend, to turn his back on the reason he was there. That kind of distraction could be deadly.

Reynard's steps slowed as he neared the doors that looked out onto the street. *Great God.*

Most of the creatures he guarded were night dwellers. When they escaped, they fled into the darkness. He chased them in darkness. What he saw outside was something he had not seen in many, many years.

Sunshine.

It slanted through a slim break in the late-afternoon clouds, angling across a roadway and some spindly trees bright with the first flush of spring growth. Long shadows followed the people crossing the street. He blinked, aching to feel the sun on his skin.

He reached the doors, pushed one open, and stepped outside. Still in shadows, he paused under the overhang of the roof. Sunlight splashed the pavement six feet ahead.

If I go any farther, I will never come back.

People passed him, coming and going. They might have been ghosts. He was staring at the rushing cars, deafened by the noise. Like London from his day, the place teemed with a thousand ever-changing lives. Excitement was a scent. It tantalized him, begging him to step forward, to feel the balm of sun and heat and toss himself into that whirling current.

Is my existence so meaningless that I could throw it away so easily?

Perhaps.

His whole body ached with loss, each throb counting again all he had sacrificed—family, friends, love, career, every last simple act of being a free human. His hands shook, a sudden fever creeping over him, along with the urge to vomit—but there had been nothing in his stomach for two and a half centuries. Nausea lurched past with nothing to latch onto. He closed his eyes, shutting out the spears of cruel, seductive light.

I will not run mad.

The sun had always been unattainable. He remembered the tall bookshelves in his family's leather-and-port-scented library. He'd been all of ten when he'd found his father's great black book with a six-pointed sun embossed on its cover. The sun was painted in gold leaf. He'd caressed the cover, tracing the bright design with his finger.

"Don't touch that!" snapped his father, swatting his hand away.

"What does the sun mean?"

"It means we were born to serve. The book isn't a plaything for little boys. It belongs to the Order."

His father had put the sun away on a high shelf, and Reynard had seen it no more. The next time he'd seen the symbol, it had been above the door of the vault where the urns were stored. By then, he knew what it was that the Order did.

They snatched the sun away from boys who grew into men.

At last, Reynard walked back inside, putting his back to the fading spring day. *Duty, dignity, and death.* There was work to be done. It was past time to get back to Ashe and see if she had any ideas where to begin his quest.

He turned, knowing where she was the way a compass knew north. Ever since that day when she'd wiped the blood from his face and urged him to live, he'd known where to find her, even from the other side of the Castle wall. To use the modern phrase, they had a connection.

Reynard crossed the library threshold and his blood ran cold.

Ashe stood in front of the desk, facing a vampire in a long, hooded coat. Two women, one old, one young, stood nearby like gaping sheep. The other clerk, Gina, clung to the counter as if it were the only thing holding her up.

Reynard dropped the paper bag he was carrying. It landed with a rattle, the extra socks and his threadbare, faded uniform spilling onto the carpet.

Heads turned his way, including the vampire's. In less than a second, the creature realized he was between two enemies.

Using the distraction, Ashe lunged with a ruler she held like a rapier. The vampire spun, snarling. The ruler caught him in the side, poking the heavy cloth of the coat but little else. Reynard heard splintering wood.

Reynard leaped forward, vaulting over a table full of books.

The vamp snarled, grabbing the young woman around the neck and dragging her to his side. She squealed like a trapped rabbit, high and desperate, curling in on herself as much as she could. She wasn't a fighter. The perfect human shield.

Reynard was just steps away. How could he get his own body between the human and the vampire? A guardsman could survive a lot.

He never had a chance to figure it out.

Grim-faced, the old lady hoisted a heavy book in both hands. "This is a library, you oaf!" she snapped, and thumped the vampire on the back of the head.

Ashe yelled, "Mrs. F., no!"

The vampire flung out a clawed hand, grabbing the thick purple fuzz of the old woman's coat. Ashe spun on her heel, slamming her other foot into the vamp's forehead in a sideways kick.

He let go of his hostages and recoiled, his attention now on Ashe. "Are you going to come quietly, or do I have to force you?"

The girl sprawled on her stomach, too frightened to move. Reynard hauled her up by the armpits and shoved her toward the door. "Go! Go!"

He pushed the old woman and Gina after her. "Now!"

Civilians. He'd forgotten how helpless ordinary humans could be. In the Castle, everyone knew enough to run at the first whiff of danger.

The vampire sprang. Ashe sidestepped, but the vampire dragged her down, pinning her beneath him.

The old woman had the right idea. Reynard grabbed a square metal object off the counter and used the heavy block to club the vampire over the head.

The vamp twisted, grabbed Reynard's left wrist, and sank in his teeth. Fang scraped bone and tendon, shearing away flesh. Reynard still had the heavy block in his right hand. The pain brought a flood of rage. He smashed the block down again.

"Reynard!" Ashe gasped from beneath the vamp. "Get this thing off me!"

The vampire's scalp was bleeding, but he clung on, teeth sunk in Reynard's flesh.

Furious, Reynard smashed again and again, a haze of

anger clouding his vision. The fangs loosened. Reynard ripped his arm away, leaving skin behind. He grabbed the vamp by his bloody hair and levered him off Ashe.

Arms now free, Ashe reared up and drove the broken ruler into his heart, then slammed it home with the palm of her hand.

The vampire went limp. Reynard shoved the body aside. Suddenly, the object he was holding seemed enormously heavy. He dumped it back onto the counter.

Ashe was still on the floor, leaning on her elbows. She started to laugh.

"What?"

"You checked him out, all right. That's the demagnetizer."

"The what?"

She shook her head. "Not important. Shit, I thought you were going to bash him to pulp. Did he bite you?"

Reynard held up his torn arm. He could feel the venom, cold as ice, speeding through his veins. In ordinary humans, it produced an addictive, orgasmic state of bliss. He just felt pain. It hardly seemed fair. "I'm immune to their bite. One of the benefits of my occupation."

Ashe raised her eyebrows. "Lucky, I guess."

"Are you hurt?" he asked.

"No, I'm fine. He wanted me for a present to his king."

Her eyes were a pure green, so bright they reminded him of sun through a cathedral window. Staring into them, he had the same sense of awe.

He held out his good hand, remembering his manners. She took it, letting him pull her to her feet. Through their clasped palms, he could feel her strength, her elasticity of muscle and joint as she moved. The venom from the bite was turning from ice to heat, spreading a glow like good brandy.

She was looking at his tight shirt.

He wanted to kiss her. He felt a little foxed, like he had been drinking too much of that brandy. Oh, well, so he wasn't completely immune to venom. Or maybe being outside the Castle weakened his resistance. Or maybe he just didn't want to be oblivious to the venom's pleasure anymore. He'd had enough of playing the saint.

"You know," he said with what he hoped was a charming smile, "while we've already agreed that *I* need *your* help, you seem to be having a few difficulties here."

He pulled off the sunglasses, trying to ignore the stabbing pain of the light.

Ashe looked suspicious, giving a feline cast to those remarkable eyes. "What do you mean?"

"I think you need my help as much as I need yours. I should be your partner while I'm here. We work very well together."

Before she could answer, he grabbed her by the waist and pulled her into him. A risky move, if she objected. Instead, she went perfectly still. Her body leaned into his, thigh to thigh, hip to hip. Her breath was on his face, coming in short, shallow gusts. She was startled, but not fighting back.

"There's a vampire rotting on the floor," she said with disgust.

"They always do that when we're around, don't they?" He grasped a wisp of her hair and let it slither between his fingers. It fell like straight, smooth silk. It was the color of ripe birch leaves when they fell, as gold as if it were made of distilled autumn light.

Oh, God, she's so enticing.

Then, remarkably, he felt her lips on his, soft but demanding. Ashe kissed with frank hunger, hiding nothing. Because she didn't hesitate, he couldn't. The instinct to match her, to best her, strength for strength, was too powerful.

He teased one lip, then the other, searching out her tongue with his. She tasted of woman, warm and earthy.

Reynard felt as if he were crumbling from the inside out, as if soon he would turn to dust, just like the vampire. It had been so hard to hold himself together over the centuries, the notion of sensual surrender felt like suicide. Like flying. Like peace.

No discipline could possibly survive this. This is heaven. No wonder vampire venom is addictive.

Ashe clasped his face, holding him as if she were afraid to miss a single drop as she drank at his mouth. His hands were on her ribs, working their way down her lean waist to the female flare of her hips. He brushed the bare skin peeking out below her shirt. It was hot, velvety, yielding. He slid his palm onto that satin skin. He caressed her, spanning the small of her back with his hand. She gave a moan that vibrated through him like a cat's purr.

A sensation grew low in his belly, a glorious, aching heat that he had long forgotten. Too bad he couldn't resurrect the vampire just long enough to say thank-you. *This is what I felt like before all the misery, the darkness, the damned curse took my life.*

I must possess her.

She smelled of soap, her warmth the only perfume. He breathed in the scent, vowing never to forget it. Ashe broke away, licking her lips, tasting him. Reynard ached to grab her again. Her lips were wet, bruised from their kiss. He was fascinated by the bow of her mouth.

More.

"You are one helluva kisser." She said it like an accusation.

"It is a mighty talent, I confess." He grinned.

Expressions passed over her face, one after another: suspicion, admiration, outrage, bald curiosity. "Don't *ever* do that again."

He stared, felt his jaw actually drop.

Not the reaction he expected. Once, women had wept with joy if he so much as kissed their fingertips. *You're not that man anymore. You sacrificed all that.*

He folded his arms, suddenly on the defensive. "Why not? You seemed to enjoy it."

She pressed her lips together. "Because I'd want to go further. You're not a one-kiss guy."

And what the bleeding hell is wrong with that?

He didn't get to ask. Mrs. F. was back with the security guards, hurtling forward like a fuzzy purple cannonball. "Where is it? Where is that monster?"

Ashe waved a hand at the vampire. "There."

It was starting to dissolve. The exposed flesh was starting to sink in on itself.

Mrs. F. fell back with a grunt of horror. The short, round security guard didn't look happy, either. He glared at Reynard and Ashe. "What happened here?"

Ashe shrugged, exchanged a glance with Reynard. "He dog-eared the pages."

Chapter 8

The prince watched his subject sleep.

Long ago, when Miru-kai had walked the earth, the fey had the power to keep their human companions from aging. True, such magic was a risky alteration to the great pattern of destiny, but it was a chance the fey were willing to take to enjoy the friendship and love humans gave so freely. But the pattern sometimes had a will of its own. The magical herbs, the stones of power, and all the other spells the fey habitually used had been lost to Miru-kai when he and his band of thieves had fallen into the trap of the Castle. Fortunately for the humans among them, the Castle's magic stopped the effects of age. It didn't stop the effects of steel. All of Miru-kai's human friends had perished in battle. All except Simeon.

Now, as the Castle's magic changed and life returned to the stone walls, whatever magic kept humans young was eroding fast. It made sense. Life was change. As the Castle lived, so the cycle of birth and death began spinning again.

Just because it made sense didn't make it bearable. Miru-kai watched Simeon and felt each passing second like a drop of his own blood leaking away. *I don't know what to do.*

His own grandfather had been human, but he had passed into the Summerland with the rest of Miru-kai's kin before the path to that magical realm had been lost. Too long ago to remember.

So this is what it means to be mortal.

The prince hadn't seen this kind of death before, at least not for anyone he loved. How did humans stand growing old?

Simeon's hair had not gone white. It would take time to grow out that way. Instead, it had lost all its sheen, gone brittle and dry as straw. His flesh had shrunk against his bones. The energy that had always seemed to roar from Simeon like a north wind had fallen silent, still, and all but dead. All this in a matter of weeks.

By the time Miru-kai had figured out what ailed his friend, it had almost been too late. Sheer genius alone had ushered the prince into the guardsmen's vault. Genius, luck, and the machinations of a demon pursuing other ends. He had used the demon's conniving to his own purpose.

Reynard and Mac had fallen into the prince's net like oafs at a county fair. He hadn't exactly lied to them, and that was the secret. A nudge here, an evasion there . . . Miru-kai hadn't lost his touch. He could sell warts to goblins.

But could he fix this?

Shadows bunched on the walls as he rose from his chair, then knelt by Simeon's bed. The old man slept, heavy breath in, heavy breath out. The mortal had been everything—his counselor, his teacher, his boon companion, the one who had bathed his wounds. If his own blood had the power to cure, Miru-kai would have opened his veins.

But no, blood was not the answer. Miru-kai rested a hand on the soft-worn sheet, feeling bones beneath. Simeon was fading fast, shrinking and shriveling even as his prince hesitated and pondered.

It was a fey's duty to protect his humans. *Is this what Simeon would want?*

He picked up the urn he had taken at random from the guardsmen's vault. There had been no chance to pick and choose, just a grab as he turned invisible and fled Reynard's unholy wrath. The urn's gold paint felt smooth under his fingers. The shape was elegant, a pleasing combination of curves topped by a slightly pointed knob at the top of the lid. Between the lid and the body of the urn was a seal of white wax. Inside was the life of a man.

This separation of body and soul made the guards all but immortal. Perversely, it also gave them two ways to die. If either the body or the soul was completely destroyed, both halves perished. If he broke the seal, both the soul and the body that matched this vessel would die.

Unless he used sorcery. He could steal the life from this pottery prison and give it to Simeon. *He would hate this idea.*

Miru-kai started to turn the vessel over to read the name on the side, but stopped. He knew many of the guards by name. Knowing whose urn it was would make using it harder. That would feel like murder.

"Kai?"

His head jerked up.

"What are you doing?" Simeon didn't lift his head from his pillow, but peered at his prince through half-closed eyes.

"Nothing."

"You look guilty."

The prince bit his lip, thinking of the many times his old friend had said that, in just such a way, ever since the prince was little. After sneaking out on one of his father's horses, for instance, or cheating at his studies.

Miru-kai took a deep breath, steadying himself. "I might have found you a cure."

Simeon looked weary. "No cure."

Frustration lanced through him. "I don't accept that

speech you gave about mortals needing to move on. Move on where?"

"I fought in the Crusades. Use your imagination."

Miru-kai swore under his breath. They had always argued philosophy—the fey pattern versus the human interpretations of fate and free will. "Surely death cannot be better than life."

Simeon's eyes drifted shut, then dragged open again. "If I can manage it, I'll come back and let you know what I find out."

"No!"

"As you wish."

"*No.* I don't need a pronouncement from the beyond. I need you here." Miru-kai ducked his head, unable to meet Simeon's eyes a moment longer.

He rolled the urn over, read the name, and froze. *Bran. Oh, no.* He'd seen that evil guardsman die in the wars last autumn. That meant the urn was empty.

Oberon's hairy balls!

He was the most cunning thief of the fey, and yet his haste had spoiled everything. He'd been too eager to snatch one of the guardsmen's souls and get away. There would never be another chance—at least, not in time for Simeon.

If I'd only taken my time, read the names, sacrificed a bit of stealth and done a proper job.

"Kai?"

I have killed him with my failure. "What?"

The answer came slowly, softly. "Don't worry so much."

"Don't you dare go!" Miru-kai's voice broke to pieces, sounding small, and young and afraid despite his long, long years of life.

There was no answer.

He felt the blossoming void when Simeon left him, that horrible blankness where once a mortal soul had been. He reached out, touched the weathered face, but no one was there. Simeon's thread in the pattern was done. Miru-kai was alone in the room.

The harsh breathing stopped a minute or two later, but it was merely the lights burning down in an empty feast hall.

For the rest of the night, Miru-kai held Simeon's hand in his. The fey didn't weep. They weren't capable of it. They did not break their hearts over the death of a fragile human.

The prince, grandson of a mortal tribesman, did both.

Friday, April 3, 7:30 p.m.
North Central Shopping Mall

I'm so screwed.

Two hours later, Ashe gathered up her coat and purse from the staff room. It was seven thirty and she was starving and unemployed. She hoped those two conditions were temporary.

As soon as the security guard had gathered his wits, he'd called the cops. Ashe had phoned her boss. The head librarian had arrived at the same time as the police.

They'd all had a lot to say: You didn't just stake patrons. You! Fine! Them! Suspension. Union rep. News media. Nonhuman-rights cases. Blah, blah. Vampire dust hard to clean out of carpet. Blah, blah.

How were the police supposed to confirm identification? Did he have any distinguishing features? *What? Like the fangs?* Look, lady, don't need the attitude. Blah, blah-de-blah.

Ashe produced the wallet card with her international hunting license. That calmed them down.

Reynard produced a government-issued nonhuman ID card. Apparently Mac, once a detective with the local police, had made all the guardsmen get them. It worked almost as well as the license, once Mac's name was mentioned. The demon ex-cop still had allies on the force.

Fortunately, Mrs. F. and Gina stuck around and gave their accounts. Both painted Ashe and Reynard as a cross between archangels and superheroes. The young student the vampire had grabbed was identified and tracked down by phone. She'd give a statement tomorrow, but right then she was too afraid to leave her house. Daylight was better.

Grudgingly, the cop in charge let Ashe go if she promised to show up at the station and make a formal statement. Hunters got away with murder as long as they signed the right forms.

Her boss was less easily assuaged. Since vampicide wasn't covered in the Fairview Library's "Interdepartmental Manual of Standards"—fondly referred to as the FLIMSy—Ashe was suspended without pay pending review by the board of directors. She was advised to call her shop steward in the morning.

By that point, she didn't care anymore. She'd care after she'd had something to eat and hugged her daughter.

"Where are you going?" Reynard asked. He stood in the staff room doorway, arms crossed, a bandage around one wrist to cover the vampire bite. He wasn't quite slouching—his posture was relentlessly upright—but the casual clothes made him look more relaxed. Or maybe that was just the buzz from a touch of after-stake snogging.

Ashe didn't reply at once, but kept stuffing all the junk she'd left in the staff room over the last couple of months in a plastic bag. If it turned out she was fired, she didn't want to have to come back to claim a bunch of plastic food containers and old magazines she'd claimed from the discard pile.

Besides, it gave her an excuse not to look at him. She wasn't embarrassed by the kiss, but it raised some questions she wasn't ready to deal with at the moment. Such as, maybe she was more ready to move on from Roberto than she had fully realized. The embrace had jolted something in her awake. Something she didn't even want to go back to sleep.

Mixed up with confusion and worry and stress, it wasn't a comfortable feeling. Still, the kiss had been . . . wow.

"It was the venom," Reynard said. "I apologize."

He sounded more satisfied than sorry.

"Yeah, okay." Ashe opened the fridge, checked the shelves for comfort food worth stealing. "The venom made you do it."

Goddess! Ashe couldn't keep on thinking about that kiss on an empty stomach. The memory made her dizzy enough as it was. It was taking all her resolve not to throw him on the staff room table and repeat the error of their ways—common sense, motherhood, and sanity be damned. And he had the gall to apologize, like he'd dinged her bumper. *Ooh, bad metaphor.*

"Is there a different apology that would please you better?" Sarcastic, this time.

"No woman likes to hear she was kissed due to a lapse of judgment."

"Blast it, Ashe!" Reynard was suddenly next to her. He grabbed her wrist, his casual strength nearly enough to lift her off her feet. "Listen to me."

Ashe stared into his eyes, letting her anger show. *No one* handled her like that and kept his fingers. "What?"

He bared his teeth, a gesture between a grimace and a snarl. "Don't you see? If I felt the venom, I'm losing the powers that being a guardsman give me. I'm separated from my life force. I'm starting to fade."

She expected to see fear in his storm-colored eyes, but instead there was furious defiance. She knew what that rage felt like. It had been riding her when she staked her first vampire.

"Then you don't have much time left," she said, fear filling her mouth with a sour, metallic tang.

"I don't have much *life* left." He let go of her wrist, stepped back. "I shouldn't have kissed you, but I bloody enjoyed it."

That sounded honest. She shut the fridge. "Forgiven."

He held her gaze intently, as if he were willing her to understand. "I have to work fast, before I decide to hell with spending eternity in a dungeon. I am far too tempted to live while I can. It's a poor choice between death and eternal darkness."

The starkness of his words took her breath away. Her tongue went thick and dry. "I said I'd help you. You're going to live if I have to take you back to Mac drunk in a wheelbarrow with your urn strapped to your forehead."

"That's a charming image."

"I play rough."

He gave her a smoking look that said the venom story was only half-true. Captain Reynard knew what he liked, and there was only a thin sliver of civilization holding him back. Had he played too long with monsters, or had he been born with that wild streak? She could nearly taste it, a trace of the savage in the air. He could change his mind in a moment, and she would be the one on the table. *Yowza.*

Ashe felt a low, sweet burning in her belly, but it was wounded by sadness. The mix of desire and sorrow reminded her too much of her husband and his senseless end. Ashe looked away, swallowing down a sudden ache in her throat. *Back to business.* She knew the head librarian was waiting outside, ready to show her the door.

"I have to pick up my daughter. The after-school care was good enough to take her to my grandmother's."

Guilt felt like a fine dust coating her skin, so ingrained it merely smudged when she tried to brush it away. Good mothers didn't miss pickup time because they were explaining themselves to the cops. *Goddess, what happens if I lose my job for good?*

Reynard seemed to read her face. A furrow of concern formed between his eyebrows, and he brushed warm fingertips down her cheek. She stiffened, but didn't pull away. The touch was caring, not intrusive. She just wasn't used to having a man around anymore.

"Do you want me to go?" he asked.

"No. Come with me. We need to talk. You came to me for help. I haven't forgotten that, and we can't waste any more time." Abruptly, she started for the door.

He fell into step beside her. "Where are we going?"

"To Grandma's house."

He gave her a sidelong look. "According to the old tales, isn't there a wolf at Grandmother's house?"

Ashe smiled sweetly. "So you've met Grandma."

Chapter 9

A she stopped at the supermarket en route. She wasn't going to show up empty-handed, especially since her grandmother had probably fed Eden dinner. Although Grandma loved Eden's visits, to Ashe it felt like freeloading unless she contributed something to the meal—and right now, she needed every scrap of pride she could cling to.

"I'll be quick," she said to Reynard, who had been largely silent throughout his first car ride. Except for a wide-eyed look, he was handling his introduction to the technological age with surprising calm.

"Take your time," he said, reaching out to run his hand over the air vent, the glove box, and the gearshift with reverent fascination. "The pictures on the television don't truly capture the feel of riding in one of these."

Ashe bit her lip. He was a man besotted. Wisdom said touching would lead to fondling, which would lead to ignition. Ashe took the keys, just in case. As little as she liked the SUV, she needed it in one piece. *Oh, honey, just wait till you get a load of my motorcycle.*

Showing off to Reynard would be oddly thrilling.

She was in and out of the store in five minutes. They

reached their destination around quarter past eight. Grandma Carver, retired witch and family matriarch, lived in a seniors' complex. The Golden Swans balanced independent living with just enough care to keep the residents healthy and safe. Grandma had raised Ashe and Holly after the death of their parents. They had all lived in the family home, but Grandma had moved to the Swans about five years ago, when her arthritis made climbing up and down a three-story Victorian too much of a challenge.

Of course, Ashe suspected the real reason for the move was the Swans' avid bridge community. More gambling went on there than in Atlantic City, and Grandma rarely lost.

They took the elevator—another first for Reynard— up the east tower and knocked on Grandma's door. She usually left it unlocked, but not this time. Rampaging vampires got even her attention. The door opened as far as the chain would let it, a sliver of Grandma's apple-doll face showing through the crack.

"Ah, it's you," she said. The door closed, chain rattled, and it opened fully this time.

"Hey, G-ma." Ashe had to bend down to hug her. These days, her grandmother barely came up to her chin. Ashe noticed that now there was more white than gray in the older woman's long ponytail.

"Who is this cupcake?" Grandma said as Ashe released her.

Ashe rolled her eyes. "This is Captain Reynard. Hands off."

"I'd say he looks old enough to look after himself. It's good to share, darling."

"I'm enchanted to make your acquaintance, madam," Reynard said, setting the bag of groceries he was carrying beside the door. He bowed over Grandma's hand, obviously thrilling her right out of her orthopedic sneakers.

He shot both women a devilish look. Grandma's cheeks turned pink. Ashe wondered if hers did, too.

"Then come on in. No point in letting the neighbors

get jealous." Grandma Carver gestured for them to follow her inside. She walked with two canes, and she used both to thump her way across the floor. Ashe winced, hoping her downstairs neighbor was hard of hearing.

The one-bedroom apartment was pin-neat and smelled of cigarettes. The decor was a nostalgic mix of old-fashioned chintz, mahogany, and crocheted antimacassars. Grandma's decorating sense was the only demure thing about her.

"Ashe, where've you been hiding this one?" Grandma demanded. "One hello and I need a smoke."

"Sit, Grandma," Ashe commanded. "I brought dessert."

"Allow me." Reynard guided Grandma to the table.

"Oh, Ashe, honey, keep him around. Just for me?"

Ashe wanted to crawl under the couch. "Grandma!" Reynard winked.

"Agh!" Ashe picked up the groceries from the hallway and headed into the kitchen. Her grandmother was wise, dedicated to their witch heritage, and loved them all fiercely, but sometimes she was also a big, fat pain.

"Mom!" Eden bounced into the room like a yo-yo, completely forgetting her dignity. She was always happiest around Grandma. "Whatcha bring?"

"Nanaimo bars. Sorry to be so long. What were you doing while you were waiting?"

"Reading. Let me get plates."

"Thanks, Eden."

"We did some basic meditation exercises today," Grandma said, her voice heavy with theatrical significance. "Eden is a young witch showing every sign that she's going to get her powers very soon."

"Cool." Ashe was proud and filled with maternal dread at the same time.

Her grandmother's look said that she knew exactly what she was thinking. "Ashe, did you notice that Eden and I are twins today?"

Eden carried the plates to the table and stood next to Grandma, draping one arm around the older woman's shoulder. They both wore black sweatpants and hot-pink T-shirts. The only difference was Grandma's orange cardigan, which featured a fleet of chopper motorcycles done in crewelwork around the hem.

Ashe grinned. "Nice sweater."

"I thought it made a statement. Gray power rules."

"Very colorful," Reynard added uncertainly.

Ashe finished making introductions. Eden was polite. Dessert was served. Reynard declined anything but water.

"Have you heard from Holly today?" Ashe asked Grandma.

"I talked to her on the phone. Little Robin is fine. Alessandro stopped by on his way downtown. I told him what you told me on the phone about your vampire at the library. He said he'd look into it."

"Mac will be interested to learn of this," Reynard put in. "It puts an entirely new layer on the assassination attempt."

Ashe put down her fork. The rich, sugary dessert—brownie, custard, and a thick layer of dark chocolate—curdled in her empty stomach. "Just add one more strangeness onto a big, steaming pile of weird."

Eden excused herself to return to the living room and her book.

Grandma leaned over and whispered to Ashe, "She was asking about her grandparents again today. Soon you're going to have to tell her what happened, before she finds out on her own."

"I know," Ashe whispered back, feeling old, familiar guilt.

"Soon." The older woman gave her a significant look. "So what else is up?"

Ashe got down to business. "I was hoping you could offer some insights. There are a few things going on."

Grandma fidgeted. She obviously wanted a cigarette but refused to smoke around Eden or Robin. "Okay, hit me. What's up?"

"For starters, we need to find an artifact that was stolen from the Castle," Ashe said.

"You're looking for a spell to find lost objects?"

"Stolen by a demon," said Reynard. "My guess is that the object would be shielded from ordinary location spells."

Grandma blinked in surprise. "Have you talked to Lore? If there's a black, gray, or even slightly dingy market in Fairview, the hellhounds seem to know about it."

"You think talking to him would be better than using a spell?" Ashe asked.

"Cast a spell and the thief, if he's any kind of a magic user himself, will know you're looking for him. Sometimes simple is safest."

"Good point." Ashe looked at Reynard. "I know where Lore works. I'll try to set something up first thing tomorrow morning."

Grandma leaned back in her chair. "So what's the object? What's going on?"

Ashe and Reynard shared a look.

"Where do we start?" Ashe said.

Grandma huffed. "I don't much care. Spill, or forget any more free advice."

They explained who Reynard was, and then filled her in, starting with the rabbit, carrying on through the lawyer's demon problem and the theft of the urn, and finishing with the death of Frederick Lloyd, the vampire in the library. The news that he was the King of the East's emissary, and that the king wanted an heir, made her grandmother's face pucker with anxiety.

"My Goddess." Grandma refilled her coffee cup. The gesture looked automatic, like she needed something to do with her hands. "Just because Holly and Alessandro had Robin, are vampires suddenly going to want kids of their own?"

"Only some of them," said Ashe dryly. "Lloyd let something slip about other vampires considering daddyhood to be an abomination. That's the same term the sniper in the gardens used."

Reynard looked grim. "You think the sniper, or whoever hired him, planned to prevent any future children by killing you?"

"Is Holly in danger as well?" Grandma snapped, although the answer was obvious.

Cold dread snaked around Ashe's limbs. If Omara, the local vamp queen, heard about the King of the East's messenger, she would freak. There'd be monster politics raining all over everyone. Fairview would become a kill zone. They had to take care of this before her fangship found out.

Ashe met Grandma's eyes, and guessed by her expression that she was thinking along the same lines. "Holly's our best magical weapon, but she said her mojo is still wonky. Any idea when she'll be back to normal?"

"Soon. It usually takes a month or two after the baby is born before a witch's powers recover. In the meantime, Alessandro will look after Holly. You take care of yourself and Eden. Protect your family. Stake half the damned vampires in town if you have to."

Rambo Grandma. Great. "It's not going to be that easy. I'm looking at a custody case. Hunting monsters isn't an approved single-mom occupation. Even if I fly under that radar, the vamps like their revenge. I'm afraid that if I make a move, it'll put Eden in danger."

"Then let me be your sword," Reynard offered, leaning forward across the table. The dim light of the dining room darkened his eyes and pared any trace of softness from his face. He was all sharp angles. Granite with an edge of steel. "There is no reason for you to risk yourself or your daughter. Not while I am here."

But you won't be here for long. "You've got your own problems."

"It's the least a gentleman can do." He gave a sardonic smile. "Besides, I thought we agreed to help each other."

Ashe sat back in her chair, feeling a sudden need for distance. This was too much, too soon. "I said *I'd* help *you*. I don't hunt with a partner. Never have, never will."

She looked him straight in the eyes, determined to make her point. She saw a flicker of what might have been hurt; then his gaze became hard and gray as the stones of the Castle walls. He'd taken her refusal as a personal rejection. Annoyance burned through her stomach. *Great. Like I have time to soothe wounded male egos.*

"Mo-o-o-om!" Eden bawled from the living room.

The air around the adults' table suddenly felt brittle with tension. The interruption only cranked it up three notches.

Ashe took a shaking breath before she called out, "Hark, I hear the sweet tones of the Princess Eden!"

"May I have more dessert, please?"

Good grammar emerged only when Eden wanted something. "Come and get it."

"But I'm *reading*!"

"Then leave your eyeballs there."

"Mo-o-om!" This time disgust.

Ashe made a face. She was pulled in too many directions.

"I'll take it to her." Reynard stood up with a cool glance at Ashe, impatience in every line of his body. He shoved a slice of the chocolaty dessert onto a plate and stalked away from the table.

Grandma shot Ashe a caustic look. "You really know how to win friends and influence people."

"Whatever," Ashe muttered.

"He'd be a good partner. He looks like he's broken a few rules in his time. You don't end up an immortal in a dungeon by doing nothing but crossword puzzles."

"I don't want a partner. You have to be responsible for a partner. I don't need that."

"Why not?"

Ashe sat back and folded her arms. "When I've done

such a good job with the other people in my life?" *Like Mom and Dad and Roberto* ...

"Take his help, Ashe. He's a big boy. He can handle himself."

"How much can I rely on a guy who's on a ticking clock?"

"It's clear from one look that he thinks the world of you."

"Is that enough?"

"You're pushing him back into his stone cell."

"Damned straight, I am. With his urn. He'll live that way."

Grandma toyed with her coffee cup. "If you don't want my advice, then why are you here?"

"I *do* need help. I need a shoulder to cry on."

Grandma raised her eyebrows. "Besides the obvious, what's the matter?"

"Everything," Ashe said in a low voice. "Like I said, it's one thing to be flying solo when it's pouring vamps and demons."

Grandma took a swallow of coffee, taking her time. "But the stakes are higher with your family around."

"I'm damn near paralyzed. I can't afford to make a mistake. The last time the monster posse showed up I had to send Eden away."

"So think like a slayer, not a soccer mom. You need to go on the offensive and get ahead of the game. Get them before they have time to make another move."

Ashe set her coffee mug on the table with an audible thump. She was pulled in too many directions to think straight anymore. "But that's the whole problem. I can't kick every ass that needs kicking anymore. Yes, I hate that. I actually like hunting. But changing who I am gives me a life that includes my daughter, and I'm not sorry. There is *nothing* I won't do for her."

Grandma shoved her plate away, the corners of her mouth pulling down. "The world does not run on absolutes. Your role in our family is as a protector. That doesn't mean you never get to be a Norman Rockwell mother. You just can't be one right now. Slay now; make tuna casserole later. Do both. Be versatile. It's the way of the modern woman."

"That sounds pretty simplistic."

"Because it is. If Fairview's not safe, Eden's not safe. The question's not whether you're going to clean up this mess, but when you're going to get busy and do it. What are your options? Let the bad vampires run amok? Send the demon a housewarming basket? The list of people who can deal with this sort of thing is very short, and you're at the top. If you're worried about safety, stay with Holly. That house is a magical fortress."

Ashe gave a single, reluctant nod. She hated sleeping in her childhood home. It held too many memories, but if things got bad, she could suck it up. "There's still the whole custody thing. I have to do this entirely under the radar."

"I understand. We'll cover you."

"We?"

"Me, Holly, Alessandro. Your family. We'll figure out how."

Ashe was shaking her head before Grandma finished talking. "I can't put that burden on you."

"Damn it, Ashe, if you want things to get easier, you have to change. Learn to accept a helping hand!"

Reynard was furious. *She cannot refuse my assistance. It's not reasonable*. Clearly she could see he was more than capable. They'd killed two vampires together. But there was nothing reasonable about Ashe Carver. She was all will and steel.

There was no possibility that she was better off without his help, and her resistance brought his own will—and, to be honest, his pride—into focus.

She could tell him he wasn't welcome. That did not mean he would accept her refusal. Ever. He hadn't survived centuries in the Castle by giving in. He had learned how to bide his time. If he had to, he would simply outsmart her.

The idea curled through him like a plume of incense, part inspiration and part nostalgia for the Reynard who had stalked the drawing rooms of yore. How pleasurable those days had been. Their sweet nostalgia lingered like a perfume. He had been a master with the women of his time. Surely he could handle one of their descendants in much the same way. For Ashe's own good, of course.

At least until he fell off his perch, he thought sardonically.

His inner conversation stopped dead when he saw Eden. The child was curled into a ball on the sofa, book clutched to her chest. Her brown eyes were wide. He set the plate on the small table beside her.

She just kept looking at him, as if she were expecting something more. Reynard's inner rake vaporized like a wisp of smoke, vanishing into the wiser, harder man.

"Is there something else you desire?" he asked gently.

Her gaze shifted toward the dining room, where Ashe and her grandmother were arguing in low, tight tones. "I thought Mom would come," she said in a small voice.

She hadn't wanted the cake; she'd wanted her mother. *Something is wrong.*

Reynard listened for a moment, trying to hear what the girl would hear. The argument sounded different from a distance, without the gestures and faces to accompany words: the old woman's low, husky voice; Ashe's was lighter, clear, and aching with tension.

His ears told him things he hadn't seen. *Anguish.*

He could tell Ashe was tearing herself to pieces, all her certainty a bluff for a terrible fear that she would fail her child. But all Eden would understand was that her mother was terrified, and a frightened mother made for a frightened daughter. Reynard was no expert with children, but he had seen soldiers' families dragged along as camp followers during war. He recognized that panicked look. In those cases, he'd always had something practical to offer—food, water, protection. Now he was at a loss.

He sat down beside Eden. She let go of the book, and it slid to the floor. He read the title: *Prince Caspian*. Nothing he recognized.

"Easier when you're a lone wolf," the grandmother said from the next room.

"Lots," Ashe replied, her voice quiet, but not quiet enough.

Eden gave Reynard a look filled with confusion. "Why does Mom want to be alone all the time?"

Bloody hell, she thinks Ashe doesn't want her here. Yet, just the way Ashe looked at the child made that idea impossible. Ashe wanted her daughter above everything else.

Mother and daughter were on a collision course of misunderstanding. Just like he and his brother had been. Families hadn't changed much over the years.

Reynard swore to himself for a moment. Seduction—he understood how to play those games. He knew how to fight, gamble, and make the witty chatter expected of a gentleman at dinner. Providing emotional comfort was something quite different, and nothing he had ever been good at. He had been raised to show no weakness, and the Castle crushed sympathy before it began. But the sinking feeling in his gut wouldn't let him back away. He still didn't know what to say to a child, so he went with the truth.

"You realize that your mother fights monsters from time to time," he said, hoping he wasn't insulting the girl's intelligence.

"Yeah," Eden said bleakly. "She's done that for a while now."

"That is why we were late. We had a problem to take care of."

She looked down, thick, dark lashes hiding her eyes. She didn't have the doll-like prettiness of some young girls, but she would grow into a striking woman.

"I heard you guys talking. There are bad vampires around." Her fingers plucked nervously at the fringe of a throw cushion. "She should let me go back to Saint Flo's so I wouldn't be in her way. I should just go."

She's far too young to have to worry about demons and slayers. Reynard wished he were Mac, who would know how to give support with a touch and the right word. He took the girl's hand in his. It was small and warm. She looked up at him, her eyes surprised and wary. He let her go, hoping she understood that he meant only kindness. "Your mother needs you here. She wishes the vampires would stay away, that's all."

"Then why is she afraid?"

Damnation. "If she's a little bit afraid, then she won't make mistakes. That's part of why she's good at what she does."

"How dangerous is it? Tell me the truth," Eden asked. Her eyes were starred with tears she seemed too stubborn to shed, but her mouth was firm and steady.

She's already lost her father. He swallowed hard, feeling the complexity of the child's world unrolling around him like a giant map. Every horizon held storms and dragons.

"I won't tell you it's not dangerous, because that would not be true," he said, inwardly wincing at his honesty. "But I'm going to be with her. That tips things in our favor."

Eden's scrutiny made him think of Anubis weighing the souls of the dead. He was being judged down to his brand-new bootlaces. "So you've got her back, then?"

Fortunately, that was one of Mac's expressions. He understood what she was asking of him. "Yes. Absolutely." *Even if Ashe doesn't accept that yet.*

Eden put her hand over his. "Good."

Her hand was half the size of his, the nails chewed and stained with blue ink. Beneath it, his own looked large and rough from long years of handling the tools of war.

Reynard realized he'd made a huge promise. He'd damned well better live long enough to keep it. His jaw set. His stomach felt as if he were betting his inheritance on a last hand of cards. He'd never been a praying man, but this seemed like a good occasion for it.

Just then, Ashe strode into the room, wearing the look of a woman at the edge of her reserves. "Time to go, kiddo."

She looked at the two of them, her bright green gaze darting from one face to the other, finally settling on Eden's. Reynard saw the look of dawning horror on Ashe's face.

"It was quite easy to hear your conversation from here," he said, a reproachful edge creeping into his voice. He couldn't help it, but then regretted the look of shame in her eyes.

Ashe blinked rapidly. "Eden, don't be scared by what we were talking about. . . ."

Eden jumped off the couch. "I'm glad Captain Reynard's helping you."

Ashe shot him a glare that withered as fast as it bloomed. She hugged the girl to her, hiding her face in the brown curls. "We're discussing that."

Reynard frowned. No one was going to berate Ashe for her mistakes harder than Ashe herself. The problem was that punishing herself wasn't the answer.

He rose, following Ashe as she herded Eden toward the door, gathering up the girl's backpack and coat as she went. The grandmother waited to see them off, leaning on her canes.

"Be sensible," she said.

"I'll do what I think is right," Ashe grumbled, but she sounded weary.

Reynard gave the old lady a respectful bow. "And I will work your granddaughter around to my way of thinking."

Grandma Carver smiled sweetly. "And I'll knock your heads together if you screw it up. And, Ashe," she said, handing her a paper bag, "these charms will keep out nightmares, whether they're your own or sent by someone else. Sleep well."

"Thanks, G-ma." Ashe hugged and kissed her grandmother.

They left. Outside the air was cold and clean. It had rained while they were indoors. Reynard filled his lungs, gulping down the tang of the spring night. He'd forgotten that sharp, sweet scent until that chase in the gardens. He couldn't get enough of it.

"Don't hyperventilate," said Ashe, unlocking her vehicle so Eden could climb inside. "Do you have someplace to stay? I've got a couch."

"I've made arrangements," Reynard said, wishing he could accept her offer. He didn't want to leave her side, but that would lead to the inevitable question of beds and pleasure and the decision of behaving like a gentleman or a desperate man with the life span of a flea. One was dull and the other lacked dignity. "What time shall we meet to go see Lore?"

"I'll call him tomorrow morning. Eden goes to the rec center for piano and swimming. I'm going to drop her off and catch a quick workout. Meet me at nine thirty at Morgan's Gym. The people we need will be up by then. We'll make plans from there." Ashe shut the passenger door with a sigh. "Of course, you don't know where the gym is."

"I will find you," he said. "That's not a problem."

"Be careful saying stuff like that. That sounds a bit stalkerish."

Reynard chuckled softly. "Your world is confusing." He looked up. "Even the constellations are hard to make out."

"Light pollution."

"Unfortunate." There were no stars in the Castle. That blankness had cut his spirit down like scythed wheat. Without even the sky above, he'd truly been shut off from everything he'd known. That loss still chilled him.

A man could go mad counting so many losses. Perhaps that was what drove guardsmen like Killion to murderous sprees.

Her eyes found his, their emerald brightness smothered by the darkness. "One thing I've gotta say. After last fall, y'know, when you were so hurt, I kept wondering if you were all right. I'm sorry I didn't call. Or write. Or whatever."

"I didn't know you remembered," he said.

Her brows drew together. "Of course I did! It was just that I—"

He held up a hand to stop her, regretting his words. "I was trapped in the Castle. You had to bring your daughter home. There is nothing to apologize for."

She shrugged. "I just want you to know that I didn't forget about you."

"Thank you," he said. He felt like he should say more, but he wasn't sure what she would have welcomed.

"Okay," said Ashe, rubbing her eyes. "Tomorrow morning at the gym. Do you need a ride anywhere?"

"No, thank you." Reynard folded his arms before he could reach out to her. "Good night."

She rummaged inside the back of the vehicle and handed him the string-handled bag with his uniform and spare clothes. As he took it, she hesitated. "We're going to make some serious headway on this urn thing tomorrow. I promise. We'll go see Lore, if he's around. Then I've got a ghost to take care of for my sister."

"I'm sure I'll enjoy that."

Her mouth worked a moment. "I didn't say you were coming along."

"I didn't say I wasn't." He met her gaze, standing his ground.

She huffed and turned away. "Bloody English bastard."

Reynard smiled to himself. He had won the skirmish. It was a start.

Ashe and her girl drove off into the night, taillights glowing like eerie eyes. He stood in the dark for a long time, watching the night. The lights went off in Grandma Carver's windows. A cat trotted by, intent on patrolling its territory.

It was pleasant to stand there in the outside world, enjoying the illusion of freedom. Perhaps that was why he wanted to help Ashe and Eden so desperately. It was a choice he made freely and had nothing to do with the duty that was his prison even more than the stone walls.

He had wrestled with that duty even before he knew it existed.

A few years after he found the black book with the sun, he'd been playing pirates with his brother. At the moment, he was a runaway slave and hiding underneath the curve of the stairway right outside the drawing room door. His parents were entertaining a few close friends inside the beautifully appointed room—Reynard and his brother were rarely permitted inside it—so Reynard was quiet as the proverbial mouse. That was why, despite the excitement of his game, he had heard them talking.

"The Order's lottery has always demanded the heirs." That was his father's voice. "Why can't they take the younger sons? The warlock families are weak enough without scything down the flower of our manhood."

Another voice answered. It was a dry, dusty, cruel voice that made Reynard squirm even farther into the protective shadows of the stairs. "Without sacrifice, where is the service to duty?"

That one sentence, delivered in the voice of a nightmare, had stayed with him, haunting his child's imagination. At the time, he had wondered what sort of games the adults played. He didn't know he and his brother were already pieces on the board.

Pieces about to find their checkmate.

It was only years later—many, many years—that he understood his father was just as much of a victim. Heirs were taken to keep the families weak, so that none could challenge the Order's ruling elite. His father had spoken out of a generations-old frustration.

Eventually, he had managed to forgive the fact his

father had hoped Reynard would play the sacrificial lamb—even if his father's wish had come true.

The memory darkened his mood too much for him to enjoy the night any longer. Reynard reached out with his mind and pulled the power from the atmosphere around him. Wind and rain surrendered their energy, letting him gather it inside his body. It spun inside him, churning, building until he lifted his hand, spreading his fingers. Then he released it as easily as he would a sigh.

The charred scent of magic filled the night. A bright dot hung just beyond the tips of his fingers. It whirred madly, spinning outward until it seemed to burn a hole in the air. The dot grew to a ragged orange disk. Reynard stretched it with his mind, pulling and tearing at the fabric between this world and the Castle. As the magic built, it crawled along his skin with prickling claws, filling his nose and mouth, coursing down his limbs like water sprayed in icy needles.

The portal was a fiery bright mouth, the Castle the darkness of its man-sized gullet. Reynard squinted against the brightness, and stepped through.

"Nice threads," said Mac. "You look normal."

"I'm in disguise," Reynard replied. "But never mind that. I've come to give a report. A vampire attacked Ashe in the public library today."

"Say what?"

Reynard had just sat down in the quarters Mac shared with Constance, his vampire lady love. The pair had a passionate and yet down-to-earth sort of happiness that radiated throughout their domain. The rooms were bright, modern, spacious, and very undungeon-like. Just like the outside world, the place was filled with color. A basket of knitting sat beside Reynard's chair. Glossy decorating magazines fanned out across a glass topped coffee table. Constance was the consummate homemaker.

Mac picked up the remote and clicked off the flat-screen TV. The fire demon was sprawled in a huge leather recliner, and had been watching the hockey game. Perhaps it was a good thing Reynard interrupted, because he smelled something burning. Mac had an unhappy tendency to scorch his surroundings when his favorite team was losing.

"It seems the King of the East is a player in our melodrama. The vampire was his emissary. Alessandro Caravelli and the other locals are finding out what they can."

"Bugger vampire politics. So much for sneaking fifteen minutes of R and R." Mac ran his hands through his hair, clearly exhausted despite his demonic strength. "Interesting. I'll follow up with Caravelli and find out what he learns."

Reynard gripped the arms of the chair to stop his hands from shaking with anger. He wanted to beat Frederick Lloyd to a pulp all over again. "Word has spread that at least one Carver woman has borne a vampire's child. Now some want to sink more than teeth into their flesh."

"Nasty."

For the second time that night, Reynard recounted everything that had happened so far. When he finished, Mac made a disgusted face. "With Miru-kai and the vampires and a possible demon escape, the only species not kicking up a fuss right now are the werebeasts."

"I wouldn't say that too loudly." Reynard sighed, paused, and realized he was too weary to go on. "On another subject, how does Stewart fare?"

"I called his mother. He'll be in the hospital for a few days, but they expect he'll recover."

"I'm going to wring Miru-kai's neck when I find him. He's deep in the middle of this, somewhere."

They sat in glum silence for a moment. Reynard could hear Constance singing to herself in another room. Her presence reminded him of the time he'd taken her son prisoner. After spending even a short time with Ashe and her child, he understood a little more Constance's pain at losing the lad. It was a wonder she'd ever forgiven Reynard for what he'd done, even if it had come out right in the end.

He shook his head to clear away the memory, and thought instead of everything he'd seen that day.

"It is hard to walk in the outside world," he said, half to himself. "It is confusing, because much is unfamiliar, and yet I remember parts of my old life that I'd forgotten." Things that would have been easier never to recall.

Mac toyed with the remote. "I wish I was able to come with you, but I've got, y'know, fairy problems. I'm thinking pesticide, but that could take a few days."

Reynard laughed.

Mac shrugged. "Do you think you can manage this urn business with Ashe's help? If you need me, I'll find a way to put everything on hold and go outside with you."

"I will be fine. I rode in an automobile today. And an elevator."

Mac grinned. "Look at you go, you daredevil."

"The modern world has much to recommend it." Reynard stood. "The cars are fascinating."

"So am I going to see you zooming around here in a sports coupe?"

"I would like to ride a good horse again."

"I've got some unicorns down in the basement, if you'd like to take them out for a spin."

"They only like virgins. I'm rather too late to that party."

Reynard walked back to his own quarters filled with a mix of weariness and impatience. Tomorrow would bring more challenges. It would bring another chance to linger in the free air of the outside world, to be near Ashe, and to find parts of himself he thought long dead. Yet, what was the point of coming back to life, only to sink once again into the sunless existence of the Castle?

He was weary of the question. There was no good answer. The Castle was both oppressive and safe. *Doomed, damned, doomed, damned.* His curse just kept on ticking.

He opened the door to his Spartan quarters. There was a sitting room and a bedchamber, nothing more. He had little need of possessions. One trunk held weapons, the other clothes. A small shelf of books rounded out the furnishings.

After the chaotic plenty of Ashe's world, he saw his rooms with fresh eyes. They looked like a monk's cell. No bright, sunny colors here. He pulled off his new T-shirt as he walked into his bedroom. His narrow bed looked as welcoming as an anvil. The paper bag with his clothes sat on the plain counterpane. Carefully, he took out his worn uniform and folded it neatly. Not all of it was original. Much of his red coat had been replaced, piece by piece, but the buttons and braid were the same. The buttonholes, arranged in pairs down the front, were carefully mended. No loose threads. Nothing frayed. With so little to call his own, the uniform had become more to him than a suit of clothes. It was everything he should have aspired to, everything he should have achieved in his life when he still walked in the world.

Beneath the uniform were the rest of the clothes Ashe had bought him. Comfortable, easy, fresh, new. If they represented anything, it was the unknown. Or maybe they were just socks and shirts—clothes blank and empty of meaning, like they were supposed to be. Normal people didn't overthink socks.

He poured water into his washbasin and bent over, looking in the spotted, faded mirror that hung above it. Swirling blue tattoos covered his chest, inked there by the magic that identified him as a guardsman. They were different from Mac's, more primitive. Where Mac's tattoos marked him with the authority of the Castle, Reynard bore the brand of the Order.

The oath—curse—had taken his life and written servitude into his flesh. He could feel the hollow ache of the urn's absence. Once he had entered the Castle, the feeling had resolved into a pain under his ribs. It was growing, reminding him that he was, for all intents and purposes, little better than a dead man. Mac had suggested that he sleep in a hotel outside the Castle, where he would be closer to the urn.

A sudden stab of pain shot through him, making him flinch and grip the sides of the washstand. He was going to have to accept Mac's offer of a hotel room after all.

He was running out of time.

And yet . . . he had seen the sun today.

Given hope to a little girl.

And he'd kissed Ashe Carver.

For the first time since—well, since he'd traded his life for his brother's so long ago—Reynard felt hope.

Chapter 10

"**G**ood evening, children of the night. You're listening to CSUP, 101.5 FM at the beautiful University of Fairview campus, and I'm Errata Jones, your hostess for the evening. For our last item tonight, here's the latest tidbit I've found about the guardsmen, thanks to Perry Baker, my favorite werewolf researcher and Internet sleuth.

"Where, oh, where did the old guardsmen come from? They were put there by the same jolly folks who built the Castle—those nine sorcerers who decided the world needed a prison for the supernatural folks. Well, it only made sense to install live-in security, I guess, especially if you were trying to cleanse the planet of anything that might be more magical than you.

"The subcommittee in charge of security was selected from the same families as the sorcerers. Nothing like keeping world domination in the family.

"An interesting sidebar: They were all warlocks.

"Another interesting sidebar: In later years, those

same families made up a supersecret society called the Order.

"Third sidebar: Warlocks, and the Order, are supposed to have disappeared from the face of the earth.

"However, if I'm reading my history right, they're actually still running the Castle. I mean, aren't the old guards all from warlock families? Whatcha make of that, listeners?

"Well, it's nearly the witching hour, and I'm Errata Jones, signing off as your hostess for the evening. I'll be back at nine tomorrow with special guest and entertainment insider Mina Arcana, and she'll be talking about the latest Howlywood headlines. I can't wait, and I know you can't, either. Addicted to the fake-blood scandal? Who isn't? I mean, a vamp that can't put the nosh on? What's up with that?

"But before I leave you, a tasty treat to wish you sweet dreams. Here's a tune from Nine and Twenty Blackbirds with the title cut from their hit collection, *Darkest Rose*. Kiss, kiss, and good night."

Saturday, April 4, 9:15 a.m.
Morgan's Gym

Ashe finished a run on the treadmill, grabbed her towel and water bottle, and climbed the stairs to the top floor of the gym. It was a large, barnlike room with an area for fencing. A long rack was hung with masks and jackets. Another rack held practice foils and épées. The equipment was basic. Competition-level fencers went to the university's *salle*, where there was an ex-Olympian coach and electronic scoring. Ashe wanted less style and more aggression, and Morgan's delivered with brutal, bruising efficiency.

No one else was in the fencing area. The early-morning gym crowd hung out in the cardio room downstairs. Ashe took a blade off the rack and began running through her drills. The épée had a bell-shaped guard and a blunted tip designed to snag on the opponent's clothes long enough to register a hit. Not deadly, but a blow still hurt.

Because she was alone, Ashe didn't bother with a mask or jacket.

Sun streamed through the tall windows, flashing on the mirrors, on her blade, warming the color of the old fir floor. She let her mind go still, concentrating on her form as she glided through the elaborate, dangerous ballet.

She'd finally slept last night, thanks to Grandma's charms. She'd still worried about her job, or lack thereof. About Eden, and the horrible mistake Ashe had made by forgetting just how often kids eavesdropped when you thought they were off doing something else. About Reynard and about the hundred and one monsters out to complicate her life. It was bad when you didn't know what to worry about first. Too many choices.

But at least she'd done it after getting a solid seven hours of vampire-free Zs. Of course, those came after another telephone marathon calling those bump-in-the-night types who might be willing or able to give her useful information. Sadly, no one had seen a thief, demon or otherwise, with an urn tucked under his arm. She began mixing moves, making a few up, pretending she was in an actual skirmish. *Thrust, step, turn, parry.* When you fought for real, you had to know how to improvise. She'd learned that from Roberto.

Her husband had been the first to teach her to fence— just another aspect of his danger-junkie lifestyle. Maybe that was why they'd hit it off initially; when they met, she'd been in a fatalistic mood. He'd picked her up in a bar in Switzerland, made her love life again, and married her four months later.

She reached the back wall of the gym, spun around, and began working in the other direction. *Thrust, parry.*

Roberto had made her forget her past, her parents, and her guilt. She would always love him for that gift.

Lunge, redouble, retreat.

Should she have pushed her husband to take fewer

risks? If she had succeeded, he would still be alive. But would he be Roberto? When was protecting someone chaining them down?

Still, if Grandma was right and she was a warrior born to protect, her track record sucked. Few seemed to survive the Ashe Carver hazard zone, aka random magic, rampaging bulls, and vampires with sniper rifles.

Now it was happening again. If Ashe couldn't find a way to help Reynard, he would die.

Dread flooded her, weighting her limbs until they dragged to a halt. She didn't want to lose him. They might only ever share that one kiss, but it had been . . . She didn't have the right words for it.

Except *first* kiss. That was the whole problem. Reynard had made her feel alive. For the first time since Roberto's death, she wanted to get back into the business of finding a mate. She still wasn't sure how she felt about that. She was still turning the emotion over and over, hunting for signs that she was betraying her husband's memory. Sure, she'd had sex since he died, but this was different. She wanted a particular man.

One logic said she could never have.

Ashe panted, feeling the sweat trickle down her back. She glanced at the clock on the wall. Reynard had promised to meet her. Where was he?

The sun pouring through the windows made the room beastly hot—apparently the air-conditioning was toast. She was wearing only a sports bra and jogging shorts, but she was still roasting. She strode to the fire escape and pushed it open to let in some fresh air.

And nearly bashed Reynard with the door.

He lounged on the stairs like a great cat, basking in the sun. He twisted his head to look up at her, inscrutable behind his sunglasses. "A half-clothed woman with a sword. I believe I had a dream like that once."

Was this smart-ass the same guy who'd been an absolute gem with her daughter? Ashe poked him with the toe of her Reeboks. "Get up. What are you doing out here?"

He lazily pulled himself to his feet. His hair was slicked back and tied tightly at the nape of his neck. It showed off the lean angles of his face. "The sun felt good. I was indulging myself, just for a minute."

He pushed the sunglasses up his nose with one finger. She didn't need to see his eyes to tell that it was a very adult look he was giving her. She'd modeled naked for a life-drawing class and felt less exposed than she did right then.

Slowly, his gaze shifted to the long, jagged scar a werewolf had torn across her stomach, and then to her épée. "What's this? Sword practice?"

"Just getting in some lunges." Glad to change the subject, she turned and walked back to the rack with the swords. "It helps when I run into a vampire from the old days."

"The old days?" Reynard intoned, amused. He looked around the room with obvious curiosity. "You mean my lifetime?"

"That's right," Ashe said crisply. "Now we just shoot each other. Quick and to the point."

His smile was sun-drunk, all heat and languor. "Some things shouldn't be rushed."

Ashe rolled her eyes.

He picked up an épée and swished it through the air, testing its weight. "Light. More like a dueling sword."

"Nothing like what you're used to," she said dryly. "Or were you the swords-at-dawn type?"

He pulled off the glasses, squinting. "I would not refuse a legitimate challenge."

"Would you today?"

He looked startled for a moment, but recovered quickly enough. A very bad-boy look came over his face. "Do you think you could best me?"

"No, I don't have your years of practice."

He smiled, but it was condescending. "Then you're not inviting me to cross blades with you?"

Ashe leaned on one hip. She didn't mind being the

lesser swordsman, but the assumption that she was a complete amateur bothered her. "You think you can beat me without breaking a sweat."

"Yes."

"You're wrong."

"You said yourself I have years of practice."

"Which is worth something."

"Absolutely."

His tone bordered on pure arrogance. It made her want to needle him.

"I have years of experience as a slayer, and yet you think I need your help."

He sighed. "We discussed this last night."

Ashe took a step back, shrugging. Her skin began to heat, the first sign of anger. "I prefer to work alone. I don't like looking after a partner. I feel guilty when they get themselves killed and, bud, you're pushing your luck with this whole urn business."

"How so?"

"You shouldn't even be thinking about wasting your time on my problems."

"Maybe putting someone else first is the point. Maybe it's the only real choice I have."

That brought her up short. "Then you've got a bad sense of self-preservation."

He flicked his blade at hers, hitting it hard enough that it jumped in her hand. "Put me to the test."

"Why bother, if I'm such a pushover?"

He slid the sunglasses back on. "I've had men with your temperament serve under me. They need to test their officers before they are willing to follow."

"That's a leap. You don't know a damned thing about me. And I'm not a great follower."

He bared his teeth in a hungry smile. "Oh, I do believe we understand each other rather well."

"What's that supposed to mean?"

"I'm afraid you'll have to beat that out of me."

"This is pure guy crap." Ashe raised her sword.

"Yes," he said with a satisfied air, "it is. But it is also

your . . . nature. You won't grant me respect until I've earned it."

He had read her well. "Damned straight. And I play for keeps."

She realized with a sick jolt that she was facing off with someone who was no doubt an expert swordsman. Worse, she was wearing nothing but spandex underwear. No masks and padded jackets. The swordsmen in Reynard's day had played for blood. Her heart started to pound, but only part of that was fear.

This was interesting. Their reach would be about the same. Reynard was well muscled and clearly heavier, but he was fast. All the guardsmen had inhuman strength and speed. *The odds suck. Good thing he plays by the whole gentlemanly conduct code, and I don't.*

Which was why she would win.

Ashe struck his sword with hers and leaped backward. The clash filled the sun-drenched room. He swept one foot back almost lazily, flexing his knees, raising his sword *en garde.*

"It is customary to salute first," he said, easily parrying her next lunge.

"This isn't the grand ball. Besides, we're already on a first-name basis. Or we would be, if I knew yours. Do you even have one?"

"Yes."

He launched a lightning barrage of moves, driving her back. She parried each one, even managed to strike the bell-shaped guard of his weapon. The slight lift of his eyebrows told her she'd done better than he expected. *Ha!*

"So what is your name?"

"Reynard."

Snarky bastard. He slid his blade under hers, then thrust up. Ashe sprang back, the shock of his sword against hers hard enough to make her arm tingle.

"Good footwork," he said.

"Did ballet as a kid."

She managed to drive him back a step or two. He kept his sword arm lower than Roberto did, wasting no energy until the last possible moment. Reynard never hinted at his next move. It was like fencing with a brick wall. *Gimme an opening, dammit!*

Finally, he lunged. She countered, following with a combination she'd practiced endlessly. Not fancy, not stylish, but by-the-book aggressive. Reynard melted back. She thrust. He disappeared to the side, letting her momentum carry her forward, then kicked her feet out from under her.

Ashe fell to her hands and knees, just managing to let the épée drop before she landed on it. "What the hell?"

He grabbed her by the upper arm, dragging her back to her feet. "Classic mistake. You assumed I would fight fair."

Ashe flushed furiously. "Why wouldn't I?"

He pushed the sunglasses onto his head and set his épée against the wall. "Do you take me for Sir Galahad? When I'm fighting for my life, I bloody well cheat when I have to. If I didn't, I would have died a hundred years ago. I'm not going to end up blood on your hands. I don't need a nursemaid."

Ashe felt her cheeks burn. Her instinct was to make him pay for what he'd just done, but he had a point. She'd misjudged him yet again.

He pulled her closer. "I'm not a relic from a chivalric age gone by. I'm about getting results. Sometimes it's right to let the beast out. We both know that."

She could smell the warmth of him, clean and male. The strength of his grip was fearsome, and yet oddly comforting. They had matched wits and weapons, and this time he had won. On a primitive level, that made him worth that first inch of trust.

"Okay. Whatever."

At that point, he should have let go of her arm. He didn't, and she didn't pull away, but their eyes did not meet. Instead, he took her other shoulder, pushing her back against the mirrored wall. The smooth, cold surface felt good against her hot skin. Sweat trickled between her breasts, tickling her.

"Look at me," he said. His voice was low, and cracked with emotion. "I'm like you. A fighter."

Instead, Ashe looked away. Reynard exhaled slowly. She could feel the movement, hear the subtle shift of cloth over muscle. He stood too close. Ashe felt invaded, as if his body were a cage around her. She could feel her breath reflected off his cheek. Against his enormous strength, there was nothing she could do. If she pushed, he would push back.

He was only half playing, and that was a turn-on. There was no telling what he'd do next.

Sadness welled up inside her, an ache for both of them. He was a man without a future, and she couldn't afford the emotional wrench that entailed. She was done with that kind of risk. *No more tragedies*.

And yet, there he was, pressed against her, hot and real. Suddenly those complexities, that risk, melted like steam from a mirror. *Just for a moment, I can have him. Just for this minute*.

She ran her lips along the clean angle of his jaw, feeling his breath ruffle her hair. She reached the tender spot where the jaw met the neck, and felt the fine trembling in his body. He was reining himself in, keeping them just this side of propriety.

"Close your eyes," she whispered, and pulled off the sunglasses, hooking them in the hip pocket of her shorts. Without them, he seemed vulnerable, his eyelids so pale she could see the network of faint veins.

She kissed them, finding a tenderness she'd rarely possessed for a man. Maybe it was because he was so strong, or because he had nearly bled to death in her arms before. Strong. Weak. She couldn't tell. Reynard was completely off her usual radar.

His hand crept up her side, finding her breast, cupping it. His lips parted, angled, and then suddenly he was devouring her, crushing her mouth under his. There was nothing gentle in it. Pure need. Pure hunger too long denied. Her back pressed into the mirror from the bruising embrace, the ridge of her bra digging into flesh.

A quick wing beat of fear pulsed in her belly, and then she gave herself to the kiss. He tasted and smelled of man, dark and musky. She traced the strong bones of his face beneath her fingers, felt the liquid movement of muscle in his chest.

Instinctively, her legs parted, making room for him. She could feel his hardness against her, fanning embers low in her body. She began to ache in all her female places. This was what she always wanted. No compromise. No holds barred.

Tears welled in her eyes. Sadness. Joy. Loneliness. Her throat ached with them.

He ran his teeth along the arch of her ear, teasing with bites just this side of pain. Unexpected pleasure melted her inside, like the madness of a sudden spring thaw.

Fingers traced the scar across her stomach, and the one that curled up her back. Loving them. Honoring them. He wasn't afraid of who she was.

Breath escaped her in a moan. She wanted to roar in triumph, like a jungle cat finally finding a worthy mate. But it wasn't that easy. Reynard wasn't hers to keep. He wouldn't be anybody's unless they found the demon thief.

And then he would go back to his prison. Success meant separation; failure equaled death. Either way was the inevitable good-bye. *Oh, Goddess.*

Ashe planted her hands against Reynard's chest and eased him back an inch or two. "I told you never to kiss me again."

"Good thing I didn't listen."

She raked a loose strand of hair from her eyes, using the gesture to wipe away tears. "We have work to do."

He squinted at her, blinking against the sun. He had that did-I-do-something-wrong? expression men got when they were shut down midseduction. She unhooked the sunglasses from her pocket and pushed them back onto his nose.

"If we're going to partner up, I need your mind on the job."

His mouth quirked. "Partner?"

Chapter 11

Invisible, Miru-kai watched the fire demon they called Mac. The prince bit his nail, wondering whether to proceed. He had several gambits in mind, but were any of them clever enough to achieve what he wanted? You never knew with demons.

Miru-kai was loitering in the doorway of the office where the guard rosters were made up. The room was a curious mix of ancient stone and modern equipment, for this was one part of the Castle where electricity could be conjured from the walls. Mac was sitting at an old metal desk, biting the end of his pen, dark head bent to his work. The desk was big, ugly, dented, and covered in a snowstorm of paper. A lamp with a green shade cast a stark circle of light in the center. The floor was bare stone.

The scene was almost comical in its contrasts. The huge demon, a massive man by any standards, was covered in blue flamelike tattoos. The heat from his presence alone warmed the room. Miru-kai had seen him battle an army of rebel guardsmen single-handed. And here Mac was fretting over paperwork like a common clerk, making neat notations, writing lists, crumpling pages into little balls and tossing them to the floor.

Like any good leader, Mac would do what it took, big or small, to get the job done. It would be interesting to match wits with him, but Miru-kai would try persuasion first.

The prince crossed to the desk, reading the papers upside down. He understood the problem at a glance. Too many shifts, too few men trying to cover the added burden of interviewing a host of suspects. Something no amount of magic, fey or demon, could solve.

He pulled the door shut behind him, making their conversation private. At the sound, the demon looked up and around the room, suddenly alert.

With a flick of his robes, Miru-kai sat down in the visitor's chair across from Mac and dropped the spell that hid him from sight.

"Shit!" Mac jumped up, pulling out one of those small firearms the new guards used. Such speed meant years of training. *Impressive.*

"Relax," Miru-kai said, sounding calmer than he felt. "I did not come to fight."

Mac's dark eyes glinted red. "Then what do you want?"

The prince set a small flask on the desk, the gesture bringing on an unexpected and real sadness. "I need a human to mourn with me." The words hurt, as if each one took a piece of his flesh.

"What are you mourning for?" Mac's gun didn't waver.

"My friend Simeon is dead. His loss feels so profound, it comes as a surprise that every being in the Castle does not know of it."

They stared at each other long enough that Miru-kai's neck began to hurt from looking up at the tall demon.

"You ambushed us," Mac said coldly. "Stewart nearly died. Don't talk to me about mourning."

The prince had heard that a guardsman was hurt, but not who it had been. A wrench of regret twisted in his chest. "I simply wanted to get away. I asked my men to make sure you were occupied, and they took that too far. I'm sorry that the young guardsman was hurt. That was far from my intent."

"I don't believe you."

Miru-kai shrugged. "As you like. At least Stewart lives. My men died."

"Sorry about that. Maybe you shouldn't have sent them to do your dirty work."

"Is it dirty work to cover my retreat?"

"It is if you're in league with a thief."

"I am a thief."

"And you have the gall to come back here?"

Miru-kai gave a slight smile. "I am not the thief you want. Coming here is quite safe for me. You're too curious about what I might say to fire that little gun."

"Oh, yeah?"

"Then blast away, demon."

Finally, Mac lowered his weapon.

The knot in Miru-kai's stomach eased. He always preferred a battle of wits to a battle of strength. After all, he was smarter than most people. "Drink with me. Drink in Simeon's honor."

Mac sat down, looking pissed off, puzzled, and wary. "I'm sorry for your loss, but why do you need a human?"

"My courtiers are dark fey, like me," Miru-kai said in a low voice. "Simeon was a mortal. He arrived here with me, as part of my court."

"So?"

"It is only fitting that another human, or someone who was once human, marks his end." Miru-kai paused. A question he hadn't meant to ask elbowed its way out. "He died well, but I don't understand that. How can you live, knowing your days will run out?"

Mac opened one of the old metal desk drawers and pulled out two glasses and a bottle of Scotch. The light from the desk lamp turned the whiskey to liquid gold. "You just kind of do. It's not like you have a choice. You don't think about it."

Miru-kai shook his head. "It would make so much seem futile." His own bluntness surprised him. *This is not like me. Perhaps grief causes one to behave in strange ways.*

Mac shrugged. "I have a demon's life span now, but not much has changed. I work. I kiss my girl at the end of the day. I watch the game. It's all about quality of experience, not quantity."

Miru-kai sighed. "We—the prisoners here—longed so much for release from eternal darkness. Ironic. As nature returns to the Castle, so does death."

Mac blinked. "Is that what happened to your mortal friend?"

"Yes." He suddenly felt exposed. He waved at the Scotch bottle. "You brought out your own supply. Do you think I intend to poison you?"

"Let's just say I'm happy to share." The demon unscrewed the cap from his bottle and poured a small measure into each glass. "So what were you looking for in the guardsmen's vault?"

Miru-kai flinched. That tone of interrogation again. The demon had been a human policeman, just like the ones shown on that television program *Law & Order*. "Ah, yes, the vault. I had hoped the chamber of the guardsmen held a cure for my friend, but it did not. Now he is dead."

"You could have asked for help. We'd have tried."

"In the end, there was nothing in the vault that helped me. And nothing you would have permitted me to take."

"And someone just happened to steal Reynard's soul?"

"I did not take Reynard's urn. If I had, my friend would still live."

Mac said nothing, but it was a loud silence.

The prince sniffed the Scotch. "This is better than what I brought."

Mac set the bottle down. "Help yourself."

"You must know the fey appreciate good manners."

"If I get you drunk, maybe you'll tell me what's on your mind."

Miru-kai tasted the Scotch. It touched his tongue like fire, whispering of wild places, starlit nights, music he could almost hear. Food was different for the fey; it affected all the senses.

He set the glass back on the desk, wanting to make the drink last. "What I have to say is plain enough. I know you assume I am your enemy, but I am not. War does not serve the interests of the dark fey."

Mac raised an eyebrow. "You surprise me. I never took you for a peacemaker."

"Don't get me wrong, demon. We are opportunists. We survive by stealing the choice cow or the best ale—but without cattle or a keg in sight, we starve. Prosperity is in our best interest. You look like you might offer that."

Mac took a sip of his Scotch. "Then you're on my side?"

"Surviving in this Castle is like playing a dozen chess games at once. I've spent centuries ensuring there was no true winner."

"Why not?"

The prince smiled. "Whom among the warlords would you choose to rule?"

Thoughts chased across Mac's face. "Good point. Are you going to see to it that I lose, too?"

"You offer a novel outcome: peace and integration with the outside world. That interests me. After this long, anything that piques my interest is worth a great deal." Miru-kai took another taste of the Scotch.

"How long have you been here?"

"When I arrived, Jerusalem had just been taken by the Christians."

"That was what, around nine hundred years ago?"

"Perhaps?" Miru-kai felt a strange sensation. Wonderment. Fear. Most of all, a need to burst out of this prison. As it came back to life, he grew more restless. Besides, there was no reason to stay anymore. The pattern had changed. He'd just buried his emotional ties to the place. "Simeon was with me the whole time."

"How does a mortal get to be part of a dark fey's court?" Mac asked.

"He was a poor knight. My father invited him to join our court in exchange for teaching me the ways of the sword. My father failed to mention that there was no release from his vow. If he set foot on his own land, he would turn to dust, because a hundred years had passed without anyone realizing it. So Simeon stayed on. For all that time, he was a steadfast friend and my second father."

Mac was sitting back in his chair, watching him, catching every nuance. "Did you do that a lot? Take mortals?"

Miru-kai tolerated the questions, hoping to trade information for a spoonful of trust. "We need humans around us. They provide much that we lack. Humans, especially their children, love more easily."

"You took *children*?"

"Don't you read fairy tales, demon? My own grandfather was a mortal, taken as a babe."

"That's sick."

"We raise those children as our own. Protect them as well as or better than their human parents ever did. Occasionally, as with my grandfather, we wed them. The ability to connect emotionally is a mortal trait we treasure. I would give much to live among humans again."

There, he had hinted at his true reason for this so-civilized conversation.

Mac gave him a shrewd look. "I don't think the outside world is ready for a prince of the dark fey."

Miru-kai gave a mournful smile, careful not to show his fangs. "You won't set me free?"

Mac laughed. "You've been fighting the guardsmen here for close to a thousand years, and you're damned good at it. You're the prince of a dark power. Plus, you're a tricky bastard. I'm not that much of a fool."

Disappointing, but no surprise. "And yet you let Reynard go. Don't you know every guardsman who leaves the Castle for more than a day or two inevitably goes mad? Did you never hear the sad story of Guardsman Killion and his murder spree? That was only a handful of years ago."

Mac didn't even blink. "Reynard is no madman."

"How do you know? The guardsmen have quite a history. Don't forget you had to kill half their number when you took over the reins of power."

"What are you saying?"

"Sacrificial lambs, every one of them. Their fates were sealed by their forefathers thousands of years ago. The Order is the type of gruesome business only humans can dream up. Worse than anything I've ever been mixed up in."

"Interesting, but I'm still not letting you go."

"There is nothing I can offer you in exchange for my freedom?"

"No."

"You let the hellhounds leave the Castle."

"Bad example. We rescued them from slavery to warlords like you."

Miru-kai rose, picked up his own flask, and slid it into the pocket of his tunic. It was time to change tactics. "Don't say that I didn't ask nicely."

Mac set down his glass, stood up. "What do you mean by that?"

"I've stayed a prisoner long enough. It's time to leave this place."

The gun was suddenly in Mac's hand again. "Not happening. Not until I know there's a snowball's chance you'll behave. What you just said about kidnapping doesn't help."

"You could win me as an ally. Think what that would mean."

"I would guess a big fat headache. You're a trickster by nature. You can't help yourself."

Unexpected anger sliced through Miru-kai. Odd, but he had wanted the demon's friendship. That surprised him. "Then know what it is to cross the dark fey!"

He saw a flicker of something on the demon's face that might have been fear. *Good*.

"Making threats only digs you in deeper," Mac growled.

It was like teasing a bad-tempered dog—amusing and scary at once. "I *will* leave this place."

Mac's face flushed, fire flickering in his dark eyes. "And how do you think you're going to do that?"

Time to go. The prince turned on his heel, pausing with one hand on the door handle. He looked back. "It's a chess game, remember? You'll have to see my moves as I make them."

"This isn't a game. You can't win. You can't escape."

"I have the means. . . ." Miru-kai grinned, this time showing his fangs. "And I'm sure I can do at least as well as a rabbit. You can't even keep a bunny behind bars."

He opened the door. *Oh*.

A handful of guards stood there, chains of cold iron ready to fetter the prince.

No fey could escape cold iron.

By Oberon's balls!

"For future reference," said Mac, "just because you don't see security, that doesn't mean it's not there. This office has surveillance cameras and a silent alarm."

Miru-kai wheeled as one of the guards grabbed his wrists, snapping metal cuffs around them. "What's the meaning of this?"

Mac folded his arms. "I don't like chess."

Chapter 12

Saturday, April 4, 11:00 a.m.
101.5 FM

"This is Oscar Ottwell with your CSUP news. Our top story is yesterday's attack by an out-of-town vampire at the North Central Branch of the public library. Leaders of the supernatural community anticipate repercussions following this unprovoked and very public incident. We'd like to remind our listeners that if you have any knowledge of strange vampires in your area, please call CSUP immediately. We'll notify the proper authorities on your behalf."

"Of course we'll look after Eden," Holly said. "Honestly, we've got it covered. Us and the four hellhounds in the front yard. When Alessandro found out about the vamp attack, he went nuts with the security."

Ashe looked at her sister, who was standing in the doorway of the Carver family home. Holly was small and dark-haired like their mother, more of a sprite than an Amazon. She stepped back, letting them inside.

Ashe felt the house welcome her as she ushered

Eden in, Reynard on her heels. Witch-built houses were sentient and self-repairing, living off the magical energy that hummed around a healthy family of spell casters. The birth of a new baby had made the place almost jolly. She could feel it in the air, crackling with the same vibrant energy as a Solstice tree heaped with presents.

"Hey, there," Holly said, looking Reynard up and down. "I have to say the twenty-first century suits you."

He gave a graceful bow. "And, if I may be so bold, motherhood becomes you."

"Why, thank you, Captain." In truth, Holly looked like she needed a good night's sleep.

"Hi, Aunt Holly," Eden said. "Mom says I have to stay here today."

"Howdy, sport." Holly wrapped an arm around Eden's shoulders. "We torture you because we love you."

Eden looked disgusted and pleased at once. "Why did I have to bring homework?"

"Because adults are cruel and perverse," Ashe said, shooing Eden through the door. "C'mon. I have to pick up the stuff for the ghostbusting job."

Holly led them into the living room, which was filled with brass lamps and bookcases. Exactly the same as Ashe remembered it from childhood, except for the addition of Caravelli's expensive sound system. They sat grouped around a coffee table made of glossy mahogany and littered with baby toys.

"I really appreciate this, Hol," Ashe said. "I know how busy you are."

"Family comes first," Holly replied. "And anything I can do to help you kick the bad guys out of Fairview, consider it done."

Eden thumped her schoolbag to the floor and sank onto the couch, folding her arms in a mild sulk. Her dark curls fell around her face, hiding her expression. Ashe left her alone to ponder her woe.

Through the window, she could see the hellhounds patrolling the grounds. Two had shifted to their animal forms—big black dogs with red eyes and pointed ears.

Holly's big tabby cat was sitting on the porch, nervously swishing his tail.

"Under the circumstances, I can cancel this ghost-busting job," Holly said, casting an anxious glance at Reynard. "You've got more pressing problems."

"Nonsense," he said. "It should be quick, and these days I don't have many opportunities to perform a service to a lady. Allow me the pleasure of assisting your sister. It will do me good."

Holly colored a little. "If you're sure."

"Completely."

Beneath the pretty words, Ashe heard a real yearning. Reynard was free, however briefly. As he had said to Ashe, helping was one of the few choices he could make for himself. Well, she'd let him help this time, but then it would be all urn search, all the time. He might be okay with gambling with his life this way, but she wasn't.

Holly picked up a tiny stuffed whale from the coffee table, squishing it between her fingers. "Alessandro filled me in last night after your phone call. He spent the rest of the night talking to the other vampires in town, but none of the locals seem to know about out-of-towners or anyone who might hire a sniper."

"That's pretty much what I expected," Ashe replied.

"Alessandro's put in a call to Queen Omara, just to give her a heads-up. He kind of had to." Holly grimaced. "I really hope she doesn't decide to pay a visit. Once she's involved, the two vampire courts will be at war."

Ashe could see the strain on Holly's face. War meant casualties, and Alessandro would be in the thick of it. "Who are these vamps? Are they all with the King of the East?"

"And how did this collector find a thief inside the Castle?" Reynard put in. "There are connections here we do not see quite yet."

"There are collector demons," Holly offered tentatively. "Gathering stuff is a sickness with them, kind of like hoarders with superpowers. They're notorious for double-crossing whomever they're working with if they're offered the right trinket."

"Who would hire someone like that?" Ashe countered. "Wouldn't they check references?"

"And forgive me for saying this, Captain, but would someone want a vessel containing your life essence?" Holly's forehead furrowed with concern.

Reynard leaned forward, resting his elbows on his knees. He had that closed look again. "I don't really know. I assume for some work of the dark arts. Magic stole my life to bind me to my Castle duties. It stands to reason the same magic could install it elsewhere."

"It's not the Castle itself that binds you?"

"No." His voice was heavy. "No more than any of the other inhabitants. The guardsmen's power itself has a separate origin. One that chains us much more firmly."

"So if the changes in the Castle's magic haven't affected the old guards, do you feel any different when you leave its domain? Do you get hungry or thirsty?" Holly asked.

"It happens more slowly with us than for the other residents. If there is too great a separation between body and soul, the spells that keep the guardsmen alive begin to weaken. That's when we begin to feel ordinary appetites."

What did that make those exquisite kisses in the gym? Ashe wondered. Most likely a really bad sign.

Holly tapped her chin with the stuffed whale. "So how did the guardsmen get started?"

"I'm afraid that was far before my time. I think they've been there as long as the Castle."

Eden tugged Ashe's sleeve, finished sulking and clearly bored by the adult conversation. She looked up, her hot-chocolate gaze at its most appealing. "Where's Robin? Can I see her?"

The interruption scattered Ashe's thoughts. She'd been on the cusp of making a connection, but it was gone now. She looked at her sister. "Is that okay?"

"Robin's in the downstairs nursery, asleep. Eden, can you be very, very quiet?" Holly asked.

"Sure," Eden replied, as if that was a completely unnecessary question.

Ashe stood, glad of the excuse to take a quick peek at her niece. "Come on, kiddo."

The room was down a short hall decorated with wainscoting and an old-fashioned striped wallpaper. Eden followed Ashe, her hands in her pockets. "I hate the idea of the hellhounds outside. The kids around here already think I'm a terrorist spy. If they find out my aunt's got a dog army guarding her house, my life is over."

Ashe tried to digest that, but failed. "Y'know, they turn into hot guys in leather at least half the time. That's pretty cool."

"Human is cool, Mom. Everyone knows that."

"Since when?"

"Since forever. They used to burn witches, you know."

Ashe stopped and took her daughter by the shoulders. She was actually shocked. "Don't you ever turn your back on your family or what they are."

Eden's face turned serious. "The kids at school . . ."

"Are complete idiots." Ashe let her go. "You know that, right?"

"I don't want to go there. I want to go back to Saint Flo's." Eden gave her hostile eyes. "I bet I could hitchhike."

"The ocean would be a problem." Ashe bit her tongue, wanting to say more, but Eden was only a child.

"Yeah, but I have to go to this school that hates me, so what am I supposed to do?" Eden was close to shouting, the anger sharp and real.

"We'll figure something out. I promise."

"When?"

Ashe made a decision. Her daughter was on the verge of getting her magic. Life was going to be hard enough for Eden, getting used to all that, and she'd run away once already. "You and I will have a talk before next weekend. Maybe there's a different school we can try."

The girl's face melted with relief.

Bingo. Ashe put her arm around her daughter, and they walked into the downstairs nursery. It used to be Grandma's room when she had lived in the house, and her Victorian tastes showed in the flowered wallpaper and pink Chinese carpet. Holly had made it into a second room for the baby, closer than the nursery two floors above.

"This room feels different," Eden said softly, remembering not to wake the baby. "Super quiet."

"It's the house watching over Robin. It will keep away anyone who means harm to one of us."

"One of us?"

"One of the family."

"Cool."

"You bet it is." Ashe kissed the top of Eden's curly head. "Here you've got the house, the hellhounds, Aunt Holly, and Uncle Alessandro to look after you. This is the safest place in Fairview."

"Did my grandma and grandpa live here?" Eden asked.

Ashe's stomach tightened; she felt the ghosts of her past circling around. "This used to be their house. Holly and I grew up here."

Eden looked up at Ashe. "Are there any pictures of them?"

"Aunt Holly would know where they are. Now, let's look at Robin."

Ashe crossed to where the baby's crib stood in the middle of the room. Robin had been born healthy but a little too soon, and was still tiny. A pink fuzzy sleeper engulfed her limbs, making her the same shape as a gingerbread cookie. Her hair was wheat blond like her father's, but there wasn't much of it yet. A single downy tuft crowned the top of her head like the curl on an ice-cream cone.

"She's so funny-looking!" Eden whispered.

"Shh. Don't say that in front of Aunt Holly." Ashe felt her heart lighten. "All babies look like that."

Robin was going to be beautiful. Ashe thought she could see something of both parents in Robin: the bow of Holly's mouth, Caravelli's straight nose. It would be fascinating to see who this miracle child turned out to be, what powers she would wield.

Ashe gripped the crib rail, aching to reach down and touch the baby's petal-soft skin, but afraid to wake her. She had wanted more kids. At least now there was another child around. Being an auntie had its perks.

Eden gave an eager smile. "I bet I get to hold her later."

"If you're really lucky, you can change her diaper."

Eden made a face at that.

Reynard and Holly came in. Despite his graceful movements, the captain seemed too large for the feminine room. He looked down into the crib and his face went soft. "Hello, darling girl."

The way he said it, with that accent, had Ashe melting where she stood. "Have babies changed much?"

Reynard looked up, his gray eyes filled with something she couldn't name. Sorrow, but deeper, as if the bad boy and the gentleman had stepped aside, and the real Reynard looked out at her for the first time.

"No," he said, his voice suddenly rough. "Not at all. My niece and nephew were just the same."

Lore wasn't going to be around until the next morning, so Ashe and Reynard had plenty of time to keep Holly's ghostbusting appointment. Ashe was glad it was going to be a quick job. She had far more interesting worries, not the least of which was the man sitting next to her. They were well into day two of the Great Urn Search, and she still didn't have a lead and wasn't sure where to begin looking. She was a slayer, not a detective.

"Pursuing any of the supernatural problems at hand will shed light on the others," Reynard had maintained as he'd wrestled with the mysteries of the SUV's seat belt. She hoped he was right.

Her tussle with Reynard this morning had nailed home the fact that, whatever her brain was thinking, her body wanted to know him a whole lot better. Her self-control circuits were seriously overheating.

She could feel herself sizing up Reynard for long-term potential. Which, of course, didn't exist. Obviously, her libido wasn't very bright. She was almost grateful when they reached their destination. She needed those last few brain cells for the task at hand.

She found a parking spot, sacrificed to the meter gods, and looked around.

The bookshop at Fort and Main was in an old two-story house. The front yard was separated from the street by a picket fence. Along the walk, a few hyacinths were just coming into bloom. The rest of the garden looked overdue for a good weeding. Ashe and Reynard walked to the porch. The paint was peeling around the windows and porch rail, and last fall's dead leaves drifted in the nooks and crannies of the steps.

A wooden sign carefully lettered with BOOK BURROW hung above the door. The name had nagged at Ashe since she first heard it, but she couldn't place why it was familiar.

"This place is neglected," Reynard commented.

"If it's a new owner, maybe he hasn't had time to clean up yet," Ashe replied. "I remember this store. Old Mr. Cowan used to own it. It was called Cowan's Books back then. He used to save the Nancy Drews for me. He had an uncanny memory for which ones I still hadn't read."

"Nancy Drews?" Reynard asked.

Ashe walked up the porch stairs. "Mystery stories. I had the whole set when I was ten years old." She paused, trying to sense anything odd about the house. It wasn't sentient, just a house, but a faint sadness curled in the air like smoke. Maybe whatever was haunting the place missed old Mr. Cowan. She turned the brass knob and went in, setting off a door chime.

Reynard followed, looking around. The floor creaked beneath his boots. "It smells like mildew."

"Maybe the roof leaks." Ashe fought claustrophobia. There had always been lots of bookcases, but they had multiplied. Now they lined both sides of the hallway, leaning precariously where the old floor buckled and heaved. Stacks of boxes jostled for space in the corners. "I don't remember it being this crowded. There's got to be twice as much stock."

Cardboard signs were tacked to the wall, each with an arrow and subject area. Cooking, this way. Military history, that way. Novels, upstairs. While Ashe scanned them, a faint sound came from the left, no more than a footfall on the thin carpet. She whipped around, far jumpier than she needed to be. There was nothing there—no monster pouncing from the shadows. She took a deep breath, letting it out slowly.

The noise had come from the room she remembered held the cash desk, where Holly's client was probably waiting. She listened again. Nothing hit her senses as a threat.

Then why am I so jumpy?

Get moving. The best thing to do was follow that noise.

She had to go carefully so that she didn't knock something over. The store's new name was apt: It was like burrowing through a tunnel of books. Reynard had to turn slightly, his broad shoulders brushing the shelves. High above, a stained-glass window shed a thin light over the mess.

The main room was much as she remembered it. The walls formed a hexagon, glass-fronted shelves reaching to a twelve-foot ceiling. The topmost books could be accessed by a library ladder that wheeled around the room. A bay window faced the street. Reynard paused to peer into a glass case. A stuffed marmot snarled from inside the dusty prison. "Why would anyone want this?"

"Yeah, especially when there's a perfectly good two-headed squirrel over there. C'mon."

He still hesitated, distracted by a collection of miniature sailing ships.

"Reynard?"

He pointed to the ship in the middle. "I sailed to India on one like that." He straightened. "It was a bit bigger, though."

Ashe envisioned Reynard on the high seas, and felt a pang of confusion. Imagining him in the past seemed right and wrong at the same time.

"Do you see anyone here?" she asked.

"No."

The service desk was where she remembered it, at the back of the room. A huge, antique cash register, covered in brass scrollwork, perched on the mahogany counter.

"Hello?" she called. The sound seemed to die as soon as it left her lips. Bad acoustics, with all those books around. "Hello?"

"I'll go look in the other rooms," Reynard said, his brows drawing together.

"Just remember he's a bookshop owner, not a demon."

He looked down his nose. "Do you think I've forgotten how to deal with common humans?"

"You looked kind of serious there for a moment. I'm just saying . . ."

"I'll mind my manners, madam," he said a touch frostily, but the twinkle in his eyes gave him away. He walked back the way they had come, a slight swagger creeping into his step. It did nice things for his blue jeans.

Ashe's heart gave a little gallop. "You do that, Galahad."

Job. There's a job, remember? She tried to tune into the house again, let her own energy fan outward until it touched the spirit of the place. Old places gathered memories, moods. It wasn't active magic, just the silt of years past.

Heavy. Tired. Sad.

It came through faintly. The presence of the books muffled the feeling, absorbing the house's energy as effectively as they did sound and light. Ashe could feel each volume, too, rows and rows of presences, individual auras rich with the trace of every reader who had thumbed their pages. A few books carried more than that, some pulsing with magic. Interesting, but not why she was there.

She pushed past the walls, reaching outward. Reynard was hunting through the rooms to the right. Mice tiptoed behind the baseboards, stopping, sniffing. Above, far above, someone waited. Not a human someone.

That presence sent a chill trickling down her body. She definitely had a ghostbusting job to do. *Why isn't the owner here?*

There was an open door behind the service desk. Through it, she could see a flight of stairs to the floor above. These were plain and steep, originally a servants' stairway. The main stairs were by the front door.

Ashe rounded the desk, ducked through the doorway marked PRIVATE. She'd never been back here before. She gave a curious look around. The room was cluttered with empty packing boxes. Mud smeared the old linoleum, leaving a crunchy film of dirt.

The place had the sour, close smell of neglect. No wonder it had ghosts. They loved undisturbed spaces.

Reynard joined her. "An eclectic collection. If only I had time to do some reading."

"You find the owner?"

"No. There is a shed behind this building, though." He leaned against the wall, the muscles of his arms and chest working the black T-shirt he wore. He could have modeled for Workrite's next catalog. All he needed was a hard hat and a sign that said REAL MEN USE HAND TOOLS.

A bead of sweat trickled down Ashe's spine, making her shiver. Nerves and lust warred with each other. Ashe looked up the stairs. She could see more bookshelves. The second floor had always been the fiction section. The Nancy Drew books used to be kept by the narrow window that looked out on Fort Street. *What would Nancy do? Would she ever jump her guy and forget the case?*

No, by now Nancy would have found the owner hiding in a secret passage, tied up the villain, and driven away in her cute blue roadster without mussing a single Titian-red hair. *Preppy bitch.*

Ashe could feel the inhuman presence above, waiting with arachnid patience. It was starting to piss her off, and she had a pocket full of Holly's charms. "I'm going to check upstairs."

Reynard nodded. "I'll investigate the shed and meet you up there shortly."

"Okay."

Reynard slipped away, quiet as a cat.

Ashe pulled a stake out of the side pocket of her pants—not that it would kill a ghost, but it made her feel better. She rolled her neck to relax the knot between her shoulder blades, and began mounting the steps. *A-hunting we will go.*

There was no handrail and the floor humped at the top of the steps, making for iffy footing. On the other hand, the second story was relatively uncluttered. She moved quietly through the romances to the mystery section, scanning the shelves and bookcases that lined each of the four upstairs rooms. The only light came from dirty sash windows, cords broken and frames painted shut. She saw Reynard outside, emerging from the shed. It didn't look like he'd found anyone.

She kept moving, looking for signs of the ghost, but the second floor was far less spooky. In fact, not much had changed in this part of the store since she'd been a kid. There were still a handful of the old, yellow-spined Nancys where she thought they'd be. The sash window by that shelf—the only one that opened—was still the same, looking onto the metal fire escape that zigzagged down the side of the house. Mr. Cowan had let her sit out there and read sometimes. He'd been a sweet old guy.

She made a circuit of the upstairs, finding nothing. Ashe began to relax. On a nostalgic whim, she slipped a copy of *The Sign of the Twisted Candles* from the shelf.

That had been the first one she'd ever read. She wondered if her old books were around and if Eden would like them.

"Have you found what you're looking for?"

Ashe raised the stake as she jerked around, ready to strike. The book fell to the floor with a thunk.

A man stood there, his hands in the pockets of his chinos. "You must be the ghostbuster I called."

"Yeah," Ashe replied, feeling foolish.

He was a few inches shorter than she was, a few years older. He had curly dark hair, big brown eyes, and a day or two's growth of beard. He smiled, showing white teeth and a set of dimples calculated to melt the female heart.

"I'm Tony," he said. "Welcome to my mess."

"You have a lot of stock."

"I got a shipment from a huge estate sale, and I'm still trying to find a place to put everything."

He gave off an easygoing, relaxed air. "I'm sorry I wasn't downstairs to meet you. I've been lugging boxes up the stairs all day. I guess I didn't hear the bell."

Ashe slowly lowered the stake and crouched to pick up the book. "I'm Ashe Carver. My partner's downstairs. You gotta ghost?"

Tony's gaze wandered from the Nancy Drew to the stake, obviously trying to put the two together. "Yeah. In the attic. I was going to use that space for storage, but no way. Not until it's cleaned out."

Then the ghost was definitely the creepazoid presence she felt.

He gave her a curious look. "I thought your name was Holly?"

"That's my sister. The agency's a family business." Not like she could say she was the second-stringer. Ashe looked around. "Where's the attic entrance?"

"This way. Appropriately enough, it's in the room with the thrillers."

He started for the door, casting a look back over his

shoulder to make sure Ashe was coming. She set *Twisted Candles* back on the shelf and followed Tony.

"So who is this ghost? The store's been around for years. I've never heard of any spirit activity, and I used to come here all the time as a kid."

"A child died in this house a hundred years ago. Don't know her name. For some reason she's acting up all of a sudden."

"What does she do?"

"She sings. Bangs around. Makes noise."

Ashe looked at him.

He shrugged. "It's worse than it sounds. She knows just how to get to you."

"Did something happen around the time the ghost first appeared? It's rare for a quiet spirit to become active."

"The old owner died. Maybe she misses him."

The attic stairs were behind a door. The door was one of the bookcases that swung out on creaky hinges, forming the obligatory secret passage. Ashe had walked right by it twice. Nancy would have found it. *Perky teen detective one, professional slayer zero.*

Tony held open the door with the air of a nervous butler. "You don't need me for this, do you?"

"Probably better you stay down here."

He looked wobbly from relief.

"Are there lights?"

"Just this."

He reached through the doorway and pulled a chain. It made a *chink* noise, and a single bulb lit a flight of painted stairs. Ashe slid the stake back in her pocket and pulled a Maglite from her belt.

"Send my partner up when he comes in, okay? He'll be here in a sec."

"You got it," Tony said. "You're set? Can I get you anything?"

"I'm set."

"Good luck." He looked worried.

Ashe ignored his expression and headed up the stairs. She'd wiped out whole vampire nests. This should be a piece of cake. She flicked on the flashlight and started up the steps.

Even though it was only April and starting to cloud up, the attic was hot and stuffy. It was unfinished—just a raw wood floor and a few piles of junk here and there. Someone had been busy with rolls of pink insulation, but had run out of supplies or ambition about three-quarters of the way across the roof. There were a couple of vents with screens to keep out the birds, but no windows. In some ways the lack of sunlight was good. Ghosts were easier to see in the dark.

Then she felt it. Fingertips against her cheek, so light they tickled. Annoyance flared. "Don't be a pain in the ass."

Wind huffed along the floor, stirring dust. Ashe heard a scampering of bare feet, quick and light as a child's. A faint gurgle of laughter. Yes, it sounded like a girl.

Oh, great. She looked around for the obligatory china-faced doll, or the rocking horse that teetered back and forth all by itself. Ghosts loved their clichés.

There was a big captain's chair shoved in the corner. Dollars to doughnuts, that was where the spook would appear. Ashe pulled a piece of chalk out of her pocket and drew a circle around the attic floor, making sure to touch each wall. Then she took out her packet of charms. Holly had used a Ziploc sandwich bag to keep the herbs fresh. Ashe pulled it open, getting a heady whiff of mint and something bitter. All she needed to do was position a few of these around the attic, light a spell candle, and she was finished. Prefab despooking even a broken witch could manage.

She felt the ghost's breath on her cheek, as intimate as if she were peering over Ashe's shoulder—which was probably true. The temperature in the place was beginning to drop. Ashe's fingers fumbled as she pulled the first charm out of the bag. It was a cheesecloth bundle the size of a walnut. She wasn't sure what was inside. This was Grandma and Holly's special recipe.

She felt for her inner compass, found east, and placed the charm against that wall. The Carvers used a simple, respectful spell to release a ghost, to sever its earthly bonds and send it where it needed to go. "Goddess of word and thought, I invoke you; cut this knot."

She felt the bloom of power as her words activated the power Holly had packed into the charm. But that wasn't all she felt. The cold deepened, chilling her till she shook. The ghost was fighting back. Some just didn't want to go.

Give me a vampire any old day. She found the south wall and tipped a charm out of the plastic bag, letting it roll into place. Her fingers were suddenly too numb to fumble with the cheesecloth balls. She blew on her fingers, warming them enough to set the charm right side up. "Goddess of sun and heat, I invoke you to this feat."

Her words came out in little clouds. Her nose was dripping. The lightbulb over the stairs—the only light in the attic besides her flashlight—went out with a fizzle. She heard the footsteps again, and the sound of a child softly crying. Sobbing. The heartbroken, wretched grief that only a young child can fully express. Ashe stopped in her tracks, the sound leaching the strength from her limbs.

How could anyone stand that weeping? It was the sheer despair of an abandoned child. Ashe felt that sadness through her whole body, clawing deep in her guts. Eden had cried like that when her father died. Had she cried the same way when Ashe left her at St. Flo's? *Goddess! Goddess, forgive me.*

Ashe felt tears freezing on her cheeks. *Don't go there. That's how the ghosts get you, through your own fears.* She had to hang on, be stronger.

West wall. It was so dark she could barely see, but somehow she got one more charm out of the bag and into place.

"Goddess of womb and heart, pull these earthly bonds apart," Ashe murmured through chattering teeth. She hoped divine spirits could read minds, because her words were barely words at all, just frozen chunks of breath.

A voice lisped next to her ear, "He wants me to go away because I can see what he is. I'm trying to stop him. Help me! He's very, very bad."

Ashe whipped around, stumbling because her feet were numb.

It had been a little girl.

Stop him? Stop whom?

The temperature spiked, the air suddenly stuffy and warm again. Ashe stood, shaking as her body tried to bring heat back to her bones. The stairway light flickered back on.

Something felt very, very wrong.

Ashe rushed to the north wall, nearly throwing down the last charm in her haste. "Goddess of earth and arctic wave, send this spirit from its grave."

She felt the circle of charms close, containing the space where serious magic would begin. The last items in the bag were a book of matches—Holly never trusted anyone else to remember them—and a candle carved with an intricate pattern. Ashe tipped them out, stuffed the bag in her pocket, and picked a nice, central spot. Getting the candle right in the middle guaranteed even coverage as the spell worked. Right above her, the roof beams met, the angles of the house pointing to its apex. *Perfect.*

The candle was short and fat, so it stood on its own. Ashe set it down and opened the matchbook.

And felt something watching her from the dark northeast corner, just outside the circle. Her shoulders hunched, instinctively protecting the back of her neck from the snapping jaws of predators. The shadow was banned from the circle, looking in, but the charms were light-duty magic. This was heavy-duty nasty. She knew the vibe. *Crap.*

This might be more than one ghost. Maybe the little-girl ghost had a friend. Or maybe the vile, nasty thing had moved in, and that had disturbed the little girl's spirit.

Keeping a tight grip on her nerves, she pulled out a match and lit the candle. "Release, release, release! I command you to your peace."

The flame stretched tall and thin, blue-white at the tip. The magic was working. Ashe breathed in the scent of the beeswax, using it to reinforce what mental shields she still had. She could smell cinnamon for opening the psychic portals, and birch, spruce, and thyme for cleansing. Oh, and lavender. Grandma used that for everything.

She closed her mind, shutting out the darkness that seemed to ooze thicker around the chalk line. It was silent, and she didn't want that to change. Chatting with the spirits wasn't always smart.

"You were only supposed to cast out the girl."

So much for silence. The voice wasn't the little girl's. This sounded like it had bubbled up from a pit of rotting carcasses.

"Are you the spirit that haunts this place?" Ashe asked, keeping her tone firm. Better not to act terrified. That was a turn-on to some of these bastards, and, technically, she should stay while the candle burned down and only then release the circle of charms. But the exit was looking pretty good at the moment.

"Noooooooo," replied the whatever-the-hell-it-was. "She's run away. It's time to put out your spell. Now. Right now."

"Does it bother you?"

"It's time to go, witchling."

"Whatever." What the hell was this thing? Nothing good, if it reacted to the magic. Any number of critters could feel the shove of a banishing spell, but not all of them had to obey it. The heavy hitters just got a big old headache—assuming they had heads.

Goddess.

She wasn't sure the circle was going to hold. She dug

in another pocket for a second stash of charms, the famous witch grenades. Holly had tucked in an extra bottle of scented oil in case the spell needed a booster. Grateful, Ashe fished it out and set it next to the candle. Then she remembered that the girl ghost had said something.

"Are you the one the spirit is trying to stop?"

Whatever it was rustled, as if it had wings made of old, cracked leather. "She is an annoyance."

The candle flared bright as it burned down to the first circle of carved sigils, releasing their power into the field of energy formed by the circle. She could feel the cleansing magic humming against her skin.

"Ah, you sting me, little witch. It bites like gnats." The voice was nasty, sneering and sarcastic. The creature seemed to hump and bulge, shadow on shadow. It might have a snotty attitude, but it was hurting.

"What do you want?"

"I want you to stop!"

And then it seemed to fan its wings, huge and tipped with claws like a great, prehistoric bird. It spread larger, thinner, a film of feathery darkness against the outside of the circle. It was suffocating, like hot, humid air. Moldy. Robbing everything of life.

Ashe felt its power then. Hunger. Angry emptiness. A yearning for . . . she wasn't sure what. It was like nothing in the world would quite satisfy her. She could consume it all, and the pit inside her would still be there.

Goddess. This was no ghost. She was in way above her pay grade.

She heard footsteps on the stairs. Reynard! He wasn't expecting any of this. "Stop! Stay back!"

Ashe jumped to her feet, accidentally stepping on the glass bottle of oil. She felt it break beneath her boot heel, splurting the spicy liquid everywhere. She didn't have time to worry about it. Ashe drew her knife and ran to the edge of the circle nearest the attic stairs. Using the blade, she drew an arc in the air, making a doorway at the edge of the circle big enough to step through. Darkness spilled across the circle's chalk line like ink. *Shit!*

She crossed through and then sealed the circle again as fast as she could, chanting the spell all over again.

She could see the dome of magic over the circle flicker, struggle to re-form beneath the clinging shadows of the bird-beast. *If I were Holly, I'd just blast it away.* But she wasn't. Her magic was barely enough to remind the circle to work. And now she was outside with the Thing.

It was oozing off the side of the dome, flowing toward her like malevolent syrup.

"What's going on?" Reynard asked, coming up behind her.

"I'm not sure, but I think it's a demon." She pulled one of the bombs out of her pocket. Like the charms, they were bundles of herbs and minerals wrapped in cheesecloth, but these carried different magic. She pressed it to her lips, then lobbed it at the flowing darkness.

It disappeared as if the dark had swallowed it.

With a new baby, Holly's magic wasn't reliable. They'd thought the bombs would be okay. Apparently not.

Crap.

"Down the stairs," Ashe said. "Now."

The stair light went out, leaving them in total darkness but for the spell candle.

Reynard grabbed her hand. "The dark won't slow me down. Stay close."

Ashe followed, letting him lead while she fumbled for her flashlight. "Where's Tony?"

"Who?"

"The owner."

Their feet clattered on the stairs, Ashe stumbling blindly behind Reynard. Finally, she managed to thumb her flashlight to life.

"Didn't see him. Door to the stairs was open."

"Then where is he?"

She felt something cold touch her arm. Wild despair filled her. She felt pain seize her heart, squeezing it under her ribs.

Reynard pulled them through the door and into the

forest of novels. He slammed the doorway shut. Ashe grabbed a shelf for support and wiped her face with her sleeve.

"Goddess, what do we do now?"

Reynard grabbed her elbow. "Run."

Blackness seeped under the door.

"Dammit!" Ashe backed out of the room, fishing in her pocket for a second bomb. She threw it, watching to see what happened. This time the bomb flared, but wavelets of darkness arched over it, pulling it under like a wrecked ship.

Maybe the charms were fine, but the demon was just that much stronger.

We're screwed.

Ashe turned and ran. The floor bucked under their feet, sending Reynard to his knees. He scrambled up, but the tall shelves weren't anchored to the walls. He shielded his face as a cascade of paperbacks tumbled out of a lurching bookcase.

Ashe looked behind them to see the darkness slithering along the floor. Before them was an alley of nineteenth-century fiction, each volume a weighty tome. *Brain damage if one of those suckers beans us.*

Inspiration struck. She grabbed Reynard's hand. "Fire escape."

But when she looked out the window at the metal stairs where she'd read Nancy's detective adventures, it was now dripping with demon slime.

She'd seen that particular shade of goo, with those particular flecks, once before. And how many demons could there be in Fairview at one time? She remembered where she'd seen the store's name before: printed on a white file label on her lawyer's desk.

Bannerman, I'm going to kill you.

Chapter 13

Demon slime was toxic, no two ways about it. Ashe thought about bringing a bucketful and dumping it over the lawyer's head.

They'd had to crawl onto the slime-coated metal stairs and slither down as best they could without breaking their necks. The second-floor exit was too high to jump, and it wasn't like they had time to pry open one of the other windows. They were all painted shut.

Which meant plenty of exposure to the toxic goo. They'd run straight to the corner gas station to get hosed off. That probably saved their lives, but not their clothes. Even sprayed clean, they smelled like rotten hamburger.

To add insult to injury, clouds had rolled in and it had started to pour by the time they'd gotten back to the SUV. The seats got soaked.

There was no time to change before making her appointment with Bannerman and her in-laws' lawyer. Stinking like a pig carcass and high on adrenaline, Ashe wasn't in the mood for high heels and pearls anyway. She was channeling Bruce Willis from *Die Hard*, and wanted someone to pound.

She made two phone calls en route. One was to Holly, telling her the bookstore was possessed. Without magical backup, Ashe was useless against a demon. Holly said she'd take care of getting an extermination team together right away. In the meantime, she'd send the hounds down to keep the public away from the store.

The other call was long-distance to a hacker Ashe employed from time to time, a guy somewhere in the South operating out of a mobile home. Getting into the land titles database and figuring out who had sold what to whom was a matter of minutes. He confirmed what she'd already guessed: Bannerman had handled the sale of the bookstore when old Mr. Cowan's estate had been settled. If good old Tony and the demon were one and the same, Bannerman *must* have known. Sure, demons could pass for human for a while, but sooner or later their real nature came out. Why had he sent Ashe on a mission to search out the demon sliming his walls when he already knew who it was? Why not just ask her to kill it? None of this made sense.

When they parked in front of the lawyer's office, they were, amazingly enough, only five minutes late. She slammed the Saturn's door and stalked toward the front door of the skyscraper.

Reynard caught up to her in a few long strides. His face was grim, mouth a thin line of tension. "I know your times are different from mine, but I cannot see that they have changed so much."

"Which means what?"

"Threats of violence won't work." His gray eyes held worry. "Lawyers have courts and judges they can use to fight back."

Ashe tightened her jaw. "Who says I'm threatening? Threats are just warm-up exercises." She burst through the door to the foyer, leaving a trail of water behind her. "I can't believe I hired that goof."

He grabbed her arm. "You made this appointment because you are fighting to keep your daughter."

Ashe shrugged herself free. "Yeah, and there's no way that jerk is going to represent my case for one second more. A lawyer is a weapon. I only use clean weapons."

She saw the flash of understanding cross his face. "I'm not an idiot, Reynard."

"You're angry."

"Anger is just another tool."

She jabbed the elevator button. There was a sign on the door saying that Bannerman, Wishart, and Yee had moved offices to the sixth floor during renovations. Maybe Bannerman had actually listened to her advice about evacuating because of the demon slime.

Reynard did stop her from bursting through the office door with all the subtlety of a drug raid. The droid behind the reception desk managed a shocked, "Ms. Carver!" as they barged in, but by then Ashe had a long stake in one hand. The woman's mouth snapped shut with a gulp.

There wasn't anyone else in the waiting room, just dim lights and the soft, hypnotic rush of air-conditioning. She had no idea if there were people in the other offices in the suite. The place had that clinical, empty feel of a bad sci-fi movie set.

The receptionist dove for the phone. Ashe grabbed the cord and ripped it out of the wall.

"Cover her," she ordered Reynard. "If she tries to push any buttons, tie her up."

Reynard nodded. He was no cleaner than Ashe, his hair fallen loose in a wild mass of wet tendrils. His shirt was plastered to his skin, showing off the muscles beneath. He frowned down at the secretary. Her eyes went wide, but a little speculative. Maybe bondage was her thing. Underneath the scowl, Reynard looked like he was having way too much fun.

Good someone is.

Ashe slammed open Bannerman's door. He was sitting at the little round conference table that filled one corner of the office. It had four chairs. The second was occupied by a man she assumed was her in-laws' lawyer.

"Sorry I'm late," she said brightly.

"Good God, Ms. Carver!" Bannerman exclaimed, falling back in his chair with a look of disgust mingled with fear. His eyes traveled up and down her body again and again, as if staring hard enough would make her disappear.

The other guy just looked confused. "This is your client?"

Ashe advanced on Bannerman like a Valkyrie coming in for the kill. "You know, if you're going to hide from a demon, it's going to take more than changing floors in the same building."

"What are you talking about?" Bannerman cried, looking wildly around.

"You're up to your 'nads in doo-doo, dude. I went in on a ghostbusting job and, lo and behold, I ended up giving your demon a migraine. The spell wasn't powerful enough to send it packing, but it got real pissed off."

"*My* demon?" Bannerman scoffed.

Okay, so he was going to deny the whole biz in front his colleague. Idiot.

Ashe planted herself on the other side of the table, leaning across it to get in Bannerman's face. "Yeah, whatcha do, sell it a haunted bookshop? Old Mr. Cowan's place? Demons really hate ghosts, by the way, one of the few types of entities they can't control, even if they are a thousand times more powerful. Like mice and elephants. Ghosts make them crazy. Ghostbusting gives them a headache. I bet old Tony didn't know that when he called for someone to despook his new store. My guess is that he's not that old, as demons go."

Bannerman said nothing, but his expression went from shocked to calculating.

Ashe leaned in another inch. "He's our bad guy, isn't he? Demons always look so nice when they're playing human. They're almost impossible to detect at first."

"I don't do business with demons."

"Of course not," said the other lawyer. "That would be illegal."

Ashe detected a note of irony in the other man's voice. He was young and modishly dressed, with the latest in tech toys arranged before him. "Brent Hashimoto," he said. "I'm here representing the de Larrochas. Excuse me if I don't shake. You—um—stink."

"'S okay. I got up close and personal with hellspawn. It's a smelly business."

Ashe inched yet closer to Bannerman, who bellowed, "Miss McCormick, call security!"

"She's tied up," Ashe said grimly. "Or else she's begging for it by now."

Hashimoto sniggered, reaching for his camera phone. Ashe raised the stake, and watched him back off with a shrug.

"Good decision." She smiled.

She turned back to Bannerman. "Now. You promised me that my custody case would get top-drawer treatment if I got rid of your demon."

She heard Hashimoto inhale. *Good.* "I said I'd do my best, but demons aren't easy to find and they're very, very hard to kill. Normally they kill you first. But hey, I was willing to at least check it out and see what could be done, for the sake of my daughter."

She rested the tip of the stake against Bannerman's chest, making him gasp. "But you, Chuckles, already knew who it was and where it was. All it took was a rummage in the database of the land titles office. It wasn't hard from there to find out who handled the sale of the estate for Mr. Cowan's heirs: Bannerman, Wishart, and Yee, Barristers and Solicitors. The place was sold to one Anthony Yarndice. Tony."

"So?"

Pushing a little on the stake, she leaned over. "Did you think a demon wouldn't care about a little spook action? Figured he wouldn't complain, because demons can't legally hold property to begin with? Figured he'd take the crap property and be grateful?"

Bannerman's eyelids fluttered, and then he broke as easily as the yoke of a half-cooked egg. "He—it—wanted a store. He got one."

Hashimoto's eyebrows shot up. "Seriously? You cut a deal with a demon? I didn't even know you did real estate."

Bannerman twitched. "Just a bit of a sideline from wills, divorce settlements, that sort of thing."

Ashe gave the stake a shove, just enough to dent his skin. "Why, Mr. Bannerman, did you put me needlessly at risk?"

"Risk? Everyone knows how powerful a hunter you are. Your sister killed a demon queen, after all. You have everyone afraid."

"Who is *everyone*?"

Bannerman didn't answer.

Impatient, Ashe tried again. "Why not ask me to simply go exorcise the bookstore owner at Fort and Main?"

Her prey was sweating, rivulets running down his temples. "I couldn't. I wanted to. I want him gone. I just . . . couldn't."

"Easygoing Tony has you running scared, eh?"

"He—it—made it so that I can't say more."

"It put you under a compulsion?"

"Yes!"

Ashe swore. Probably the moment Bannerman had started to deal with the demon, old Tony had made the lawyer his unwilling flunky.

Hashimoto looked fascinated. "Did you sell it any other properties?"

Bannerman was turning red. "I can't say!"

Which meant he had. A negative answer would have been straightforward.

"Where?" Ashe demanded.

Bannerman made a sound between a choke and a quack.

"That's too obvious," Hashimoto said, coming out of his seat and around the table. "The demon would have thought of *where*." He rubbed his nose, a nervous gesture, but his eyes were alight with an almost gleeful interest. Ashe could picture him in the courtroom, winding up to question a witness.

Hashimoto leaned over Bannerman, his face inches from Ashe's. "*What kind* of places did the demon want?"

Bannerman's eyes flicked from face to face, fear rolling off him like a fog. "A place for its collections."

Ashe fell back a step, jolted by his words. "Collections?"

Hashimoto looked up. "That mean something to you?"

"Yeah." The lawyer's demon, Holly's client, and the thief who took Reynard's urn were all the same creature. Reynard was right. Everything was connected, but they were only starting to see the big picture.

Another thought lit up like a neon sign: Hadn't Holly said collector demons were hoarders? That would explain the congested mess the bookshop had been in.

She fell back another step. *But if the demon has more than one property, where's the urn?*

Sound burst from the front office, including the shrill complaint of the receptionist. The door slammed open, Reynard's shoulders filling the doorway. "Mr. Bannerman's associates have questions. I thought you would prefer that I didn't actually maim them."

The moment Ashe looked away from Bannerman, he launched himself from the chair, knocking Hashimoto aside. He wasn't a fighter, but he was heavy. Distracted, Ashe didn't see the tackle until he grabbed her. She dropped the stake to avoid driving it into his gut. After all, she hadn't really meant to kill him.

But he bowled her over until her head smacked on the edge of the desk. She went down, ears ringing. Then, for a split second, everything went black.

Damn!

Bannerman's weight shifted away and she heard Reynard ordering people around. He had that tone that made people pay attention. After a struggle, Ashe blinked her eyes open, feeling queasy. Bannerman's voice drifted from the front office, full of anger, but she couldn't focus on the words.

She sat up carefully. She wondered how much time had passed, because now she was alone in the office except for Hashimoto. He held out a paper cup, the type that came from a watercooler. His dark eyes looked worried. "Drink this."

What does hitting your head have to do with being thirsty? She drank the water anyway and gave him back the cup. Gripping the edge of the desk, she got to her feet.

Reynard came back in and closed the office door to shut out the noise. He put a hand on her arm. "Are you all right?"

"Yeah. Thanks for dealing with the natives."

He looked satisfied with himself, and the smile he gave her was pure deviltry. "The senior partner assures me there will be no legal action against you for assaulting their colleague. Bannerman's poor judgment in clientele is enough of an embarrassment to the firm for them to keep this altercation quiet."

"That's the best news I've heard so far today." She took his hand, squeezing it and wishing they were alone so she could kiss him. "Guess I need a new lawyer, though."

"Not necessarily," said Hashimoto. "Custody settlements can be mediated."

Ashe squinted at him. For a moment she'd forgotten he was there. "What do you mean?"

He shrugged. "If both parties agree, a mediator can help them come to an arrangement without going to court. It takes conflict off the table and focuses on a plan everyone can live with."

Ashe opened her mouth to speak, but Hashimoto held up a hand. "I know this isn't the time to talk, but let me say this much. The de Larrochas don't like your lifestyle, but they're more upset about not getting to see their granddaughter because she's not in Spain anymore. If you cut them a deal on visitation, I think they'd back off on the unfit-mother routine."

A ping of surprise made her frown. "I never said they couldn't see Eden. I just want her living with me."

Hashimoto handed Ashe his card. "I can't see how an adversarial court case is going to help either of you. As for you, Ms. Carver, you've got too many strikes against you as far as a traditional judge is concerned."

Ain't that the truth. I nearly staked my attorney.

He bobbed the card in the air, urging her to take it. "Call me if you want to talk about alternatives. Mediation isn't necessarily a walk in the park, but it's your best option."

Ashe took it. "Aren't you doing yourself out of a job?"

"I've mediated for clients before, and I'd rather have a reputation as a problem solver than a shark. Plus, I've wanted to kick Bannerman's ass for years." He gave a toothy smile that made him look a lot less sophisticated.

"I'd have paid to see that."

Ashe put his number in her pocket. "Thanks."

"Nah," he said, packing up his slim attaché case, "the pleasure was entirely mine."

Hashimoto gave a casual salute and left the office.

Chapter 14

A she pulled into her driveway. The house looked quiet, as if all the neighbors were out. By the front fence, tulips shivered in the fitful wind, their pinks and yellows almost painfully bright in the gloom. As they got out of the SUV, Ashe pondered Reynard's quest. Or really, their quest. Everything led back to the collector demon. At least she didn't have to feel guilty anymore about taking Reynard away from his mission. Their enemies were the same.

Reynard stood contemplating the flowers as if he hadn't seen anything blooming for centuries. Maybe he hadn't. With his hair loose and damp, she could see a chestnut tinge in the waves. It softened his face, except for the eyes kept secret behind sunglasses, even though it had started to drizzle.

"What now?" he asked, clasping his hands behind his back.

She kept her voice businesslike, as if she didn't want to bury her fingers in that hair. "We need to strategize, but first I have to clean up."

"I should do the same."

"Do you want to come in?"

"My clean clothes are in the Castle."

The statement was simple, but nuances lingered underneath his clipped tone, taking her back to the gym that morning. To the memory of his crushing her between his body and the mirror. She shivered, disappointed and relieved that she wouldn't be trying to shower and change with him there. Her brain could sure do Technicolor when it needed to. Hot running water, soap suds, and Reynard was a combination akin to a tsunami. It would wipe everything else off the map.

But oh, my Goddess, talk about temptation.

"Come find me when you're done. We've got a lot to talk about." She turned and walked away, leaving him standing beside the flower bed.

If she didn't, she was going to jump him right there.

Saturday, April 4, 6:30 p.m.
101.5 FM

"This is a CSUP news bulletin.

"There is a fire in the twelve hundred block of Fort Street. Traffic near the Fort and Main intersection has been blocked off by police. Motorists are asked to take alternate routes through the downtown.

"The Book Burrow, formerly known as Cowan's Books, is engulfed in flames. Fire crews are concentrating on containment. Neighboring businesses are in no immediate danger, but that could change at any time. Due to the extreme nature of the blaze, which seems to have begun in the attic, firefighters have not been able to enter the building or search for survivors. However, arson is suspected.

"Cowan's Books, a Fairview institution, had been in that location since 1965. It was recently sold to new owners after the death of the previous owner, William Cowan.

"We will provide updates as more information becomes available."

* * *

Ashe switched off the radio, a rock in her stomach. Spilled oil. Candle. Attic. She finished toweling off from the shower, put on a robe, and then phoned Holly. More and more, she was calling her sister when she needed to talk something out.

"How's Eden?"

"Enjoying spaghetti, meatballs, and television."

"No wonder she loves going to your place. Thanks again for looking after her. I know you're swamped."

"Not a problem. She's actually not a bad little baby-sitter."

Ashe felt an almost irrational pride in her daughter. *Way to go, Eden.* Then her mind flipped into business mode. "Hey, you hear about the fire?"

"Yeah."

Ashe hunched, feeling the loss of her childhood bookstore like a physical pain. "I think I might have started it. I spilled the extra oil you sent. I left the candle burning when I had to run."

"I don't know if that's enough to make a blaze that hot." Holly sounded doubtful. "There was a lot of magic going on. That can change things. Plus, that place is stuffed with old paper."

"Oh, Hol, all those old books. I *loved* that place."

"At least we're sure that poor little-girl ghost is freed."

"What if the urn was in there?"

"Did Reynard say anything about feeling it?"

"No."

"Then probably not."

Ashe was silent for a moment. "I burned down Mr. Cowan's bookstore."

Holly's voice dropped to her special talking-Ashe-off-the-ledge tone. "You don't know that. The demon might have done something. If he tried to shut down the spell, that might have made something go wrong. Don't jump to conclusions. You went there to cleanse the store. Maybe this is how it had to happen."

Ashe was silent. If only demons burned as easily as

vampires, but the Tony demon would still be out there, and now it would be pissed.

Before Ashe could dwell on that horrific idea, Holly brought up something else. "Alessandro's going to meet Lore down there as soon as it's full dark. Lore's hounds were guarding the place when it went up, but from the sound of it, they didn't see anything. Sandro's going to check the place over for himself."

Ashe looked out the window at the fading light. "Alessandro's leaving you and the kids on your own?"

"I'm not helpless, Ashe. Plus we've got more hell-hounds digging up the flower beds outside."

Ashe smiled at her sister's disgusted tone. "You don't mind keeping the kiddo a bit longer?"

"Let her stay overnight. It's safe here. No vampires. No demons. You should come stay, too."

"Thanks, Hol, but I've got to meet with Reynard. Did your esteemed vamp-in-residence find out anything about the visiting fangsters?"

"He's got the locals out looking, but so far no joy."

"Damn."

"It won't take long to find out where they're staying. Vamps are territorial, so the natives are motivated. So, what's with you and Reynard?"

"There's nothing to tell." Ashe could tell she sounded grumpy.

"Yeah, right. You like each other."

"Sure we do. That's it. There's way too much going on to complicate things."

"Too bad. I mean, the guy'll probably get out of the Castle only this once. Someone should show him a good time."

Ashe laughed, but it sounded forced. "He's got no soul. I'm so over men like that."

"Well, we're only talking a couple of nights here at most."

"He deserves more than a pity fuck. And don't talk about him like that." Ashe bit off the next thing she was going to say, bewildered by her sharp response. "Sorry. His situation's gotten to me."

"Sure, yeah. And I shouldn't be joking like that, anyway. But y'know, Grandma said he was great with Eden."

"He was pure gold."

Holly was silent for a moment, as if not sure where to take that thread of conversation. Then she jumped tracks altogether. "How'd the meeting with the lawyer go?"

Ashe filled her in on everything that had happened that afternoon. "He's so fired."

"Shouldn't he be arrested?" Holly asked. "He's doing business deals with a demon, and not a nice one like Mac!"

"I'm pretty sure his office partners are building a big legal fortress around him as we speak. But I've got a better idea. I'm going to tail him. Wherever Tony goes next, now that his bookstore is gone, Bannerman is sure to be at his beck and call. We'll find him that way."

"There's a spell—"

Ashe heard Robin's cry in the background.

"You need to go," Ashe said. "That sounded hungry."

"Yeah, catch you later." Holly hung up.

Ashe disconnected, setting the phone back in its cradle. She wished Holly had left Reynard out of the conversation. There were a handful of people she'd do anything for: Eden, Grandma, Holly, a few of her hunter friends, and, on a good day, Alessandro. Reynard's name was starting to creep onto that list, fading into view like invisible ink slowly revealed by the heat of a flame.

Reynard needed far more from her than a booty call. He needed someone willing to fight for him, to break the chains that bound him in darkness.

And when she was done fighting? That happy-ever-after thing always slipped through her grasp. She wasn't Sleeping Beauty or Cinderella. She was one of the knights, slapping the prince on the back and buying him a round after they ganked the dragon.

Awkward.

An interval of quiet followed, but it was short-lived. Ashe had barely pulled on fresh jeans and a tank top and started to make herself a sandwich when the burned-toast smell of a portal came drifting from the living room.

"Hello?" she called, holding the butter knife in one hand. She set it down and shoved open the window to clear the air before the fire alarm went off.

Reynard sauntered into the kitchen, clean, tidy, and looking around with a speculative air. He set the sunglasses on the pale yellow counter. Ashe looked at them, then at him.

"You can see okay?"

"I'm getting used to the light." He looked around, still squinting a little. "You have a comfortable home."

Ashe buttered bread. "It's small, but it's all right."

"Where is Eden?"

"Still at Holly's. She's safest there, protected by the magic of the house. Caravelli should be up soon. And the hounds are still camped out in the yard, making like super-ugly garden gnomes. I phoned to check in."

"Garden gnomes? I thought they lived farther south."

Ashe put the lid back on the butter dish. "Imports."

He watched her open the fridge and bring out containers of leftover chicken, mayo, and salad. He pulled up one of the café stools and sat on it as she worked. It was all weirdly domestic, and it made her twitchy.

"So tell me something about yourself I don't know," she said.

"Such as?"

"We're usually trying to kill something when we're together. Or on the move. I'm not sure what to expect now that we're just sitting in a kitchen."

He gave a slight smile. "Once upon a time I was considered a skillful conversationalist. I used to have more talents than fighting."

Ashe pulled the lid off the salad container and started searching for bits of lettuce that still looked more green than brown. "Oh, yeah? Like what?"

"I was an excellent sportsman. I rode almost before I could walk. I have a keen interest in astronomy and navigation. Handy when you've traveled as much as I did."

He leaned against the counter, the posture casual but the muscles in his body still coiled. A man doing an imitation of somebody relaxing. "It was part of a young man's education to tour Europe. Then, when I took up my career with the military, I went to India with the Royal Regiments."

"That must have been a culture shock."

He tilted his head, his look far away. "It was an experience. Many of the officers weren't interested in anything outside their own gentlemanly circle, but I wanted to learn whatever I could. The language. The life in the villages. How the common soldiers lived. That's where I got the Brown Bess you so adore."

Ashe returned his smirk. "That wasn't your usual weapon?"

"Not exactly." He warmed to the subject a little. "Officers didn't do the actual shooting in battle, but I liked knowing how to use it. By understanding the arms, I had a better idea of what the men who used them were faced with."

Ashe thought about that for a moment, and the sound of his voice. She had always become lost in the refined English accent, but she could hear the nuances of emotion now. Rough sadness, layers of irony, respect for the men under him. He wasn't a stranger anymore. She liked that.

"How long were you there?"

"Four years. Then I was wounded and sent back to England to recover."

"And then?"

Reynard looked down at the countertop. "My next trip led me to the Castle. There was no more traveling after that."

Ashe waited for more, closing up the chicken sandwich and cutting it in two. She wanted details about the guardsmen and about how he ended up in an interdimensional prison. No more words came, however.

Would pushing be a mistake? The wrong question at the wrong time might make him clam up, and she was tired of that closed-off look of his. It was like talking to the cardboard Legolas the bookstore guys had left outside the library. She wasn't going to risk losing the rapport they had going.

The downstairs neighbor pulled up in front of the house, slamming the car door. Ashe closed the window, starting to feel cold.

"Well," she said quietly, sitting on the other café stool. "What do we do next?" She bit into the sandwich, all the salt, pepper, and mayo doing a happy dance on her tongue. She was so hungry, it hurt.

Reynard picked up a stray twist tie, looking at it with furrowed concentration. He had apparently lost none of his taste for discovering new cultures. "The urn wasn't in the bookshop. I would have felt it if it were."

He said it casually, but she heard uneasiness buried under the sangfroid.

"Then we have to find the demon's other hangouts," she said after swallowing. "The bookstore burned down, anyway."

He gave her a sharp look. "Pardon?"

"It was on the news. It might have been the spell I was doing, or something the demon did afterward." She looked down, mourning again the loss of all those books. "It won't kill the demon, just make it run someplace else. We find it, we find the next possible urn location."

"The person you called before was able to find out that Bannerman sold the bookshop. Could he discover what other sales that firm handled recently?"

"Good idea." She took another bite.

He was watching her eat, his eyelids half-closed. He reached out, stealing a cherry tomato from her plate, and put it in his mouth.

He was eating something.

Ashe stared, forgetting to chew. Reynard bit down, eyes closed in concentration. His eyelids fluttered, then opened, a look of shock tensing the muscles around his nose and mouth.

"You okay?" she asked around the bite of sandwich.

He gulped. "That tasted . . ." He trailed off, shaking his head.

"Like a tomato?"

"Yes." He ran his tongue over his teeth. "I'd forgotten what they were like."

His gaze traveled back to her plate.

"Are you hungry?"

He shot her a wild look that he shuttered almost before she truly saw it. Something beastlike, driven by deprivation. She felt her heart stutter, filled with fear and pity, then shoved her plate across the counter toward him. "Go ahead. I'll make myself another."

The knowledge of what his hunger meant passed between them. He looked away, almost shamefaced, then picked up the sandwich and bit into it. She heard his sigh and wondered how long he had been denying the urge to eat. Her own appetite vanished at the thought.

What the hell can I do for him? All he wants is to live a little.

And we're not going to find that vessel in time.

She picked up the phone and walked into the living room to call her hacker contact. She stood in the semidarkness, glaring at the glowing screen of her cell phone.

Goddess!

She needed her vision to stop blurring so she could read the list of contacts.

*　　*　　*

The complex textures of the sandwich filled Reynard's mind, blotting out everything else. Soft bread, the crunch of greens, the rich tearing of meat. He tasted butter. Holy God, he'd forgotten how good that was. Some things didn't quite line up with memory. The bread was different, but that didn't matter. It was food, that basic connective tissue that bound man to man, regardless of race or creed or culture. Hunger was their shared inheritance, relieving it a universal rite. After so long, he was part of that brotherhood again.

And it tasted so good.

He could feel his body seizing on the food, realizing he must have needed to eat long before he knew it. Dizziness swept over him as he crammed the last bite of chicken into his mouth. He wanted more, but he'd seen prisoners of war make that mistake when they were finally liberated and fed. Too much at once ended in sickness. He couldn't risk that.

He slid off the stool, washed his hands, and filled a glass with water. He gulped it down, feeling the coolness slip over his throat. Even water suddenly tasted like heaven.

Ashe came into the kitchen behind him. "My contact's going to call me back."

Reynard set the glass in the sink. "Then we wait."

He turned to face her. Her expression was horrified and dazed, much like he had felt when a piece of artillery had blown up too close for comfort, taking the gunner with it. He wanted to wipe that look from her eyes, but what could he say? *Yes, my dear, I'm perishing faster than a beached fish, but I feel marvelous.*

And he did. There was the hollowness where his soul should be, but there was so much emotion. Bit by bit, his heart was unfreezing. Joy, liberty, and affection were his again. Instead of groping for memories, he was experiencing life. He pushed away from the sink and crossed over to her, his boots a slow tattoo on the tile floor.

She set the phone on the counter, finding the right

place by touch. Her emerald gaze was glued to his face, filled with a mix of concern and something a lot less maternal. That look was worth everything. He'd walked out of the Castle into freedom, and a beautiful, fierce woman cared what became of him. As victories went, it was magnificent.

I wish I could make you understand. He put his hands on her bare arms, feeling the soft skin and hard muscle beneath. She was exactly his height and every bit as talented a fighter as he was, but also oddly delicate. There was nothing heavy-boned about her. She was all speed and grace.

In a just world, he could have promised her everything. All he had was his body, but he could use that to take the sadness from Ashe's eyes. She knew what was happening to him, but she couldn't see the joy he felt. Where words failed, there were other means to make himself understood.

"What are you thinking?" she asked.

"About this," he said, and brushed her lips with his, once, twice, and then took her mouth without holding back. She retreated a fraction, but then gave in to her response, as if coming to a decision. Her lips parted under his, letting him in.

She wound her fingers though his hair, pulling out the tie that held it back. Her teeth nipped at his bottom lip, not breaking skin but marking possession.

"I want you," she whispered. "I shouldn't, but I do."

"Then I shall be your sinful pleasure."

Reynard pulled Ashe into him, holding her hard against his chest. She felt so warm, so soft and strong at once. He grasped her shoulders, feeling the bones and muscles move as she wrapped her arms around his neck, then slipped her fingers down his shoulders. His own hands cupped her cheeks, running his thumbs along the fine ridge of her jaw. The pulse in her neck fluttered against his fingers, as if reaching for his caress.

Ashe was mortal, her life spent in an instant. Like him, she was more than human but she had none of the guardsmen's indestructible power. The magic she had was all but destroyed. Or so she said. He could feel the remnants of it clinging to her, as ephemeral as cobwebs and yet curiously strong.

Her mouth found his neck, leaving nips as she tasted his flesh. Clean, silky hair brushed his cheek as she caressed him. The sunny softness of it reminded him of home—of meadow flowers and random feathers found by the banks of a wild creek. Ashe belonged there, in that land of freedom and instinct. The land where sensation weighed heavier than thought.

There was something oddly innocent about that, and it charmed him.

She leaned her weight against his chest, forcing him to fall back a step. Retreat signaled a change of tactics. She swerved, pushing him against the wall. His shoulders thumped against the hard surface.

"Take off your shirt," she said, her words half whisper, half growl.

"La, madam," he murmured into her ear. "Do you mean to strip me of my virtue?"

She looked up through her lashes, her eyes sharp and hungry. "First things first, boy. Shirt. Off."

The challenge was too much. "The devil I will. You'll have to work for it."

"You'll pay for that." Grasping the hem of his T-shirt, she started to pull it up his stomach.

"Not so fast."

He grabbed her by the waist, lifting her feet from the floor as if she were no more than a naughty child. In response, she wrapped her legs around his middle, holding on with the strength in her thighs. The motion turned them in a half circle, knocking over a floor lamp that fell with a clatter. Neither of them stopped to assess the damage.

Ashe pulled the shirt off over his head. By that point, he had to cooperate and raise his arms or she'd tear the shirt. Possibly with her teeth. Besides, the feel of her against his bare skin was too enticing to resist. She waved the garment for a moment like a victory flag, then let it arc to the floor.

"I always get my way eventually." Releasing her grip on his waist, she braced herself on his shoulders and slithered down his front until her feet touched the floor. The movement made him wish for that wall to brace himself against. Friction was exquisite torture. All of a sudden, his knees were not at their most reliable.

Her hand cupped the front of his jeans just for a moment, a quick, possessive gesture. Reynard caught his breath. *Blood and thunder, if I don't hurry this along, I won't last beyond the opening pleasantries.*

Roaming up her ribs, his hands could find only flesh beneath the top she wore. He felt a brief pang of disappointment—he had fancied an encounter with one of those frilly bras he'd seen in modern magazines—but warm female breast quickly occupied his attention. He circled her nipples with his thumbs, bringing a groan from her throat. Her hands raked through his hair, then fell to his shoulders, then slowly ran down his arms, caressing him until she cupped his own hands where he touched her.

She turned, pulling him down and falling onto the couch in one graceful motion. The fabric that covered it was a deep green, her bare arms ivory against it. Reynard knelt, straddling her legs, knocking throw cushions to the floor as he settled. Ashe was on her back, underneath him, as he'd fantasized so many times.

Only this time, there was no Castle to throttle that desire. The pounding in his loins was as raw and real as it had been in his youth. The scent of her skin filled his nose, his lungs, seeping into his blood like a drug. A flush of desire was creeping over her, turning the ivory to rose. He could feel the warmth of it, and he heated in turn.

Her eyes widened with appreciation of the tattoos that crawled over his chest.

"These are so funky," she said, tracing them lightly with her nails. The butterfly touch made him shiver, hardening his own nipples into pale peaks. Her hand moved to a scar that curled from his shoulder down to his chest. "What's this?"

The impulse to talk was fading fast. "The sword thrust that sent me home to England."

"And here." She ran her fingers over his abdomen. "There should be a scar here, from last fall, but there's no mark. That ax wound was deep."

Reynard began to play with the waistband of her pants, hoping to lure her back to the task at hand. "I have scars only from before I became a guardsman. The rest heal completely, given time."

"That's right. You've got superpowers of recovery. That should come in handy tonight."

Tonight. It might be all they had, but he would make her remember it. Reynard pulled up the hem of her shirt and pressed his lips to the soft flesh just above her navel, tasting it, nuzzling his way upward between the arcs of her rib cage.

Seeming suddenly impatient, she peeled the peach-colored tank top over her head, revealing small, firm breasts. Her nipples were the delicate pink of seashells. He took one greedily, using his tongue to bring it to a peak. She arched into him.

"Tell me what you want," he said, kissing the hollow of her collarbone, the soft spot just below her ear. He used his hands and his mouth to make her breath come quickly, short gasps of need that made the back of his own neck prickle.

"It's all good," she whispered.

"But all women have a key," he murmured into her ear. "A secret wish that unlocks them every time."

"You wouldn't like it."

"How do you know?"

"It's not pretty."

Ashe writhed as he pulled down her stretchy slacks, tossing them to the floor. He nearly fell to the floor right along with them.

"Bloody hell."

She was wearing nothing underneath, not even the

usual triangle of hair. His imagination hadn't predicted that one, but it was sure to be included in any future scripts.

"That would be *your* key, would it?" she said slyly. "Or perhaps calling it the lock would be more anatomically correct."

Reynard cleared his throat, but there would be no more talking as her fingers found his zipper and slid it carefully open, giving him blessed relief. Her breasts rose in a quick inhale as he shed the rest of his clothes.

"Sweet Hecate, no wonder they locked you up."

"You have no idea," he said, keeping the irony out of his tone.

She shifted, welcoming him into her arms. The sensation of touching skin to skin, the complete freedom of nakedness, filled every sense. She was smooth and lean, long legs wrapping around his waist. It had been so long since he had felt anything like this, the physical world began to blur. Nothing was left but the painful, throbbing need to possess.

"I can't wait," he said through gritted teeth.

"Then don't."

"It will be rough."

"Perfect." Her gaze was unfocused. "Completely perfect. Don't hold back."

She shifted again, her hand guiding him as he pushed inside. The hot tightness of her made him cry out. A growl came from her throat. Sharp nails dug into his shoulders, the pain only increasing his desire. He moved inside her carefully, biting his lip, doing everything he could to slow down and give her some chance at pleasure. Her muscles clenched around him, the delicious agony of it turning his vision to starbursts.

Then rhythm took over, each thrust making her gasp and the couch moan. He heard the sounds, but they had no meaning. All he could feel was the gathering storm, and the hot wetness surrounding him. Quickening pulses spasmed deep inside her as his rhythm broke and he began to pound, taking her too hard and too soon.

But he could tell she needed the raw frenzy of their joining as much as he did.

"Oh, Goddess!" Ashe cried.

He felt the release like a bolt of lightning, blanking every nerve in exquisite torment. It felt like it went on and on, making up for an eternity of denial.

Ending too soon.

He gripped the couch, arm muscles quivering. There was no room to collapse, not without smothering Ashe or tumbling to the floor. They were both breathing hard, sticky with sweat. She looked startled, like he'd done something remarkable. *Maybe not all my skills are lost?*

"Do you sleep on this couch?" he demanded, his voice hoarse with panting.

Her hair had come loose, scattering around her in a ragged, tawny sun. She shook her head mutely.

Carefully, he found his feet, making sure his legs could still support him. "Show me your bed and I'll do that properly."

Ashe frowned. "But you did it just right."

"Of course I did. And now I know what you like. A tiger to your tigress."

"Hot damn," she muttered.

Taking her had only kindled his need. Her flushed cheeks and swollen lips turned the flame into a blaze. He pulled her up and into a deep, hungry kiss.

This time, she melted in his arms like sorbet left in the sun. *Ah, yes.* He cupped the cheeks of her firm bottom, the feel of the warm flesh starting the heaviness in his belly all over again. He felt himself hardening already.

Immortality had its advantages.

She broke away, catching his hand. "This way."

He registered nothing of how they got there. It was growing dark, lights glowing here and there on clocks and appliances. There were noises in other parts of the house—voices, doors closing—but it only served to enhance a sense of stolen privacy.

Halfway down the hall, Ashe stopped, her grip on his

biceps rough. He let her shove him into the cold, rough plaster of the wall.

"How hard are you willing to play?" she demanded.

"How hard do you need it?"

She took his mouth, then the flesh of his shoulder in her teeth, biting down. Pain and pleasure shot through him like shards of light. Unbearable, and yet the throbbing in his groin flared into an ache. He grabbed her around the ribs, picking her up. Her tongue traced the side of his neck, her hair falling around them in a silky curtain.

"Take me," she whispered. "Let me fight you."

"I'll win."

"Make me forget everything but you."

"With pleasure."

Chapter 15

Hours later, Ashe lay beside Reynard, sore and exhausted. She was on her stomach; he was on his side, one arm curved around her. A blanket covered them. The top sheet was a poly-cotton shred-fest somewhere on the floor. She thought they'd broken a lamp, but she wouldn't be sure until she got up. It was pitch-black in the room.

She felt quiet, content. Spent. Rage—about her life, her mistakes, her destiny, and the fact she had been alone for so long—had burned away. After they had bitten and wrestled and pinned each other down, Reynard took her with all the tenderness she'd never wanted before. Incredibly, he made her feel she deserved it. Although it might be his only chance at a night of passion, he had made it about her.

Rough and gentle, he had delivered them both, delighted in them both. That was better than oblivion. That salty-sweet combination was, as he had put it, her key. He was the first lover to discover her private need for both.

Roberto hadn't. It was something she barely understood herself.

Ashe listened to his steady breathing. He was drifting in and out of sleep, as tired as she was. Reynard had given her everything she asked without judgment, and yet she had no sense that he was in any way deprived. He had taken his fill of pleasure, too. Reynard had strength to spare. Strength enough to master her—and to care for her.

He was everything she'd ever wanted in a lover.

She rolled onto her side, her back curling into him. His breath gusted across her neck, warming her skin. A faint snore said he was lights-out. The sound of it made her smile. It was kind of cute.

It's been too long. For the first time since Roberto had died, she was able to float in the after-bliss of lovemaking feeling whole, clean, and cherished. Worthy of love.

It wasn't a question of falling in love. That was something softer, something that came only when this first piece had fallen into place. On some deep, biological level he had earned the right to be with her. More than that, he had taken her. Every cell. Every pulse of her heart.

Ashe felt slightly awestruck, even as her eyelids drifted closed.

Boredom was the largest difference between being held a prisoner in the Castle, and being held a prisoner in one of the Castle's cells. Miru-kai could not complain that he was mistreated. Mac had shut down the old cells that were no more than caves with doors. By contrast, the room where he had put Miru-kai was small but clean, the stone walls whitewashed to take away some of the gloom. There was a shelf with a thin mattress and a dark blue blanket neatly folded at the foot. Not princely, but palatial compared to what it might have been.

Still, it was a lockup. A grate of iron bars striped the white stone. The door was made of iron bars. Magic would not work in a room lined with cold iron. He saw no one but the occasional guard with his jingling ring of keys. There was absolutely nothing to do.

Boredom was an ingenious form of torture. He'd

begun to listen for the guards' footsteps as a means of passing the time. Miru-kai lay on the mattress, his hands folded across his stomach, and tried to relax. He was used to the bustle of his encampment. It was literally too quiet to sleep. All part of the complimentary torture service.

Miru-kai opened his eyes and stared at the stone ceiling. He could count the blocks of stone, but he had to save some excitement for later. He slipped off the bed and stood at the barred door, careful not to touch the irritating iron. He could see out, but there was nothing there but corridors of stone, the same view as anywhere in the Castle.

I shouldn't be here. None of the fey should be here. Fairykind knew how to repair the earth the humans plundered, but the humans knew how to make the earth yield crops. Once, the two species had worked side by side—or so Miru-kai had been told. That was before his time, before the bulk of his people had retreated to the Summerland, closing the gates behind them and leaving their brethren to struggle on alone.

I could have been dancing in dew circles if my venerated parents had gotten off their royal backsides and left with the rest. Instead, he was stuck here, dealing with the dregs of the Castle.

Footfalls echoed in the corridor. Miru-kai drew nearer the bars. The heavy silk of his clothing rustled as he moved, reminding him he was a prince and not just a prisoner.

His visitor was Mac, his large form backlit by the flickering torches.

Once he saw who it was, Miru-kai backed away, not wishing to look too eager to talk. Still, he couldn't resist some of those *Law & Order* phrases. "Now that you've let me—what is the expression?—*stew in my own juices*, have you come to *tune me up*?"

"Maybe I just want to gloat a little bit." Mac stopped outside the bars, folding his arms. He didn't come too close, either. "Mostly, I've got questions."

Miru-kai crossed his own arms, mirroring his jailer's posture. "I have one or two of my own. To begin with, I wonder why I thought a civil conversation about freedom was even possible."

"It was and always will be possible. Whether I agree to it depends entirely on your track record. You came to my office thinking you could charm your way out. I'm not that easily conned."

"My word of honor counts for nothing?"

"I'd rather have a month's worth of incident reports without your name all over them."

"The fey are misunderstood. We don't respond well to petty rules."

"Uh-huh. And what happens when you get outside the Castle and start buying cars? Rush hour in Fairyland must be really interesting. Road rage with goblins."

"You mock me."

"You bet, but there's a point to it. If you played well with others, I'd hold the door open myself."

Miru-kai said nothing, annoyed by the demon's confident air. He was a prince. A little groveling and trembling would have gone down well about now.

Mac gave him a sharp look. "Exactly how much did you have to do with the break-in at the guardsmen's vault?"

Walking to the bed, Miru-kai sat down. The cell was small enough that it made no difference to the conversation, except now he was comfortable. Princes sat. Lackeys stood.

Mac's expression didn't change.

Miru-kai considered his options and chose a strategy. "In all honesty, I simply played the role of opportunist. Perhaps bodies do not easily break free of the Castle's chains, but news travels by sorcery, by whispers, by means even I cannot fathom."

"Like the bulletin board at www.SeeSparkyRun. com?"

"I may be an old soul, but I can surf the Web," the prince replied, putting one hand to his chest. "Though

I concede calling a fire demon of your stature 'Sparky' is a touch disrespectful. Some of the fey can be insolent wags."

"Which is why only this part of the Castle gets wire-less anymore."

Damn it all! For the first time in hundreds of years, the prince had found a reliable link to the outside world, and now it was extinguished. Miru-kai swore silently, but shrugged as if it didn't matter.

"If you want out of this cell, you're going to have to give something up," Mac said sternly.

"I have professional standards. Confidentiality to maintain."

"Since when have you done anything but protect your own interests?"

"You wound me."

"No, but I can. A good friend of mine is counting on me to figure this out."

Mac's expression packed its bags and went to the dark side.

Miru-kai sighed. It was better to offer up information while it still had value. The whole sorry affair was going to come out soon, anyway. "I heard of an individual who wished to steal a guardsman's urn. How he found out that they even existed is quite beyond me, but no mat-ter. He required a thief who could, with the proper in-struction, circumvent all the wards upon the door of the vault. I gave a referral."

"And collected a finder's fee?"

"Of course."

"I'm guessing you let the demon through the forest gate?"

Miru-kai nodded. "Yes. There. I confess. Let me out. I found my client a certain kind of demon who is expert at acquiring valuable objects. He is your thief."

Instead, Mac's brows drew together. "A collector demon?"

"Yes."

"You *knew* he was a collector demon, and would

never, ever give up whatever he took." He made it a statement, not a question.

"His species is extremely rare. I deserved a bonus for being able to locate such a prodigy. Even if I was hired for my quick wits and extensive knowledge of the Castle and its inhabitants and, yes, my extensive information network, this . . . *this* was a coup."

"Yeah, yeah," said Mac impatiently. "And then?"

"It is not my fault that my client wasn't specific about the *character* of the thief. He simply wanted one who could procure what he wanted. I did what I was asked. The fey always keep their bargains." Miru-kai gave a toothy smile. "Though we tend to give what our client deserves. He was a trifle pushy. Vampires, you know."

Mac was unamused. "Your client was Belenos, King of the East?"

"How well-informed you are."

"I'd heard he was hanging around Fairview. I'm not the only one working on this case. Where is Belenos?"

"I don't know."

"Are you sure about that?"

"Positive."

"How did you get paid?"

"In goods. As for the demon," Miru-kai went on, breezing past the question, "it is my understanding that the first thing he did upon double-crossing his employer and running away with the urn was to find a successful lawyer and bind him into service. So much for the good old days, when an army of rotting corpses was the best line of defense. These modern days lack a certain sense of theater."

Mac pondered that. "You let the demon thief out of the forest. How did he get out of the Castle?"

"Two weeks ago, Lord Belenos secured one of the nine keys to the Castle at a very, very, *very* private auction. While it's not as powerful as your master key, with a lot of extra sorcery he managed to get the demon past the portal barriers. That was no mean feat of magic. And the key has allowed Belenos to come and go from here ever since."

Mac's face froze; then his voice emerged thunderous. *"What?"*

Miru-kai licked his lips, savoring the moment. "That's probably why your allies on the outside can't find him. King Belenos has been sleeping here, right under your guardsmen's noses."

Ashe woke to find herself sitting on a headstone. Startled, she jumped down, her mule-slippered feet landing on the cold, crumbly loam of the grave. Claw-sharp pine needles poked at her heels.

Where the hell am I? The graveyard looked familiar, with the ocean sighing against the rocks to the south. *Where's Reynard?*

But she was alone. Overhead, the moon dodged a lacework of clouds. Not enough light to really see, but it looked like Saint Andrew's Cemetery. Big trees, old graves, the smell of cold sea air. She hadn't been there for a while, but she'd walked through it often enough as a kid.

I'm dreaming again. That thought made her relax a notch. She'd neglected to set Grandma's charms in place. Well, she'd been a little distracted.

She stepped off the grave, leaving a slipper behind. Cold, damp loam touched her bare sole, giving her instant goose bumps. She stuck her slipper back on her foot, then emptied the other of crumbly dirt. One crappy detail was that the night was freezing cold and she was wearing nothing but an oversize *Ghostbusters* T-shirt. Better than the nothing she was wearing curled up beside Reynard, but why couldn't she have dreamed herself in a nice, warm coat?

But part of her knew it wasn't quite a dream. A frisson of dread crawled over her flesh like a horror cliché lurching from the grave.

Ashe whirled around, trying to see in every direction at once. It was too dark, the moon in and out of the clouds just enough to see shapes a few feet away. The clumps of cedar trees were no more than patches of rustling blackness. She could just make out the name on the tombstone where she'd been sitting: Marian Carver.

Mom. Ashe's hand went to her mouth, a weak gesture she hated.

She'd been sitting on her mother's grave. The mother she'd killed with her stupidity. Her sense of balance seemed to melt, leaving her weak-legged and sweating despite the cold. If this was some sort of trip through the basement of her subconscious, it was doing a good job of freaking her out. Maybe it was punishment because she had actually been happy for a moment.

She pushed her hair out of her face and took a long breath, forcing herself to stand straight. *Get a grip. Figure this out.*

Now she knew exactly where she was. Memory filled in the details the wavering light glossed over. They were close to the cliff edge that looked over the water, in a triangle where two walkways crossed. There was a pair of white headstones flanked by yew and rowan trees. Her dad was in the next grave over, her grandfather about fifty feet to the west.

Why am I here, of all places? The answer had better come soon. She was starting to shiver and she was way past pissed off.

A cold hand fell on her shoulder. Ashe spun, leading with her elbow to deliver a blow, but stumbled against— nothing. No one was there.

Oh, crap. She really wasn't up to ghosts. *They're always whining about something. Like, get dead already.* Ashe let her temper heat, doing her best to counter a growing sense of vulnerability.

"Ms. Carver," said a voice behind her. Or were those low, velvety words all in her head?

Obviously, whoever or whatever this was couldn't be smacked down like a common mugger. Ashe turned, this time moving at a normal speed. And there was nothing common about the figure standing there. Inwardly, Ashe gulped. *Holy Hecate!*

He was far too close, forcing her to look up. The speaker was at least six-five and built with a fighter's physique—hard, broad, and lean—but the poor light gave away nothing of his features. Ashe opened her mouth to speak, but could find no words. It was like coming nose-to-nose with a timber wolf. There was nothing adequate to say, even if it was—almost—just a dream.

Electricity skimmed her skin in a subtle, deadly tease. One of the few scraps of magic left to her was at work, identifying and reporting what she'd already guessed. *Vampire.*

A very, very powerful bloodsucker to boot. She had no weapons. Beating him off with a slipper wasn't going to work. Her mouth went dry with apprehension. If she were awake, she'd be fighting by now, or at least running. Instead, she felt stupefied.

"You brought me here," she managed to say.

"Of course I did." Vampires could enter a person's dreams, but it wasn't a beginner's trick. Only the most powerful could pull it off.

He raised a hand, and a gauzy white light bloomed from his cupped palm as if he were cradling an infant star. Ashe's breath caught in her chest, tangled in terrified wonder. Many vampires used sorcery, but she'd never seen a move that smooth.

Her eyes went from his hand to his face. Most vamps had eyes with a gold or silver cast. His glinted topaz, if topaz could melt and burn with the intensity of an alchemist's forge. His face was more masculine than pretty, the strong, straight features softened only by the fact that he had been Turned young.

The vampire's hair was russet, the red of a fox's pelt. It fell thick and straight to his waist, woven through with bits of gold and beads. He wore other gold, too—heavy cuffs and a twisted torque that sat on his collarbone, both decorated with red stones that glinted in the weird light. Only his clothes—just a dark shirt and slacks— were everyday.

"What do you want?" Ashe asked, pleased that the words came out sounding normal. "Not to sound rude, but the whole nightie/vampire/graveyard-at-midnight thing is best when it's kept brief. Especially since I was, y'know, busy."

"This seemed the safest way of speaking to you. You and your guardsman friend destroyed my emissary Frederick Lloyd." He blew on the light he held, and it floated to the ground, still glowing like pale, fey campfire.

"You're Belenos, King of the East."

"Correct."

"And all this time I thought you were just a series of anxiety dreams."

"I've been called worse."

He bowed, raising his fist to his heart in a gesture she guessed was as old as the Caesars. She wasn't reassured by the courtesy. Vampire monarchs weren't the kind of people you wanted to notice you, no matter how nice they were pretending to be. He rose, the ornaments in his long hair making a gentle clatter that made Ashe think of bones.

"What do you want?" she asked, then added, "Your Majesty."

He looked amused. "Good manners from Ashe Carver, the famed huntress?"

"That was a freebie. You have to earn anything more than that."

"Very well."

"What's with the graveyard?"

"I thought you would be at home here."

"In a cemetery?"

"You deal out death to my kind. I am a king of the once-dead. Your thoughts dwell with your dead more than with the living around you. It seemed appropriate."

Ashe shuddered, partly from the cold, partly from the truth in his words. "People around me tend to die." *Like*

Reynard will, if I don't get that urn back. A new and profound pain hit her in the belly. He had mattered before. Now he was vital to everything she hoped for.

Belenos tilted his head, watching her as if she were an interesting worm. "Then you understand a little of what it is like to be of my kind. The living inevitably wither away, and the only thing we can do to save them is to share our dark gift."

The world rocked slightly, as if she'd had too much to drink. She felt the sadness in his words, as tantalizing as a delicious scent. They shared the same melancholy. Before she knew what she was doing, she took a step closer, responding to the too-human sorrow in his eyes. He put a hand on her arm, lightly touching her skin. The cold seemed to fall away, allowing her muscles to relax.

Her gaze lingered on his mouth, almost feeling the curve of his lips against hers. They covered fangs, soft sensuality over a killing hunger. *Erotic.*

What had she been doing before the graveyard? Her mind struggled to remember, but it was like running through an ocean of thick, golden honey.

Belenos was suddenly even closer, his fingers pulling the elastic from her hair. It tumbled from her ponytail, sweeping like pale wings against her cheeks. She wore it down like that only when she was with a man. When she was seducing or seduced.

No, not with this one. Not with a vampire.

He ran the tips of his fingers down her cheek.

Reynard.

"You're hypnotizing me." With all her will, she managed to raise her hand, pushing his touch from her face. She stumbled back, away from him. Cold flooded in, as if she'd stepped outside of a protective bubble. Her heart hammered, pulse pounding in her throat.

"I'm just making you more comfortable." He closed the gap between them, making all her struggles useless. She was frozen, unable to move away one more time. He cupped her face in one hand, running his thumb over her lips as gently as the brush of a butterfly's wing. "The man you're with is all but dead. How am I any different?"

Ashe couldn't answer. Despair seemed to seep out of the grave dirt, crawling up her limbs like a foul tide.

Brushing his lips against her forehead, Belenos breathed in her scent. "That's why you kill us, isn't it? I've shared your nightmares. I know your secrets. You're already half in love with death. It's a magnet to you. Safer to snuff out temptation before you join those who've already crossed over."

"Why did you bring me here?" Ashe said through gritted teeth, wanting her strength back, wanting weapons to rend Belenos's dead flesh. "Why have you been in my dreams?"

"I want your attention."

"Well, you've got it. What do you want?"

"You. I can promise you freedom. No more guilt. No more shouldering the weight of a losing battle. You can't protect everyone, Ashe. Let it go. Let yourself go."

"And what? Die? Suck blood for a living?" She felt dizzy, as if the ground were slowly falling away under her feet. The feeling was spiked with terror that he understood her all too well.

Belenos's lips brushed the fine hairs by her ear as he leaned close to whisper, "Think of the risks you take. Think of how you dance on the edge of death, greedy for that rush of adrenaline to make you feel alive. You're already in the darkness, Ashe. Give in to it. Thrive on it."

He bent down and kissed her forehead. She cringed, even though his lips were warmer than she expected, the kiss tender. He brushed her eyelids, the corner of her mouth, and then took her in a full-on embrace.

"Get off me," she muttered. She couldn't pull away. Her strength had fallen to dust, staked in its turn. "I don't belong to you."

"Not yet," he said, the words sinking down to her bones.

And yet, there was nothing lewd in his kiss. It was

careful, the merest suggestion of fang and tongue. A promise. Forgiveness. Almost a benediction.

As if he knew just how she would have wanted a first kiss from her king.

He released her, holding her face in his hands. The topaz eyes trapped hers. "If you accept my dark gift, I'd be happy to keep you by my side. Or I could offer you ultimate peace." His gaze traveled to her parents' graves. "Or I could simply let you go. Any of these outcomes are acceptable, as long as you give me what I want."

Ah, here comes the punch line. Cynicism sliced through whatever mojo held her still. She shook him off, and he let her go. He had already made the point that she could wander only as far as he allowed.

"Your minion said you wanted an heir." She said it bluntly, maybe to shock herself awake. It didn't work. "Save your efforts; I'm on the pill. Oh, wait—vampires can't have babies. Looks like there are some logistics to work out."

He looked away, laughing almost shyly. "Perhaps, but the birth of your sister's child opened a realm of possibility none of the Undead had ever dreamed of. The Carver witches are indeed remarkable."

Ashe folded her arms. "Fuck you. Holly is taken."

Belenos gave a slight shake of his head. The gold ornaments clattered softly. "Of course. Caravelli is a formidable warrior and a favorite of Queen Omara, for all that he is a headstrong subject. Even I hesitate before taking his woman, which is why I have come to you. You have no one."

I have someone. I'm sleeping beside him right now. But how long would that last? *Never mind that. Five minutes with Reynard is worth eternity with this loser.* "You're out of luck. My powers were destroyed years ago. I can't do what she did."

His eyes flared a moment. Was that news to him? If so, he shifted gears like a pro. "And yet you are still of the Carver bloodline. Genetics count, and what magic you lack, I can provide. I planned for contingencies."

Ashe scoffed. "How? Sure, you're a vampire king and all, but you're not a witch. In fact, you're dead."

"There are ways." Belenos gave a derisive smile, a dangerous look on that warrior face.

Ashe didn't understand, but she summoned enough will to fall back another step. "Can't you just adopt?"

"Most vampires were born into a feudal world. They understand dynasty, clan, and rule through the right of blood. I can give them a prince. I can give them new hope and a future."

"Just by having a kid of your own?"

"I can give them a living heir. A prince who is theirs but who can still walk in the sun. A blood ruler who will ultimately sacrifice himself to take his place as my equal and their lord. Such a triumph has never been dreamed of. The vampire species will recognize our right to rule all."

"All?"

Belenos smiled, and for the first time she saw the long, strong eyeteeth of a male vampire. She felt a tightening in her gut, fascination and terror. *This guy would Turn his own kid.*

"You know yourself the cruelties of the humans," he said. "They execute us for the slightest cause; they deny us the vote; in many places they still dictate where we can live. We are stronger, faster, better. Why should we not be at least equal? Why not more than equal?"

"You get all this from having a kid?"

Ashe didn't understand. Maybe she couldn't. She was modern and mortal. All she knew was that he scared her down to her bones.

He cupped her cheek again. "My son will grow to be as great a warrior as me. No one will stand in our way."

"Well, someone wants to! There was an assassin. . . ."

"Yes. There are those that oppose my plan. The demon, for one, double-crossed me and kept the urn. He thinks he is clever enough to escape my wrath."

Thunderstruck, Ashe stared. "You hired the thief? Why?"

"The urn holds life. I can use that to live, for a time. Long enough to sire a child."

For a moment, Ashe relived thrusting the stake into the assassin's soft heart, only this time it was Belenos she exterminated. "You sick bastard!"

"I would have called it inventive, but there you are."

"That's someone else's life. That's *Reynard's* life!"

He opened his hands in a shrug. "Was he putting it to good use?"

Ashe lunged forward, forgetting everything in a need to rip and tear his flesh.

Belenos caught her by both wrists, holding her in a grip like granite. "Let me protect you. Let me seduce you. I want you to come to me of your free will, just as your sister came to love Caravelli."

"I hate you!"

"Hate is love's cousin. You're mourning Reynard. So be it. He will be gone soon enough."

Hot rage dried the tears in Ashe's eyes. "You can't force me to want you."

He laughed, a deep, confidential sound that resonated deep in her flesh. "I can strip you of your pride, imprison you, even torture you to do my will, but what sort of legacy is that for my child? You would be no better than a venom slave. My son's mother must be a warrior, like you. I won't harm you, Ashe."

He kept holding her, his grip bruising as she struggled. "I don't expect you to desire me simply because I ask. Persuasion is a complex art. Conquest is the interesting part of the game. And it's a game I play very, very well."

"I'm shaking in my slippers."

"So you should be. Death always wins."

"Screw you."

Chapter 16

Reynard woke to the sound of the phone ringing. He couldn't figure out what it was until Ashe moaned and grabbed the handset from the bedside table.

He sat up, feeling long-forgotten muscles. The room looked like a herd of trolls had stampeded through. Bedclothes everywhere. Clothes nowhere. Sun was filtering through the curtains, giving a muffled brightness to the room that his eyes finally seemed to take in stride. His stomach was raging for food. He was *alive*.

"Hello?" she said to the phone.

Ashe's scent lingered on his skin, awakening his need for her all over again.

He looked down at Ashe, who had one arm over her face, blocking out the light while she talked. Pride and wonder rushed through him. He had bedded the Amazon queen, and lived to tell the tale. More than that, he had found her softer instincts, the generous and gentle woman she guarded inside. The one who would give up hunting and take a humble job to see that her child had a home. He could see that part of her now in the shape of her mouth, the grace of her hands.

The better man inside him had fallen on his knees to that hidden goddess, but the rough-and-tumble adventure of finding her had been everything he'd dreamed. Ashe was not the kind of woman who would ever be dull or predictable. She was the princess and the dragon both.

Just looking at her made his heart speed.

"Yeah, okay." Ashe grabbed a paper and pencil off the table, pulling them onto the mattress so that she could write. "Go ahead."

He watched the sleek muscles in her back move as she scribbled notes. The night had changed everything for Reynard. He had been grateful for one night of life and love, but now that wasn't nearly enough.

He had bedded an army of women in his day, from courtesans to countesses, but he had felt like this only once before.

Elizabeth. Back then, he'd been no more than one and twenty, but the possessive hunger had been the same. This need to keep Ashe beside him wasn't going to fade. His first love had stayed with him for centuries. This one would burn even hotter, because he wasn't going to let her slip away.

Somehow.

There had to be an option besides imprisonment or death, because that wasn't a choice at all. Not when returning to the Castle meant eternal nothingness. No food, no drink, no love—nothing but slaughter. *That is why Killion and the rest went mad. They saw their future and could not bear the sorrow.*

Long ago, he made a sacrifice for all the right reasons, but hadn't he paid long enough? There had to be a way of slipping the chains that bound him. Loving and dying or loving and leaving Ashe behind—neither was an acceptable outcome.

The urn's absence was a hollow in his gut. Before

long, he guessed, his strength would start to ebb. Fear niggled at the edges of his mind, but he forced it to stay there.

"Sure," said Ashe. "I know that place."

Her gaze traveled to him, her eyes wide-open now. "Thanks. Bye."

She hung up the phone and fell back to the pillow, pulling the blanket up around her. "That was Lore. He gave me the address where he'll be this morning. I guess he left a message on my cell phone late last night but called back when he didn't hear from me." She sounded sheepish.

"When can we see him?"

"Anytime." She put a hand over her eyes. "I just had the worst dream."

He lay back down beside her, resting on his elbow. He put a hand to her cheek, turning her to face him. "What was the dream?"

"The King of the East paid me a visit." Her eyes said there was more than just a social call involved.

"Then it wasn't a dream."

"No. Belenos hired the demon to steal your urn, but his thief double-crossed him."

"Belenos." Reynard gave a bitter smile that hid his mounting anger. "A vainglorious Undead monarch. It's fitting that he was duped. Still, it's nice to know my life essence is in high demand by the very best people."

"He wants to use it as part of his plot to sire a child."

A vampire would use his soul to hurt Ashe? Fury blazed through him, twitching in his muscles. It was a struggle to think, to put the facts together. "I would have guessed as much. The transfer of life essence is very old black magic."

She sat up, looking down at him. "But why you in particular?"

Reynard thought long and hard about answering that one. "Perhaps because I was the last of the guardsmen. I was the newest and, in some ways, the strongest."

"How? Why is that true?"

"As the fey would say, I broke the pattern. There were no more guards after me."

Ashe looked at him for a long time. "Did you mean for that to happen?"

"I shed blood to make sure I was the last," he answered in a tone meant to end the conversation. "I made sure it wouldn't happen again."

He didn't want to remember that horror. Not with her sitting there like a promise of everything new and clean.

She looked at him long and hard out of those spring-green eyes. "Okay." She slid out of the bed.

He followed, catching her by the arms and kissing her. Finding the demon and the urn was the first step, but the journey to happiness suddenly felt urgent. He had to hurry before it drained through his fingers like water.

"My name is Julian," he said, realizing it was a complete non sequitur. "The guardsmen don't use Christian names because they hold too many memories. It's easier if we break all our ties to those we love."

The statement hung in the soft bedroom air like the confession it was.

A shattered look crossed Ashe's face, and then her expression grew clean and hard as a sword's edge. "Well, Julian, we've got an urn to find. Let's go see a dog about a demon."

They took Ashe's Ducati Superbike 1198S. The bright red motorcycle was her favorite possession. She'd traded up to a bigger bike with dual seats when she discovered Holly loved riding as much as she did. Once Holly could bear to leave Robin for an hour or so, they had begun hitting the open road. Other sisters got mani-pedis. The Carvers went cruising. As sister bonding went, it worked for them.

It worked for Reynard, too.

The technical details of the machine were lost on him,

but by the rapt expression on his face, one ride had revealed his inner speed junkie. He got off the bike a little unsteadily, his lips parted with breathless wonder. "I had an Andalusian mare, but even she was not that fast."

Ashe pulled off her helmet. She'd taken the long route to Lore's shop, finding a stretch of highway to show off a little. What the heck—it was a beautiful spring morning, and the detour was only a few minutes. She looked fondly at the bike. "I love this baby. But, hey, a horse is probably better company."

"She nipped." Reynard straightened, now fully recovered from the ride. "I still miss her, though. She had a strong personality."

Talking about horses seemed perfectly natural. They were in an old parking lot behind brick buildings that had been warehouses long ago. Age and pollution had blackened the name of the feed company that was painted on the fourth story of the old building directly ahead. The rutted alley that led to that spot could well have been designed for carts instead of cars. Only the telephone poles and a battered Dumpster disturbed the old-time feel of the place.

They started across the lot, the air heavy with the smell of sun-warmed earth and car exhaust. "This area is called Spookytown by the locals," Ashe said. "Johnson Street runs in front of these buildings. It's one of the busiest streets in the downtown. Most of the nonhumans in Fairview live right around here."

Reynard looked from side to side as if expecting an ambush.

"It's actually pretty peaceful," she added, recognizing her own first reaction to the place. "The crime rate is lower than average. The nonhumans want equal rights. They're doing their best to be model citizens."

Ashe led him to an old door in the side of the building. It had peeling white paint and small, dirty panes of glass at the top. She tried to look through the locked door without success, so knocked instead. She could hear faint music, as if someone had the radio on inside.

Was that Def Leppard? She knocked again, louder this time.

The music died. After a few seconds, she heard a bolt draw back and the door opened. It was Lore, the young alpha of the hellhound pack. Like all the hounds, he was tall and lanky, with big bones and shaggy dark hair. He wore coveralls splattered in grease and paint and an expression that gave away nothing.

"I expected you, Ashe Carver," he said. "I did not expect the captain of the guardsmen to come to my door." He spoke a little haltingly, although he didn't have a defined accent. It was the speech of someone translating their thoughts as they went.

"Is that a problem?" Ashe said, putting some steel into the words.

"The hounds are free from the Castle. That was guaranteed to us."

Reynard held up his hands in the universal not-armed gesture. "I am here only for information. You and your people are safe from me."

"Do you give your word, guardsman?" Lore asked. The question had the weight of ritual.

"I do." Reynard made no move until the hound nodded.

"If it is you who swears, then I will accept your truth. You are one of the few guards who always keep your word. Come inside."

They followed him into the cavernous warehouse. It seemed to be hollowed out inside, with only a mezzanine above for offices. Large windows let in air and light, but it was dark enough that Reynard slipped off the glasses. Metal shelving surrounded the open area. A moving van was parked beneath a rolling steel door that opened onto busy Johnson Street. A dozen hounds were moving what looked like freshly upholstered furniture into the van.

"What kind of business is this?" Reynard asked.

"Humans are wasteful," Lore replied. "We take what they throw away and make it new again."

"Furniture refinishing?" Ashe queried. "You've gone into decorating?"

Lore gave her a look that might have been amused. Hellhounds were notorious for their poker faces—for them, showing emotion was a private gesture. Lore was more expressive than most. An effort to blend in with the humans, she supposed.

"Among other things." He shrugged. "Engines. Appliances. Whatever we can fix."

Reynard said nothing more, but looked around with intense curiosity.

There was a kind of coffee nook in the back with a few folding chairs gathered in a loose circle. As they approached, the four hounds sitting there glanced up. As one, they rose and went to help the movers, leaving them alone.

Lore stopped beside the coffeepot. "May I offer you something to drink?"

"Yes," said Reynard unexpectedly. "I would be honored."

"Captain Reynard fears he will insult me," Lore said in response to Ashe's puzzled look. "Our elders do not take it well if hospitality is refused."

"Then, sure, I'll have some coffee," Ashe replied. "Whatever makes the elders happy."

"That is what I say, all too often." Lore found three clean mugs and poured from what looked like a fresh pot. "Please help yourself to cream and sugar."

It was real cream. The coffee tasted like hazelnut. The recycling business must have been doing well.

Lore sat in one of the folding chairs. "How may I assist you?"

Reynard sniffed the coffee experimentally. He looked pleasantly surprised. "We are searching for a thief."

Lore's dark brows came together. "And so you came directly to me. Am I to be flattered or insulted?"

Ashe blew past that one. "This thief is probably dealing in high-end valuables or curiosities. That includes goods from the Castle."

Lore sat up straight, his eyes dark with carefully banked anger. "I once traded supplies with the Castle warlords to free my hounds from slavery. You think that means I know every thief and smuggler who sets foot in the Castle?"

"There aren't many rumors the hounds don't hear," said Reynard quietly. "That's why we are here. You are the best source of information we could hope for."

Lore sat very still. Ashe felt queasy with the tension in the room. She preferred fighting to info gathering, hands down. Hitting someone over the head was easier than convincing them to cooperate.

Reynard went on, his face grim. "We think this thief may be a demon."

"The same one who owned the bookstore that burned down yesterday," Ashe broke in. "Y'know, the one Holly asked your hounds to guard so no humans blundered inside? We think we're dealing with a collector demon."

Lore looked confused. "Then if you know who the demon is, why are you asking me?"

"Because the store burned down, and now we don't know where he's gone. If we know who he hangs out with, or if he's on the market for more stuff, or, well, whatever the rumor mill can tell us, we might be able to track him down again."

Lore nodded, confusion fading to thoughtfulness. "Such as . . . perhaps he is pursued by a vampire?"

"Are you serious?" Ashe stiffened. *Bingo!*

"Hellhounds cannot lie. That is our nature, as you well know." The annoyance was back.

Reynard sat forward. "Tell us. Please."

"There's not much to tell, but the incident was unusual." Lore got up, put his cup on the counter, and turned. "I worked here late last night. Around midnight a vampire knocked on my door. He asked the same questions that you are."

"Goddess," Ashe breathed. "Who was it?"

"I don't know. He was a stranger. He was powerful. Tall, red-haired. Very, very old. I smelled anger on him.

He, too, had heard that the hounds knew about trade in stolen goods. By the questions he asked, I am certain he is hunting for the same thief."

"Belenos." Ashe stood up, too wired to sit still. "He's the King of the freaking East."

Lore's brows drew together. "I wondered. There were others with him, but they stayed in the shadows outside. He's traveling with a guard."

"Did he do more than ask questions?" Ashe asked.

"Wait here a moment." Lore started across the warehouse at a jog-trot, heading for a small office stuck in the corner.

Reynard rose and set his cup on the counter. It was half-empty. He held the handle a moment before letting his fingers slip away, as if reluctant to let it go. "That tasted good."

He's dying. She knew that, but it hit her with a gut punch all over again. Ashe tried to keep her eyes steady as she searched his face. "You don't look upset."

"It's hard to explain what it's like to really taste something after hundreds of years." He gripped the counter a moment.

"Are you feeling okay?" Ashe said tentatively.

"Of course." He turned to face her.

Like the hellhounds, he was a crappy liar.

Oh, Goddess. Guilt made her turn away, cursing under her breath. "I should have a plan of action by now, and I'm not sure where to go next. I thought Lore would be more help."

"But he has been. We know our visiting vampires may lead us to the demon's door. If we find one, we'll find the other."

"I've got to come up with something." She paced a few steps, digging deep to find the clinical calm that had taken her through so many hunting missions. "This is taking too long."

But she didn't have time to think further. Lore was returning, a pink object in his hand. He stopped, an unhappy look on his face. "The vampire king left this. He said others would come asking about the collector, and they would know what this meant."

Lore held out a pink stuffed rabbit. "Do you understand this?"

Reynard stiffened. "It's a threat."

Lore looked flummoxed. "A rabbit?"

Ashe took the plush toy. It looked expensive. Reynard turned over the gift tag tied to its paw.

"'For Eden, hugs and kisses,'" he read aloud.

Ashe felt her heart freeze. "Goddess, I've got to get to my daughter."

Chapter 17

"This is Oscar Ottwell at CSUP, coming to you from the University of Fairview. We're interrupting regular programming with a request to our listeners to be on the lookout for a lost little girl. Eden Carver is ten years old, with brown eyes and brown curly hair. She is wearing blue jeans, a long-sleeved pink T-shirt, and is probably wearing a blue jacket. She was last seen at around noon at her aunt's home in the Shoreline neighborhood not far from St. Andrew's Cemetery. If you see Eden, please call the station immediately at 555-CSUP. Volunteer searchers are also requested."

Miru-kai moved silently through the Castle, freed to roam the prison once more. Mac had finally run out of questions and let him go. Or, more precisely, Miru-kai had chosen to run out of answers. He had given enough good information to buy himself out of that cell.

Mac wasn't fully satisfied, but couldn't afford any

more time to spend on the prince's evasions. Belenos with a key to the Castle presented a bigger threat.

A fortunate turn of events, because Miru-kai had to find the vampire first. Today he was scheduled to collect his payment from Belenos. Just because the thief had turned out to be a despicable double-crosser, that didn't mean the vampire wouldn't keep his part of the bargain. No one broke a deal with the fey. That carried with it an automatic curse no amount of time or distance could cure.

It was the prince who had buyer's remorse. This was a bargain he should never have made. And yet the gem Belenos offered had been too much for even his jaded soul to resist. Over time, the stone had been given various silly names: the Stone of Darkness, the Treasure of Jadai, Vathar's Bane. It was a fey treasure, and though other species knew it was potent, few even knew what it did. How Belenos had gotten his cold, clammy hands on it was anybody's guess.

The gem solved a fundamental problem for the prince. No fey could leave the Castle, even with a portal standing wide open. The wizards who built the prison had put extra safeguards in place for those, like Miru-kai, who had the power of invisibility. If they tried to walk out, a wall of power sent them hurling backward like a ball slammed with a racket. That hurt. A lot.

The gem, in the hands of a powerful fey like Miru-kai, meant freedom at last. He had made the pact with Belenos without a moment's hesitation. He wanted that stone!

But so much had gone wrong.

He had promised delivery of an urn. *Not an urn with a soul in it.* Again, wording was everything in these deals.

Miru-kai had told the demon *very specifically* to look for Bran's urn—the same empty urn Miru-kai had picked up by mistake. Ironic? Definitely.

The idiot demon had stolen Reynard's instead—probably grabbed the closest pot to the door in his bumbling haste. But Miru-kai could hardly make him take it back and fetch another, could he? He'd found out about the mistake too late to cover his tracks. The pattern mocked him.

So he had decided to tell Reynard about the theft. Make the game a little more fair. That was the fey thing to do. And, of course, by then he had discovered it was necessary to get an urn for himself—for Simeon. The fact that Reynard's soul was at stake made it easy to get into the vault.

That was the only thing that had gone right.

First, Miru-kai had picked up the wrong urn.

Then Simeon had died days before Miru-kai could rescue them from this hole.

And now, by picking up bits and pieces of information from Mac's questioning, Miru-kai understood what Belenos meant to do with the urn. What a disaster!

So much for making a hasty bargain in his desire to leave the Castle. A fey child would have known enough to ask more questions before sealing the deal. Carelessness like that was unforgivable in a prince—in him! A warlord! A sorcerer! The great Miru-kai!

A vampire dynasty? Projects like that always ended in a bloodbath followed by a snowstorm of gloating memoirs. What a pompous fool. Bravo to the double-crossing demon thief for putting a wrench in *that* idiotic plan.

However, Belenos was a pompous fool with something the prince still wanted.

Miru-kai reached the meeting place, a cavern where the roof was so high, it was lost in shadows. Here the rock was unhewn and the boulders a soft gray with veins of white. Pebbles covered the floor, marking where a river had run long ago. A mere stone's throw away, a cliff face thrust into the darkness. Deep runnels gouged the rock, hinting that a long-ago waterfall had splashed from at least forty feet above.

Miru-kai searched the darkness. An ever-burning fire flickered in a brazier at the mouth of a tunnel. Flames cast a tiny puddle of light, drawing blade-sharp shadows on the rocks.

The cavern was empty. The others had not arrived.

Before Miru-kai, the dry riverbed wound through the cavern. Behind him, a narrow passageway led back toward the gated wilderness where the phouka and demons roamed. He looked up at the blackness above. Perhaps it was his imagination, but he thought the dark held a different quality tonight. It looked almost like, well, sky instead of rock so high it was lost in shadow. It had to be his imagination, because there were no stars, or moons, or any glimmer of relief in the velvet black. He wanted to be free so badly he was imagining things.

He yearned for the weave of his existence to change.

A tiny figure darted out of the tunnel, its wings whirring like the flight of a dragonfly. Miru-kai got to his feet as the little fey zipped around the brazier, circling the light.

"Greetings, Shadewing," said Miru-kai.

The fey's body was no longer than Miru-kai's hand, spindly and frail. The skin was dark blue, with hair the color of forget-me-nots. The overall effect was waif-like, if one missed the needle teeth, claws, and eyes that glowed like hot coals. Shadewing was a bringer of nightmares, the one who soured milk and made babies cry in the dead of night. In other words, a nasty little bastard at the best of times, and one of the prince's most clever emissaries. Miru-kai had trusted him as a go-between on many occasions.

"The vampire king sends his warmest wishes," Shadewing said with a voice that was lovely and yet chill. It made Miru-kai think of the frost on fallen autumn leaves.

"He did not choose to come in person?" Miru-kai said with sarcasm. "How like a vampire to take what he wants and then never call."

"The vampires sent me ahead. Belenos is no more than a minute behind me." The little fairy twisted in the air, looking behind him. "Less than that."

A pair of goblins, hulking brutes in bronze-plated jerkins, gold rings glinting on their tusks, lumbered from the mouth of the tunnel. Those were Miru-kai's guards. Dark-suited vampire guards stood behind them, their pale faces seeming to float in the shadows. In their midst stood the tall, red-haired King of the East.

Belenos stepped forward, moving like a tall-prowed ship cutting the sea. The image was apt. There was something of the plundering marauder still lurking in his topaz eyes.

Miru-kai schooled his expression to hide his contempt. The prince and the king faced off at a polite distance, making formal bows.

"I, Belenos, monarch of the Eastern Kingdom of the Vampires, surrender your payment."

He was holding a yellow gem no bigger than a peppercorn, held by a claw of gold.

"I, Miru-kai, prince of the dark fey, accept your payment."

Miru-kai held out his hand. Belenos dropped the gem into his palm. Miru-kai's fingers closed over the dainty object, feeling the jolt of power as soon as he touched it—fey magic calling to fey magic. It would take him time to learn the gem's secrets, but now he held a world of potential in his hand.

"Our business is concluded," Belenos intoned. Obviously, he was already feeling his inner emperor.

Vomitous cretin.

Miru-kai slipped the loop of chain over his wrist, sparing a glance for the gaggle of vampires standing a few yards away. What did one call a group of the Undead? Flock? Herd? Fang? A suck of vampires?

There was something very obviously not a vampire in their midst. He could just make out a small form, one that glowed with life. "Is that a human child?"

He loved human children.

This one was female, just on the cusp between child and maiden. She was wedged in between the vamps, corralled by their lifeless bodies. *Panting like a bird*, he thought. Trying not to breathe too deeply lest her frame brush the dark coat sleeves of her captors. He could see it in her fine shudders of disgust.

Poor chick.

Belenos's mouth twitched, just the hint of a self-satisfied smirk. "With your help, Prince Miru-kai, I have found the means to create a living dynasty."

He paused, giving Miru-kai a moment to be impressed. The prince gave the ghost of a bow.

The vampire continued. "That is the daughter of the woman I seek to fulfill my plan. My human servants took her this morning."

Miru-kai frowned. "Why?"

"Leverage. I'm going to let the child's mother stew until she's desperate. Then I will lead her into a trap. Perhaps here in the Castle? It's an atmospheric place for an ambush, don't you think?"

Miru-kai, who had experienced a millennium of the atmosphere, shrugged.

Belenos went on. "Once the mother comes to find her, I will take both back to my kingdom."

A chill dread dragged over Miru-kai's skin, like the tail of a silk shroud. "If you are referring to the magic of the Chosen, I thought it required affection freely given."

It was Belenos's turn to shrug. "Captivity can teach affection. If that doesn't work, I have the daughter. I can raise her to love me. She carries her mother's magic. Perhaps both shall make good wives. Plus, I still mean to regain the urn. As the expression goes, there is more than one way to skin a cat. I will have my heir."

Now the vampire's mouth moved, not to a smirk but to a smile that turned the prince's stomach. Miru-kai looked at the girl. Her eyes were huge, brown, and frantic, her face almost as pale as the dead pallor of the vampires.

Apparently free will was a slippery concept for the king.

Outrage began to bloom in Miru-kai's gut, a pinprick of bitter heat.

* * *

The hunt for Eden had moved outside of Holly's house. Reynard took charge of the search, dividing up the streets and assigning volunteers to each small segment of ground. Of course the police were there, doing everything possible, but there were only so many officers available and a lot of streets to cover. The neighbors had come out to help, human and supernatural alike. Reynard had sent Ashe to lead the door-to-door search because it was clear she needed to be moving, not organizing. On the other hand, taking charge and assigning tasks was his strength.

He just wished he felt better. He could deny the drag of the urn's absence, but it was still there, a nagging fatigue that grew with every hour. But there was no time to think of that. Not now.

Twilight was falling, and a new and unfamiliar terror rose in his gut. Someone vulnerable, someone he had started to care for, was in danger. He had fought to protect innocents before, but never one who had wound herself around his heart in the space of a few hours. This was new and, bloody hell, it was awful. He felt helpless.

The house had already been searched, both physically and magically. There was no sign of struggle. No one had seen anything. Everything pointed to the conclusion that someone—almost certainly the minions of Belenos—had scooped up Eden and carried her off. Holly thought perhaps Eden had left by the side door, slipped past the hellhounds, and gone to the corner store. Kids broke rules sometimes just because they were there, and Eden had a history of running away.

Damnation! His heart hurt for her, for Ashe. He had never dreamed that he would hold Ashe Carver while she wept. It hadn't lasted long before she pulled away, whipping herself to action, but he had felt her grief through his whole body.

She had turned to him for comfort. He treasured the gift of her trust, and yet it was the greatest condemnation of all. He was a guard. After the bizarre attack in the library, he had anticipated another strike—but he had never dreamed it would be directed at Eden.

Thrice-damned idiot! By God, he would fix this. He'd organized everyone within an inch of their lives. Then he marched back into the house. He had the beginnings of an idea. Fortunately, because the searchers were turning up nothing.

Now he truly understood the loss Constance had felt when he'd separated her from her son, and he hated himself anew for causing such desperate pain. It felt like a stain—dark and twisted as the guardsmen's tattoos—blackening the hole where his soul should have been.

I have to fix this. For Eden, for Ashe, and perhaps to make amends for his past crime. *Whatever it takes.*

There was one place no one had thought to look for Ashe's daughter.

The house felt heavy and sad, as if in mourning. Maybe it, too, blamed itself. Reynard jogged up the stairs to the second floor, where he knew Holly had a separate room to work her magic. She was the only adult still inside, and she was trying to cast a tracking spell.

He paused in the doorway, catching his breath after the run up the stairway. Not something he had ever had to do before. He was growing weaker. Reynard swallowed hard, pushing down fear for himself. The safety of a child came first.

Holly's room was lit with myriad candles, except for the corner where Robin's wicker crib sat, the baby fast asleep inside. The floor was covered in a plain blue carpet ringed with a white circle. Stones were carefully placed along the ring, marking the points of the compass. In the center was a square of silk threaded with glinting silver. On it sat Holly's magical tools and a brass bowl with sweetly scented incense. Holly knelt in the circle, a map spread before her. She held a crystal on a long silver chain, waiting for it to point the way Eden had gone.

Reynard waited in the doorway until Holly looked up. Her green eyes, so like Ashe's, were wet with tears. "I can't make it work. It's like she's shielding us, but that's not possible. She hasn't come into her magic yet."

"Or else someone else is shielding her." His idea was taking shape, pieces fitting together like shards of broken pottery.

"Who?"

"Have you looked inside the Castle?"

Holly's eyes widened. "Why would she be there?"

"Because we know Belenos has connections there."

"Who?" Holly wiped her mouth with the back of her hand, as if she felt sick. "I sound like an owl, don't I?"

"Just do it." Reynard's voice was harsh.

She swallowed. "I need something from the Castle."

He crossed the room in two strides and picked up the white-handled knife that sat on her silvery cloth. It was poor etiquette to breach a witch's circle, but that was just too bad. He sawed through a lock of his hair and handed the knife and a clump of brown strands back to her.

Holly took them, astonished.

"I was there for centuries. Part of my body should suffice."

"Okay," she said uncertainly. "Give me a minute."

Her skin brushed his, warm and buzzing with magic. She was so like her sister, and so different. Reynard realized he would have given anything to reach out and grab Ashe's hand. The images flickering in his imagination were enough to drive any man to need comfort.

Holly looked up from her spell to give Reynard a long, considering look. "I think you're right. I think she's there, but the trace is faint. Just like she's being hidden."

Now she had a hand-drawn map of Mac's part of the Castle on the floor before her. The crystal was moving to the left of what she'd drawn, the point lifting away from the chain like a dog straining against its leash. It wobbled a little, as if uncertain, ranging over a small area of the uncharted paper as if trying to find its mark.

That meant Eden was weakened, or else someone with a lot of magic had her captive.

Reynard swallowed hard. The air around him lost its warmth. *How much strength do I have left?*

Realistically, they had made little progress in finding his urn. Its absence was telling on him. When he had returned to the Castle even just long enough to change clothes, it had drained him badly. If Reynard pushed himself too hard, he would simply perish.

For a moment, he closed his eyes, feeling the weight of the decision he had to make and knowing that there was only one possible outcome.

What choices did he have? Die slowly, taking what pleasure he could as his humanity came back in one last hurrah, or die quickly, and perhaps save Ashe's daughter? *Duty, dignity, death.*

An aching lump worked its way up his throat, as if all the arguments for life scrambled for breath at once. He choked them down in one hard swallow.

At the last moment, he let his gaze linger on Holly's baby, softly sleeping in the corner. As his last vision of the outside world, the innocent infant was a good one. She was a symbol of everything love could achieve. Life from death.

He couldn't make life, but he could save it. He could do his duty.

"Will that crystal work outside the circle?" he demanded.

"Sure, the spell's got an hour or two left on it."

"Will it work for me?"

"Yeah—"

"Then give it to me." He held out his hand.

Reluctantly, Holly handed it over. Her elfin face was filled with questions.

Reynard took a deep, steadying breath, finding the discipline that had kept him strong for centuries. He pulled himself straight. "Tell Ashe that I know where her daughter is, and that Eden will be safely home by morning."

"Wait a minute," said Holly, her voice rising with tension. "What are you planning? You know you can't go back into the Castle. It makes you sick."

Reynard couldn't help smiling. It was so nice that someone cared what became of him. He hadn't always had that. "There's no time to argue. I know the Castle. I can find Eden faster than anyone else."

As he spoke, he pulled power from the air, grabbing the scraps of Holly's magic and the wild anxiety of the searchers roaming the streets and calling Eden's name. He spun it, letting it build fast and hard.

Holly grabbed a slender wand from where her tools were arranged, her knuckles turning white as she gripped it. "Reynard? Don't go all cowboy on us."

He shook his head. "The vampire is working with the dark fey. I'm sure of it. No one knows what fairies might do, much less their prince." *The fey take children, and Miru-kai has been in the thick of this from the start.*

"Dark fey?" Holly demanded, the words cracking with fear. "What are you talking about? What's happening to Eden?"

He released enough energy to make a portal. The charred scent blasted the room. A spinning dot appeared and spread like oil poured in a pan, growing to man height in a wash of bright orange, prickling energy.

"Talk to me, Reynard, or I'll zap you," Holly warned, raising the wand. "Don't think I won't!"

He would have rather told her all that he knew, explained his choices, but every second counted. Eden's welfare trumped everything else. "Tell Ashe I'll make everything right."

The portal swallowed him with a pop.

Chapter 18

Miru-kai stared at the little girl, delight in his heart. A human child! Who would have thought such a prize would come to him here, in the dismal Castle?

She stared back, terrified but struggling not to cry. With the aid of Shadewing and the goblin guards, it had been a matter of moments to snatch her away from the vampires. As a feat of arms, it was barely a challenge. Miru-kai was a commander of armies and every bit Belenos's equal in battle. After that, Miru-kai's knowledge of the Castle had made it child's play to lose them in the maze of corridors.

The vampire's outraged howl had been a delight. Proud Belenos hadn't anticipated anything but fawning admiration. From a prince of the fey! *Idiot.*

Just to add insult to injury, Miru-kai had sent Shadewing to tip off the Castle guards that there were unwelcome visitors afoot. An excellent way to win points with Mac and send Belenos on a merry chase. All in one fell swoop. Priceless.

Now Miru-kai was alone with the girl. Terrified, she sat curled into a ball, knees drawn up to her chin, eyes watching his every move. He'd sent the goblins away, hoping that would calm her. He was the first to admit their appearance took some getting used to.

It had worked. Now, for a very frightened child, she was remarkably loquacious.

"What's your name?" she asked.

A fey prince had many names and titles, so he offered something a child could remember. "Kai."

"Kai."

"Yes." Hearing the name tugged at something deep inside him. Only the closest of friends had ever used that name. Friends like Simeon.

The emotion doubled his desire to keep this human as his charge, safe and sound. No vampires would steal her from under *his* nose. The fey took better care of children than that.

She gave him a serious look from large, dark eyes. "You sort of look human, but you're not, are you?" Her tone was all accusation.

"My grandfather was human," Miru-kai replied, keeping his voice gentle. "But the rest of my ancestors were kings and queens of the fey."

She narrowed her eyes. "What's a prince doing in here?"

He allowed himself a slight smile. "My arrival was an inconvenient accident. I'll be leaving shortly."

"Uncle Mac is going to let you go?" She looked even more suspicious. Not a stupid girl, this one.

"Of course," he said smoothly. Now that Miru-kai had the gem, Uncle Mac had little choice in the matter. "It's time to join the modern era."

But it wasn't just himself he was thinking of. All of his people wanted freedom as much as he did, but whether the new human world and the dark fey were ready for each other was another story. How he approached integrating dark fairies into the twenty-first century would depend on what he discovered beyond the Castle door. He had heard the hellhounds hadn't found the outside world particularly welcoming, and they were as human-friendly as monsters got.

He had his work cut out for him.

"Captain Reynard and Mom will come get me, you know."

The girl's statement snapped Miru-kai's mind back to the here and now. "How do you know the good captain?"

"He likes my mother." The girl looked down, frowning at her hands.

Oh-ho, what have we here? "Does he?"

She tucked a curl behind her ear. "They kill things together. He's okay."

Reynard's been gone how many days? The old fox works quickly!

She gave him another narrow look. "Are you one of those creepy guys who touches little kids?"

The prince shook his head. "I give you my word; I simply enjoy your company. No harm will come to you while you are with me."

"Are you sure?" Her chin stuck out stubbornly. "The first bunch put a bag over my head when they stuffed me in their car. I think it was a potato sack. I smell like dirt."

"I am *not* personally responsible for the sack. Those were vampires and their servants. Nasty things. And you do not smell like dirt. You smell like human."

She looked faintly embarrassed. "What does that mean? Do I need a bath?"

He laughed, something he hadn't expected to do ever again. Not after Simeon. "It's hard to put into words. Humans smell like their houses. Warm. Like food. Yours has a scent of magic. And you've been near a baby."

Eden made a face. "Yeah, Robin stinks. She can't help it."

The girl looked away. Her cheeks held the bloom of health and sunshine, despite the circles of fatigue under her eyes. *What is her story?*

"My mom will get those vampires."

"Your mother is a Carver witch?" Miru-kai already knew the answer. Belenos was after a witch who could mate with a vampire. There was only one such case in recent memory.

"Yeah, but she's lost her magic."

Miru-kai sucked in a breath, putting scraps of information together. *Not the one who already has a vampire husband, but the monster-slaying sister.* He'd heard tales about that one.

"Then your mother is Ashe, the elder daughter of Marian Carver."

"How did you know that?"

"I try to know everything."

"Even the first name of my grandma?"

"People still talk about your grandparents."

"Why?"

"Because your mother killed them with a spell, of course."

The child started where she sat, as if he'd pinched her. Her eyes flooded with dismay, then tears. "That's a lie!"

Oh. Miru-kai cursed under his breath.

He'd blurted out the wrong thing. He was used to dealing with monsters, not the nursery. Wanting to comfort, he rested a hand on her thin shoulder, but she shrugged him off.

"I want to go home now," she said in a small voice. "Leave me alone."

Miru-kai straightened, folding his arms and contemplating the small, huddled form at his feet. *Simeon would know what to do.*

But Simeon was dead. Miru-kai was on his own with this weeping child. He tugged the ends of his mustaches, at a loss.

He might be a slippery, conniving thief, a warlord, a sorcerer, and an all-around bad sort of fellow, but he had softer instincts. He could well protect this child, at least until he was able to unravel the magic of the gem and make his escape. He might even keep her after that. He so wanted to have a human at his side again. . . .

There was much to ponder.

Ashe was heading back to the house, her cheeks stiff with dried tears. The crying came on and off, uncontrollable. Her nerves crackled as if she'd downed an oil tanker of coffee. Though her mind was clear, her body was manifesting all the fear she couldn't acknowledge and stay sane. Breaking down wouldn't help her daughter, but nobody'd told her shaking hands.

But she had found nothing.

No one had.

So far, there was no ransom, no demand. Whatever game the vampire was playing, she couldn't figure it out. She really hoped Reynard had a clue what to do next, because her exhausted brain was full of nothing but panic.

Ashe stopped dead in her tracks. Holly was running out of the house with Robin in her arms, calling for help. Ashe sprinted across the street to join her, along with a crowd of other volunteers.

Alessandro, Holly's vampire mate, reached her first. He was tall, with long, wheat blond curls and amber eyes. "What's going on now?"

"I should have zapped his ass!" Tears streaked Holly's face. Robin woke and started to fuss, making tiny, frustrated cries. Holly hushed her as they gathered around.

"Who are you zapping?" Ashe demanded. "And why?"

"Captain Broody, that's who!" Holly hiccuped.

"Reynard?"

Alessandro put his arm around Holly, a gentle, affectionate gesture. "Hey, come on. Calm down." Then he put his other arm around Ashe.

Ashe clutched her arms, feeling the night chill more than she should have. She was low on fuel. She hadn't eaten. She couldn't.

"Reynard thinks he knows where Eden is," Holly blurted. "He went to the Castle to get her back."

"Is she there?" Ashe made a confused sound. "Do you think he's right?"

"He said something about dark fey working with Belenos."

"Oh, Reynard," Ashe choked out, her face growing cold with dread. "He's going to fade if he goes in there. Why is he doing this?" But of course she knew why. Because of Eden. Because Reynard was who he was. Gratitude and anger collided. *I can't lose either of them!*

"He said there was no time. He was afraid of what the fey would do."

"Son of a . . ." Alessandro started swearing in a language she didn't know.

Ashe vibrated with desperation, her stomach so knotted it hurt. "Goddess! I have to get there. I'm going to kill whoever has Eden! I've got to get him out of there!"

Alessandro Caravelli's red T-bird was parked at the curb. Ashe took off, bolting across the lawn toward it. Alessandro beat her to it by seconds.

They got into the T-bird and took off with a scream of tires.

Once inside the Castle, Reynard followed the crystal's direction. His boots echoed on the stone floor, every scuff rustling in the dark recesses of the corridors.

So far, he felt well enough to carry on with his mission—which wasn't saying much. Like so many others from his time, he had marched under the scorching sun of India while dressed in a wool uniform suited to Britannia's fog and rain. He was used to soldiering on through discomfort.

Still, he could tell the urn was far away—a different dimension counted more than miles. Strong as he was, there was a limit to his energy. It was draining like sand in an hourglass, each minute depleting a little piece of him.

He had anticipated this, so he paid attention to those occasions when the crystal took him near one of the patrolled areas. He meant to find a guardsman and send for help.

Unfortunately, no one was at their usual post. Had something happened to call them all away? His plan counted on reinforcements; if he couldn't finish the search for Eden, someone else had to.

He walked on, his pace brisk. The corridors criss-crossed with mindless regularity, pools of torchlight just bright enough to give the shadows shape. The stone walls exhaled a clammy chill.

At the next post he reached, he called out. The echoes of his voice faded into the dark, drifting like dust. The dark halls were empty. No one was there to help.

Reynard paused for the barest fraction of a second and then pushed on, calculating the distance to the next post and how far he could go before he ran out of strength to generate a portal to safety.

And if no one was at the next post, either?

He had chosen this risk. He would see it through. *Am I being an idiot?*

Ah, well, he had dueled while drunk more than once. He had gambled and lost fortunes. He had bedded women who were as adept with poisons as pleasure, full well knowing that night's death might be of the literal rather than the poetic kind. He *was* an idiot. Or at least he had been, before he came to the Castle. He didn't take unnecessary chances anymore.

Now he knew the real face of danger. He had lost everything, all his choices.

Except this one. He chose to save the little girl who had given him hope. For her, he would gamble with the last scraps of his life.

For Ashe, who had given him back a taste of joy.

Reynard froze, listening. There was a scuffle of foot-steps, soft soles on cold stone. Almost too soft to hear. Moving very, very fast.

Before he could draw into the shadows, a group of five vampires rounded the corner, moving smoothly as a school of sharp-toothed fish. Their pale faces floated in the dim light, eyes seeming lit from within. They came to an abrupt halt, staring at Reynard.

A tall red-haired male stood in the center of the

group. The others surrounded him like an honor guard.
All were armed and disheveled, as if they'd been in a
fight. One had a gash in his temple, already scabbed
over, a trickle of dried blood trailing down his cheek.

Well, that answered the question about who had
drawn the guards away from their posts. They were forming search parties, looking for this group of intruders.

"Stand aside," growled the red-haired one in the
middle.

Belenos, I'll wager. A cold smile spread over Reynard's features.

Eden was silent as she walked with Miru-kai through the
Castle's grottoes and torchlit halls. Deep in thought, she
barely seemed to notice her surroundings. Or perhaps
she was too afraid to be curious about the dark, stony
prison. She was probably thinking about her grandparents.

Sadly, fey magic didn't include taking back words he
had no business speaking. The prince cursed himself.

It wasn't like a fey to wonder about a human's
thoughts, but Miru-kai had human blood. It made him
ponder things no other fey would worry about. For instance, every child taken by the fey changed the future.
Their threads dropped from the weave of human history. Deeds would be left undone, future children never
born—the effect as absolute as if they had lost their
lives. Did the fey have the right to cause such changes
in the pattern?

Right now he wished he were fey enough to simply
grab the girl and count his blessings. Instead, his rudi-
mentary conscience—a very human attribute—was
forcing him to think hard about what he was going to
do next. What futures might he alter by interfering with
her destiny?

He could feel her unhappiness. Empathy was something Simeon had tried to teach Miru-kai, and now
he couldn't shut it off. The very air around the child
screamed with how much she wanted to go home.

How did humans get on in life with everyone else's feelings to worry about? It was exhausting. On the other hand, he couldn't indulge in emotion all the time. He had to keep several thousand monsters in line. That called for a cool head.

"Sometimes," he said, "it is difficult to be a prince."

"Why?" Eden responded, startling him.

He hadn't realized he'd spoken out loud. He looked down at her, and then decided to finish his thought. Listening and advising. That was what human companions were good at. That was what Simeon had done for him.

"I was a pirate once. That was much more fun. Gratuitous amounts of robbery and liquor."

"So, why'd you change jobs?"

Miru-kai sighed. "The fey were weak. They needed a leader, and I was a prince. Then others came along—changelings, goblins, the unwanted and ugly species no one would take in."

"Why do you want to rule them, if no one else seems to?"

"I understand what they need."

Miru-kai stopped. They had reached a vast space ringed with balconies. In the center was a dark pool rimmed by white marble, the carved lip of the stone fluted and curving outward. The overall shape of the pool was squares overlapping squares in a geometric pattern. Rather than torches, fires burned in the four corners of the space.

The hall had seen better days. Tiers of stone benches rose up a sloped balcony, but many had been broken during the last battle inside the Castle. The curious fact was that some kind of night-blooming plant had begun to grow there, twining around the ruins and breaking them down to rubble. And yet, there was neither sun nor water. The sweet-scented vine had to be a freak of the Castle's errant magic.

Eden reached out to touch one of the red-veined trumpet flowers, but the prince caught her hand. "I wouldn't touch that. I'm not sure if it's safe."

Her face turned to him, and his heart grew still. There was gratitude in her eyes, and a glimmering of trust. The look made his chest hurt. Few people ever looked at him that way.

Eden put her hands back in her pockets and sat down on a stump of stone pillar. She looked sleepy. Dimly, he remembered that children needed rest.

"There used to be a dragon here," he said, nodding toward the pool. "But they had to put it back downstairs, where it was warmer."

"A dragon?" she asked. "My mom and Uncle Alessandro fought a dragon once. I wonder if it was the same one."

"I think it was."

She seemed to ponder a moment. "I thought dark fey were bad." Eden made a face. "Sorry, but you seem nice. Not at all like what I've been told."

Miru-kai blinked. That was the thing with children. They were blunt. "The dark fey are tricksters, but we're part of nature's cycle. Sometimes we're the necessary chaos that breaks down old, dead patterns. Sometimes we give people what they deserve and they call it bad luck. That's why they're afraid of us. We're not evil. We're just uncomfortable."

"And light fey?"

"They dress better, but they're not that different. They don't like to be around humans as much."

"Why not?"

"It's complicated. The last light fey I talked to still referred to humans as an upstart ruffian species that deserved to be exterminated like an unwanted invasion of ants."

"Whatever." She yawned. "Bring 'em on. Ants bite back."

He tilted his head, amused. "I wonder how like your mother you are, and if Reynard knows what he's getting himself into."

Her mood, which he had so carefully eased, flattened.

She began picking at her fingers, head bowed. "Why do you say my mom killed my grandparents?"

"It's just something I heard," he said lightly. "It's probably not true."

She gave him a withering look. "You said it had something to do with a spell?"

"So it was rumored."

Eden pursed her lips, looking out over the dark pool of water. "I've asked and asked, but no one's ever told me how they died. My grandparents weren't sick or anything, were they?"

"No."

"And no one suspected it was something magic?"

"Very few people had any idea there was anything out of the ordinary."

"So it wasn't like a mugging or something?"

"No."

She fell silent.

"What are you thinking?" the prince asked uneasily.

"About something Mom said once. About how a selfish spell broke her powers."

"What was the spell?" As soon as he asked the question, the prince felt a sudden need to change the topic. Talking about this was only going to make the child unhappier. "Have you noticed how sweet these blossoms smell?"

"It was to give Grandma and Grandpa car trouble so they wouldn't come home and find out that Mom snuck out to a concert instead of babysitting Auntie Holly."

"Ah," said Miru-kai. "Would you like to visit the gargoyles? The hatchlings are really rather comical."

"I don't want gargoyles or flowers!" Eden snapped, then lowered her voice. "I just want to know the truth."

Miru-kai considered long and hard. "A spell like what you describe is meant for two people. If your mother tried to perform it on her own, it would have been difficult to control."

"Is that what did it? A car crash?"

Miru-kai looked down at his hands. "According to what I heard, your grandfather's car went out of control." He didn't say the vehicle had fallen down a cliff, crashed to the beach, and burned mere feet from the ocean. In his experience, truth had to be adjusted to suit those who heard it.

Tears welled in Eden's eyes. "I hate my mother."

"Don't be so hard on her," Miru-kai said gently.

"She killed my grandparents. She cast a selfish spell that went wrong and they died."

He winced. "And she's had to live with that every day since. If she did not tell you before, it's because she was afraid of losing your love."

Eden looked at him from under dark lashes. "How do you know that?"

Miru-kai didn't answer at once, but stared across the ruined amphitheater with its strange, fragrant vines. Images of the white blooms shivered in the dark pond, the water stirred by a breeze too faint to feel upon his skin.

"Because I'm very old, and I've made a lot of mistakes. Many were for selfish reasons. As I said, I was a pirate. A thief. Then I became a warlord. Those are occupations where mistakes are catastrophic. I don't imagine being a young witch is any simpler, with powerful magic and the wildness of youth in one's veins."

"What she did was wrong."

"Of course it was. But how does your anger fix anything at all? Does it make her a wiser person? Does it bring your grandparents back to life?"

"She should have told me."

"She probably thought you were too young to understand. Perhaps she has not forgiven herself, and so finds it hard to ask forgiveness."

"Why?"

"That's something, sadly, you will learn in time. Think about it. If you were in your mother's place, what would you think of yourself?"

Eden hugged herself, looking small and frail amidst the ruins of the hall. "No wonder she always seems so sad."

"She's a prisoner of those memories. Perhaps telling her you forgive her will set her free."

Reynard drew his Smith & Wesson and fired all in one motion. A vampire head exploded. Two of the other vamps fired their weapons. Reynard dropped to the ground, tucking into a roll that took him backward. With four on one, room to move was essential.

He came out of the roll and into a crouch, bringing up his weapon again. *Blam!*

The corridor rang with the noise, hell on vampire ears. He missed, but they flinched. *Blam!* Another head exploded.

Three on one now. Reynard ducked into another roll and scrambled to take cover where this corridor crossed another. A bullet *chinged* on the stone near his ear, sending prickles of alarm in waves down his neck. Reynard jerked back from the corner, gripping his gun and pulling in a breath of stale air and cordite.

A small blue fey zigzagged down the corridor, wings humming. One of the vampires fired at it, sending sparks flying off the stone wall.

Silence, then a hum of magic. Reynard felt it crawl over his skin, vibrating in his back teeth. Carefully, he peered around the corner.

Just in time to see a portal close behind Belenos and his last two henchmen.

Damn and blast.

He had heard from Mac that Belenos had a key. Unlike the guardsmen, who could open a portal at will, a vampire would have to activate the key's magic—chant a spell or do a dance or however the blazes the keys worked. Reynard had never needed to use one, so he didn't know the specifics.

But that answered why the King of the East and his minions were in this deserted corridor. Belenos had probably been looking for a quiet place to make a door and get away—a bit of a challenge with the Castle guard in pursuit, but he'd just managed it. *Damnation!*

Reynard clicked the safety on his gun and slipped it back into the holster beneath his jacket, reciting a litany of curses compiled over several centuries.

The skirmish had been over in less than two minutes.

As he would after any of his daily battles in the Castle, Reynard checked for injuries—bruises, but nothing noteworthy—and carried on. He would report the fight to Mac as soon as Eden was safe.

Unfortunately, the skirmish had cost energy. As he pulled out Holly's crystal and resumed his search, Reynard's feet felt heavy, and an odd ache beneath his breastbone began pulsing with every heartbeat. He pushed himself, hurrying as fast as he could manage. He was running out of time.

The trail led him to a familiar room, one nearly destroyed by a cataclysmic battle last autumn. To one side, his silk garments an exotic splash against the stone, sat Miru-kai. Across from him, Eden perched on a lump of rock, looking hunched and tired. Reynard's heart bounded at the sight of the girl.

Silently, Reynard pocketed the crystal, sending a prayer of thanks for Holly's magic. Then he pulled the Smith & Wesson again.

"Miru-kai."

The prince looked up, his face tightening as he saw who had interrupted his conversation. "Well, old fox, it seems you've sniffed us out."

Eden's head whipped around. "Captain Reynard!"

She leaped up and streaked across the room, thumping into him in an ecstatic hug. The force of it nearly made him stumble. "You've come to take me home!"

Reynard put a hand on the dark curls, the child's warmth so vibrant against the cold, dead air of the prison. His strength was ebbing fast. His knees were shaking with fatigue. It felt odd, for one immortal. He'd forgotten what illness was like.

That memory was coming back with a vengeance.

But he'd meant it when he said Eden came first. He hugged the girl and pushed her behind him, putting his body between her and Miru-kai. She grabbed the back of his shirt, as if she was afraid he'd vanish. Then one hand slipped into his.

He kept the gun trained on the prince.

He didn't mind the anchor of Eden's grip. His head was clear, but his gut was a solid knot of apprehension. In a weakened state there were too many things that could go wrong. "I'm taking Eden back to her mother."

"Are you sure?" said the prince, his eyes a mix of anger and amusement. "You look like you're about to fall over. What did you do, wrestle every troll between here and the Castle door?"

"I ran into a group of Undead. We'd no sooner become acquainted than one of your fey buzzed past. A little blue fellow. Are the fey in league with the Eastern vampires now?"

The amusement vanished. "No. For one thing, we had a falling-out over the girl."

"The fey never give up their prizes," said Reynard, his tone pure acid. "Not once you've won the game."

The prince gave him a sharp look. "It's not in our nature."

"And you always play by the rules."

"Precisely, when they're rules we like. However, young Eden was in Belcnos's tender care. He didn't seem to be daddy material, whatever his delusions, so I liberated her."

That was interesting. But was anything Miru-kai said ever true?

"And now I liberate her from you." Reynard meant to simply turn and go, but his vision narrowed, darkness eating away at the edges of the world. Cold sweat stuck his shirt to his skin.

Miru-kai flashed a brilliant but cold grin. "And you are a more able caretaker? I am a fey prince, and you are one guardsman looking a bit tattered around the edges. You offend me, Reynard."

Then, without warning, Reynard's legs gave way. He

fell to his knees, sprawling forward. The gun clattered on the stone, slipping from sweat-slicked fingers.

"Captain Reynard!" Eden grabbed his sleeve. "Captain Reynard, are you all right?"

Miru-kai rose from his seat in a whisper of heavy silk robes. "Reynard?"

He didn't respond, instead shaking his head to clear it. He thought he could hear guardsmen in the corridors, calling orders and running. He thought he heard Ashe's voice calling him, and his heart raced with terror and love. His own existence had gone so very wrong, and this was the one thing he could do to make Ashe's better. Except he wasn't quite finished. He really had to get up and take care of loose ends.

Where was he?

What had he just been doing? Memory was flickering in and out of focus.

Oh, yes. He started to climb to his hands and knees, but melted to the right, losing track of his hands and feet.

There was a terrible, terrible pain in his chest.

"Captain Reynard!" Eden shook him with all her strength as the world went black.

Ashe strode in Mac's wake, Alessandro swift and silent behind them. They had found Mac easily enough. He'd been firing questions at a little blue fey no larger than one of Eden's fashion dolls. The thing was trying to explain something about vampires and kidnapping and children. When Ashe showed up, argument stopped and they were on the move again.

The demon stormed into a huge, dark cavern. Angry heat blasted from him in waves. As soon as she could, Ashe stepped sideways, finding cooler air. The minute they reached open ground, she broke into a run.

Reynard sprawled in the middle of the cavern, Eden clinging to his hand.

"Baby!"

Eden gave a wordless cry and bolted across the

stone floor. Ashe wrapped her child in both arms, holding her tight. An agony of relief ripped through her as she breathed in the smell of her child and felt soft skin against her own.

"Captain Reynard's sick!" Eden sobbed. "And the prince disappeared when he heard you coming!"

Reynard! Behind the relief came cold anger, then panic. Alessandro and Mac were already beside Reynard, who was having trouble getting to his feet.

"Get him out of here," ordered Mac. Other guardsmen were trickling in through the doorway, drawn by the emergency. "Make a portal. Get him back on the other side of the door. Get him to Holly. Maybe she can do something."

Alessandro picked up Reynard, slinging one arm over his shoulder. Vampire strength made light work of the full-grown man. "Lead on."

The fey prince had to be guilty. Why else would he vanish the moment the authorities arrived? Ashe released Eden and stood, pulling a foot-long knife from her boot. "Goddess! Where is that bastard fairy?" It came out as a rasp. Frantic bursts of fear and relief and horror came one after the other, tearing her to shreds.

Mac rose, running to the entrance to the cavern, flames surrounding him in a white-hot corona. He filled his lungs and roared to the darkness, "*Guardsmen, find the fairy bastard!*"

The walls shook with the noise, as if the Castle itself cringed before his anger. Wherever the guards were, they heard.

"But he didn't do anything wrong!" Eden insisted. "He was nice to me!"

But no one listened to a child. No one ever did.

Chapter 19

"We're joined here today for an exclusive telephone interview with Belenos, King of the Eastern Vampires. Your Majesty, I cannot begin to express how honored we are that you condescended to join us."

"Thank you for having me, Errata. Let me begin by saying how much I appreciate the opportunity to speak to your listeners in the lovely Pacific Northwest."

"It's entirely our pleasure, Your Majesty. What would you like to speak about?"

"Interspecies relationships. The human media has long maintained that mixing human and nonhuman societies will inevitably lead to disaster."

"Not all human media."

"But most. I'm here to say it isn't true. Peaceful relations can be maintained."

"How do you propose to do that?"

"Humans outnumber us, so we assume they are stronger. I don't think that's true."

"Why does it matter who is stronger?"

"Errata, my dear, half the time you wear the skin of a mountain lion. Surely you understand the law of fang and claw. Sovereignty belongs to the hunter, not the prey."

"Excuse me, Your Majesty, but we need to cut to a commercial break."

Reynard knew he was unconscious, because he'd had the dream so often before. It was New Year's Day, 1758, at about ten in the morning. He rose from his bed in the big family home in Surrey, discovering that he had slept in his clothes. Drips of wine spotted the front of his shirt and breeches. *Well-done, Reynard.*

Through the fog, he recalled being rude to his older brother, Faulkner, again. He couldn't fix on the details. But then, his brother had been drunk, too. His memory would be no better. Hopefully. Reynard wished he could remember what the devil he'd said. Uneasy, he pulled the bell rope to summon a servant.

Outside, he could hear his nieces and nephews shrieking with excitement. He winced at the pitch of the noise, then cringed again when he pushed back the curtain to admit bright sunshine. A soft, feathery coating of new snow lay on every branch and stone, intensifying the dazzling light. He squinted at the scene. The children, bundled in wraps and mittens, were in heaven.

Noisy little buggers, Reynard thought, but fondly. He had played under the same snow-dusted trees in his time.

Then Elizabeth emerged from the house, wrapped in furs, her hands tucked into a muff. She laughed with the children, walking toward them with cautious, tiny steps. The paving stones must have frozen over with ice.

Lizzie. A poet could say how beautiful she was, how soft her fawn-brown hair, how smooth her skin, but Reynard was no poet. The sight of her killed the words inside him, striking him dumb, and empty, and full of lost echoes. She had that power over his spirit. She had kept him from loving anyone else.

Elizabeth, his brother's wife. She had been his, but then Faulkner, with the title and fortune of the firstborn son, had come along. Elizabeth claimed her parents had made them marry, but he had always wondered. She'd fancied a coat of arms.

After that, Julian Reynard, dashing cavalry captain, was merely a comet that came blazing through from time to time, wakening dreams and stirring discord. If he loved his brother, if he loved Lizzie, he had to let her go.

Reynard started awake. *Where the hell am I?* He'd never been in this room before. He looked around, his tongue coated with the ashy taste that came from overusing magic. He was bone-tired, his limbs like sodden bread. He moved his gaze over the furniture. It looked new? Old? How could he tell? Everything looked modern to him. He closed his eyes, too tired to keep them open. He was thirsty, but sleep claimed him again before he could think any more about it.

He was dreaming, back in his old home, same day and date. He rinsed his face and smoothed back his long hair, tying it with a black ribbon. He pulled on his new uniform, thinking he would go out and about. A bit of gold lace impressed the ladies.

Reynard descended the stairs, still buttoning his coat. The bright, snow-reflected sun flooded the high-ceilinged hall, casting shards of light through the bevels in the window glass. Rainbows bounced off the crystal droplets dangling from the candelabra, ricocheted off the cut glass of a vase. The unforgiving light hurt his wine-soaked brain.

He stopped before the open door to the morning room, his gaze quickly spotting the coffee service sitting on a table by the window. The sun flooded in here, too, turning the steam from the coffeepot into a gossamer haze.

Faulkner, as fair-haired as Reynard was dark, and another man were sitting on either side of the fire in identical armchairs. Faulkner's guest, an older man with a black coat and a full-bottomed wig, looked just the same as when he had visited their father years ago, but Reynard couldn't remember the fellow's name. Bellamy? Barstow? Beelzebub?

Bartholomew. That was it.

Faulkner was leaning forward, his elbows on his knees, his hands gripped together in an attitude of brooding worry. He flinched as Reynard strode across the Turkish carpet. Faulkner was either very tense or he had an equally vile hangover.

There were no servants in the room. Without a word, Reynard poured himself coffee and took a large bite out of a buttered biscuit. He wolfed down the food, standing with his back to the other men until he had something in his stomach. Rude, yes, but his temper would be far less risky if he was fed. He swallowed the last bite and picked up another biscuit, looking out at the prospect of the park and garden. The windows in the room were twice as tall as a man, draped with loops of sky-blue velvet. Beautiful, but they let in the cold as if there were nothing between the room and the snow outside. Dusting off his fingers, Reynard refilled his cup and moved toward the warmth of the fire.

All the while he had been eating, he had been eavesdropping on his brother's conversation. His hearing had always been exceptional. Often he heard things he should not.

"So what is this nonsense?" He stopped, facing his brother. "You say your name came up in a lottery? What lottery? And what is this Order you speak of?" The name rang a bell, but he could not think why.

Faulkner lifted his head. "It's not nonsense. I wish it were."

"Then why did you never mention this Castle, if it's so bloody important?"

Slowly, his brother sat back in the chair. "The odds of this happening were remote. The fewer people who know about the Castle, the better."

"If something can turn your face as white as the snow outside, I have a right to know about it." His point made, Reynard walked back to the table and neatly returned his cup to the tray. His life might be in all manner of disarray, but the army had instilled some need for order into his soul.

Bartholomew spoke for the first time since Reynard had entered the morning room. "Perhaps if the details are explained now, we can disregard what should or should not have been said in the past."

The dry, dusty voice jolted him. The cruelty in it brought back memories of hiding under the stairs as a child. Another time he heard things that had confused him. Inwardly shaken, Reynard returned to his position, glaring down at his brother and folding his arms.

"Very well," said Faulkner.

The older man shifted in the chair, leaning forward to look into Reynard's face. "In the event that you do not remember me, my name is Bartholomew. I—as well as your father—have belonged to something called the Order for centuries. We look after—we guard—a particular castle."

Faulkner buried his face in his hands. At the sight of his brother's distress, a queasy sensation began invading Reynard's gut. It was no longer the aftereffects of a night of drink. He recognized the cold seas of fear. "This is no ceremonial duty, I take it."

"No," said Faulkner, his voice quiet. "It is as dangerous as anything you faced in India. And it is absolutely, utterly real."

Reynard's mind groped for some point of reference. Despite Faulkner's reaction, nothing about this conversation seemed believable. "Where is this castle?"

Bartholomew rose, restlessly pacing with his hands clasped behind his back. "That is the hardest question to answer."

"How so?" Reynard protested, but Faulkner cut him off with a wave of the hand.

"Think back to the tales of the Dark Ages," Faulkner

said softly. "The stories of fey and demons, monsters and ghouls. Did you never wonder where such creatures went, why they walk the earth no more?"

"Not really," Reynard said with a bark of laughter. "Those are nursery stories."

"On the contrary," said Bartholomew, his eyes meeting Reynard's. "The sorcerers of old imprisoned all the evils in an infinite dungeon between the worlds."

Realization nudged Reynard, not a bolt of brilliant insight, but the subtle bump of a stranger in a crowded room. He stared for a long moment, remembering scraps of conversation from childhood. Adults hushing as the children grew close, but not quickly enough that some shreds of their fantastic, gruesome news did not fall upon young ears. A book with a golden sun. Talk of warlocks. Talk of the Order.

So this is what all those mutterings were about. He tried to deny the thought, but it clung like cobwebs. Old, bad dreams revived in the dark places of his memory. In spite of the coolness of the room, he felt sweat trickle down his ribs.

"And the service you speak of?"

The old man shrugged. "A castle needs guards. The families of the Order send their sons."

"You need one of us," Reynard said, indicating himself and Faulkner, "to go on guard duty to keep evil locked away in a castle between the worlds?"

"Yes," said Bartholomew.

Reynard's sense of logic rebelled.

"And which worlds would those be?" Reynard's tone slipped into sarcasm. *There will be holes in this story I can—I must—use to disprove it all. Demons? Fey? More likely a brotherhood of thieves and murderers. Perhaps an imaginary game played to chase away the boredom of balls and hunting parties.*

"All the worlds. I don't even know what they all are. No one who goes into the Castle ever returns to tell us."

"They said that about certain establishments in Calcutta, yet here I stand."

"You fancy your chances, do you?" Bartholomew said with a derisive smile, resuming his seat.

Reynard turned away, facing the coal fire. *Villains are flesh and blood. Fearsome, perhaps, but nothing new to me.* "Tell me why I don't throw you down the steps."

"Our father's lineage," Faulkner said in a flat voice. "Our family name demands it."

"Then let me deal with this little man and his castles."

"Your bravery is commendable, Reynard, but it is not required," Faulkner put in, rising from the chair. "I am the firstborn. The duty is mine. I will answer the call upon our family's honor."

So like Faulkner. "And what of Elizabeth and your children? If men truly go into this Castle and never return, have you no thought for them?"

"Of course. What would they think of me if I turned away and let you take my burden?" Faulkner stopped speaking, and Reynard could hear the heavy, determined intake of his brother's breath. "You will look after them. You're a man of honor. I know this house, this title, is everything you have wanted, deep in your heart. Now is your chance."

He didn't mention his wife, yet Elizabeth was present in both their minds as surely as if she stood in the room.

Elizabeth.

Damnation. Reynard doubted Bartholomew's tale—what sane man wouldn't question it?—but Faulkner clearly believed every word. Perhaps their father had told him more. Faulkner was the eldest son.

That heaped doubts on doubts. If there was the slightest chance any of it was real, Reynard couldn't let his brother go. Faulkner had a loving family who needed him.

And Reynard knew far better how to handle a den of thieves.

He spun, his fist connecting with his brother's jaw in a resounding crack. Pain exploded in his hand as Faulkner dropped to the floor. Nursing his knuckles, cursing, he watched the still form of his brother. Faulkner sprawled, the lace of his cuffs stark against the ruby-red pattern of the carpet.

Reynard's lip curled into a snarl. "I am looking after your family, you idiot. What do you take me for?"

Faulkner remained unconscious, his chest rising and falling in a mockery of sleep.

"Nobly done. I hope you didn't break his jaw in the process," Bartholomew observed dryly. "But your heroism is useless. It has to be the firstborn."

Reynard considered, tilting his head. Faulkner's face looked normal enough, though it would probably bruise. No matter. Reynard would leave, and his brother would keep his honor.

"Too bad. You get me or nothing."

The outburst of violence had restored his equilibrium, putting all those vague, fairy-story fears back in their childhood place. He would take care of this Castle nonsense and be on the first ship back to India.

Unexpected emotion welled in his eyes. Faulkner was upright, brave, humane, and would not last an hour in the face of true danger. Clenching his teeth, Reynard willed his softer sentiments away. "Tell me where I need to go to fulfill this lark."

Bartholomew nodded slowly. "This is unprecedented, but very well. We leave at once. Have a servant pack your bags, whatever you would take on a long campaign. And bring as many weapons as you can carry. I will meet you by the gatehouse."

Despite years of moving camp at a moment's notice, the sudden order was unnerving. "Will I need provisions?"

Bartholomew looked oddly embarrassed. "No."

Reynard's eyes snapped open, his breathing slowing when he realized he was just reliving the distant past. It wasn't real. He was in the same unfamiliar room. It was dark, with one lamp burning in the far corner, and he ached all over.

But Ashe was lying on the bed beside him, watching. Her bright green eyes were muted by the dim light.

"You're awake," she said softly, stroking his forehead. "We're in Holly's house. It's more protected here."

"Eden?"

"Eden's safe. Mac has Miru-kai captive."

He felt better. He put a hand over his chest, where the pain had hit in the Castle. The throbbing was gone. Some of that, he knew, was being in the same dimension as the urn, but the healing seemed deeper.

Ashe was reading his face, her eyes serious. "Grandma and Holly came up with a medicine. It should help for a while. Buy us a little time."

"How much time?" She seemed to be wearing nothing but a long T-shirt that skimmed her knees and left her shapely calves bare.

The past was suddenly just that—over and done with. With Ashe there, it seemed possible to look forward.

He'd take whatever future he could get, as long as she was in it.

"What were you dreaming?" she asked. "It looked like a nightmare."

He told her. She was the first person he'd ever told. It was the first time that he could let the words go. "Bartholomew informed me there were a limited number of families with the right kind of magic to be guardsmen—abilities that passed down father to son. Those were the warlock families who made up the Order."

"Warlocks?" Ashe said in surprise. "I thought they'd died out long ago."

"If they did, I'm not surprised. Every ten years one of the firstborn sons was chosen by lottery, and he had to go to the Castle. It was a magical pact the Order had set up to keep the monsters under guard. Replacements were needed over time. That year it was our family's turn to pay."

"And it was a complete surprise to you?"

"Yes."

"Huh." Ashe frowned. "So what happened once you met that guy at the gatehouse? Who was he, anyway?"

"Bartholomew was the one who went from place to place with the bad news. He was an immortal himself, and had done that job since the pact was set up thousands of years before."

Ashe blinked, a frown creasing her brow. "He was part of the spell that made the guardsmen, or a carrier of it?"

"Part, I think. At first I thought he was lying, or perhaps I just hoped he was. When I finally accepted that what he said was horribly true, it was too late for me." Reynard looked away, looked up at the shadowed ceiling. "So I drew my sword and killed him. He wasn't going to show up on any more doorsteps, destroying families and thrusting young men into hell."

"That's why there were no more guardsmen," Ashe murmured.

"I broke the spell by destroying Bartholomew. At first I savored the thought, believing myself a secret hero, until I understood that it meant the guardsmen fought a losing battle. Until Mac, there were no more recruits to help us keep the Castle under control."

"You saved your brother's life," she said, lacing her fingers through his. "And who knows how many others who would have come after you."

"Killing a man is still a terrible thing. It doesn't matter why or how many times one does it."

Ashe lay down, putting her head on his shoulder. "I cast a spell when I was sixteen. It killed my parents and destroyed my magic, and it nearly destroyed Holly's, too. That's not what I'd meant to do, but it was where my arrogance led me." Her voice had an edge of desolation, but it was soft, like cloth handled too often.

He curled his arm around her and kissed the top of her head. "We're quite the pair."

She was quiet a moment before she murmured, "It's easier to think about it when I'm not alone."

The words tugged at his heart. He knew just what she meant. They lay like that for several minutes, Reynard drowsing in the combined warmth of the bed and her body.

Finally, she rolled over, resting on his chest and cushioning her chin on her hands. "I've never met a warlock before. As I said, I don't think there are any warlock families left."

Maybe that means the Order is dead and gone. "We are just like witches, but the magic goes through the father's side rather than the mother's."

"But you didn't know you were a warlock? I mean, witches come into their magic when they're about Eden's age. There's no mistaking what's going on."

Reynard pondered that. "It must be different for us. Now that I think back, there were signs—I've always had unusually good hearing, for instance—but nothing that couldn't be explained away. Warlock magic has to be awakened. I only ever learned what was necessary to perform my duties as a guardsman."

"Like making that rifle shoot straight?" Ashe gave him a teasing look through her lashes.

"Just so."

He felt the words drift away into the soft twilight of the room. He wasn't thinking about Bartholomew anymore. He was remembering the last time he lay wounded in Ashe's arms as the battle for the Castle raged around them. She had looked after him then, too, at once gentle and fierce. Such comfort never came to the guardsmen, and yet here he was, basking in it a second time.

He might be cursed, but he was also blessed.

Ashe stroked his forehead as he fell into a dreamless sleep.

"You saved my little girl," she whispered. "I will never, ever forget that."

Chapter 20

Early the next morning, Ashe sat across from Eden on the floor of her old bedroom in the Carver house, listening to her daughter tell the story of her kidnapping again, from start to finish. Eden had gone through it the night before in front of everyone—Mac, Alessandro, and Holly included—and then again with just Ashe holding Eden in the narrow, pink-quilted bed. Ashe was relieved that Eden was physically unhurt, but couldn't bear to think what might have happened if Reynard hadn't thought to look in the Castle.

This was the room where Eden slept when she visited her aunt. It was mostly emptied of Ashe's old things now, all the teenage paraphernalia packed away, but the yellow curtains were familiar, as was the angle of the sun on the floor. It brought back memories both sweet and painful.

Every so often, she reached across, brushing the dark curls of hair from Eden's face, unable to stop touching her. Some part of Ashe needed that physical contact to reassure herself that Eden was really safe.

"I was just scared," Eden said. "No one actually hurt me, and Miru-kai was really nice. I mean, I was so glad to see Captain Reynard, but I was okay."

Eden had told the story several times already, but each time something new emerged. Today, it was the fact that the fairy prince knew exactly how Ashe's parents had died. That wasn't impossible—a very few in the magical community had that information—but it showed how thorough the prince's network of informants was.

More important was the fact that he'd told Eden. In Ashe's book, that was a crime in itself, whether or not he'd meant to do it. It wasn't his secret to share. Still, it seemed he really had saved Eden from the vampires. The jury was still out on what he had meant to do with her himself. At the moment, according to Mac, Miru-kai was swearing up and down that he'd meant to return her to Ashe.

They'd probably never know the truth, but dark fey kidnapped children. Mac had no plans to let the prince go anytime soon.

"Do you need me to forgive you for casting that spell way back when?" Eden asked, looking up through her lashes. "Because I do, y'know. Everyone makes mistakes, sometimes bad ones. Look at Uncle Mac. He got himself turned into a demon, but we still like him, right?"

Ashe was stunned, her stomach doing a strange flip. Where had that come from? "What I did isn't something that can be forgiven. Not really."

"But I forgive you. So it happens." Eden gave her a crooked smile. "And I need you at the top of your game for when I get my powers. You're going to make sure I don't make any big mistakes."

For a moment, Ashe couldn't meet Eden's eyes. "I don't have any game anymore. I lost my powers."

Eden's smile got bigger. "That doesn't mean you're not my mom. Moms always have game."

Ashe snorted. "Tell me that after six loads of laundry. By then I'm all game-over."

"Look." Eden closed her eyes, holding out her hand, palm up. Ashe watched her with a mix of curiosity and maternal alarm, wondering what was coming. For a moment, there was only sunlight, the curve of Eden's cheek, the peaceful feeling of the house. And then it happened—a cluster of bright blue sparkles hovering over Eden's hand. Tears blurred Ashe's eyes. She recognized the conjuring spell at once. It was one of Grandma's first magical exercises.

"You're growing up," she said huskily, picking up the ball of blue sparkles and rolling it along her fingers. "Far too fast."

"Hey," said Eden, watching her mother play with the light. "I thought you said you couldn't do magic."

"I'm not a complete null," Ashe retorted. "I'm still a witch."

There were some things she would never tell Eden. Foremost among them, Ashe had never looked for a cure after the spell had taken her magic. She might have found one. After all, Holly had eventually healed.

No, Ashe didn't know whether or not her powers could be revived, and that was the way she wanted it. When her parents had died, there had been no law on the books for manslaughter by magic, so Ashe had made her own sentence. She lived deaf and blind to everything but the most basic energy fields. There were senses she used to have but didn't anymore. That was her punishment.

Witches could be immortal if they were powerful enough, but, without using a lot of powerful magic, Ashe would age and die like a human. Some witches made that choice. Grandma, for one, had chosen to join her human husband by letting time have its way. In the meantime, Ashe was going to live her mortal life well. That way, there would be opportunities to make what amends she could for her mistakes.

But there was one exception to her self-imposed sentence that she was prepared to make. Ashe blew on the blue sparkles, snuffing them out. "Give me your hand," she said to Eden.

Eden complied. Her hand was warm and soft, just starting to hint at the fine-boned elegance of a woman's. "Is this going to be slimy and disgusting?"

"Would I do something like that?" Ashe said brightly.

"I'm just saying. . . ."

Ashe closed her eyes and reached into herself, finding the emotion that bound her to Eden. She pictured it in her mind's eye, running like a constant golden flow from her heart, down her arm, and through her hand to Eden's. She focused on that flow, seeing it like a stream of living blood, cell by cell, giving health and life just as when Eden had been in her womb. Then, without willing it, she could see the flow in reverse, a paler gold but just as strong, bringing love from Eden's heart to hers.

Was it her daughter's newfound magic that let her see that second stream? Or was it a remnant of her own? At that moment, it didn't matter. It was what she needed. *Despite everything, she loves me.*

Ashe said the words that once her mother had said over her:

Child of mine, child of mine
Your love will bind your heart to mine.
I will know, I will know
Whatever steps your journeys go.
And where I go, you shall see
Where I venture constantly.
Blessed be.

Ashe felt the spell slide into place. She opened her eyes. Eden was staring at her with awe. "What was that?"

"Just a little magic. A very, very simple, small spell." Yes, she felt like apologizing, but no judge in the world could fault her for this. "This way we'll always be able to find each other if we want to. No vampire or demon or fey can keep us apart. You matter more to me than anything."

Eden grinned. "This magical GPS is going to suck when I'm sixteen."

"Hey," said Ashe. "You said you wanted me at the top of my game."

Monday, April 6, 5:30 p.m.
Carver House

Reynard woke himself by sitting bolt upright. Alessandro Caravelli stood at the foot of the bed. Reynard's scalp tightened, primal instinct telling him a vampire wake-up call was a dodgy thing.

Caravelli tossed a pile of clothes on the bedcovers. "Here's something clean to wear. The sun's been up for hours. You're watching the house now. I'm going to bed."

Reynard glanced around, disoriented. "Where is Ashe?"

"Downstairs."

"Any sign of Belenos or the demon?"

Caravelli gave an unpleasant smile that did nothing to relieve his look of exhaustion. The daytime hours were telling on him. "Nothing yet, but allies are arriving from out of town. Wolves and vampires who owe me favors. Belenos cannot escape long. He's moved himself from annoyance to threat by touching my mate's family."

Caravelli began heading for the door, but paused. "Once you have your urn, what then?"

The weight of his amber, predatory eyes reminded Reynard of a tiger he had seen in India. The difference was the tiger had seen him as mere meat. The vampire had a much more complex agenda.

"I don't know," said Reynard. "I didn't expect to survive."

Alessandro gave a slow blink. "Ashe and I have had our differences, but I would regret seeing her unhappy."

Without another word, he left the room.

Reynard stayed where he was, propped up on his elbows, feeling the cool air of the room on the skin of his chest. The simple, forgetful pleasure of falling asleep with Ashe stroking his hair seeped away with the warmth of the bedclothes.

He understood the vampire's last words. *Don't hurt her.* He'd received that same warning often enough in the past from fathers and uncles and brothers. This time, though, it was different. He had changed. Back then he sought to forget the woman who'd chosen his brother instead of him. He'd bedded his way through dozens of women out of anger and revenge. He'd squandered his substance on liquor, cards, and danger.

Now . . . now he wanted a way to stay right where he was. The man he was now loved, wanted, *needed* Ashe, with her stubborn strength and hidden vulnerabilities. Being with her was like admiring an exotic, spiny seashell, and then finding its secret entrance to the pearl-pink luster inside. He wanted to protect that private chamber, make it his.

At some point during the night they'd talked again. She'd told him about her husband, who he was and how he'd died. Her affection for Roberto de Larrocha had been plain in her voice. It made him want to be by her side even more, because Ashe Carver clearly knew how to love. It made Reynard long to have her think of him with such tenderness.

Reynard rose, showered, and dressed. He started down the long hallway outside his bedroom door, trying to guess where everyone else was in the huge house. He could smell the sea, and wondered how close they were. He longed to see the endless silver of open water again.

There was a window seat in the upstairs hallway. He paused, peering through panes of colored glass. The day was overcast, the sky heavy and grim with rain. He unlocked the casement, pushing it open. A cold blast of wind ruffled his hair, the stinging chill a welcome and familiar slap against his skin.

Below, the rich dark earth of the flower beds already showed spatters of rain. Tulips tossed on their stems, the bright reds and yellows luminescent in the muted light. Here and there, hellhounds stood beneath the trees, dark shapes in the shadows. There must be a dozen. No one was taking any chances.

It was late, nearly dusk. Reynard had more than slept around the clock. No wonder Alessandro had looked so tired. The rest had done him good, though. Whatever Holly and her grandmother had given him made him feel almost back to normal.

He wondered how long it would last.

Reynard pulled the casement shut, locking it. The house settled, like a bird ruffling its feathers. He could believe it was sentient.

What would he do once he found his urn? He would survive, but could he bear going back to the Castle? In the course of time, everything he had felt and done in the last few days would fade to shopworn memories. Piece by piece, the incredible gifts of hunger and thirst, lust and true joy, would fall away, leaving a numb eternity behind. He was doomed and damned.

A jittering panic wrenched his gut. When would he have to face the choice between duty and freedom, the Castle or death?

A sudden, visceral memory twisted inside him. The clanging of the old cell doors. Bargaining, bullying, pleading with the warlords to keep peace in a place where the guardsmen were outnumbered a hundred, maybe two hundred, to one. His second in command, Bran, losing his wits and taking to flaying the inmates who crossed him, pinning up the hides like trophies on his cell wall.

Discipline had kept the despair at bay. Reynard had written logs every day, copious records of incidents, rosters, patrols, and supplies. Filling page after page with trivia no soul would ever read. *Today, Guardsman Phillips found a box of firearms in the outer chambers. Today, a sighting of the griffin on level three.* In the end, who really cared what Phillips did or what they saw? The events were all forgotten in the darkness of the Castle, along with the men who witnessed them.

All that pride—the tidy logs, the neat uniform, the refusal to give in to chaos—it was all whistling in the dark. Mac had made things better, but too late for Reynard. He hadn't broken, but imprisonment had worn him to the bone.

He took a long breath, then another, calming himself until the sudden chill of dread left his body. *What if I simply refused to go back? Two hundred and fifty years of service is enough.*

There had to be a better answer.

Reynard rose from the window seat and found the stairs. Moving through the warm, pleasant house quickly lulled him into a sense of borrowed peace. His nose led him to the kitchen and he stood in the doorway for a moment, enjoying the scene. Holly was making soup; Eden was at the table with her schoolbooks. Ashe was reading a cookbook with a perplexed frown.

"How many cupcakes are you supposed to take to the school bake sale?" Ashe asked her daughter.

"Twenty-four," Eden said without looking up from her schoolbook. "With pink icing."

"That's a double batch," said Holly. "That's a lot of ingredients."

"Mrs. Flammand specified pink icing?" Ashe said skeptically. "Are you sure those aren't your specifications?"

Eden looked mutinous. "With chocolate sprinkles."

"I don't think we have chocolate sprinkles," Holly put in, stirring the soup. "We have food coloring, though. You sure you don't want me to do the baking, Ashe?"

"I can fight a demon. Surely I can make cupcakes."

"I dunno," teased Holly. "Those little paper cups can be tricky."

"I'm tougher than that." Ashe got out of the chair and took the cookbook to the kitchen counter. "Whoever heard of asking parents to bake on short notice? What is this, like a command performance or something?"

"Welcome to the dictatorship of the parental fund-raiser," Holly said dryly. "I've heard all about it from the moms in the baby clinic."

"Janie's mom called Mrs. Flammand the cupcake Nazi," Eden piped up.

Holly snorted. "Better watch our step, then. We can send one of the hellhounds for sprinkles."

Reynard watched and listened with a happy feeling he'd forgotten. Bantering women, the smell of good food, domestic bustle. This was something he'd never take for granted again.

"The soup smells wonderful," Reynard said.

"Hi!" Ashe and Holly said in chorus. They looked at each other, a bit embarrassed.

"It's not soup," said Holly. "It's a tracking spell for the demon. We've given up trying to be subtle."

"By now it knows we're on its trail," Ashe said. "It has to."

He sat down opposite Eden and looked at her book. It was upside down to him, but he knew what it was right away. "You're studying the stars?"

"For science." Eden took a sip from her glass of sticky brown milk—chocolate milk, he thought she'd called it. He'd have to try it when he got the chance.

"You don't have to do homework today if you don't want to," said Ashe.

"It's okay," said Eden. "I kind of feel like I should be good for a couple of days."

Ashe looked at her daughter with concern. "I'm not complaining, but are you sure you're feeling okay?"

The girl shrugged. "You said I was grounded until I was forty for running away again. I thought maybe I should start sucking up."

Reynard exchanged an amused glance with Ashe. "Currying favor usually works better if you at least pretend to be sincere."

"I am sincere," Eden said blithely. "Mom rocks."

Ashe gave an exaggerated shrug.

"When this is all over, are you going back to the

Castle?" Eden asked Reynard, coming with a child's instincts to the one topic he didn't wish to discuss. Which apparently everyone else did, starting with Caravelli.

"Why do you ask?"

She gave him a wary look. "Is it *all* really horrible there?"

Yes. He had to answer this one carefully. He didn't want to frighten the girl. "There are some wonderful people there. Your uncle Mac, for one. Lore and his hellhounds lived there until a little while ago."

"I like the hellhounds. They play fetch."

Reynard's mind boggled a moment. "Good for them."

"Do they have other animals in the Castle? I didn't see any."

"Yes. Parts of it are a bit like a zoological garden." *A bizarre, nightmarish one.* "Your mother and I saw a rabbit there the other day."

"Are the animals in cages?"

"Not all of them."

"Don't they eat each other?"

"No. The Castle makes it so no one's hungry or thirsty. You weren't there long enough to notice that."

"You don't ever eat in there?"

How many questions can she ask in under a minute? "Never ever. At least not the old-timers, like me."

"That sucks. What about Choco-puff cookies?"

"Fortune is a harsh mistress."

She made a face. "You're laughing at me."

"A little."

"I'm just a kid."

"Don't underestimate how wonderful that is to an old soldier like me."

She wrinkled her nose. "You're not old. Grandma's old."

"I am, too. I've lived a long time and traveled a great many places."

"You talk like you're from England."

"I was. I've been other places, too. Flanders. Italy. Germany. India."

"India? Did you see elephants?"

"Of course. And a few lions and tigers as well."

"And bears?" Eden's eyes twinkled.

"No bears," he said, thinking that now she was laughing at him, though he couldn't figure out why.

She pushed a bag of cookies his way. "Have a Chocopuff."

He took one and bit into it. It was disgustingly sweet. He ate it anyway.

"Why did you go to India?" she asked around a mouthful of chocolate.

"The king sent me. And I wanted to get away from home for a while." From his father. From Elizabeth. From the fact that she had borne his brother a son. Oddly, the memory didn't burn the way it used to anymore.

Eden watched him intently, the way children do. "Did you get homesick?"

"Yes, but I watched the night sky, like in your book there. When you travel the world, somehow knowing the people at home see what you see in the sky helps a lot. And it helps you sail your boat home again."

"You can find your way with them? Could I find Spain with the stars?"

"Stars are like a map. You can find your way anywhere if you know them well enough."

"Are there stars in the Castle? I didn't see any stars."

"No. There are no stars." *There is no connection to anyone else there. You are truly alone.*

Eden looked glumly at the book. "I can't remember this map, and we have to name the stars on a test."

Reynard tilted the book to see it better. It was a map of the night sky, with lines and dots marking the major constellations. He looked at the window over the kitchen sink. It was just starting to grow dark. Not dark enough to teach her the way he had learned, from simply looking at the sky with his tutor.

He thought for a moment. "Sometimes it helps to remember them by the story they tell. Do you know your Greek legends?"

Eden wrinkled her nose. "Like gods and goddesses?"

"They play a part." And he started to tell her the stories he knew of Hercules' lion, of the twins Castor and Pollux, and Orion the Hunter, pointing to each of the players where they danced in the night sky.

Ashe listened with half an ear as she worked, measuring flour and trying to double the recipe without miscounting. Reynard's voice was soft, his stories steeped in the elegance and heroism of another time. She didn't know about Eden, but she wasn't going to forget a word of his tale.

But when the story ended, her mind drifted. It had been a busy day, an urgent search through books with Holly and Grandma to find the perfect demon locator spell, dozens of phone calls in search of news of demons or vampires, and keeping an eye on Eden and Reynard to make sure they were all right. She'd tried contacting her hacker friend again to see what other properties the demon might have purchased. No answer. She wasn't worried—every so often he seemed to fall off the planet only to reappear days later, but it was a bad time to pull one of his vanishing acts. Then she'd got Mac on the phone to see what he'd learned from questioning Mirukai. Even if she hadn't been banging on doors, the last hour was the first reprieve from the search for the urn, Belenos, or the demon.

One other thing had happened. Earlier that afternoon, Brent Hashimoto, the lawyer who was presumably not a demon-possessed nut job, had phoned with a proposal for her. Roberto's family wanted to spend the holidays with Eden. That meant summer vacation and Christmas in Spain. In return, they'd back off about Ashe's suitability as a parent. As Hashimoto said, their real concern was losing touch with their only grandchild.

That gave her something to think about. Ashe agreed

that Eden should have a relationship with her grand-parents. The sticking point for her was, as always, safety issues. As long as they agreed to work through those, she was willing to talk. Hashimoto was smart: Confront-ing Ashe head-on only made her hostile. Appealing to her reason engaged her. Acknowledging that nothing came before Eden's well-being had her willing to play ball.

Perhaps it was possible that at least something in her life could be settled without a knock-down, drag-out fight? It would be nice to think it was possible.

Eventually, she started spooning chocolate batter into paper-lined muffin tins. They'd had just enough eggs. Ashe's mood was good. Cupcakes seemed easy after the last few days. Holly's spell was bubbling. Reynard was looking better. Eden was safe and sound.

Eventually, finished with his astronomy lesson, Rey-nard came to lean against the counter. Something in his expression reminded her of a stray cat confident of a handout.

"Wicked with a stake, and she cooks, too."

"Don't mock the woman holding the food."

He looked from her to the bowl as if both were filled with tasty goodness. Ashe ducked her face away before she blushed or started to giggle. Even leather-clad ac-tion babes got giddy with relief some days. The memory of Reynard naked wasn't helping her concentration, ei-ther. If lust could be stirred into a recipe, these cupcakes were going to be rising high on pure desire.

She picked up the baking pans and slid them into the oven, then set the timer and dumped the dirty bowl in the sink, where Holly was washing dishes. "There's one more for ya, Hol."

Holly stuck out her tongue, but her eyes were full of mischief.

"Hey, Eden," Ashe said. "We're going to eat supper in a little while. Why don't you take a break and put your books away for now?"

"Put them in my office," suggested Holly. "Move the

cat off the desk if you want to play on the computer. He likes to sleep there."

Eden slipped off the chair, gathered her books, and wandered off. Ashe watched her go, wondering if her daughter really was that calm after her adventure with Belenos and the fairy prince, or if it simply hadn't hit home yet.

The phone rang before Ashe could pursue that thought. She picked up the cordless handset. "Hello?"

"I thought I might find you at this number."

Belenos. She turned her back to the others and walked into the living room, not wanting them to see what must have been horror on her face. From there she could see out the front window. The streetlights flickered on, pools of yellow light backlit by an indigo sky. It was still a half hour to full dark.

"Aren't all good little vampires still asleep?" She dropped her voice and tried to add a pinch of menace. *Does he know this address?* The house was secure, but they still had to come and go.

"I am neither good nor little. However, I did think congratulations on retrieving your daughter would be appropriate. Of course, it would not have gone so well for you if that meddling fairy hadn't turned up. We missed our opportunity."

For what? For me to fall at your feet? Ashe glared at the handset a moment. It wasn't like Reynard's departure would leave a job vacancy she'd have to fill. In fact, she was trying hard not to think about post-Reynard at all. The notion of it left her empty, like a nut shelled to find only cobwebs inside, the meat long shriveled away. "I'm not having this conversation with you, Red. Take your sicko fantasies and go home."

He laughed, low but not menacing. He sounded genuinely amused, and that pissed her off even more.

She heard Holly and Reynard leave the kitchen, retreating to the library at the back of the house. Reynard was asking something about the Order; Holly was of-

fering to look something up in one of her books. Ashe
suddenly felt very alone.

"Aren't you going to ask why I'm calling?"

"No. I doubt you have anything interesting to say."

Belenos sighed against the mouthpiece of the phone.
The sound of rushing air was so intimate, she could have
sworn it brushed her cheek. "You mistake me for someone who gives up easily."

"Maybe I mistake you for someone with half a brain.
You might be able to sell this trip as an effort to fix a
business deal gone bad, y'know, with your thief turning
traitor and all that. But if you keep pissing people off,
you're declaring war on the local vamp queen. You pull
that, and everybody loses."

"Perhaps we are already at war," Belenos said softly.
"I will protect you, if you let me. I will even protect those
you love, if you ask."

Ashe felt the muscles down the back of her neck
tense. "What are you talking about?"

"Have you forgotten the assassin you killed? I certainly didn't send him. So who wants you dead? Have
they given up? Perhaps I have an answer for you."

Ashe opened her mouth to speak, but breath wouldn't
come. The assassin. She hadn't forgotten about him, but
too much had happened to dwell on a threat that wasn't
in her face right that moment.

"I'll be at your mother's grave in an hour."

The phone beeped, and then the sound of a dial tone
filled her ear. Ashe hit the disconnect button.

"Damn it!" She fell into a chair. At some time during the call, the light in the room had turned the corner
from dim to dark.

A dark that had been relatively inert a few moments
ago. Now it crawled with suspicions. *What the hell kind
of a game is Belenos playing?* Was this an elaborate
setup to make her grovel to him for protection? Or was
he telling the truth? Was there another killer with her
name on a contract?

Nah, it was a transparent trap, and he was too arrogant to think she'd refuse to come.

It was tempting to grab her stakes and go. She needed something to fight, not these vague, faceless enemies. Not a voice on the phone. Not a figure in a dream. A sniper on a hill. Tension clawed her shoulder muscles, sending the first flickering lights of a bad headache arcing through the darkness.

Time passed. Ashe wasn't sure how many minutes she sat there, turning over everything that had happened since the phouka had attacked in the gardens. There was a connection, perhaps something fairly obvious, that she was missing.

She heard Alessandro leave, start the T-bird, and drive away. He was going to pick up some of his friends from the airport shuttle. The supernatural community at large had taken an interest in Fairview's situation and was starting to mobilize.

It was about bloody time.

Ashe jammed her fingers in her hair. Bunny. Demon. Vampire. Fairy prince. Yes, Miru-kai was a possibility. Which one wanted her dead the most?

What was she going to do about Eden? There had been one horrible night, back in Spain, when Ashe had awakened to find a vampire creeping down the hall toward Eden's pink-and-white bedroom. She'd killed it, of course. She had cried afterward, suddenly and explosively. Ashe had not truly known fear before that night. The next week, she began looking at boarding schools. What was she going to do this time? Send Eden away now, or risk waiting?

She heard Holly's slippers scuffing on the kitchen floor. "What's burning?"

Shit.

Chapter 21

A she walked through the graveyard, part of her brain worrying about where she could buy two dozen chocolate cupcakes on a Monday night because she'd been so wrapped up in the call, she hadn't heard the oven timer. Holly had pulled two pans of charcoal briquettes from the oven, the pink crinkle cups lightly smoking. *How late does Safeway stay open?*

The rest of her was in slayer mode, alert to the rustling night. She could hear the ocean to the south, just at the bottom of the cliff. The slow roll of waves on the shore would cover a lot of stealthy sounds. Ashe strained her ears, trying to hear past the water and the wind in the trees.

Belenos and no doubt his underlings were somewhere nearby. She could feel the tingle of vampire energy dancing on her skin.

She hadn't come alone. Reynard and the hounds had spread out through the cemetery, keeping watch. The thought eased the pinch of tension in her neck just a little. Once upon a time, she would have been happy to walk into a trap just to prove she could beat it. Not anymore. She had too much to lose.

She wasn't just a slayer. Ashe had known that since she came back to Fairview, but in the last few days she'd come to understand that fact on an emotional level. It was more than having an overfilled date book.

She was a mom with cupcake problems, a lover with someone to look after. She had a job—fortunately, the library had called her that morning to say she was forgiven for getting vampire all over the carpet—and she was part of her family and community as a whole. Grandma had been right: It was time to embrace all the roles she played. To appreciate approaching life with the laundry basket in one hand and a stake in the other.

Whatever. She'd have to work on that metaphor. The bottom line was that she felt the chaos all those job titles implied, but it made her somehow complete. She wasn't just a finely crafted weapon. She was a person who mattered to other people.

That gave her strength. She picked up the pace of her stride. It was a beautiful night for a hunt. Especially when she was after the vampire who'd dared to touch her daughter.

Colt in one hand, she followed the path that led around a stand of trees and approached her parents' graves. The ocean was louder here, the crash of water on rocks an insistent exclamation.

She stopped.

Belenos was already waiting. Instead of a ball of light, this time he'd brought a long torch. It thrust from the soft loam beneath a trio of huge cedars. Ashe wondered if he'd swiped the torch from the Castle.

The oblique light dazzled on the baubles in his Titian hair, molten gold caught in a flood of silky fire. He was dressed for travel: Windbreaker, twill pants, and baggy cashmere sweater. The sight of him put Ashe's every muscle on alert. He was pretty, but then, so was a cobra.

She mentally measured the distance between them,

making sure there was a healthy patch of ground between her flesh and his fangs.

"Thank you for seeing me," he said. "I notice you brought your guardsman along. Does he object to waiting on the sidelines?"

"He knows there are some things a mother has to do."

"Well, I brought friends to keep him and his dogs busy while we chat."

Ashe felt a prickle of anxiety, but she knew she didn't have to worry about Reynard. He'd proved to her he could look after himself.

"Do you plan to kill me?" Belenos asked, his voice like hot satin.

She felt the pull of it, but shook it off. This wasn't a dream now, where she could be so easily seduced. "I'm sure as hell going to teach you a lesson."

"Really?" he said, pulling something from his pocket.

"No sudden moves, Red." Ashe raised the Colt. "Silver bullets. They'll sting for sure." Her tone said they'd do a whole lot more.

Slowly, he raised the object in his hand. "Chocolate bunny?"

Ashe narrowed her eyes. "I suddenly find myself on a diet."

"Bad associations?"

"Was it you who tried to shoot me?"

He was as still as a wax figure, finely sculpted and utterly dead. "I did not send the assassin, my lovely huntress. I want you very much alive."

"Then why the rabbit theme? The stuffed toy, now this?"

Belenos returned the candy to his pocket. The breeze rippled the sleeve of his Windbreaker. "Because it is a symbol of threat and a reminder of your unknown enemy. If it frightens you a little, that's useful to me. But let me assure you someone else hired that goblin to release the phouka."

"Why?"

"To draw you out. You're the great monster scourge. What better way to lay a trap than by giving you a great monster to chase?"

Ashe digested that a moment. Somewhere in the darkness, one of the hounds gave a deep, bell-like howl.

Belenos spread his hands. "Don't you see? You're the famous Ashe Carver, a witch who kills with a stake instead of a spell for the pure, bloody thrill of thrusting through flesh and bone. Your reputation has little monsterlings shaking in their beds. Not only can you take out a clan of vampires single-handed, but everyone believes that you are as magically gifted your sister. She destroyed a demon queen and bore a vampire's child. Who can allow such power to roam unchecked?"

Obviously, Belenos couldn't. Not without wanting it for himself.

"But it's not true. I don't have any magical ability to speak of."

"Most people don't know that. You've made no effort to contradict the rumors." He gave a cold smile. "It is only natural that a freshly released demon would do his best to remove a threat like you from his new territory."

"Damn."

The smile fell into a twist of disgust. "Of course, my double-crossing thief was too cowardly to face you himself. I understand he got that lawyer of his to make the arrangements. Bannerman has contacts in the supernatural community who hired both the goblin and the assassin."

"Huh." Ashe tightened the grip on the Colt, feeling oddly blank. Her ex-lawyer had paid good money to end her life, and had actually been a bit creative, with the phouka and all. "Well, thanks for the heads-up. The lawyer's already on my to-do list, but that kicks up the urgency a notch."

She'd be outraged later, but right now her mind was

in overdrive. She wondered whether Holly had been included in the assassin's contract, and if Bannerman had any other hit men on his speed dial.

Belenos gave something between a nod and a bow. "As I said, it is in my best interests for you to remain alive. At least for the time being."

Ashe exhaled slowly, forcing herself to be just as calm as the vampire appeared. She didn't trust him in the role of helpful informant. Logic said he was luring her to drop her guard.

That didn't mean she wouldn't pump him for information. "One thing I don't understand. The assassin chose to die rather than talk. Bannerman's just not that scary."

"Have you met Mr. Yarndice in his demonic form?"

Ashe remembered the thing in the bookshop. "Got it."

Another howl curled upward to the cloud-shrouded moon. A human cry of rage followed. Ashe forced herself to stay focused on the vampire. Forced herself to trust in her partner.

Belenos's lips moved in a smile that didn't touch the rest of his face. Utterly mechanical. Utterly horrific. "Now perhaps we can get down to discussing your terms of surrender?"

Rage zinged through her. "The only thing getting surrendered here is the Castle key you've got. Then you're getting on a plane back east with a magically binding oath that you'll never, ever come back."

"Is that so?" He took a step forward, which made her take a step back.

"The only reason I haven't splattered your brains all over these gravestones is because killing a king means war. War between the vampire kingdoms would make bad headlines."

He shifted his weight, obviously preparing to move closer. "So hostile. So outraged. It thrills me."

Her stomach ached with tension. He was going to do

this the hard way. With her left hand, she pulled a stake out of her thigh pocket. "Let me make this simple. Stay away from my child."

"I shall if you come to me willingly," he said in a soft voice. In the flickering light of the torch, he looked like an old master's painting, his features outlined by stark shadow. "You belong to the dead. I would still have you as my queen. You are"—he paused—"magnificent."

Ashe felt her eyes widen as she struggled not to snort out a laugh. "Thanks. I'm over the whole broody thing. I'm thinking pastel bike leathers."

Belenos raised a hand, as if beckoning. "Come now; would you turn your back on your essential nature? You belong with the dark."

Ashe felt his power crawl over her like some chitinous beast. She thought she'd brushed aside his attempt at controlling her. Now she realized he'd been holding back. Belenos was old. A king of vampires. He might be Fruit Loops crazy, but he was no lightweight. She closed her eyes, because to meet his gaze would be a terrible mistake. Vamps, if they were good enough, could hypnotize as easily as they breathed.

Perhaps that was what he'd been waiting for. She could feel rather than hear him drawing closer. He seemed to absorb the energy from the air around him, the weight of his magic blotting out the life in the night wind. She swayed slightly from keeping her eyes closed, but trusted her senses to tell her exactly how close he was.

Any slayer worth her salt knew how to fight blind.

He was waiting for an answer, so she gave one. "I liked the dark because it hid the stains on my soul. But now I'm coming to accept that people forgive my past. It's spring. I'm in love, and with a living guy to boot."

"Ticktock. Reynard still does not have his soul."

Ashe concentrated on a cramp that was forming from holding the gun so still. Pain would help her keep her focus. "Yeah, the urn's still missing. Which means you don't have your supernatural Viagra."

"Perhaps we don't need it. I could teach you to love me. You could Choose me."

"And what drugs are you on?"

He was close now, drawing closer. A predator ready to pounce. "Perhaps I could heal your powers. You could be the witch you once were."

It was the one thing he should never have said.

Ashe opened her eyes. He was mere feet away, deadly close. She curled her lip. "You're such a waste of space."

Ashe pulled the trigger.

Belenos flew back, arms splayed in a graceful arc. He was a large male. The force of the bullet didn't take him too far, but he toppled with a crash worthy of one of the great cedars sheltering the graves. A circle of dark blood bloomed on his chest, black in the torchlight.

Ashe switched weapons, now grasping the stake in her right hand, the gun in her left. One bullet wouldn't kill a vampire this old, unless it ripped through his spine. She was counting on it knocking him cold for a good eight hours.

She stood before the fallen vampire, their boots nearly touching. "By the way, I'm not an idiot. My brother-in-law brought along two dozen of his closest friends to mop up your henchmen. The fun and games are over, Red."

Eight hours should be long enough for the local vamps to take the Eastern vamps to Queen Omara. The monarch of the Northwestern territories could punish Belenos in ways no witch or mortal could dream of, and all within the letter of the vampire laws.

She wished she could watch.

Ashe knelt over Belenos, pressing the point of the stake over his heart. He looked like he was out cold, his hair strewn around him like an exotic mane, but she wasn't taking any chances.

The bullet hole was a little to the right, just where she'd wanted it. Not quite a killing shot. Ashe could smell raw meat. That would be where the custom silver-coated slug had torn its way out his back, making a big mess along the way. Cruel, but if you tangled with a vampire like Belenos, you had to mean business.

She heard footsteps, and recognized Reynard's tread.

"I've got him," she said. "What about the others?"

"They've been dealt with. Do you want me to search for the key?"

"Please."

Reynard knelt on the other side of the fallen vampire.

"Do you think others vampires will show up, wanting children?" she asked.

"According to Caravelli, Queen Omara will make it clear what a bad idea that would be."

"Good."

He began fishing in the vampire's pants pockets, and pulled out a small gold disk. It bore a six-pointed sun. Their gazes locked, Reynard's eyes grim, as he gave it to her. "Are you all right?"

"Sure. I just did what any mother in my place would have done."

Early the next morning, Ashe's hacker contact finally called back, but only to report that he had no leads on any properties recently purchased by Anthony Yarndice. He'd tried every search known to hackerdom and then some. Bannerman, however, seemed to be constantly buying estates and selling them at a profit. He gave Ashe three addresses the lawyer had purchased in the last six weeks.

Ashe had just gotten out of the shower. Reynard was still in the bathroom, discovering the joys of a massaging showerhead. "Yeah, okay," she said into the phone, trying to write and adjust the towel wrapped around her hair at the same time. "Thanks, bud."

She wrote down the last address and hung up. *Bingo!* Ashe did a victory dance, losing the towel in the process.

Reynard appeared in the bedroom doorway and watched the performance with speculative interest.

"What is it?"

"A hit! A palpable hit!"

Reynard raised an eyebrow.

Ashe waved the notepaper with the addresses. "Bannerman bought three properties. One location corresponds with the demon-tracking spell Holly cooked up last night. We have Tony's new location."

Reynard's eyes turned a cold silver. "Where?"

"North Central Shopping Mall. Where you met me at the library."

Reynard picked up Ashe's towel and handed it back to her. "Well, my dear, then let's go *check it out.*"

"Har, har," she said. "I hate librarian jokes. You know that, right?"

He gave her a look that mixed mischief and affection. "Why else would I make one?"

Chapter 22

Since Holly was the only one among them who'd actually bagged a demon, she agreed to meet them at the mall as soon as Grandma arrived to watch the kids. While Ashe was making those arrangements, Reynard called the hellhound guard post outside the Castle door and reported that the errant demon had possibly been found. Mac and the other guardsmen should be on standby.

Those errands done, Ashe and Reynard took the Ducati, roaring through the streets with the abandon of teenagers on spring break. She could feel his excitement in the play of his body behind her, in the tingle of his power dancing along her skin. It was a Tuesday morning and traffic was light. They sped past empty playgrounds, silent houses, and schools with throngs of children standing outside the doors. Coffee shops had tables out on the sidewalk, patrons reading the paper and sunning themselves. Except for the task at hand, it was a beautiful morning.

Hellspawn had a way of souring the mood.

Ashe tried to remember everything she knew about

demons. There were many different kinds—the term "demon" was about as specific as "bug." Some were born. Hellhounds were a kind of half demon. Born demons tended to be fairly sane and law-abiding. Others were parasites that infected human hosts. Most of those demons were far more powerful and very bad news. Fortunately, they were rare.

Ashe had killed a few lesser demons, but none bigger than a bread box. The big guys had to be banished, and that took magic powers. The Carver witches had performed a banishing spell exactly twice. It had been the same soul-eater demon both times. Ashe's ancestor Elaine Carver had died the first time they'd booted it out of Fairview. The second time, Holly had killed the demon and ripped open the doorway to the Castle. Ashe hadn't been present at that battle, but she'd heard it took a whole lot of magic to get the job done. Holly had pulled earth magic from a nexus of ley lines that converged right where the battle was being fought. Where that had been an ocean of power, the area around the mall was a trickle. Plus, Holly's powers were just coming back online. They couldn't count on her providing that boatload of power. The best they could hope for was, like, a kiddie pool's worth. Or a salad bowl. Or a butter dish. Even if a collector demon wasn't the badass that the soul eater had been, how the hell were they going to get rid of it?

They pulled up to a stoplight. It was only chance that made her glance down almost at the same time that Reynard tapped her shoulder and pointed at the brand-new BMW 5 Series sedan next to them. Ashe recognized the driver. *Bannerman.* A hot wave of dislike itched its way across her skin. Was he out and about doing business for Tony? Were they picking out curtains for more demon hidey-holes?

At that moment, the lawyer looked up. Even through the tinted glass of the car window, she could see him pale as he figured out who was glaring into his passenger window. His expression said he was terrified of Ashe.

Gratifying, but . . . Sure, she'd roughed him up a bit, but not enough to explain the sudden tears in his eyes. That made her plain curious. Had something new happened?

Suddenly the silver BMW swerved out of its lane, moving to the right to slide into the turning lane that led to the highway. An evasive maneuver, if there ever was one. That doubled Ashe's curiosity. Did Bannerman somehow know that she knew he'd hired the assassin to kill her?

The moment he began to pick up speed, the light changed. Ashe cut across two lanes of traffic before the other drivers could react. Like a shot, she was after the lawyer, Reynard letting out a whoop as the Ducati's engine opened up with a snarl.

The gorgeous BMW had plenty of horses of its own, and Bannerman had a head start. They were on the four-lane stretch of road that would eventually head to the ferries. Ashe was cautious about weaving around cars, especially with a passenger, but she pulled past the pickup in front of her to get a better visual of Bannerman's car. The pickup honked, but it was mere background noise. She had the roar of the engine in her head, the vibration between her thighs, and a hot and happy male pressed against her back. She was born for moments like this. Her heart seemed to beat in her throat, straining like a horse fighting its bit.

Bannerman was two cars ahead now, and signaling to pass a third. They swept beneath an overpass, the heavy band of shadow a sudden coolness on her face. The BMW changed lanes, sped up. Ashe guided the Ducati into the space between two lanes and let it rip. She felt Reynard's hands tighten around her waist.

In twenty seconds, she slid into a space only a car length behind her quarry. She saw Bannerman looking in the rearview, squirming, rubbernecking from side to side for an escape.

Why was he so afraid? It wasn't like she had punched him out or anything.

He took a risky dodge into the left lane. In another second, he turned, flooring it before three lanes of southbound traffic could T-bone his beautiful car. Ashe swore, but more for form's sake. She simply pulled an illegal Uey at the next break in the meridian.

"Bloody hell, woman!" Reynard roared in her ear.

"Suck it up; we've almost got him."

Okay, so that was a little optimistic. By the time Ashe reached the turnoff, she saw the BMW silhouetted against the bright April sky. Bannerman was heading southeast on one of the narrow roads that led through the maze of hobby farms north of Fairview. If they lost him in that neck of the woods, the trail would grow cold fast.

There was nothing but empty field between her and Bannerman's car, but the winter rains had turned the ground into a muddy slough. She found herself slowing to compensate for dirt and gravel left behind by farm vehicles crossing from field to road. Bannerman was slowing as well, bumps in the road threatening to bottom out the expensive car. The lawyer was more cautious than he needed to be, but that was fine with Ashe. She was gaining on her timid prey.

The BMW crested a hill and disappeared over the other side. Ashe did the same. Pulled up behind Bannerman. Pulled alongside him. She glanced over, saw the mix of fury and fear in his eyes.

As the hill began to descend, she took a risk and put on the speed. The Ducati swooped ahead, Ashe dodging most hazards but gambling with her control when the road bumped too hard. A half mile ahead, the road forked. That was all the space Ashe had to stop Bannerman. When she had gained just enough distance, she slowed the bike, turning it to block both lanes. Tires chewed the pavement as she slowed to a stop. A plume of dirt and dust kicked up.

Reynard jumped off, grabbing his helmet off his head. He looked ashen, but he ran to put himself between Ashe and the oncoming car, drawing his Smith & Wesson as he went.

"Whoa! Stop!" Ashe yelled, steps behind him.

For a moment, she thought they'd both be a hood ornament. Only at the last second did Bannerman stand on the brakes, bringing the vehicle to a lurching halt.

Ashe stood very still, partly to show no fear, partly because she thought her knees would collapse.

The passenger door flew open and Bannerman shot out in a panicked sprint toward the main highway.

You've got to be kidding.

Reynard set his helmet on the bike. "Shall we go wish Mr. Bannerman a good morning?"

Ashe was right behind him. "Oh, yeah, I'm looking forward to this."

Reynard caught up to him in a burst of guardsman superspeed. He grabbed the lawyer by one arm, dragging him back before he'd gone a hundred feet. Reynard pinned him against the shiny BMW.

Despite the cool spring air, Bannerman was sweating, his hair limp against his skull. The skin under his eyes looked puffy and dull. He seemed to have aged ten years since Ashe had met him only a few weeks ago.

The lawyer was apparently getting what he deserved.

"Going somewhere in a hurry?" Ashe asked.

"Let go of me!" Bannerman snapped, but his eyes were begging.

What does he think we're going to do? Not that she couldn't think of a few things.

Ashe tried to guess what Bannerman was seeing. She and Reynard were both dressed for action in dark leathers, denim, and sunglasses. They probably looked like rejects from a metal band. Reynard took his hand off the lawyer's arm, but stood close enough so the man still couldn't move.

Ashe folded her arms, a bit of a trick in a tight leather jacket. "So how is good old Tony this morning?"

"Don't ask me about him. I can't talk about him."

"Yeah, right. The compulsion."

The skin around Bannerman's eyes puckered. "It hurts."

Reynard nodded. "Some silencing spells work through pain."

"Is that why you ran just now? Because you were afraid we'd make you talk?"

Bannerman bobbed his head once, his face going gray. Sweat shone on his upper lip.

"Damn." Ashe hated this. Bannerman was a creep and had earned a lot of payback, but she wasn't into torture.

"Is the demon at the North Central Shopping Mall?" Reynard asked. "Yes or no?"

"Yes." The lawyer writhed as if something had pierced him through.

Reynard leaned closer, his expression showing regret, but neither did he shy away from the task at hand. "Has he purchased other places?"

"Not yet."

So the two other addresses the hacker had given them were Bannerman's own investments and not for Tony. Good to know.

"Are you in the process of arranging such a purchase for the demon?" Reynard asked.

"Yes." Bannerman gasped.

"How many?"

Bannerman twisted and fell to his hands and knees, retching. Ashe jumped back before he puked on her boots. The sound made her mouth water in sick sympathy.

The lawyer held up three fingers.

The demon was trying to buy three other places.

Bannerman crawled to his feet, wiping his mouth with a handkerchief. Reynard hauled him up until he could lean on the car. Bannerman's head fell forward. When he lifted it slowly, Ashe could read the exhaustion in every line of his body.

"It seemed simple at first," the lawyer said. "He seemed normal, even nice. He just wanted a bookstore. I was settling the Cowan estate. I thought, why not? But then things changed." Bannerman's face twitched, but he had the look of a man gone beyond pain to numb surrender.

"How?"

"It's like he was part human when he first came into the office. I couldn't even tell he was a demon at first. Now he's all demon, all the time."

"How is he choosing his properties?" Reynard asked. "Are there certain strategic locations he's after?"

"I don't know. He just wanders around town. Once he settles on a place he likes, it's up to me to convince the owner to sell. And up to me to pay for it." Bannerman hung his head as if he'd lost the strength to lift it. His eyes were screwed shut. "You've got to stop him. I can't."

It dawned on Ashe that Bannerman had just volunteered information, despite the pain. She flashed back to her first interview with the lawyer, when his office had started dripping slime. In a roundabout way, he had asked her to save him from Tony then. He still wanted her to save him now.

"And if the owner declines to sell?" Reynard asked.

Bannerman shook his head. "I don't want to know."

Ashe felt another layer of anger spreading over her soul. "I am so going to ice this hellspawn."

Reynard stepped back from Bannerman and reached into the car. When he straightened, he had a file in his hand. "Does this give the particulars of the sales?"

Bannerman opened his eyes and nodded.

Ashe took the file and glanced at the papers. She was no lawyer, but it looked as if every last detail of the transactions was documented there. She couldn't stifle a grin. "You're not getting a retainer, are you?"

Straightening, the lawyer returned a look meant to boil flesh from the bone, suddenly the Bannerman she'd first met. "I could still file for assault, you know."

"But you won't. You need us to save your skinny ass."

"You violent, arrogant . . ."

"I wouldn't throw stones, bud. You're the one who hired someone to kill me, right?" Ashe shot back.

"You can't prove that!" But Bannerman turned the color of bread dough, his eyes going wide. "As far as a court's concerned, that's pure speculation." He was panting, his short, shallow breaths wheezing painfully.

Ashe let her disgust show. "Is that the demon talking, or just your own cover-your-ass legal bluster? Grab a brain. You just finished saying you needed us."

Reynard peered over the top of his sunglasses, flagrantly unimpressed. "Shall I blow his head off for you, my dear?" Despite the breezy tone, Reynard's fingers tightened on the Smith & Wesson.

Ashe put a hand on his arm, reluctantly letting go of her anger. "As much as I hate to admit it, he was under compulsion."

"Yes." Bannerman nodded feverishly. "I wasn't responsible for anything."

"Except greed and stupidity," Reynard replied in an icy tone, raising the gun with a casual air that said he'd have no qualms about pulling the trigger.

"No," Bannerman said, flailing against the car in his terror. "Oh, God, no, I beg you!"

Reynard turned to Ashe. "It's up to you. He'll be a threat at least until the demon is banished."

Ashe gritted her teeth in frustration. It was tempting to let Reynard do it. Neat, clean, quick, and final. But illegal. Bannerman wasn't a monster. He was a demon's thrall. If they could get rid of Tony, the lawyer would most likely revert to being ordinary scum instead of homicidal, hit man–hiring scum. She could throw him that lifeline, at least—if not for him, for the family she'd seen in the photo on his desk.

"Let him go," she said regretfully.

Reynard lowered the gun and stepped back, eyeing the lawyer with contempt. "I think we're done with you."

Bannerman was in the car as fast as mortal limbs could manage. The motor started with an expensive purr.

Ashe pounded on the window. Bannerman lowered it a crack. "What?"

"Where in the mall is he?"

He gave her a hollow look. "Oh, you'll find him."

Ashe had to jump back before he ran over her feet.

Reynard caught her, one hand to her back. "I would say he doesn't appreciate our good efforts."

Ashe flipped the file open again. There were legal documents, printouts from the Internet showing warehouses, shops, and even an auction house. "We've got to stop Tony before Bannerman hits the Multiple Listing Service. Y'know, I almost feel sorry for the guy. He's kind of like a Renfield."

She closed the cover and slid the file inside her coat.

"Most demons start out as human servants," Reynard said. "Another reason to stop this specimen. We don't want him making friends. Demons are an epidemic waiting for an opportunity."

That had always been one of those irrational, late-night terrors for Ashe: a world where demons slowly infected every human around her. Families, cities, countries would fall to their insatiable hunger. She couldn't handle the thought that those paranoid fantasies might come true. "If they're an epidemic, then I'm a great big bottle of antiseptic."

She took out her phone and started dialing.

Reynard looked at her. "Who are you calling?"

"The police. I don't care what kind of a legal wall Bannerman's buddies are building around him; that folder you grabbed has clear evidence that he's been selling property to a demon. That's good for five to ten years if he's convicted. Even if he isn't, it should keep him on ice long enough for us to clean up this mess."

"How very crafty of you."

"You didn't think I'd let him off that easily, did you?"

She looked across at Reynard. Now that Bannerman was gone, his face had fallen into lines of weariness. The fight had cost him. Whatever grace period Grandma and Holly's magic had provided was running out.

It took them another twenty minutes to reach the mall. Just as they got off the Ducati, a red T-bird turned into the lot, heading for the underground parking.

"That's Holly and Alessandro," Ashe said, setting a rapid pace toward the parking entrance. "Come on, let's catch up."

They started to run. Reynard slowed suddenly, pulling his sunglasses off and scanning the front of the mall.

"What's wrong?" Ashe asked, skidding to a stop.

"My urn is in there. I can feel it." He suddenly looked energized, as if someone had put in fresh batteries.

"Great. Let's go get it." Ashe grabbed his hand, pulling him into the shadows of the underground parking garage.

Alessandro was already out of the T-bird by the time they approached. "Hey, fang-boy," Ashe said.

He grunted and clapped her shoulder by way of greeting. Beneath a long, leather coat, the vampire carried a broadsword that contained enough silver to be fatal to most magical creatures.

A fatality was a distinct possibility when dealing with a vampire roused before dusk. He looked bleary and cranky.

Holly got out of the driver's side of the car and promptly yawned. "I suppose we don't have time for coffee before saving the city from the ultimate evil?"

"Sorry," said Ashe. "The coffee they sell here is the ultimate evil."

Then she did a double take, looking at Alessandro and then Holly. "He let you drive his precious Thunderbird?"

Holly gave the vampire a sidelong glance that spoke of a barely cooled argument. "No way I'm letting him drive during the day. He may look awake, but I'm not convinced."

Alessandro narrowed his eyes, but Ashe couldn't tell if he was annoyed or drowsy. She handed Holly Bannerman's file. "Put this in the car. It's a file with the future addresses of our demon."

Reynard had drawn near the car and touched the glossy red hood with his fingertips. It didn't take a mind reader to see the auto lust in his eyes. A low growl from

Alessandro prompted him to remove his hand with a guilty jerk.

"What's the plan?" Alessandro asked. "I've called other vampires who can walk in the daytime, as well as the hounds and wolf packs. They're on standby."

"We met the demon's human on the way here," Reynard replied. "He is under a compulsion to serve his master. There is every chance the demon has been warned of our approach. It would be wisest to assess the field before deploying your troops."

"Bannerman said the demon would be easy to find," added Ashe.

"That can't be good." Holly shut the car door and looked from one face to another. "I mean, what the hell is it doing?"

Ashe grimaced. "We need to see for ourselves."

"But how do we look without revealing our location?" Alessandro asked.

She pointed to a service door. "We can get to the back entrance to the library from here. If the thing is expecting an attack, it won't be looking for someone skulking in the young-adult section."

"I do not skulk," said the vampire, giving Ashe an owlish glare.

Holly glanced at her mate and stifled a sigh. "Let's do it."

Ashe led the way. Reynard followed, then Holly and Caravelli. The heavy door groaned and clattered as Ashe pulled it open, the hollow vault of the parking area echoing with the noise. She took a set of narrow concrete stairs that zigzagged upward to the main level. The metal handrail was nearly devoid of paint, mere chips showing that it had once been an industrial green. Footsteps bounced and whispered in the empty space—the heavier tread of the men, Holly's light step—until Ashe opened a second door that led into the service hallway behind the mall stores. Each plain white door had a number stenciled on it. Boxes of packing materials, dress hangers, and other junk sat here and there, waiting for pickup.

They all wrinkled their noses. Demon stink hung in the air.

Ashe turned to the right. "This way."

They rounded a bend in the corridor and nearly ran headlong into a reed-thin young man smoking a cigarette. He ground it out hastily as they approached.

"Ashe!" he said, and it sounded angry.

Ashe stopped in her tracks. "Gary! What's up?"

He was one of the bookstore clerks and a ringleader in the practical-joke wars, but he didn't look like a light-hearted prankster now. He twitched nervously, his long, slender fingers working their way over his Book Box monogrammed polo shirt.

"It's not funny." Gary was obviously scared out of his wits, but trying to keep it together. "The cardboard guys, the Easter eggs, maybe it was a bit of a mess, but no one got hurt. This is too much."

"What's going on?"

"Things are going wrong all over the mall." Gary gave another twitch. "Really strange stuff. Things flying. Wicked smells. The bookstore's been hit with something bad. There's stinky slime running all over the bestseller wall."

Caravelli arched an eyebrow. "Perhaps a demon reviewer expressing his opinion?"

Gary gave him a panicked look. "Oh, God, a vampire."

Ashe took the guy's arm and shook him a little to drag his attention back from Alessandro. "This isn't a joke by the library staff, Gary; it's a real demon."

Gary's mouth curled in a sneer. "This not-a-joke stuff part of the joke?"

"Sadly, no," said Alessandro, pulling out his huge sword and flashing his teeth.

"Oh, God!" Gary pressed the heels of his hands to his eyes. Ashe wasn't sure if he was going to cry or faint. "A demon. A vampire. Swords. This is like a really bad role-playing game."

He started to hyperventilate. Ashe shook him hard

enough that he dropped his hands and looked at her. Panic gouged lines around his eyes and mouth.

"Get it together, bud," Ashe said in a hard voice. "We're the cavalry, so don't make me put on my mean face. Show us the demon."

"O-okay. This way." Gary pulled open the door marked with the number eight. Ashe saw that his hands were shaking.

"Sorry about the boxes," he said. "We were unpacking a shipment when all this started."

It wasn't easy to get through. Boxes were piled in towers that reminded Ashe unpleasantly of the Book Burrow. A few were open, releasing the sharp scent of newly printed pages. Compared to the rotten smell of demon slime, the ink was as good as high-end perfume.

"Hey, there's the new Linda Howard," Holly commented as they edged past a table littered with paperbacks and pricing guns.

"If we save the world before store closing, I'll buy you a copy," Alessandro said dryly.

They emerged out of the stockroom into the flickering glare of fluorescent lights, Ashe and Reynard following last. She knew the store well. Three aisles and a big discount table held most of its stock. The walls were floor-to-ceiling displays of magazines, bestsellers, and the latest fitness DVDs.

"The urn is very near," Reynard said quietly. "I can feel it like a magnet."

"We're all over getting it back," Ashe replied, bumping her shoulder against his. "Can't have your soul end up a demon's doorstop."

He gave her a look that mixed exasperation with affection. Ashe looked away, a flutter of emotion beneath her breastbone. Her cheeks warmed. *This so isn't the time to flirt.* It was time to hunt. They fanned out beside the back entrance of the store, getting a good look at the place.

"Holy slimefest," said Holly.

Gary was aghast. "This is so much worse than it was a few minutes ago."

It was no big surprise that the store was empty of staff and customers.

Blue-green slime drizzled down the walls. Perhaps the mess had started in the bestseller section, but it had spread to every shelf in the place. Magazines curled and sagged beneath the weight of the goo. Cardboard dumps once filled with featured titles had melted into glistening mounds, books sticking out like the ribs of a sinking ship. The worst was the discount table, which was completely engulfed by the ooze. Every so often it formed a bubble that burst with an evil-smelling *ploop*, spouting a rivulet of slime like a miniature volcano from hell.

Ashe held her hand over her nose, trying to filter the smell. "Let's go where there's more air. This stuff is toxic."

They started for the main aisle of the mall, Holly dragging the stunned clerk by the hand. The floor was slippery, so what started as a quick march slowed to a careful skate. Ashe braced her hand on Reynard's sleeve more than once, on the verge of falling into the blue-green mass.

When they reached the dimly lit aisle of the mall, Gary pulled the fan-fold door across the front of the bookstore. "It's not like anyone's going to go in there, but it makes me feel better," he explained. "I think we're shut for the day."

Ashe turned to Reynard. "Is this payback for the fact that the Book Burrow was torched?"

He shook his head. "I don't know. That business appears to be in the same condition."

Ashe looked where he pointed. It was a Goth-wear store. A metal-studded bustier in the display window dripped slime. She felt a pang of sorrow; she'd secretly wanted it even though it cost a mint. "Anyplace else?"

"Not that I can see," Reynard replied.

In fact, the mall looked almost empty. She'd expected terrified mobs, hostages at slime point, demonic demands for unlimited access to the shopping channel. Instead, she could make out every note of the easy listening cover tunes echoing around the mall. Tuesdays were usually quiet, but it looked like only a handful of the curious were braving the smell to snap cell phone pictures of the trailing ooze.

"Where's mall security?" Holly asked.

Gary shrugged. "We tried calling, but nobody answered. Maybe whatever did this took them out first." He turned to Ashe, seeming to recover his nerve. "What can I do?"

Ashe gripped his shoulder. "Get everyone you can to leave. Try to convince the stores to close up and send the staff home. Then go yourself. This is going to get nasty."

Gary nodded, taking them all in with a grave stare. "You rock."

"We try," Ashe said. "Now go, grasshopper."

He went, striding up to a couple of the picture takers to send them on their way.

Good. Ashe glanced at the others. "Anyone see a demon lair?"

"Not yet," Holly said.

"Then we start looking. Split up or stay together?"

"Stay together," Alessandro said, looking at Holly. "If there are still shoppers coming and going, the demon does not control the entire mall yet. If we're lucky, his influence will be localized."

Ashe nodded, and they began to tour the mall as a group, walking slowly and checking out every store for signs of demonic possession. A small part of her brain flashed on high school and cutting classes with a gang of friends. Even some of the stores were still the same. *Weird.*

The demon hadn't touched the stereo shop, the store that sold vitamins, or the career-woman boutiques. The toy store looked like it had been looted by Viking raiders. They followed a trail of toy knights and plush animals—one that looked like a cousin to the bunny Belenos had left with Lore—around the corner to a different arm of the mall. There, kitty-corner to where they stopped, they spotted the demon's hoard.

"As shoppers go," Holly said slowly, "I'd say he was pretty unfocused."

"I'd say he was escalating," Ashe said. "Maybe losing the bookstore tipped old Tony off the edge."

She couldn't help gaping. The demon had moved into one of the empty storefronts, breaking the gate open and turning on the lights. They glared down into a space devoid of fixtures or furniture, but not of stuff. A jumble of heaps and piles made it hard to recognize half of it. Gourmet cookware formed a precarious tower of gleaming copper and stainless steel. There were books and DVDs and toys, a lawn mower, ornately glazed outdoor pots for holding small trees, and a collection of fancy stepping-stones for the garden. The demon had apparently hit Sears's gardening center. There was a sofa and matching love seat in white leather. A pair of matching end tables—very nice ones with a hand-rubbed walnut finish, and Ashe knew that because she'd had a moment of longing the other day for something besides bargain pine with dents—held faux Tiffany lamps. But what she saw most of was collections. A mountain of fashion dolls with their cars, houses, and bewildering wardrobes. Kitchen knives. Boxed sets of TV shows on DVD. Boxed sets of flatware and stemware and Royal Doulton dishes with gold trim.

"Where do you draw the line between collecting and hoarding?" Alessandro asked softly, as if speaking to himself.

"About fifty movie action figures ago," Holly replied. "I'm surprised the thing didn't go for a city lot full of storage lockers."

"Display is half of its pleasure," Reynard replied. "I have met this creature's kind once or twice before."

"Any insights we can use?" asked Holly. "How do the guardsmen deal with demons in the Castle?"

"They are not allowed in the general population. Certain areas of the Castle are sealed off for the demons, where they can do no harm."

"What if one gets loose?"

"One or two guardsmen cannot manage a large demon like this. It takes at least a dozen, and then only within the Castle. If it were merely a matter of rounding up our friend under guard, Mac would have sent reinforcements. He can help only once the demon is inside the Castle walls."

Holly gave him a surprised look. "What have you done in the past with cases like this?"

Reynard gave a resigned sigh. "We rely on the help of sorcerers and witches. The old guard used to have sorcerers in our number, but the years have taken their toll. I have some magic, but not enough for this."

"I have the key Belenos was using," Ashe said. "Is that any help?"

"The keys don't work with fey or most demons," Reynard replied. "They won't pass through doorways made by the keys. There were safeguards put in place against the most dangerous species, and only additional sorcery can open a door for them. However, I can open a portal using guardsmen's magic. It will pass through that well enough."

Ashe cursed. "So we treat this like we did the rabbit: You open a portal, and the rest of us get old Tony into Mac's loving care?"

Reynard nodded. Holly and Alessandro exchanged glances and agreed.

"Shouldn't we look for the urn while slime-boy isn't around?" Ashe suggested.

"I'd rather know where the demon is first," said Holly. "That could be a trap."

"You're quite right," Reynard agreed. "I had best let Mac know we are ready to proceed. He needs to alert his men to be standing by."

"Why not open a portal now?" Holly asked. "I mean, to me that's the hard part. Get it over with."

"I don't want to alert our friend that there is a guardsman in the house. Surprise is an advantage." He turned to Ashe. "May I borrow your cell phone?"

Ashe fished in her pocket. "They get cell reception in the Castle?"

"No. We relay messages through the hounds guarding the gate."

Reynard took the phone, opened it carefully, and began deliberately punching numbers. He held it up to his ear. Ashe took it away, hit send, and gave it back with a smile. He gave a sheepish grin. She loved a man who wasn't afraid to laugh at himself. She didn't have to walk on eggshells.

As Reynard made the call, she took a few steps away from her friends. *We've found the demon's treasure, but where is the demon?* She looked down the gloomy corridor at the largely empty mall. She'd spent so much time there over the years, she felt protective of the place. She searched out each display window, checking to see which ones were still okay. The watch store and the florist looked okay. So did the bridal shop.

She took a few steps toward Louise's Weddings, running her eyes over the gown in the front window. With a thrill of relief, she saw her favorite dress was still un-slimed. It was a long, strapless white sheath, plain but classic. She'd had a quickie civil ceremony, over before the ink on the paperwork was dry. She didn't like fuss, but that dress made her think a little might be nice. Champagne, photographs, a honeymoon . . . sirens.

She could hear sirens approaching. Distant, but moving fast.

She started toward the mall door to see what was coming. Had somebody figured out the slime wasn't a maintenance issue and called the cops? Maybe the gas company, mistaking the bad smell for a leak?

More humans on site meant bad news. Casualties would be blamed on the supernatural community as a whole, and the nonhumans were barely tolerated anyway. All the more reason to wrap this up, fast.

"We've got company," she said to the others. "Emergency vehicles are on the way."

"Look at this." Alessandro pointed. Halfway down

the aisle was the Easter Bunny's throne, where kiddies sat on the Bun's knee and wished for bushels of chocolate eggs.

Given her current feelings about rabbits, Ashe was glad His Floppiness was off that day. "What about it?" Ashe asked. *Why is this important?*

The throne was surrounded by displays of fuzzy chicks, jelly beans, and cardboard lambs in unlikely pastel colors. The nearby card shop replicated the scene in their window, with the addition of a tiny Easter-themed village complete with moving train. As Ashe drew closer, she heard a small, asthmatic wheeze meant to be its whistle.

She felt Alessandro walking beside her; the vampire made no noise. "The card store sells this Easter village," he said. "The individual pieces are collectible and expensive."

Ashe suddenly understood where he was going with this. She drew the Colt she was carrying at the small of her back. "The store has only one of the churches. That piece costs hundreds of dollars."

Alessandro's face grew grim as he gripped his sword. "I can't see our demon passing up such a prize, can you?"

They stopped their advance a few yards away from the card shop's entrance. More slowly, they edged toward the door. Ashe risked a glance behind her. Reynard was with them now, gun drawn, Holly behind him.

She peered around a big display of souvenir mugs and into the store. *Shit. Hostages.*

Tony sat on the cash desk, an affable smile on his face. He was opening every box that held a piece of the collectible village and setting the miniature beside him. About twenty customers and staff huddled on the floor. He was using this store for his holding cell. Ashe counted five under Eden's age, and two elderly women. She turned and waved at the others to stay out of sight. *He's got to have taken out mall security. Someone would have seen all this on a surveillance camera!*

But maybe someone had used their cell phone to sneak a call to the cops? She'd heard sirens—where the hell were they?

"I'm still missing the bridge," Tony said. His pleasant expression didn't reach his voice. It was flat and cold as a dagger.

The saleswoman hurried to a cupboard with a sliding door. She opened it, rummaging frantically through what looked like dozens of identical boxes, reading the labels to find the thing he wanted. She finally found it and rushed back. "Here you are, sir."

Carefully, Tony eased open the lid and pulled out a block of Styrofoam. He pulled that apart to reveal a small stone bridge ready to take the *Easter Express* across an imaginary river. A delighted smile played on his lips until his face suddenly fell.

"There's a chip in it!" He held it up, pointing to something Ashe couldn't see. He rounded on the saleswoman. "This is *flawed*!"

"I'll get you another, sir," the woman squeaked, and hurried back to the cupboard.

The demon hurled the offending bridge against a glass display case. The safety glass exploded with a resounding boom, sending a shower of chips to the floor. The saleswoman screamed, and two of the children started to cry.

"Give me another!" Tony roared in an unearthly voice.

Ashe used the moment to slide inside the store unnoticed, Alessandro on her heels. Reynard and Holly headed to the other side of the store. She was pretty sure a bullet wouldn't kill a demon in human form, but it would hurt and maybe incapacitate. All they had to do was shove Tony through a portal, and they were done.

A woman squealed when she saw the gun, but with the crying children the noise made no difference. When Ashe had a clear head shot, she squeezed the trigger. She felt the recoil and heard the *blam* a microsecond later.

In the next eyeblink, Tony slid off the counter, the bullet between his thumb and forefinger. "You're starting to annoy me."

Ashe felt a ripple of earth magic. Holly was gathering her forces. *Thank Goddess her magic's back.* Ashe faced off with the demon, keeping his focus on her. "Well, you're past pissing me off, so we're even."

"Get out. Leave me alone. I own this mall."

"Demons can't hold property. Not so much as a post-office box. Any agreement Bannerman drew up is a fraud."

"Possession is nine-tenths of the law, and believe me, demons are good at possession." He laughed at his own joke, and tossed the bullet aside.

"Why the hostages?"

"The policemen I hear pulling up outside." Tony flashed his dimples, looking almost jolly. "Hostages keep them civil."

She felt Holly pulling in earth energy again. Ashe stalled some more, giving her sister more time. "What were you before you were a demon?"

"An estate appraiser. All those lovely things, none of them mine. It was a sad life." He grabbed the second box the saleslady had brought. "Now I can have whatever I want."

"Have you noticed that it's mostly junk?"

He chuckled, opening the box. "Who says it's about the dollar value? Having things makes me all warm and happy inside."

Ashe could see Holly now. Her sister had moved up behind where Tony stood. Holly let loose a flash of power. Tony jolted like he'd been electrocuted, smoke seeping from his skin. At the same moment, Alessandro dropped from the ceiling, sword flashing.

"Go!" Ashe screamed at the hostages. They scrambled, but not all of them were quick. She heaved the two older women to their feet, pushing them out of harm's way.

But not fast enough.

Furious, Tony hurled Alessandro into a rack of cards. The blast of energy knocked three of the fleeing humans to their knees. Reynard was suddenly there, hustling them out the door. Another angry wave of power followed. Ashe staggered back, bruising her shoulder on a shelf bracket. She holstered her useless gun, thinking fast.

The demon's human form wavered like an underwater image, the colors that made up his clothes, the definition of his features growing dark and indistinct. A second later, he dissolved into a billow of smoke, wings unfurling from his swirling form and filling the width of the store. Ashe got an impression of teeth and beak.

Great Goddess, they had to contain this thing. They had to distract it from the running hostages. She saw the miniature church on the counter and had an idea. Tony's Easter village wouldn't be complete without it.

Near the front of the store, Holly dropped her arms, realizing her spell hadn't been powerful enough. Ashe grabbed the miniature church from the counter and hurled it at her sister. "Catch! Run for the hoard!"

Holly's eyes went round as she caught the thing, but she obediently bolted. The demon thing whirled, tendrils of smoke seeming to flow around its fluid move. It shrieked its displeasure, hurling mugs and little houses after her.

Reynard used the opportunity to open a portal right on top of it. Enraged, the demon lashed out. Cards exploded into the air. Paperweights and gift boxes flew in crazy figure eights. Something heavy caught Ashe in the back of the head. She stumbled, tripping over the edge of a low display shelf. Once she was down, every airborne object zoomed toward her like hostile snow: envelopes, bows, pens, notebooks, photo frames, and tree ornaments. Ashe rolled facedown and covered her head with her hands, trying to get her knees under her. The flimsy cards felt weirdly heavy, like they were brick instead of paper, and more and more piled on top of her. Ashe tried to thrust out a hand, but the edges of

the cards and envelopes seemed stuck together. Light
filtered through the curtain of paper, a checkerboard of
pink and white and pale green, but she couldn't poke
through the cocoon.

Panic set in. She wriggled, but every movement increased the weight of the trap. Her legs were pinned and
she couldn't kick. Ashe stopped, listening and panting.
She was conscious of the worn carpet inches from her
nose and mouth, a mashed piece of gum just beyond her
cheek. Fake cherry scent didn't mix well with the reek
of demon.

She couldn't hear a thing. Crushing down on her ribs
and spine, the pile of paper was grinding her to the floor.
A burn started in her lungs as they struggled to inflate. It
felt like every object the demon had ever collected was
piled on her back.

Not even her fingers could budge. Every nerve in her
body seemed to fire, begging to move her muscles, but
all she managed was a shudder. Hot, salty tears of frustration ran over her lips and into the scratchy carpet.

*Where is everyone? What's going on? Why can't I hear
anything?*

Whatever air was inside the cocoon, she'd used it up.
The edges of her vision were growing dark. She closed
her eyes so she couldn't see the creeping blackness.

Her breath came in thick, wheezing gasps.

And then stopped.

Chapter 23

Reynard's portal wobbled and slowly began to fold in on itself, the disk of burning energy collapsing like a wilted flower.

Holly caught the church, held it over her head, and danced backward. "Hey, you! Over here!"

But Tony couldn't be distracted anymore. He was clearly fighting exile to the Castle—fighting and winning. Reynard swore. A portal was hard enough to maintain without a demon trying to slam it shut. He could feel the other guardsmen beyond the opening, doing what they could to help, but Reynard was the strongest.

Not strong enough, at least not this time. The collector demon might not be as powerful as a soul eater or a fire demon, but it was still hellspawn. There would be no quiet surrender.

Reynard let the portal go, dropping his arms as it swirled shut.

They needed to regroup.

He knew from experience that demons were more often caught through persistence than force. Backing off now wasn't defeat, just the beginning of a testing process. Reynard would find the creature's weakness. He was the captain of the Castle guard. Fighting monsters was what he did.

He wiped his hands on his jeans, getting ready for the next round. A perverse part of him was enjoying the challenge—but he was tired. Being near the urn wasn't enough. He needed to find it and get back to the Castle.

That was the last place he wanted to go. Then again, he might not make it there. An end was coming either way, but Reynard couldn't afford to think about that right now.

The thing that had been Tony the bookseller opened huge, fanged jaws and screeched like a banshee, the sound rattling bones and teeth. The sour stink of demon magic rolled through the store as it stretched nightmare wings.

Huge and dark, the demon swelled to fill the front of the store, its shadow creeping across the ceiling like an advancing tide. The air grew dark, as if the lights were fading. In the false twilight, there seemed to be nothing to breathe, the air itself robbed of vitality.

Holly threw a ball of energy. The dark tide shrank back, but only for a moment. She turned and bolted down the aisle, the miniature church under her arm. With a huge rush of air, the demon flapped its wings and launched into the air, sailing after her like inevitable doom.

Reynard charged forward to intervene, but it was too late. No sooner had Holly's feet touched the tiles of the main mall than the demon grabbed her shoulder in its beak, plucking her into the air.

Reynard lunged for her. Holly's hand brushed his, but couldn't catch hold. The miniature church fell from her grip, exploding into a rain of stinging shards as it smashed to the floor. They scattered with an oddly musical sound.

With a snarl, Alessandro sprang, sword ready for a two-handed blow. The bound took him ten feet in the air, using the vampire's power of levitation. As the silver blade arced through the air, the demon faded into mist.

Holly dropped like a stone, but Alessandro caught her in one arm, holding her as they landed.

Reynard kept his eyes on the demon. It spun, winding itself to a long rope of black mist, and threaded itself between the plain doors across the mall marked, STAIRWAY TO PARKING. His first instinct was to storm after it, but a jolt of panic pushed everything else aside.

Where was Ashe?

Ashe sat bolt upright with a rasping gasp, nearly colliding with Reynard's concerned face. Someone had rolled her over and pulled the paper off her face. She was mummified in drawings of baskets, chicks, and bunnies. "Get. This. Off of me!"

Three pairs of hands began unwrapping her. Holly was to her left, Alessandro at her feet. The vampire gave her a look from under his brows, amber eyes amused.

"It's not funny!" Ashe snapped.

"You look like an Easter egg," he replied, all suave calm.

"I thought you had smothered," Reynard growled, deadly serious. "How do you feel?"

"Fine," Ashe said automatically. She was panting, trying to catch up on lost oxygen. Her head hurt—but she wasn't broken or bleeding, so that made her fit for duty.

Reynard's expression said he understood her need to fight.

Ashe shook off the last of her wrappings and clambered to her feet. The card store looked like a snowstorm had hit it. Drifts of pastel paper covered the floor, but at least they were mercifully lifeless. *I'm sending e-cards from now on.*

"The demon headed for the stairs down to the parking area," said Reynard. "My suggestion is that the trip downstairs is a diversion. Sooner or later, it will return to its hoard. We can trap it there."

Alessandro nodded. "Got it."

"I'm just afraid Tony's gone back to human form and driven away already," Ashe said.

"Not with those sirens going," Alessandro put in. "The police are cordoning the place off. We've got about two minutes before they find us here."

Ashe checked her weapon. "Then let's get to it."

Alessandro took Holly's hand and strode toward the store entrance, cards kicking up around his feet like autumn leaves. Ashe and Reynard followed.

By the time Ashe and Reynard reached the main mall corridor, police and reporters were everywhere. From the corner of her eye, she saw Gary, the bookstore clerk, trying to shoo some of the reporters back out the front door. It was a lost cause. The press had found a breach in whatever official barrier had kept them out, and the whole notion of security had collapsed like a paper bag full of water.

"What is this?" Reynard snapped, raising his voice to be heard above the babble of voices.

Ashe dragged him from the path of a determined-looking woman brandishing a mic. "Welcome to your first modern disaster scene. Smile for the cameras."

The city had only three TV stations and a handful of radio stations, but there seemed to be more press than that. Of course, police officers, firefighters, paramedics, mall management, and what looked like the health department added to the fun.

She also saw hellhounds, werewolves, and some groggy-looking vamps she knew by sight. Alessandro must have called in his troops.

Ashe had lost track of her sister. She elbowed through the crowd, which was growing thicker as they neared the demon's hoard. She couldn't see Alessandro, either. Growing less and less polite, Reynard began clearing a path. She had to admit, there was something about pure male aggression that worked like a charm when it came to managing a milling crowd.

An invisible line held the crowd back a dozen feet from the demon's lair. Still too close for common sense, but at least no one was sticking a tape recorder into the demon's beak. The hounds and wolves were moving forward, helping the cops move everyone back. Ashe shoved through to the front, ignoring the curses raining down on her from the cameramen as she spoiled their shots.

The demon was looming in the corner of the empty store, wings spread wide, black eyes glistening like something wet and foul. For the moment, it was pinned down. Holly and Alessandro crouched behind piles of the demon's shopping, Holly zapping the hellspawn whenever it tried to move, Alessandro protecting her from the objects the demon sent spinning their way.

Reynard ran forward in a crouch, ducking a set of copper-bottomed pots sailing through the air.

Ashe hurried after him, thinking hard. There was nothing she could do to beat up this demon. She was strong and a good fighter, but this needed high magic, and she had none. A sick feeling bubbled up in her, expanding to fill every cell to bursting with acid knowledge that she had once had that power and thrown it away.

Reynard was opening the portal again. It hovered over their heads, swirling energies of green and orange. The edges of it seemed burned, reality melting away like film caught in a projector. Ashe thought she caught a glimpse of Mac on the other side, ready with his men.

Standing poised, his lean swordsman's body a study in leashed potential, Reynard raised his hands. A cold glow began to gather around them like spectral gloves. Ashe caught her breath. She had never seen this kind of magic before.

The light spread from hand to hand, growing in crystalline geometry. Cold as Jack Frost, precise as a spider's web, the chill radiance rose as far as the ceiling, holding the demon's darkness in a snow-white cage.

She stood spellbound a moment, but then pulled herself away to search the fallen piles of debris for the urn. She moved as quickly as she could, but the magic in the air was so thick every motion dragged, like walking underwater.

Holly's fight with the demon had been brief but destructive. China had fallen and smashed. Books had been trampled, toys broken. Worry clenched her lungs, making breaths come hard. *He said the urn was just pottery. It can't be safe in this mess.* She followed the piles to the other side of the store, forcing herself to focus. If she let her attention wander, got sucked into the spectacle of the portal and the crowds, she'd never make it through the mass of things the demon had gathered.

But she could tell the demon was fighting, struggling to stay in the world. A shock wave shuddered the floor. People screamed. Boxes toppled. Ashe grabbed the wall to steady herself.

And there she saw it, where the boxes had fallen. A stoppered pottery jar, decorated with gold, and beautiful in the simple curves of its shape. She began to run toward it, the heavy magic in the air making everything happen in slow motion.

Reynard felt the demon straining against the pull of the portal, like a huge dog fighting its leash. Reynard had learned from their earlier skirmish, and adjusted his technique. A regular portal wouldn't drag the demon through, but with the added strength of the guardsmen on the other side, and with Holly Carver beside him, Reynard had made the portal into a vacuum. They could not fight the demon hand-to-hand, but the combination of their magic could suck the creature right back to where it belonged.

If this went well, no one else would be hurt, and no more property would be destroyed. That did not mean it would be easy.

Reynard made himself the focus of the spell. Power crashed through him, a raging torrent fed by sorcery and witchcraft. His body was mere flesh and bone, not enough to contain it all, but his warlock blood directed the magic like a wick in oil. It was brutal but effective.

Burning pain flared like an awl piercing the length of his nerves. He hurt worse when the demon struggled, every thrash, every twist against the portal's pull a searing jolt. The moment the demon faltered with exhaustion, the punishment stopped. Reynard felt hollowed out, a dry sponge with mere membranes to shape the nothingness inside.

And then the demon began fighting again.

In a remote part of his mind, he was conscious of sweat gluing his clothes to his skin. He dropped to one knee, bracing himself. *I am a guardsman. I am a weapon.*

The demon's voice slid into his mind. *Let me go. Take your soul, but let me go free.*

Reynard didn't answer, refusing to let his mind waver for an instant.

All I want are a few things to amuse me. Is that so terrible? A few pots and pans? A few books? This world has so much. Surely it can spare a bit?

The demon strained forward, beak snapping, wings thrashing, trying to cover its treasure with the stain of its shadow. Reynard roared at the agony, letting out the pain before it broke his mind. The demon reared, flapping its great wings.

Freedom! You want it, too! I can taste the bitter gall of yearning in your thoughts!

That was Reynard's weak spot, his Achilles' heel. No matter what he achieved, no matter how many lives he saved, he was forever chained to the misery of the Castle. No matter how this battle ended, there would be no joyous future, no hero's triumph.

So there was no reason to spare himself. *Duty, dignity, and death.*

Resentment and frustration had boiled inside Reynard for centuries, but he could use that. Furious, he thrust all the power he could hold at the creature.

Holly and the others dug deep, answering the demand of Reynard's attack. He hammered at the demon, rage lending strength.

The onslaught pushed, shoved, drove the dark shadow into the portal. He felt the magic of the other guardsmen sink claws into the demon's body. But the creature would not surrender its hoard. It made one last lunge forward, desperate to claim its treasure—chained by its lust for objects as surely as Reynard was chained to his curse.

The magic broke, like an elastic band strained beyond endurance. Power recoiled, slamming into the demon, smashing it to smithereens. The explosion ripped through the empty store, hurling the piles of lamps, toys, movies, and everything else into the walls.

Reynard, the guardsmen, and everyone else flew like discarded dolls. The last thing Reynard remembered was that the blinding pain had finally stopped as he was sucked into the Castle along with the demon.

Ashe dove for the urn, letting the huge force hurl her toward the fragile vessel and the life inside.

Chapter 24

A she jumped to her feet and began pounding on the wall where the portal had been—where Reynard had been—a moment before.

"Reynard! Mac!" She slammed on the plain white surface of the store wall with the flat of her hand. "Let me in!"

She stopped a moment, cradling the urn in her arms. Her head hurt. Her stomach hurt. Every part of her ached with worry.

After working that much magic, Reynard would be weakened. He wouldn't survive long in the Castle. She had to get in there and deliver his urn.

"Let me in!" She began banging again, because she wouldn't, *couldn't* stop trying to save him.

Holly got to her feet, shaking debris out of her hair. Some of the ceiling tiles were damaged and raining down a fine, white dust. "Sandro?" she called.

Alessandro had already picked himself up but had been swamped by the reporters. With no demons around, a vampire was the next-best news bite.

Holly grabbed Ashe's arm. "The portal's closed. We'll have to go downtown to the Castle door."

Ashe kicked the wall savagely. "Dammit!"

There were emergency vehicles everywhere, police cordons, news reporters. They'd never get out.

Then she had a sudden inspiration.

Belenos's key!

There was one well-thumbed magazine in the cell. Miru-kai had found it abandoned in the corner when he arrived the first time Mac had put him in this tedious place. Now he pulled it out from under the mattress and settled down for a third trip through the pages. Like the television shows he had seen, it described the human world as founded on a lust for material goods, reverence for the athletically gifted, and a rabid hunger for gossip. In other words, not much had changed in the many years he'd been in the Castle.

He shut the magazine with a disgusted flutter of pages. He was bored. It had been bad enough being locked up for knowing too much about the theft of the urn—that at least made sense. Now he was locked up for having stolen Ashe Carver's daughter. Which wasn't true. He'd *wanted* to, but he had actually begun to change his mind when Reynard had charged in to save the day.

How could he be blamed for something he hadn't done? Why not wait a bit, until he actually was truly guilty? In Miru-kai's case, that would have been only a day or two, anyway.

Humans were odd, frustrating creatures. Mac might not be human anymore, but he still thought like one. Miru-kai heaved a martyred sigh.

There was a niche in the wall with a pitcher of water and a cup. An unnecessary civility—as with the other long-term residents, he did not require food or drink—but it was a nice touch nonetheless. He poured himself a cup of the cool water purely for something to do.

He had to get out of there. He had the gem to get him out the Castle door, but that was useless unless he could get *to* the Castle door.

He tasted the water. He could sense all the metal,

and the new substance called plastic, that had surrounded the drink on its way from a man-made lake
somewhere with tall pine trees and ice. The guardsman
who had poured the water into the jug had been thinking about his woman. Those thoughts tasted sweet, like
the honey made from wild meadows. *Ah, whoever, he
is, his heart swells with love.* Humans felt everything so
keenly.

Despite what Mac thought, Miru-kai didn't wish harm
on the guardsmen. They had their duties just as he had
his. In some ways, their lot was every bit as miserable—
no sun, no joy, few creature comforts. Prisons incarcerated the guards just as much as the inmates.

The prince set the cup of water back into the niche,
saving it for later. He could not afford to get lost in the
guardsman's longing daydreams. He hoped they did not
belong to the unfortunate Stewart.

From far away, Miru-kai heard a commotion. Mac's
voice, the deep masculine rumble of guardsmen's voices.
Something had been going on for hours, but whatever
was happening now was rich with urgency. Best of all, it
was nearby. At last, something interesting!

Then he heard women talking, their words urgent
and upset. He recognized the voice of Eden's mother.
Had something happened to the child? A stab of anxiety
brought him near the cell door.

That's the Carver woman. And another. The timbre of
their voices was so alike, he was willing to wager both
Carver sisters were there, together. They were just down
the corridor to the right.

Without thinking, Miru-kai grabbed one of the iron
bars as he leaned forward for a better look. The blast
of pain sent him reeling back, a red welt rising on his
palm.

"Oberon's balls!" He grabbed his wrist with his other
hand, hissing through his teeth at the pain. He'd taken
sword thrusts with manly fortitude, but cold iron hurt
more.

But he forgot his discomfort as the owners of those

voices walked past, because then he could see what the tall, blond Carver woman held.

"You found Reynard's urn!" Miru-kai blurted out.

The woman wheeled, gave him a raking glance up and down. "I did."

She reminded him of a wildcat, taut springs of energy just waiting to uncoil. To strike.

"You're Prince Miru-kai. The one who let the demon out to steal this urn. The one who took my daughter."

Her face, pale and tight with fatigue, was a kaleidoscope of burning emotion—fear, triumph, remorse, anger. Miru-kai had the uncomfortable feeling his schemes were the root cause of much of that heat.

"I am Miru-kai," he replied, oddly glad of the iron bars between him and this Amazon. He sketched a polite bow.

She stared at him again, her bright green eyes holding his for a long moment. "I've never met you, and yet you've turned my life upside down."

"That sometimes happens when the dark fey touch another's life."

"Why?" There was no ducking that question. Her tone said she'd break his head if he tried.

"We are the storm that breaks old patterns."

"And leaves room for something new." That was the dark-haired sister, Holly.

Miru-kai bowed. There were very few who understood the role fey played in the world. Most people thought they were simply evil. "I take it the demon is defeated."

"Destroyed. And what was left of it returned to the Castle," said Holly, her voice heavy. "But it took all that Reynard had to do it. We hope that bringing him the urn will put him back on his feet."

"Ah." Now he understood the look in Ashe's eyes.

She could save the old fox, but only to lose him to his old life. He would be trapped forever, always a guard in an old, cold stone dungeon.

Miru-kai knew a thing or two about being trapped.

Mac strode up to them, looking massive in a tight black T-shirt. "They've put Reynard in the infirmary," he said to the women.

So it is serious, then.

Miru-kai felt a pang of conscience that Simeon would have applauded. After all, it was at least partially Miru-kai's fault this whole sorry business had begun. *I'll grieve for you, old fox.*

He thought about how Eden had run to Reynard with all the pure affection of a child. About how, sometimes, the weave of the pattern just seemed to go wrong. The guardsmen's thread had been flawed from the start.

We are the storm that breaks old patterns.

"Demon," he said to Mac.

"No time." Mac began ushering the women past the cell door.

"Wait!"

Mac stopped, wheeling impatiently. "What?"

Miru-kai spoke fast, before Mac changed his mind. "Do you remember that I tried to heal my friend by taking something from the vault?"

"So?"

"Did you never stop to think what, or why?"

Ashe and Holly were looking at him with puzzlement. Mac just looked irritated.

Miru-kai smoothed his mustache, thinking again of how that brave child had touched his heart. "I'll make you a bargain if you let me go. I have something to trade. I know many of the Order's secrets."

Mac's frown deepened. "Don't mess with me."

It was Ashe who understood first. "Goddess!"

Miru-kai gave a feline smile, enjoying himself.

The guardsmen's sacrifice—now, that was a cruel, unnatural pattern worth breaking.

"I know how to put body and soul back together."

Chapter 25

". . . and so ends the remarkable tale of the guardsmen. Originally they numbered in the thousands. Now a few hundred of the old guard remain: Romans, knights, cavaliers, Celts, warriors from every conceivable time and place. Through some mysterious means, they are now all free to go and explore our world. It's a brand-new and mysterious world to them. Listeners, can you find it in your hearts to make them welcome?

"The story has an interesting footnote. Shortly after the liberation of the old guards, a star appeared in the Castle above the black lake, the scene of last autumn's horrific battle. Are these two miraculous events related? Or is it mere coincidence that ending a millennia-old injustice sped the healing of the Castle? What changed to make any of this possible?

"Food for thought, girls and ghouls.

"This is Errata Jones. Good night."

*   *   *

Saturday, April 11, 6:00 p.m.
The Castle

Reynard's quarters were military perfect. Of course, there wasn't enough here to make a real mess. The guy had no stuff. There was a small living room and a bedroom, but neither screamed "live" or "sleep." The front room had an armchair and two battered old trunks, plus a tiny bookshelf. The books were the only thing that struck Ashe as personal.

Of course, she wasn't here to give decorating advice.

She leaned over the bed where Reynard was sleeping and peeled down the coverlet, knowing very well that he wore nothing beneath. The skin of his sculpted chest was marble-pale. Bare of tattoos.

"You see, they're gone."

She started. "You're awake."

"I keep waking up to find you taking care of me."

"You have a problem with that?"

He reached up, brushing her cheek with the backs of his fingers. "Never. You're as welcome as the sun after centuries of darkness. And I know what that means. It's not just poetry."

She leaned over him, finding the warmth of his lips. He was safe. He was free.

He'd been sliding in and out of consciousness for a few hours. Now his gray eyes were dark with fascination, his hair loose around his muscular shoulders. Dark stubble showed off his sharp cheekbones—the kind cameras loved and plastic surgeons ached to re-create.

He should model for a pinup calendar. *Hot Historical Heroes.* Sir September. The Duke of December. Marquess of May—or May Not. Reynard could have starred on every page.

His gaze stayed on her face as the slowly slipping bedcovers revealed his lean abdomen, each set of muscles cleanly defined. *Nothing like daily battles for a few centuries to develop the old six-pack.*

His hand caught hers before the coverlet could descend those last critical inches. A dare burned in his eyes. "You wouldn't take advantage of a man when he's down?"

"Sure I would." She grinned. "Without apology. And, y'know, you're not entirely *down*."

"You witch."

"Guilty." She sat on the edge of the bed. "And what am I going to do with you now that you're in one piece?"

His gaze made suggestions. "You mean now that I'm not half in a clay pot?"

"A nice pot, though." She lifted her eyebrows, her expression pleased. "Not that you'll need it anymore." She looked over at the urn, sitting on the stand that held his washbasin.

He squinted. "I haven't seen it for hundreds of years."

"I caught it just as the place exploded. When you forced the demon back into the Castle."

"Then you saved my life."

She allowed herself a small smile. "Maybe."

He squinted harder. "Is that duct tape stuck to my urn?"

Ashe looked a bit sheepish. "I caught it before it smashed, but I think the blast cracked it a bit. I didn't want your soul leaking out. Tape was the only thing I could find fast enough to do any good."

Reynard began to chuckle. "Witches, werewolves, vampires, and a castle full of guardsmen on hand, not to mention police, firefighters, paramedics, and the media—and the only thing that could save my soul was a roll of duct tape."

The chuckle turned into a guffaw.

Ashe looked down at him with a mixture of shock—she wasn't sure she'd ever seen him really *laugh*—and pique. "I was doing the best I could. It was all chaos and demon bits!"

He touched her cheek, his fingers threading through her hair. Reynard was giving her that smoking look again, the one that made it feel as if her insides were turning to chocolate syrup. He cupped her head, pulling her mouth down to his. The kiss was urgent and vulnerable, as if he were making up for the centuries of emotion that he'd missed.

When they broke apart, he still held her, his breath warm against her ear.

"How did Prince Miru-kai get your life out of the urn and back into you?" she asked. "You were gone for three whole days before they put you back in your chamber."

"I'm not sure. I was unconscious."

"I waited for you here as much as I could."

He kissed Ashe again, and she completely lost verbal skills.

"Three days," he murmured. "Three whole days. I only have another forty years or so. I don't have time to waste."

"Forty years is a long time."

"I've been alive for nearly three hundred, and I'm not sure I've made good use of my time. I have some catching up to do."

There was real regret in his words. He sat up, the sheet pooling around his hips. Swallowing hard, Ashe rested her hands on his shoulders. There was a lot of naked Reynard right there in front of her. "I'll do what I can to help."

He suddenly laughed, his gray eyes alight with humor.

She unbuckled her holster, setting it on the chair beside the bed. Reynard's laugh faded. One by one, she shed her knives, the stakes, the second handgun at the small of her back. She made a show of it, taking her time. By the time she got to the wrist sheaths, he looked deadly serious.

"Do you want to help me with the rest?" she asked.

He slid out of the bed and knelt at her feet, the motion graceful and fluid. And without a sheet.

Oh, Goddess. He was clearly feeling hunky-dory.

"Allow me." He lifted her foot in his hands and drew off her right boot, then her left. The stone floor was cold through her socks, worse than an unheated basement, but all she let herself notice was him. It wasn't difficult. His full lips curved in that bad-boy smile.

She reached down and picked up one of the stakes she'd dropped, running the tip along her thigh as she straightened. "Want to play hunter and vampire?"

Reynard quirked his eyebrow. "Madam, I came equipped with my own stake."

"Whoa! Points to the old guy."

He sprang up, snatching Ashe off her feet in the same motion, proving that he'd lost none of his amazing strength. "You consider me old?"

Ashe yipped with horror. "You toss me over your shoulder and I'll stake your butt, mister!"

With a grunt, Reynard dumped her onto the bed, making the springs squeak. He was breathing hard, but not from exertion.

She grabbed his arms and pulled him down, devouring his mouth. He tasted spicy, like sin melting on her tongue.

Her clothes were off in moments. Their lips met again, starved by the few seconds it took to undress her. Ashe could feel the magic of the fey still clinging to him as they bonded skin to skin. It was far subtler than a witch's power, as gossamer silk was to heavy wool. It hung like smoke around them, filling her senses with the impossible: rainbows that shone only at night, music that fell like a shower of daydreams.

As Reynard ran his hands over her, she saw a stately home dusted with snow. His old house, back in the day? The scene shivered to a storm of color as the needs of her body pushed away the thrall of magic. The house was gone, and he was touching her, testing her wetness as she clenched around his probing fingers. Salty skin, the musk of man surrounded her.

Ashe arched into him, letting pleasure ride her to the first crest of release.

Then she was back in the vision, riding a horse at breakneck speed through a field, the sunset glittering on rain caught in the grass. "Memories. I'm seeing your memories."

"It's my life coming back to me, one moment at a time."

Then they were lost in the heat, finding sweet release. Mouths met again, nurturing, nourishing. She slid down, the length of her body stroking his as they curled beneath the covers of his narrow bed. His hand found her hair, fingers weaving through it. Ashe pressed next to him, glad of his warmth in the cool room.

She turned his hand in hers, feeling the weight of it, the calluses where he held his sword. His fingers were long, but the tips were blunt and his palm square.

"What do you see in the lines of my hand, Madam Gypsy?" he asked. His voice was deep and intimate in the tiny room.

"If I'd looked at your hands first, I might have understood you better."

He folded his other arm behind his head so that he could see her better. Amusement played around his lips. "How is that?"

"You work hard."

"I always have."

"Really?"

"You thought I didn't?"

"I wouldn't have assumed . . ."

The lines around his eyes crinkled. "I had my fun, but I was a second son, love. I had to make my way in the world. Either that, or marry an heiress."

Ashe laughed. "Well, we still have a few of those around."

"I never could bring myself to wed for money. Now, for that motorcycle of yours, I might make an exception."

His hand explored beneath the covers, stroking her

waist and hip in a long, possessive sweep. "I seem to be recovering my strength."

"You're just thinking about my bike."

"No." He quirked an eyebrow. "I'm wondering how a man courts a woman in these times. Are there still balls?"

"Nightclubs and coffee shops. A lot less formal."

"What do you like to do?" His smile was wicked, bad boy present and accounted for. "You have such a poor opinion of my aristocratic kind that I ought to show you how a gentleman born can make a woman happy."

Ashe felt herself smiling in response. She'd all but forgotten this back-and-forth with a man. "Skiing. Mountain climbing. Horseback riding."

"Riding?"

"I like a good stallion," she said. "A good, frisky one."

"Really?"

She moved under the bedsheet. He drew his breath in suddenly, touching her face, sliding his hand down over her breast. Angling over her, he left a long, lingering kiss on her lips. "You're so beautiful. If a trifle impatient."

She felt the softness of his hair, the harsh brush of his stubble. The contrast of textures was exciting. Then his mouth was on her breasts, her stomach, then nipping the soft flesh of her thighs. He was just this side of masterful. That was what she needed. She didn't feel like proving herself tonight. For once, she wanted someone to simply want her—nothing complicated, no thinking required.

His mouth was on her, tasting her, sending a sweet-and-sour need through her belly. She felt her heels dig into the sheets as the tension grew, desire sharp as the finest steel. Cursing under her breath, she felt the waves of sensation pounding through her as he brought her to the edge of oblivion, then backed away, then brought her there again, only to steal her finish once more. She flung her head back, arching her neck, eyes squeezed shut in delicious frustration.

"Goddess, I'm not immortal; let me go before I break!"

"Are you asking nicely?" he teased, closing his lips around the peak of her breast at the same time his fingers slipped inside her.

And that did it. With a wild gasp, she opened her eyes, the pool of lamplight by the bedside dissolving into a golden aura as tears of release spilled down her cheeks. She came under his hand long and hard.

She was still burning with pleasure when he slipped his hard length inside, easing in with a few leisurely strokes. His chest muscles did an interesting dance as he shifted his weight onto his arms, doing a slow, slow push-up to bring his lips down to hers. Ashe could see a vein in his arm pulse as he hovered there, intimately inside her, yet holding himself apart. Her nipples just brushed his skin, trembling against him as she breathed. She began to pant, her inner muscles spasming, clenching around him.

He groaned, giving in to the urge to thrust. She felt the slide through her whole body, a friction that overflowed her senses. She rose to meet it, slick with anticipation. His next thrust was harder, barely banked power.

"Again," she breathed, reaching up to grab the bars of the headboard. "You don't need to hold back."

He let his mouth trail over her neck, down between her breasts, and then the rhythm took them both—slowly at first, Reynard lingering over the motion, then more and yet more greedily, driving into her without mercy. She came first, the sound of his name on her lips bringing him to climax in a shuddering rush.

Afterward, they lay entwined, reluctant to separate. Finally, sweat drying in the chill air, Ashe began to shiver. Reynard made the first move, retrieving the covers to pull over them. Ashe curled into his chest, basking in the lassitude after lovemaking.

It had been perfect. Epic.

There was no reason for this to ever end. She had him. Life was good.

"My love," Reynard said, running one finger down her cheek.

"What?" Ashe curled deeper into his side.

"You have very, very cold feet."

She swatted him with her pillow.

Turn the page for an excerpt from
Sharon Ashwood's next Dark Forgotten novel,

ICED

Coming soon from Signet Eclipse

Talia might be dead, but she still had a bad case of the creeps.

The scent of blood swamped her brain, swallowing sight and sound. She hesitated where she stood, her vampire senses screaming that something was wrong. That much blood was far too much of a good thing. The elevator doors whooshed shut behind her, stirring a gust of recycled air. Stirring up that maddening, tantalizing, revolting smell.

Talia blinked the hallway back into focus. This was her floor of the condo building, and home and Michelle were at the end of the hall. She fished her door keys out of her purse and started walking, the glossy pink bag from Howard's banging against her leg as she walked.

Now her stomach hurt and her jaws ached to bite, but more from panic than hunger. That much blood meant someone was hurt. There were a lot of elderly people in the building. Many lived alone. One of them might have slipped and fallen, or maybe cut themselves in the kitchen. Or maybe someone had broken in. . . .

Talia quickened her stride, following the scent. She pulled her phone out of her shoulder bag, the rhinestones on its bright blue case winking in the dim overhead light. She flipped it open, ready to dial Emergency as soon as she figured out who was in trouble. She was no superhero, but she could force open a door and control her hunger long enough for basic first aid. If there were bad guys, oh, well. She'd had a light dinner.

She passed units 1508, 1510, and 1512, her high-heeled ankle boots silent on the soft green carpet. She paused at each door—1514, 1516—listening for clues. A television muttered here and there. No sounds of a predator attacking its prey.

Unit 1520, 1522. The smell was coming from 1524, at the end of the hall. *Oh. Oh!*

Unit 1524 was her place. *Michelle!*

She grasped the cool metal of the door handle and turned it. It was unlocked. The door swung open, and the smell of death rushed into the hall like surf, drowning Talia all over again.

Instinct froze her where she stood, listening. There was no heartbeat, but that didn't mean much. Lots of things, herself included, didn't have a pulse. Reaching out her left hand, she pushed the door all the way open. The entry looked straight through to the living room, where a big picture window let in the glow of city lights. It was plenty of light for a vampire to see by.

"Michelle?" she said softly. *There's no one here. She must have left.*

Talia couldn't—wouldn't—believe anything else. She set down her purse and shopping bag and slid her phone into her pocket. *Get a grip.* But her hands shook so hard, she had to make fists to stop them.

She left the door open behind her as she tiptoed inside. She'd lived there for two months, but suddenly the place felt alien. Lamps, tables, the so-ugly-it-was-cute pink china poodle with the bobble head . . . They might as well have been rock formations on another planet. Nothing felt right.

Her boot bumped against something. Talia sprang backward, her dead heart giving a thump of fright. She stared, organizing the shape into meaning. A suitcase. One of those with the pull-out handle and wheels. Big and bright red.

It was Michelle's.

"Michelle?" Talia meant to shout this time, but it came out a whisper. "What the hell, girl?"

She groped on the wall for the light switch, suddenly needing the comfort of brightness. The twin lamps that framed the couch bloomed with warm light.

Oh, God.

Her stomach heaved. Now she could see all that red, red blood. Scarlet sprayed in arcs across the wall, splattering the furniture like a painter gone all Jackson Pollock on the decor. Talia shuddered as the carpet squished with wetness.

The smell could have gagged a werewolf.

She dimly realized one of the bookshelves was knocked over. There had been a fight.

"Michelle?" Her voice sounded tiny, childlike. Talia took one more step, and that gave her a full view of the living room. *Oh, God!*

Suddenly standing was hard. She grabbed the wall before she could fall down.

Her cousin, tall and trim in her navy blue cruise-hostess uniform, lay on her side between the couch and the coffee table. Drops of drying blood made her skin look luminously pale. Beneath the tangle of dark hair, Talia's gaze sought the features she knew as well as her own: high forehead, freckled nose, the mouth that turned up at one corner, always ready to smile. Born a year apart, they'd always looked more like twins than plain old cousins.

They still looked almost identical, except Michelle's head was a yard away from the rest of her body.

Talia's eyes drifted shut as the room closed in, darkness spiraling down to a pinpoint.

Beheaded.

Talia's grip on the wall failed, and she started to sink to the floor. The wet, red floor. Sudden nausea wrenched her. She scrambled to the kitchen, retching into the sink. She'd fed earlier, but not much. Nothing came up but a thin trickle of fluid.

Beheaded.

She heaved again, the strength of her vampire body making it painful. Talia leaned over the stainless-steel sink, shaking. The image of her cousin's body burned in her mind's eye. Whoever had done it had meant to kill *her.* Taking the head was the usual way to execute vampires—a lot more certain than a wooden stake.

She died because of me. They thought she was me.

Talia's breath caught, and caught again, air dragging through her lungs in tiny gasps that finally dissolved into sobs. She pushed away from the sink, grabbing a paper towel to mop her eyes. There was no time to fall apart.

But she did. She pressed the wadded towel to her mouth, stifling her moans. The tears were turning to a burning ache that ran down her throat, through her body, and out the soles of her feet.

This was no good. She had to get out of there.

Before whoever murdered Michelle came back.

Before someone called the cops and they blamed her, because she was the monster found next to the body.

Talia braced herself against the counter and stared into the sink until her eyes blurred and she squeezed them shut. This was the moment when the movie hero swore revenge, made a plan, and went after the bad guy.

All she felt was gut-wrenching grief.

A rustling sound came from the hallway, as if something had brushed against the shopping bag she'd abandoned by the door.

Talia spun around, terror rippling over her skin. So much for her earlier quip of *bad guys, oh, well*. Macabre images flashed one after another through her mind. Sheer willpower pinned her to the floor, making her think before she bolted straight into danger.

Normally, she would worry about hiding her scent from another predator, but the place stank so badly, that wasn't an issue. Plus, whoever had killed Michelle had to be human. Nothing else would have confused one of its own with a vampire.

Slowly, she peered around the edge of the kitchen doorway. A figure hulked in the threshold to the condo, backlit by the lights from the hall.

Oh, God! It's—he's—coming this way.

Talia shrank back into the galley kitchen, squeezing into the corner between the refrigerator and the wall. She shrank down, making herself small, bending her head forward to hide her pale skin with the dark fall of her hair. There was no need for her to breathe, as the absolute stillness of the dead would in this case work to her advantage.

Except terror made her want to run so badly her muscles cramped.

The fridge hummed, the hard surface vibrating against her arm. *Trapped!* Through the curtain of her hair, she could see the stranger's wide shoulders blocking the hallway between her and the door. Her heart gave a single painful beat, jolted back to life by the adrenaline rushing into her blood.

Tears of outrage stung Talia's eyes. She was frightened, absolutely, but she was also furious. Someone had killed Michelle, and now they'd come back. *Realize you screwed up?* she thought bitterly. *Figure out this is human blood all over your hands?*

It galled her to be so helpless. Talia had weapons, but they were stuffed in the top of the hallway closet, gathering dust. She'd thought she'd never have to use them again. Prayed for it.

Apparently no one listened to a vampire's prayers.

You're hiding in a kitchen filled with knives. Maybe she wasn't so helpless after all.

She could see the figure's shadow slide along the wall, stark against the bright patch of hallway light. His silhouette showed he was tall and big boned, moving with surprising grace for such a large man. She caught a sharp tang of smoke and chemicals, as if he'd been near an industrial fire. The smell drowned her vampire senses, choking out anything else his scent might have told her. He was coming closer, pausing after each step, his feet all but silent on the carpet.

Just a few yards more and he would be past the kitchen door. Then she could make a break for it. Even a fledgling such as her could move faster than a mortal.

Closer, closer. The hiding place where she crouched was just inside the kitchen entrance. If she reached out, she could brush the toes of his heavy work boots with her fingers. Her fingertips itched, as if they had already grazed the dirty leather. He was so close that she dared not lift her head to look at him. All she got was a good view of jean-clad shins.

And then he was past. She rose in a single, smooth motion, balancing on her toes. One careful step forward, and she reached the counter opposite the fridge. Silently she slid a kitchen knife out of the block. *Just in case*. It was smarter to run than to fight, but he might corner her yet.

She heard his intake of breath as he reached the living room. She froze, the cool handle of the knife heavy and hard against her palm.

The urge to vomit washed over her again, but she didn't dare make a noise. Not even to swallow. She could hear him, just a few yards to the right, the brush of cloth on cloth as he moved around the gory, glistening carnage in the next room.

Three, two, one.

Talia darted toward the hall, inhumanly fast.

He was faster.

Huge hands grabbed her upper arms, hauling her into the air. She kicked, hearing a snarl of pain as the sharp heel of her ankle boot dug into his thigh. She tried to turn and slash, but the angle was wrong. Wriggling like a ferret, Talia twisted, using Undead strength to turn within that big-knuckled grasp.

She flipped over, dropping through the air as her attacker lost his hold. With an upward slash, she scored the knife along the flesh of his hand.

Ha!

His other hand came down like a hammer, aiming for the weapon. Talia spun and kicked, wobbling in the heels but still forcing him back. She used the motion of the kick to fall into a crouch, sweeping the blade in a whispering arc, claiming the space around her body.

Force the enemy to keep his distance. One useful thing her father had taught her. One of the few.

But as she came out of the turn, he grabbed her by the scruff of the neck—how long was his reach, anyway?—and heaved her to the ground like a bag of laundry. Before Talia could move, she felt a heavy knee in the small of her back. She tried to arch up, but he was at least twice her weight. Rage shot through her, riding on a cold slick of terror. She hissed, baring fang.

His hand was pinning her wrist to the carpet, immobilizing the knife. Gripping it hard, she twisted her hand, snaking the point toward his flesh. His other hand clamped down, peeling her fingers one by one off the hilt.

She did her best to scratch. A female vampire's nails were as sharp as talons.

"Give it up," he growled.

She made a sound like a cat poked with a fork, half hiss, half yowl. The knife came loose. He sent it spinning across the floor, out of reach. Then she felt something cold and metal click shut around her wrist. The chill sensation made her flail, the motion jerking her elbow up to connect with solid flesh. His jaw? For a glorious moment, she felt him flinch.

Only to shove her back down and snap the handcuffs around her other wrist.

"There's silver in the alloy." His voice was hard and low. "You can't break them."

Talia rolled over, baring her fangs. The slide of metal against leather told her a gun had left its holster. She next thing she saw was a freaking .44 Magnum Ruger Blackhawk aimed between her eyes—loaded, no doubt, with silver-coated hollow-point bullets.

Their fight had brought them closer to the living room. The glow of the table lamps cast a wash of light over the attacker's face, at last giving her a good look at the man. Or what she could see of him around the muzzle of the minicannon in his hand.

Shaggy dark hair, thick and straight and a bit too long. Dark eyes. Swarthy skin. Killer cheekbones. Not classically handsome, but there was something heart-stopping in that face. Something wild.

She'd seen him before. What was his name? Lorne? No, Lore. He lived somewhere on the sixth floor.

"Great," Talia ground out through clenched teeth. Everything was catching up to her, emotions fighting their way through shock. She was starting to cry, tears sliding from beneath her lashes and trickling down her temples. *Oh, Michelle, what happened?* "Just great. I'm about to be blown to smithereens by the boy next door."

He leaned forward, pressing the muzzle of the gun into her flesh. "Be silent."

Talia hissed.

The corner of his mouth pulled down. "Did the smell of her get to be too much? You needed a taste?"

"Oh, God, no." Talia caught her breath, feeling beads of cold, clammy sweat trickle between her breasts. Fear. Guilt. She'd been so afraid of hurting Michelle, been so careful. Accusing her now wasn't fair. "How can you say that? She's right there. Right over there."

"Then tell the truth."

Talia gulped, tasting death on her tongue. "I didn't do this."

"All the vampires say that."

"Wasn't this *your* doing?"

"I don't hunt humans. I go for bigger game."

The statement made her shiver. His hand was bloody where she'd cut him, but he didn't smell like food. Not human, but nothing she recognized. The realization came like an extra jolt of electricity. *What the hell is he?*

"Then why are you here? Who are you?" She struggled to sit up, awkward because her arms were pinned behind her back. He pressed the Ruger hard against her skin, but she barely noticed.

"Who is your sire?" he demanded.

Talia clamped her mouth shut. His dark, angry gaze locked with hers. It wasn't the cold stare of so many killers she'd known. His eyes were hot with emotion, a righteous, remorseless fury.

"Who made you?" His voice grated with anger.

Talia blinked hard, her heart giving another jerking thump of fright. "No, please. If you send me back to my sire, I'll be lucky if he only kills me."

"That's what happens when a vampire goes rogue."

Now she was starting to sob, ugly little gasps that caught in her throat. "You can't send me back. I didn't kill her. I loved Michelle." She was begging, and put every ounce of her soul into it, holding his dark, burning stare.

A crease formed between his eyebrows. "Damn you."

The wail of a police siren ripped the night. Lore pressed the muzzle of the gun like a cold kiss against her forehead. "I don't trust you. I can't tell if you're the killer or not. But I believe you're afraid of your sire."

Her mouth had gone paper dry. "What are you going to do?"

His mouth thinned as if he didn't like the question. He looked her up and down, all that anger turning to a smoldering frustration. Talia could almost feel it heating her skin.

"I'll give you a choice. Take your chances with the human police, or . . ." He trailed off, clearly mulling over his next words.

"Or?" The single syllable came out in a croak.

"Or you're my prisoner. Take your pick."

Also Available from
SHARON ASHWOOD

RAVENOUS
The Dark Forgotten

Holly Carver is a witch who sometimes relies on
the help of Alessandro Caravelli for her family's
preternatural investigations business. Alessandro
is the oldest and strongest vampire in Fairview—
and he's made no secret of his desire for Holly.
But while she aches to succumb to his suggestive
wiles, she knows it would be an invitation
to trouble.

Alessandro's queen, Omara, complicates matters
when she turns up in Fairview to enlist his help.
Sultry and manipulative, she is jealous of
Alessandro's feelings for Holly, and demands he
use Holly to trap Geneva—the most evil demon
of all.

**Available wherever books are sold or at
penguin.com**

Also Available from
SHARON ASHWOOD

SCORCHED
The Dark Forgotten

Ex-detective Macmillan has a taste for bad girls, but his last lover really took the cake—and his humanity. Now a half-demon, Mac's lost his friends, his family, and his job. Then a beguiling vampire asks for his help to find her son. Suddenly, Mac has a case to work—one that leads him deep into the supernatural prison where Mac learns that cracking the case will cost him his last scrap of humanity.

Available wherever books are sold or at
penguin.com